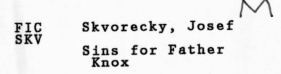

FIC
SKV

Skvorecky, Josef

Sins for Father
Knox

$17.45

DATE		

SINS FOR
FATHER KNOX

SINS FOR FATHER KNOX

BY JOSEF SKVORECKY

*Translated from the Czech
by Kaca Polackova Henley*

W · W · Norton & Company · New York · London

Copyright © 1973 by Josef Skvorecky
English translation copyright © 1988 by Kaca Polackova Henley
All rights reserved.
Printed in the United States of America.

The text of this book is composed in Galliard, with
display type set in Woodcut. Composition and
manufacturing by the Maple-Vail Book Manufacturing Group.
Book design by Antonina Krass.

First Edition

Library of Congress Cataloging-in-Publication Data
Škvorecký, Josef.
[Hříchy pro pátera Knoxe. English]
Sins for Father Knox / Josef Škvorecký; translated from the Czech
by Kaca Polackova Henley.
p. cm.
Translation of: Hříchy pro pátera Knoxe.
I. Title.
PG5038.S527H713   1989
891.8′635—dc19   88–15205

ISBN 0-393-02512-8

W. W. Norton & Company, Inc., 500 Fifth Avenue, New York, N.Y. 10110
W. W. Norton & Company Ltd., 37 Great Russell Street, London WC1B 3NU
1 2 3 4 5 6 7 8 9 0

Contents

Introduction

Sometimes life doesn't turn out the way it should, and then it's a good idea to make a change, if you can. But because you usually can't, it's a relief to be able, at least, to retire to a world created for just such circumstances. To the London in each of us, where Sherlock Holmes's carriage rattles over the cobblestones, and where murder isn't a sin but a game.

I've always enjoyed playing that game, so I invented these sins, not against the Ten Commandments they taught me long ago in catechism class, but against a decalogue compiled by a certain priest who once played the game in Sir Arthur Conan Doyle's lovely city. His name was Ronald Arbuthnott Knox; he lived between 1888 and 1957; he was originally an Anglican but converted to Catholicism. He made quite a decent career for himself in the Church, and made contributions to theological literature that were not insignificant. He was also friendly with many writers, including G. K. Chesterton. Perhaps it was from Chesterton that he acquired his love for detective stories.

He not only read them, he wrote them himself. But his name will remain in the annals of the detective story not for his novels, but for two theoretical accomplishments that are truly Chestertonian in spirit: he wrote a humorous essay in which he portrayed Sherlock Holmes as a historical personage, thus founding the entertaining body of pseudoscience known as Holmesiana; and in 1929 he issued the ten commandments that you will find following this introduction.

This was the golden age of the British detective story, and its foremost champions, led by Chesterton and Anthony Cox (alias Anthony Berkely, alias Francis Iles), founded the famous Detection Club—a society made up of devotees of fictional homicide. Like every proper association, the club needed some bylaws, and Knox's decalogue served famously. In them the theologian created what is widely recognized as the best codex of what is and is not permissible in a detective story.

And I took those ten commandments, and then I took some clay of subconscious origin and created an ideal woman (ideal in a platonic sense, that is—not in the sense that certain people refer to as moral) and made her commit a variety of sins, some of them against those commandments.

In the tales that follow, as in every detective story, the reader is called upon to determine the culprit, the motive, the method, or all three. But unlike other detective stories, these tales also pose a further question: which of Father Knox's ten commandments has been violated? Each one sins against only one commandment, but determining the answer—as every experienced reader of this decadent form of literature knows—means not guessing, but deducing and being able to support the deduction logically.

I have no doubt that many will be successful. I only hope the reader will not be annoyed by the other sins committed by the jaunty yet melancholy young woman who plays a somewhat incredible Holmes here. At times Eve uses language that is less than literary, and although she is unmarried she does what is human, and what everyone does.

Still, there are people walking the earth who are more immoral than she is—a certain aging lieutenant, for example. Though even he isn't such a bad fellow, in spite of his inappropriate desires.

J.S.

FATHER KNOX'S
TEN COMMANDMENTS

I. The criminal must be someone mentioned in the early part of the story, but must not be anyone whose thoughts the reader has been allowed to follow.

II. All supernatural or preternatural agencies are ruled out as a matter of course.

III. No more than one secret room or passage is allowable. I would add that a secret passage should not be brought in at all unless the action takes place in the kind of house where such devices might be expected.

IV. No hitherto undiscovered poisons may be used, nor any appliance which will need a long scientific explanation at the end.

V. No Chinaman must figure in the story.[1]

VI. No accident must ever help the detective, nor must he ever have an unaccountable intuition which proves to be right.

VII. The detective must not himself commit the crime.

VIII. The detective must not light on any clues which are not instantly produced for the inspection of the reader.

IX. The stupid friend of the detective, the Watson, must not conceal any thoughts which pass through his mind; his intelli-

[1]This was not a display of racism on the part of the good Father, but simply his reaction to what was one of the most hackneyed ploys of cheap detective stories.

gence must be slightly, but very slightly, below that of the average reader.

X. Twin brothers, and doubles generally, must not appear unless we have been duly prepared for them.

(If you're not sure which commandment is being violated by which story, you can find out by turning to the ab-solutions at the end of the book.)

SINS FOR
FATHER KNOX

SIN NUMBER 1

An Intimate Business

Lieutenant Boruvka told himself it was conscientiousness that had brought him to the women's prison. When he'd considered the matter in the police car on the way there, he'd been willing to admit that qualms of conscience might also have had something to do with it. But he would have denied with all his heart that it could be the somewhat faded countenance of this fair-haired girl in the coarse prison jacket. He would have denied it because it was the truth.

She sat across from him in the otherwise empty visiting room; the table between them was covered with carved hearts and other, less decent, symbols of love. The lieutenant wondered what miracle had put the carvings there, when conversations at the table were always so closely guarded. But experience had long since shown him that there are truly more things in heaven and earth than can be explained by pure reason. Besides, the table might not always have been here; maybe other girls used to sit around it, and not girls like this one.

Now, looking at her face without the camouflage of makeup, he saw that the years couldn't be denied. Thirty-five? More? Maybe a little less? But she was a slender young women—under the jacket, apparently made out of rug fabric, he observed a pair of narrow, girlish shoulders—and her gray, widely spaced eyes really knocked him out, although he was of an age where he preferred younger women. Preferred . . . but then, he was vulnerable to beauty of every sort.

She had never confessed at the trial; that was why his conscience kept bothering him. All the evidence had pointed to her, so they'd put her away. But the lieutenant still had the uncomfortable feeling that he'd overlooked something.

Yet everything at the trial had been against her. The autopsy had incontrovertibly indicated the presence of hyoscine, and hyoscine was the poison missing from the stocks of her pharmacist landlady, Mrs. Korenac. It had also come out that Mrs. Korenac was a serious morphine addict, so that it was no problem for her tenant to obtain something from the chaotic stores in her pharmacy. And the girl did admit to one criminal offense: with the help of her landlady, and occasionally without it, she had supplied her midnight colleagues with benzedrine.

Moreover, she had the classic motive for murder by poison. The words from the transcript of the trial had engraved themselves on the lieutenant's memory:

> PROSECUTOR: Would you kindly tell the court, miss, just what you saw on Tuesday, June 7 at three o'clock in the afternoon, in the corridor by Director Weyr's dressing room?
> WITNESS: I was just coming from the makeup room, and as I was passing the director's door Eve Adam came flying out, her eyes all red from crying.
> PROSECUTOR: Did you hear the defendant say anything on that occasion?
> WITNESS: I did. She turned around in the doorway and she said, or I should say she screeched, "Just wait, you—" and then she said a terribly bad word. . . .

"It's the truth, Lieutenant," said the girl in the rug-fabric jacket. "Though I can hardly believe it myself. Even at my relatively young age, I ought to have more sense. But sometimes a woman just doesn't. I could have a brain like a bookkeeper—in fact, I do—but then a rose-colored cloud settles around me and I act like a crazy young fool. You wouldn't understand."

The lieutenant wasn't unfamiliar with the condition. He wanted to say something to that effect, but she didn't give him a chance.

"If only I *had* done it, the rat. If I at least had him on my conscience, like Shura—" She broke off.

"Like who?" the lieutenant asked suspiciously.

"Oh, just somebody I know. She's locked up already, don't worry. She's sort of royalty here in the clink. She doesn't do any work, the gypsy girls do everything for her. They even do her nails, and they give her food from their own rations—she's twice as big as she was when she came in here."

"For heaven's sake, why?"

"Well, her boyfriend was squealing to the cops. He was sentenced to death by a secret gypsy tribunal and Shura carried out the sentence. Then the gypsies made mincemeat out of him, sewed him up inside a dead horse, and dumped him in the Váh River. Only the horse swelled up—"

"I'm sorry you have to be here in that kind of company," said the lieutenant. "In fact, that's why I came."

"Well, the company isn't all that bad. I have a girlfriend here, her name is Annie Preclikova, and she—" The girl stopped herself again. She had almost yielded to her native volubility and divulged the secret of certain gold items from a certain robbery successfully executed by her friend. They had never got Annie to confess where she'd hidden the gold, and Annie had promised her a share of it when they got out. Fortunately she caught herself in time. She gave the policeman a probing look, and then relaxed at the sight of his round face, his blue eyes, and all the other physiognomical clues to a simple soul: guileless, rather naive, even bordering on dense. How can this chump be a detective, she thought. She scolded herself for talking too much—and started right back in again.

"The thing is, I was gone on him, Lieutenant. Completely, head over heels. That's me all over—never do anything by halves. But if I ever get out of here, to hell with love, to hell with emotional attachments! I'll only do it for the sake of my health, only out of calculated self-interest, I swear!"

"I have come to help you," said the lieutenant, a little pompously and a little out of context. The girl, who was used to thinking the worst, wondered briefly whether this was an immoral proposition in response to her last declaration. But at that moment he looked practically simple-minded, and she squelched the thought.

"That's nice of you," she said. "Only it's a shame you didn't think to do it sooner."

The criminologist reddened. The girl registered this, and straightened a strand of hair that had fallen across her gray eyes. The lieutenant decided it had looked better over her eyes.

"The thing is, I saw him as a god," she continued. "Not because . . . not *just* because he was a famous director and he gave me that bit part. The thing is, I believed in him. He talked a blue streak, I should have recognized his ulterior motive, I'd heard all that often enough over the—I mean, enough guys have tried it," she went on, and the lieutenant grew sadder. Unlike the girl, who liked to drop literary references now and then, he wasn't very well read, and her mention of some sort of "motive" aroused his suspicion that she was mixed up in something after all. "Only I was playing the fool all over again, Lieutenant. That's why it really shook me up when I saw him with that little brat. I hate to admit it, but I acted like a darned female, I just blew it."

"You were startled, were you?" asked the lieutenant, trying to understand.

"Exactly!" She nodded vehemently. "Imagine me—a crazy young fool sitting on cloud nine, all red-hot to do the world a good deed. So I took the stint singing at the lounge at Barrandov film studios, subbing for my friend Lidka, who'd just found out her rich Italian boyfriend was in town. My own gig over at the Lucerna Bar didn't begin until eleven, so I thought I'd do her a favor. And no sooner did I climb up on stage and start singing 'Have I got good news for you' than it's to hell with good news—I saw them right there in front of me, at the first table by the dance floor. Rudolf and that nitwit. It was such a shock that it didn't really sink in for about twelve hours. And not only did I have to look at them, not only did my professional position force me to watch Rudolf making time with her—using the same method he'd tried with me, down to every last detail—but I had to keep right on singing that 'nobody needs to be alone,' because the show must go on, that's the rule in show business, no matter what happens. And I was so wiped out by the whole thing that after I finished singing I just stood there in front of the mike like a pillar of salt, Jarda Strudl had to poke me in the behind with his saxophone, I was that rigid, and then they picked up and left, arm in arm, and Rudolf was murmuring sweet nothings into her silly, eighteen-year-old, piggy little ear—Sorry," she apologized, and a pink tinge showed through the prison pallor. "I don't give a darn any more, you know," she added, unconvincingly. "It's just that every time I think of that moment I—especially since I recognized that brat from the magazine photo, and realized she's exactly Petr's age, so she could be Rudolf's daughter. And that bast—sorry," she apologized again, and her gray-eyed gaze touched on the lieutenant's fishy eye.

At that moment the lieutenant wasn't seeing those eyes, but rather the article and the photograph:

> Director Weyr has entrusted the roles of the brother and sister to an interesting pair. The brother will be played by Petr Weyr, a student at the Academy of Theatrical Arts and the director's own son, while the part of the sister had been given to a young medical student, Petra Heyduk. The coincidence of the first names has a certain charm, but another circumstance is particularly worthy of note. Although the younger Mr. Weyr has the year 1948 on his birth certificate and Miss Heyduk has 1949, they are in fact exactly the same age. Petr Weyr was born several minutes before midnight on New Year's Eve, 1948, while Petra Heyduk first saw the light of day several minutes after midnight on January 1, 1949. Heaven knows if there isn't a touch of destiny in that. . . .

That, four dots and all, was how the reporter Mrs. Malinovska wrote it up in *Vlasta,* a magazine for women—socialist women, but women all the same. The article was accompanied by a photo of two young faces, tilted towards each other more like sweethearts than like siblings. The pose, set up by the reporter, was apparently meant to imply the direction that destiny would take beyond the four dots.

"Petra!" declared the girl with distaste. "If she had to be a silly little cluck, did she have to have such a silly clucky name too?" she said, with a voice full of poison. "Sorry. So the next day in his dressing room, I just did my nut."

"You . . . lost your cool?" the lieutenant prompted her uncertainly, searching in his mind through his daughter Zuzana's vocabulary for any such expression.

"You bet your life I lost my cool," she retorted. The lieutenant knew from the records of the case that she had started singing in revues back in the year Petr Weyr was born, and had moved to nightclubs later, once they were permitted again—mainly in the border country, in the uranium empire near Jachymov. That was probably where she'd picked up the coarser elements in her language, he thought, and excused her. "Just like a darned female," continued the girl. "So then, in the dressing room, I called him a bastard—sorry—and slammed the door, and that's when that makeup lady saw me. And that was it: I was on my way you know where, flat on my you know what, and I'm still here."

The lieutenant was all too familiar with the dramatic sequence of events that had followed.

> PROSECUTOR: So, Miss Synkova, you say you worked on Director Weyr's staff as a so-called clapper. Can you tell us what you observed of the victim's behavior towards the defendant on Wednesday, June 8? That is, the day after the scene in the corridor as described by the witness Miss Moselova?
>
> WITNESS: The director had been in a nasty mood every since he arrived, and the one to catch it the worst was Eve Adam, I mean the defendant. She had the first two scenes that day. And the way he treated her, he didn't yell but he was sarcastic, you know? He kept

putting her down. Like he said to her, "For heaven's sake, if you can't fix it with makeup, would you at least try and sound like you're twenty-five?"

PROSECUTOR: How did the defendant respond to that?

WITNESS: Normally. She started to cry. She'd been pretty damp in the optical department all day, they had to keep the powder-puff handy, and—

PROSECUTOR: (Interrupts) I beg your pardon. You said something about some kind of optical department. . . .

The prosecutor's fleeting hope of an espionage or sabotage connection came to nothing. But the girl was found guilty of murder all the same. The lieutenant stared at her pale face and suddenly realized that he kept thinking of her as a girl, although she could have been Zuzana's mother. He couldn't help himself, though. She just wasn't in the same category as Mrs. Boruvka, no matter what her age. He recognized the danger of a man of his own age viewing a woman of the prisoner's age as anything so dewy-sounding, shook his head, and urgently tried to recollect the section of the court records that really did refer to optical equipment:

PROSECUTOR: And you, sir, live in a villa that has a direct view of the victim's home?

WITNESS: Yes sir, right across the street. I have a telescope on my balcony there. I'm an amateur astronomer—

PROSECUTOR: What did you see the evening before the murder—that is, on Tuesday—in the second-floor window?

WITNESS: That's where the movie director's bedroom is—or was. It was dark already, about nine o'clock, when the light suddenly went on in there. I was just looking at the evening star, and I saw that lady over there—

PROSECUTOR: The defendant?

WITNESS: That's right. She had her hand on the light switch, but just then the director walked in and turned the light off. Then the curtains were drawn across the window and the light went on again.

PROSECUTOR: And did you hear anything?

WITNESS: I did, but that was later. Before eleven. Some woman was having fits over there.

PROSECUTOR: You mean to say she was shouting?
WITNESS: That's right, shouting. I could hear it all the way back in my bedroom.

"Anyway," said the girl, "I went there to throw that bit part right in his face. I had the crazy idea that I'd make him mad, because he'd have to do those two scenes over with somebody else, and that costs money."

"Did he accept your resignation?"

"No problem," said the girl. "My idea of what it costs to make a movie was kind of naive. And he turned the light out in the bedroom because he noticed that his curtains were open. He was being naive too—he thought nobody knew about him. And then he gave me a lecture. An awful one."

"About what?"

"I . . . I can't repeat that. He was talking about women, talking as if they were chickens or something, you know? From the point of view of his stupid male superiority. The thing is, he was probably right. Or maybe he wasn't—it's all a matter of what your values are. And your priorities. You understand?"

The lieutenant didn't understand, but he nodded.

"Like falling in love and making a fool of yourself," she explained. "Or that coldness of his, like a dog's nose, all brains and meanness."

The lieutenant nodded again. "Yes, well . . . you've got something there. It's all a matter of your point of view, as you say. So there was another argument that night, that the neighbor heard?"

"Not an argument, that was when I acted like such an idiot, like I said," sighed the girl. "And that neighbor's a fine example of a Peeping Tom, repulsive old creep. He's even got a telescope installed for his hobby! Evening star indeed, the old pig!" She almost lost her temper again, but caught herself. "But never mind that. I was so dumb that the next day I even had second thoughts, wondering if I'd gone off half-cocked, quitting the part like that. Not that I regretted it—not a whole lot, that is—but I thought maybe I'd misjudged him, maybe he'd recast Petra's part on account of me and the scene I threw for him on Tuesday in his dressing room, the day the makeup lady saw me. I didn't know he'd recast it before the night I was at his place, he never told me. I didn't find out until the next day that Petra had been replaced. He just let me go ahead and make an ass of myself—sorry—in front of that slob from across the street. Misjudged him? The hell I did. Heaven knows why he recast her part, but it certainly wasn't on my account."

Of course, the lieutenant knew why Director Weyr had decided to break up that ideal pair of good-looking kids. There was a perfectly credible story about that in the court records:

I got my hands on that *Vlasta* magazine on Monday. A patient brought it to my office, asked if I'd seen it, and when I said I hadn't, she said to take a look. There was the article about how Weyr cast our Petra in the part opposite his son in the film. But I couldn't allow anything like that to happen. Why? Listen, the medical profession is hereditary in our family. My great-grandfather was a doctor, and my grandfather, and so was my father. I'm the first one who didn't have a son. I couldn't have any children, I mean I couldn't have any more children—I suffer from testicular azoospermia. So Petra had to take up the torch. But she didn't seem to mind at all. She's wanted to be a doctor ever since she was a little girl. And she'd done so well in her first year at medical school. And now, put yourself in her place: a girl like that, pretty, cheerful, an excellent medical student, and suddenly she finds herself in the movies. There's one important thing I forgot to tell you: her mother, my late first wife, was an actress. Not that I put too much stock in heredity, mind you, but environment means a whole lot. At home Petra always lived in what I might call a hospital atmosphere, and if she once got a taste of films and glory—I didn't want to take the chance. So I set out to see Rudolf. That's right, Weyr. We'd known each other for years, ever since high school in Brno, and it was my first wife who introduced Rudolf to his wife. We used to get together for a few years after they married. We played tennis, went to the cottage, you know how it is. But naturally, a film director hasn't got much of a future out in Brno, and Rudolf got a job in Prague—his father-in-law was head of some production group at the Barrandov studios there. So we stopped seeing each other. Later on I was transferred closer to Prague, to Pardubice. But there just wasn't enough time. I met Rudolf once or twice when I came to Prague on business, but that was all. The kids practically didn't know each other. So when I saw that article, I went to see him. It turned out he'd cast Petra in that role just to please me. When I explained how worried I was, how Petra might turn out to be a lousy movie star when she could have been an excellent physician, he admitted that I was probably right. No, I didn't tell Petra. Rudolf promised me he wouldn't tell her either, he'd blame it on screen tests or something. He'd say Petra wasn't photogenic. No, I know she is, I know it all too well. She's my daughter, but maybe I can say it and it won't sound like boasting— if she weren't my daughter, and if I were a quarter of a century younger . . . That's another thing. Petr is an attractive young man. And studying medicine is hard enough without having other things on your mind, not to mention a baby underfoot. No, no, I want Petra to be a doctor, and it will be a whole lot better for her to be able to diagnose a case of appendicitis than to play walk-ons in the movies or wait on a movie-star husband. I explained all this to Rudolf, and he heard me out, and followed through.

And a few more sentences from the flustered testimony of Petra Heyduk, medical student:

The truth is that I wondered why he took the part away from me. As for the screen tests being bad, he can save that for his dumb extras from the Film Club. I thought he was mad at me because I slapped him.

PROSECUTOR: Slapped him?

WITNESS: I slapped his face in the taxi on the way down from Barrandov. He was really after me, and with no encouragement, either. So I said to myself, it's probably true what they say about film directors and the casting couch, you know what I mean?

PROSECUTOR: I don't want you to hold anything back, now.

WITNESS: I haven't go anything to hold back. That little part wasn't worth it to me. So I gave up on the fame and glory of the silver screen. Besides, I was having problems in histology on account of it, and my dad would have been awfully unhappy if I'd flunked the exam. So I never gave another thought to why they took the part away from me. But . . .

PROSECUTOR: Go on, please!

WITNESS: Well, when he cast that phony little twit in the part. . . I do wonder, now. Maybe she went along with him. In fact—

PROSECUTOR: Thank you, miss, that will suffice.

"No way, he didn't recast it because of that," sighed the gray-eyed girl. "But it's a mystery why he did. Did you see the Lastovicka girl that he had time to cast in the part before, as you say, I did him in?"

"I don't say you did him in, miss," the lieutenant declared, offended. "If I thought that, I wouldn't be sitting here today. I believe you are innocent. But we need evidence."

"If the evidence you need to get me out of here is as flimsy as what it took to put me in—" She waved a hand. "I don't have any illusions. That's the way it goes, it's always a lot easier to get into trouble than it is to get out of it. But did you see that Lastovicka girl?"

"I did," admitted the lieutenant. "She still has the part. The film is being completed with Burdych as director, and she, Miss Lastovicka, well. . . ."

And he recalled the testimony of the assistant director:

He phoned me up, that would have been on Tuesday, the day before the murder. It was about eight in the evening. That reporter, Mrs. Malinovska, was just over at my place, so she had it in the paper the very next day. He wanted me to get hold of Miss Lastovicka right away, that night, and tell her she'd be taking over the part from Petra Heyduk. I wanted to object, but he said Petra's father had forbidden her to do it and that was that, and he hung up on me. The next day it was all over the papers, thanks to Mrs. Malinovska: that Petra Heyduk gave up the part on the wishes of her father. "Allegedly," it said, "so that work in motion pictures not interfere with her studies. But who knows . . . ?"

"It boggles the mind, doesn't it? A girl like Lastovicka!" She was indignant. "He boots out a cute little thing like that silly Heyduk girl, and hires a mug you can only shoot from behind, if you don't want to scare everybody in the movie house. Explain that to me, will you?" She was really quite upset, and an almost rosy color glowed through her prison pallor. She was a very dynamic girl, the lieutenant thought. All the sadder that she had to be in prison. And again he felt a pang of conscience for not having been as diligent in this case as he might have been.

"Though, to be perfectly honest," she added, brushing a strand of fair hair out of her beautiful eyes again, "no matter what she looks like, I kind of like the Lastovicka girl better beside young Weyr than I did Petra. I don't know how come, but the two of them . . . I just couldn't see them together."

"No?" The lieutenant was genuinely puzzled. He took a photograph out of his breast pocket, the one he'd clipped out of *Vlasta*. Those two little heads tilted towards each other in a pretty pose. He passed the picture to the girl.

"No way," said the prisoner. "They just don't go together. Don't you see what I mean?"

The picture traveled back to the lieutenant. He saw nothing odd about the picture, except that any two young people should be so attractive. He thought of a similar picture, a snapshot that immortalized himself and his sister when they were about the same age as these two. The photographer hadn't even put it in his show window. He and his sister had looked a lot alike, and the only thing that could be said about the lieutenant's appearance at the age of eighteen was that he was a dead ringer for an amiable but somewhat dull Simple Simon.

"Really?" He cleared his throat. "I don't know what's odd about them. I think they seem like an ideal couple, I mean for a movie. Don't you?"

And the photograph traveled back across the table. The girl bent over it and furrowed her blonde brows. A little wrinkle formed between them; the lieutenant's eyes rested on it, the girl noticed, and the wrinkle vanished.

"An ideal pair of lovers, maybe," she said slowly. "But in this film they were supposed to play brother and sister."

She thought a moment. "It's probably just female intuition, an advantage we chickens occasionally have over you lords of creation. Or do you ever have intuitions yourself, Lieutenant?"

"No, I don't, he said sadly. "I work purely by deduction. And occasionally"—he turned slightly pink—"I get a little help from coincidence."

"If only you could get some help from coincidence in my case," sighed the girl.

"I wish I could," declared the lieutenant, and he flushed bright red. The girl looked at him and her intuition suggested something to her. Unfortunately it wasn't anything that would prove that on the night of Wednesday, June 8, she hadn't murdered Rudolf Weyr.

. . .

On the contrary, everything still pointed to her. The lieutenant realized it again and again that evening as he pored over her file, plugging his ears so as not to hear his progeny, eighteen-year-old Zuzana and thirteen-year-old Joey, indulging in their devotion to the music known as rock. The clapper the director had sent to pick up his medication on Tuesday, the day before the murder, might have had the opportunity to substitute a capsule of hyoscine for one of his regular ones, but in her case there was a conspicuous absence of any sort of motive, let alone access to the poison.

And the capsules were something special. The director suffered terrible migraines, and common run-of-the-mill painkillers didn't work for him. His capsules were prescribed for him by his brother, head of the Pharmacological Research Institute, who was in fact personal physician and health adviser to the entire Weyr family. True, he had a profound interest in toxicology, but—like the clapper—he had no motive. Besides, the batch of capsules that included the fatal one had been made up at an ordinary pharmacy. Weyr carried them in a silver pillbox in his hip pocket except at night, when he put the box on his night table within reach of the bed. Whoever smuggled the poisoned capsule into it must have been very close to him. Hyoscine acts mercifully but definitively, by putting one to sleep, and according to the coroner death had occurred shortly before midnight.

It was abundantly clear that the clapper hadn't planted the hyoscine. True, Weyr had given her a lift on the day of the murder, but the only important thing about that ride was her testimony that he took one capsule from the silver pillbox in the car, and complained of especially severe pain. He also voiced his doubt that a single capsule would be enough, stating that before he went to sleep he would have to take another dose of "this poison." He surely didn't mean anything by the metaphor. He didn't know it wasn't a metaphor.

He let the clapper out on Wenceslaus Square and around half past seven arrived at his own villa. The astronomer across the street had set himself up on the balcony for his observations, just as he had the previous evening when he glimpsed the girl in the director's bedroom. When he saw that the director had arrived, he went inside to have his dinner. He returned to his post at eight o'clock and remained there, in spite of a consistently cloudy sky, until eleven. The lights in the director's study were on all that time, but the blinds were drawn. At about half past ten the light came on for a while in the bedroom, and a female silhouette crossed in front of the curtained window. She stood for a moment—as if in hesitation—and then went back and switched off the light. Because there was no interesting shadows to enliven the blinds in the study, thanks to a poorly placed lamp, the witness got bored around eleven and went to bed. At a quarter past eleven Weyr phoned his assistant to say that he didn't feel well and that it was entirely possible he wouldn't be coming in the next day. He gave him instructions to direct the shooting of several detail shots without any actors. He said he had pains in his left side and was having trouble breathing. Probably the flu, even though it was June. . . .

The expert medical witness of course recognized the pains as typical symptoms of early hyoscine poisoning, just preceding the critical moment when the victim falls into a deep sleep.

Naturally the prosecutor wanted to know who the female silhouette was. Weyr and his son had lived alone in the house for the whole month of June, and his son hadn't returned home that night until late, so it couldn't have been any ladyfriend of his. Apparently between seven-thirty and eight, while the witness was at dinner, some woman had come to the house and Weyr had let her in—unless of course she had come in the back way, in which case it could have been earlier or later. Maybe she always came in the back way: Weyr would have been afraid of her presence being discovered. Be that as it might, the defendant had no alibi for the time in question—she claimed she'd been at home, but she had no witnesses—and so it could very well be her silhouette that was observed by the astronomer behind the drawn curtains. According to the prosecutor, it probably was. Around half past ten, he postulated, an argument ensued and Weyr sent the defendant to the bedroom to bring him a capsule from the pillbox on the night stand. The accused was just waiting for an opportunity like that. She walked into the bedroom and turned on the light, but she didn't go over to the night stand at all. She didn't have to. She had the capsule with the hyoscine all ready. She waited a moment— which appeared to the witness to be a "hesitation"—and then returned to the study and handed the capsule to Weyr. Weyr swallowed it and the defendant left soon thereafter. It could have been after eleven, when the witness had already gone to bed. The coroner testified that by midnight, precisely according to hyoscine's schedule, Weyr was dead.

The defendant of course denied all this, maintaining that the prosecutor's hypothetical reconstruction was based on a total unfamiliarity with psychology, at least that of the female of the species. Having got into a violent argument with Weyr earlier, she would never have allowed him to make an errand girl out of her that same evening. She insisted on her innocence, the prosecutor insisted on his reconstruction. As is usually the case in Czechoslovakia, the judge was inclined towards the side of authority. . . .

The lieutenant looked up from the file. In the whole dark room the lamp with the green shade illuminated only his face—a face that kinder people compared to the moon, and more malicious

ones to a pancake. The orgy of noise in the next room was esca-
lating, a bleating voice from the television set was singing something that seemed to be about St. Vitus Cathedral bringing
somebody down—no, it must be something else, how would a
cathedral get into a rock song? All the same, the lieutenant got up
and opened the door a crack. He saw Zuzana staring wide-eyed
at the screen, where a sleazy-looking youth writhed repulsively
and twanged on a guitar. Sure enough, the great cathedral of St.
Vitus rose in the background.

Sighing, the lieutenant shut the door and sat down in an armchair. The aesthetic ideals of his daughter's generation mystified
him. He would have understood it if Zuzana had been infatuated
with, say, young Weyr. But when he had brought home the picture of that sweet young couple, Zuzana had remarked to a friend
of hers, "She's all right, but that pretty boy—I don't think I've
ever seen a slicker, creepier guy in my whole life. Have you?" And
the friend had agreed.

An infinitesimal hope began to dawn in the lieutenant's breast:
after all, he himself certainly didn't belong to the category of pretty
boys. . . . But the hope died as he realized that the girl in jail
didn't belong to his daughter's peculiar generation.

He closed his eyes, and in his memory he returned to the thin,
eager, but desperate face, bare of makeup or any other artifice.
"Look at me," the face said urgently. "Would I be capable of that?
I was bewildered for a while, I was crazy over him and that's the
truth; if you'd found him strangled in his bed, then it could have
been me who did it. But I always get over things in an awful
hurry. You know what I told you, about how I behaved at his
place the night before? Well, I was already feeling uncomfortable
about that on the way home, and in the morning I almost went
and apologized to him, but then I read about the Lastovicka girl
and it occurred to me that he'd recast that horror in the part on
account of me. Lieutenant, I could have strangled him in the throes
of emotion, he was a fine example of a womanizing bast—sorry.
But could the throes of emotion last long enough for me to steal

the hyoscine, steal an empty capsule, put them together, and then carry that seed of death around with me day and night? I had no idea there *was* such a thing as hyoscine. If I'd have wanted to poison somebody, I'd probably have gone hunting for toadstools. They didn't pay much attention to natural sciences at the classical lyceum I went to."

"You went to a classical lyceum?" asked the lieutenant, amazed.

"I did. A bishop's lyceum, at that," said the girl. "That's why I sing in dives."

The lieutenant almost asked her to explain, but then he recalled a period when graduates of religious high schools had a lot of difficulty continuing their studies at universities. She must have been graduating just about then.

"Well, what do you say, Lieutenant? Would the throes of emotion last long enough for me to dig up a book on toxicology? For that matter, these little fingers could easily have handled that whoring old throat of his—sorry!"

"Don't mention it," said the lieutenant. "Anyway—ahem—there have been such cases. I mean, of intense emotion lasting over an extended period. With such—ahem—erotically motivated murders, things happen that are truly incredible. For instance, did you ever read about the case of the security guard in Komarno?"

The girl shook her head. "Did he use hyoscine, too?"

"No," said the lieutenant. "A pistol. But that's not the point. The security guard, you see, was a particularly short man—"

"Inferiority complex."

"As a matter of fact, you're right. And when he was passing a garden on his way home from work one Saturday afternoon, he saw a young machinist he knew by sight from the plant. He was sitting there—ahem—with a very pretty girl. You understand: he knew the young man only by sight and he didn't know the girl at all. But that was enough."

"Did he shoot them?"

"Not them," said the lieutenant. "By virtue, as you so cleverly remarked, of his inferiority complex, he found himself in the throes of emotion, ran back to the plant—it was almost three kilometers—broke into a locker, grabbed a pistol, and returned on foot to the garden."

"You're kidding!"

"It seems improbable, but that is what he did," said the lieutenant sadly. "The two of them weren't sitting in the garden any more so the guard broke into the house, but they weren't there either and so, out of accumulated envy, he shot the young man's parents and two brothers. The throes of emotion lasted," concluded the criminologist, "all of three hours."

"Well, now you've wiped me out," declared the girl. "Nobody's going to believe me after that. It just shows that in cases like this, anything's possible." She had no idea how true her words were—or how often she would prove this to herself during the next two years.

. . .

The lieutenant turned a page in the file and started rereading the testimony of the director's son. It made matters even worse:

> Yeah, I heard some kind of argument. Just vaguely. I have an attic room and I'm not interested in my father's girlfriends. Some woman was screeching there, I don't know if it was the defendant. Screeching women all sound the same. Yeah, that was on Tuesday. On Wednesday I made a late night of it, I didn't get in till after midnight. The house was quiet by then. And in the morning I went to wake up Dad, because Mom had been in Podebrady for treatment for more than a month. We were supposed to go to the studio together early that morning, but he just lay there and he was—sort of—done for. I can take a whole lot—but when I realized Dad was stone cold, I felt sick. I nearly passed out.

Of course, he didn't pass out. He called the police instead. And when the lieutenant got that far in his reminiscences, he suddenly seemed to revive. He jumped out of the armchair, staring into the darkness of the room. Before him, approximately where the framed certificate naming him an exemplary public servant hung on the wall, he visualized the face of young Weyr, the face that Zuzana accused of slick prettiness. And beside it, in his mind's eye, he saw the face of the doctor's daughter, permanently and somewhat overly wide-eyed, saying, *When he cast that phony little twit in the part . . . I actually do wonder, now, why they took the part away from me. . . .* And then the two faces vanished, and the girl in the jacket made of rug fabric reappeared. She wasn't sitting behind the table any more, she was standing, shaking his hand in her callused palm torturing him with her gray eyes, and then she thought of something. "Lieutenant—show me that picture again! The one of those two charmers." When he brought out the magazine clipping, she stared at it and declared, "Sure, I know what's odd about those two. It's perfectly obvious! They look too much alike!" And he had gaped, finally seeing it—a delicate, subtle resemblance, as if the face of the doctor's daughter had somehow penetrated into the features of the director's son.

The lieutenant rubbed his forehead and looked around his study with his mouth open. Then he stumbled over to the bookshelf, searched for a while, and pulled out a fat volume, a reference book. He brought it over to his desk and with impatient fingers flipped it open at the end of the letter A. He soon found the reference:

> Azoospermia, Testicular—the absence of sperm in the ejaculate. It is to be assumed that the original sex cells did not travel to the embryonic gland when it was forming in the 6th–7th week of intrauterine life. Prognosis very poor, and no substantial improvement can be expected from any course of treatment.

The lieutenant rested his gaze on a point in the distance, smiled a little, and quickly grew sad again.

> Now you are in possession of enough clues to name the murderer and the motive. But which of Father Knox's commandments has been violated? Remember, it's all a question of deduction!

She sat opposite him once again, and there was still a table between them, but this time it was a marble table in the art deco Paris Café. The gray eyes were bordered with the monstrous but beautifully professional makeup that was all the rage. Now her face disclosed only about two-thirds of her actual age, and the lieutenant was stewing in the juices of suppressed emotion. But there was nothing to be done about that.

In an alto voice which confirmed that she was a singer, the girl said with admiration, "Lieutenant, it's even more incredible than the story of the security guard!"

"I mentioned that—ahem—under the influence of the erotic, nothing is impossible," he said. "She had long since come to terms with his mistresses, as well as with the knowledge that he didn't love her any more. What she couldn't accept was the realization that he had never ever loved her—not even right after the wedding, when she was totally convinced of his feelings for her. She couldn't bear the fact that he hadn't married her for love, but because her father could advance his career."

"And all it took was the photo?"

"That was all. She noticed it just the way you did. In short, woman's intuition. I could use some of that." The lieutenant gave her an aching glance. "For instance, if you were in my investigation unit . . ." He added hesitantly, "One comrade policewoman just got married, I don't know if she intends to stay with us, but you have your high school diploma, you could take a course and—"

The girl shook her head.

"I couldn't," she said. "Don't be angry, Lieutenant, but I've had enough of murder for a lifetime. I just signed a contract with Pragokoncert, to work abroad."

The lieutenant's face did what they describe in novels. It fell.

"Abroad?" His voice registered profound disappointment.

"That's the way it is," sighed the girl. "The fact is that they cleared my name—rehabilitated me, as they say—but you know people, nobody will ever altogether forget it, especially with a woman in a case like this. Heaven knows what actually happened, they'll say, some sort of nightclub singer, we know her type! All she has to do is make eyes at the judge—he's just a man, after all. . . . You know how people are, lieutenant, I don't have to tell you anything." The lieutenant turned pink, taking this differently from the way she meant it. "So I'll just be an export nightclub singer in all the bars of the world. Pragokoncert will get a percentage of my income in foreign currency, so our beloved socialist state gets something to make up for the shame I'll bring down on it by my behavior in all those bars. I can get away with it there because nobody will know me. They won't know that I was supposed to have poisoned a guy and that I only got off because I slept with three prosecutors and one senile judge." Her voice was bitter.

"It wouldn't be all that bad," the lieutenant tried to suggest, but the singer just waved a hand and took a deep drag on the Philip Morris cigarette he'd given her. He'd bought the package for her. He didn't smoke, except for an occasional stogie when there were no young girls around.

"Never mind that, all right? Just finish telling me what happened. So she noticed the resemblance too?"

"She did, and to top it off, she read in the magazine the interesting detail about their dates of birth, December 31, 1948, and January 1, 1949. And in the second article she found out that the Heyduk girl had turned down the part on the wishes of her father. Then all it took was for her to remember how close her husband had been to the Heyduks in Brno, back when they were in the process of getting married, and for a while thereafter, before they moved to Prague. She didn't even need to know about the doctor's ailment. She guessed intuitively why Dr. Heyduk was dead set against his daughter getting too closely acquainted with young Weyr."

"And the poison?"

"Weyr's brother is a famous toxicologist, and she had free access to his office. His apartment, too."

The girl shook her head and said, illogically, "Poor Mrs. Korenac. How much time do you think they'll give *her*?"

"A lot, I'm afraid," said the lieutenant.

"And she's innocent."

"Well—"

"I mean, in the case of Weyr's murder."

"In that case she is," agreed the lieutenant. "Of course, she had a mess in her pharmaceuticals and her prescriptions. She claimed she'd used the hyoscine for a medication that someone brought her a prescription for, but she couldn't find the prescription and she couldn't remember the patient." The lieutenant paused. "It took Mrs. Weyr a little over an hour to come by car to Prague from Podebrady, where she was in a sanitarium for medical treatment. She climbed out of a window after lights-out—she had a private room on the ground floor—and was in Prague by half past nine. She entered the villa by the back door, so the astronomer didn't see her arrive. Incidentally, he got probation for voyeurism," said the lieutenant.

"Serves him right, the old scarecrow. Amateur astronomer my foot! They needn't have bothered with probation."

"They couldn't help that. He had a clean bill of health otherwise. Anyway, Mrs. Weyr found her husband with a terrible headache. She explained that she'd come to pick up some things, they bickered back and forth for a while, and at half past ten her husband sent her upstairs for a capsule. By midnight she was back in her room in Podebrady."

The old criminologist fell silent. The art deco café was pleasantly bathed by the dusky evening light so conspicuously absent in the public places of the plastic era, and it buzzed with the conversations of old women over their teacups. The girl was silent too. Old-fashioned brass buttons gleamed on the front of her stylish blue blazer. She went to a lot of trouble to keep up with fashion, and Lieutenant Boruvka was somehow moved by that. Maybe because it was probably a little too late . . .

He suppressed those four dots in his mind and said, "It is in fact a case full of—ahem—eroticism. Dr. Heyduk wasn't so much afraid that his daughter would drop out of medical school but that she might—"

"Might sleep with her own brother. Or maybe even with her own daddy," the girls said matter-of-factly. "A lovely little Oedipus story. She and Petr didn't have the faintest idea that they were related?"

"No. The late Mrs. Heyduk had never told anyone, and the doctor didn't figure it out for himself until after he married a second time. They couldn't have children so he had himself checked out. Testicular azoospermia is congenital."

"Oh, what the hell," said the girl, which seemed a little cynical to the lieutenant. But he quickly excused her—he remembered all those low nightclubs in the mining district, "They could have had some fun, those kids," she said. "In this decadent day and age, it wouldn't be the most degenerate thing going on."

"Well, maybe not," admitted the lieutenant, unprofessionally. "But I don't think it would have happened anyway."

"Oh, come on, it happens almost every day," the girl said cheerfully.

"I know. But young Weyr is—you might say—too good-looking. Today's young girls—at least if I can judge by my daughter—like ugly men better. Like Mickey Rooney," he said. "Don't you like Mickey Rooney?"

The girl shook her head. "Personally, I like Gérard Philipe," she mused. "And after him, not anybody, really."

The lieutenant grew sad again. Then a faint hope arose.

"They're playing one of his old films, *Fanfan the Tulip*. Would you—" he cleared his throat predictably, unaware of the adolescent cliché he was acting out, "some evening, if you could find the time . . ."

The girl looked over at him with her gray eyes. She didn't need intuition to see it any more, it was written all over his face. Only she was just three days out of prison, and she'd had enough. For a long time. Or she thought she had, at least at that moment. She wasn't thinking about the fact that she owed her freedom to the lieutenant; girls are always ungrateful. And she shook her head even before the lieutenant finished asking.

SIN NUMBER 2

Mistake in Hitzungsee

A young woman walked into the dining room. She was slender, dressed in an elegant suit, and had her blonde hair gathered into a meticulous hairdo. She carried a paperback in her hand. She looked around, sat down at a table near the bar, and ordered breakfast.

The bartender thought she looked familiar. He kept looking back at her the whole time he was fixing the *smørrebrød,* and then through the steam from the espresso machine. He was a friendly sort, he didn't like to see guests sitting alone, especially if they were young women. When he placed the breakfast tray in front of her, he made an attempt at conversation.

"You've never been to Hitzungsee before, have you, miss? Surely not, I would have remembered you. I have an excellent memory for faces. Once I've seen one, I never forget it. Ever. And you, miss—" he smirked unprofessionally "—I've never seen you before."

The young woman measured him—very professionally—from head to toe. He was a stout middle-aged man of a certain type. She replied maliciously, "Do you know where I've been all your life?"

The smirk wilted on the bartender's face. He said unctuously, "Unfortunately not, miss." Then he stiffened and replied, with equal malice, "Or may be fortunately!" He walked over to a table where a couple of old regulars had just sat down. Bitch, he thought, and a foreigner to boot, from heaven knows where. No Swedish girl would be that snooty. But where have I seen her before?

Meanwhile the snooty foreigner had opened her paperback and started reading. She chewed away at her *smørrebrød,* and the way she held the book in her left hand, the title on the cover, *The Man Who Was Thursday,* was visible from the entrance. So when a huge man in a plaid cap appeared in the doorway, that title was the first thing he saw.

The man looked keenly around the room, his wrinkled brow suggesting that not much escaped him. He wore a striped, double-breasted suit, a little tight for his burly torso. In one hand he carried a case of the sort obstetricians carry, although he didn't look the least bit like a doctor. In his other hand he held another object that didn't seem to go with him, a paperback with the conspicuous title *Thursday's Child.* He looked around one more time, his gaze coming to rest on the book the blonde was reading; then he raised his own book to his face and seemed to be examining its title syllable by syllable. He shook his head, looked again at the girl, pondered, and appeared to come to a decision.

He waddled over to the table and sat down heavily on the chair opposite her.

She glanced up. She saw a big man grinning at her like a rather atypical traveling salesman, and in his ham of a hand holding up a book so the title faced her. She reflected that in the case of this fellow's smile, "from ear to ear" was no exaggeration. She filled her eyes with an icy look, but as she turned back to her mystery the man said, with an American accent, "There was a mixup with the books."

"What's that?" she asked, and the ice melted.

"There was a mix-up with the books," repeated that man, pointing a finger at the title of his. The finger was only a little bigger around than the girl's wrist. She looked up at his face. She liked what she saw; it said that he hadn't had a particularly easy life, and that the complications hadn't been the trivial sort that had befallen the pudgy bartender. She felt a certain amiable charity towards the stranger, and glanced again at his paperback. *Thursday's Child.* Being a clever girl, she caught on. Being even more curious than she was clever, she didn't correct his mistake.

"I couldn't find the right one either," she said instead.

"That's all right," he reassured her. "It's almost the same. One book's as good as another, right?" He hooted over his shoulder at the bartender with an order for double Scotch on the rocks, then turned back and gave the blonde another broad smile.

"It's funny, isn't it?" she said.

"Oh well, that's the way it goes sometimes," replied the man, adjusting the plaid cap that he hadn't seen fit to remove. "The whole thing's rotten, it makes me sick. That's why I'm here."

"It's very nice of you," she said, to keep the conversation going.

"What's nice about it? I'm a gentleman, that's all."

"That makes you an exception. Gentleman are, to all intents and purposes, extinct."

"No kidding?" He was apparently flattered. "But you're just saying that because you've had a rough time, babe. Not all guys are bastards. You should have been more careful."

The gray eyes turned to him inquiringly, but he took the look as a reproach. "Sorry, I don't mean to hurt your feelings. I know you can't help yourself in a situation like that. 'Specially if you're a woman. Don't worry, I'll take care of the bastard."

"Are you sure?"

"Easy. I'm an old hand at this, doll. And I'm dependable. I know all about these hotel fiends. By tonight you'll be able to forget the whole thing. Look here!"

He raised the obstetrician's bag from the floor, but just then the bartender approached with the whisky; he stared at the case, which didn't suit the man any more than the book had. The man put the bag back on the floor, and looked so annoyed that the bartender dropped the glass within reach of his gorilla's paw and cringed away. The man took a swig that was in keeping with his dimensions, spread his oversized lips in another smile, and leaned intimately across the table toward the blonde. Forgetting that he'd wanted to show her something in the case, he said, "So not to worry. By the time you and me get together this evening, you can be sure *he*"—referring again to some man whose identity was a total mystery to the girl—"won't be making your life miserable any more."

"That's very kind of you," squeaked the blonde. "And where will we be seeing each other this evening? And when?"

"Wasn't it the Moulin Rouge?"

"Y-yes."

"Okay. So tonight, when the coast is clear, all you have to do is phone here and ask for MacMac." He leaned across the table again, placing his paw on her manicured little hand. The corners of his mouth nearly met at the back of his head as he repeated, "But make sure the coast is clear. Don't forget, babe! MacMac!"

The girl shook her head with a pleasant smile. She rose and went to pay her bill, but the big man who was a gentleman stopped her. So she smiled again pleasantly, and walked out into the sunny Scandinavian morning.

Beside the entrance was a bit poster that read:

EVE ADAM
THE ROCK HIT OF PRAGUE
NIGHTLY AT THE
MOULIN ROUGE

Above it was a large photograph of the blonde.

The pudgy bartender was staring thoughtfully out the glass door into the sunshine, still wondering, where the hell have I seen that face? I have such a good memory for faces. . . .

He felt someone looking at him from behind, and turned around to face an alarmingly angry glare. "Don't get any ideas, you hear?"

said the huge man menacingly. "She's a buddy of my best buddy. And she's married!"

The bartender quickly turned to his other guests.

. . .

"Clearly he got me mixed up with somebody else," the blonde said in Czech about half an hour later, in her hotel room. "So I didn't tell him any different. Isn't that a gas, Zuzka?"

"You haven't heard the last of it, either," nodded the girl by the mirror. She was much younger than her companion and she sat in front of the mirror without any clothes on. She had enchanting dimples, and a lovely figure, full breasts and long legs. "What do you think it's all about?"

"I couldn't ask him, now, could I?"

The girl at the mirror got up and stretched. The northern sunshine outlined the curves of her body—and suddenly there was a noise at the door.

Both girls were startled rather than frightened. The undressed one put her finger to her lips, and the blonde tiptoed to the door. The undressed one performed a few teasing bumps and grinds, and the blonde quickly jerked the door open.

There was no one there any more. But a little way down the hall, the small porter in his striped apron was assiduously watering some cactus plants.

"Watch out you don't drown them. They can't swim," said the blonde, and the fellow glared at her. She shut the door.

"What do you think of that?" demanded the stripper. "This is the third time. Last time I almost poked his eye out with the door handle, and he made like he was picking up cigarette butts off the carpet. Dirty old man! And silly me, I was even nice enough to him at the beginning. But then the chambermaid told me he's been in trouble this way before. So now they all run around naked and tease him through the keyholes."

"Poor old thing," said the blonde. "It's just terrible what it can do to a person."

"Don't I know it. . . ."

The blonde caught the hint. "All right, who is it this time?"

"Eve, wait till you see him! The best-looking guy in Hit-SongSea."

"Single?"

"I don't know. We never got around to that. But wait till you see him—"

"What does he do?" The blonde interrupted Zuzka's enthusiasm in the same even tone.

"I don't know that either. But he's got money. He lives here in the Cloister, in a suite off the terrace. And he always spends his evenings at the Moulin. That's where he and I—"

"Oh, I get it! He saw you exhibiting yourself!"

"He doesn't mind. He—"

"I'll bet he doesn't." The blonde gazed at the dancer, and nodded maternally. "Take care, Zuzka. Listen to somebody older and wiser. Nab yourself a middle-aged, settled-down Swede that you know who he is and what he does and if there isn't a wife somewhere. Playboys throwing money around at the Moulin can only mean trouble.

Zuzka scowled. "Thanks, Grandma. But don't worry. For trouble, I've got the pill.

.   .   .

Later in the morning, the blonde took a stroll through the resort town that she and her friend referred to as HitSongSea. She wandered along the clean little streets, spent an hour in a department store, and finally, after much deliberation, bought herself a cheap fountain pen with a vulgar photograph of a bathing beauty on it. For some unknown reason, it inspired her. For lunch she went to a restaurant which looked modest enough on the outside but turned out to be posh, so she just ordered *smørrebrød* again, and a beer.

There was a noisy group at the next table consisting of three girls in student caps and three young men in tennis shorts. The restaurant was lit by candles, and their muted glow flattered the blonde. That may be why she caught the eye of a tall, fair-haired young man with his arm around one of the students. He can't be a day over twenty-five, she estimated gloomily. Opening her purse and digging out a mirror, she determined to her satisfaction that in intimate lighting she didn't look any older herself. They carried on a very practiced game with their eyes until the *smørrebrød* was gone, and then it gradually tapered off; he was too busy with the giggling students.

The blonde sat there for a little while longer, then paid her bill and, a little annoyed, headed for the room labeled *Badrum*.

There was a big mirror there, and although it was only a quarter of an hour since she'd looked at herself, the blonde stepped up to it, helplessly attracted by that merciless witness to the tooth of time. She confronted her round face circled by a pretty hairdo, her widely spaced eyes, and thought, well, I don't know—a face like this, and such rotten luck. How come? The question drew a wrinkle between the eyebrows of her reflection. She quickly erased it and fished in her purse for her compact, but it wasn't there—of course, she'd left it on the dresser. As she looked unhappily at the shine on her nose, a mild voice said to her, "Would you like to borrow some makeup or something?"

She turned around. A nondescript woman of about forty was smiling at her with thin lips.

"Oh, thanks a lot. That's terribly nice of you!" She accepted some powder from the faded lady and turned to repair the insignificant imperfection. The woman's face appeared beside her own in the mirror, and she said, in admiration mixed with sadness, "You're so pretty. . . ."

"Thank you."

"You must be very happy, too. . . ."

"Yeah, that's me," the blonde answered with a sigh. "I win a lottery a week, and there aren't enough hours in the day for all the gorgeous men chasing me. . . ."

• • •

After commiserating for a while, the blonde and her new acquaintance, Mrs. Lundquist, walked through the park together. Mrs. Lundquist said, "I know what you mean. It's just terrible what it can do to a person."

"You're telling *me*," said the blonde, with a vague notion that she'd heard this before.

"Naturally, all he was interested in was my money. Everyone tried to dissuade me, but I didn't listen. He was twenty and I was forty-two. You can guess what happened."

"Girls?" the blonde asked matter-of-factly.

"Except they weren't all that young. At least, after I quit giving him an allowance he started hanging around women who were older. Their financial status was higher, too."

"Why don't you divorce him?"

"I can't. I come from a strict Catholic family and—I just can't. But I've moved out on him. I was afraid. . . ." She paused and pressed her thin lips tightly together. The blonde looked at her curiously.

"I think I understand. You were afraid he might . . . kill you?"

Mrs. Lundquist seemed startled. After a moment she replied, "No. I actually wouldn't mind that. Life doesn't mean that much to me any more, you know? I was afraid of something else. . . ."

She was silent for a long time. Finally the blonde couldn't stand it any more, and asked, "Of what?"

"That I might kill him."

· · ·

They walked past the tennis courts. The low sun of the northern summer cast diagonal shadows on the grass of the courts. The girl playing on the court nearest to the path was quick with the tennis racket, and she had the slim but muscular legs of a dancer.

She was indeed a dancer.

When the blonde recognized her, she gave the girl's partner a perfunctory glance. And she blinked. The fellow in white shorts who was chasing the ball looked remarkably like the fair-haired young man who had been so taken with the students at noon.

The two women stopped by the wire fence, and Mrs. Lundquist reached inside her purse. "Isn't it nice, seeing young people having fun?" she said. "Those white outfits against the green grass—

if only I weren't so near-sighted." She finally found her glasses and sighed, "Ah, what a lovely girl!"

"That lovely girl is my roommate," said the blonde. "We share a room at the hotel."

"I see. You must introduce her to me. And that young man of hers—"

As Mrs. Lundquist turned to the young man, something like a sob emerged from her throat. Her face turned red, and then quickly paled. She looked like Ophelia betrayed.

"Quick, let's get out of here!" she gasped, and fled down the gravel path. The blonde caught up with her.

"What happened? Aren't you well?"

Mrs. Lundquist caught her by the hand, as if she needed to hang on to something. "That was . . . my husband! I had no idea he'd be in Hitzungsee. I wouldn't have come. But now I'll leave, of course."

"There, there," the girl consoled her.

"I know it's awkward," the woman went on, her voice quavering. "It must sound like nonsense to you. But I hate him! I could . . . I'm going to. . . ."

When she finally put the agitated woman to bed and fed her a sedative, the blonde sat down in the lobby; she was curious, and she liked to watch the world go by. Once, long ago, the Cloisters Hotel had indeed been a convent. It was built of stone, and had walls a meter thick that rose in a strange asymmetry against the Swedish sky. A fire blazed in the fireplace in the lobby, and over in the corner, at an antique table, the little porter in the striped apron was polishing some brass utensils.

This time the girl got a good look at him. He was a squarely built dwarf, not an old man at all. Under his nose was a Hitler moustache, on his forehead a thatch of slicked-down black hair, and his eyes didn't know how to be anything but wild—black and madly passionate. Her own gaze met his, but only for a split second. His eyes immediately sidled down to her knees, and although she usually didn't mind being looked at like that, this time she almost shivered. She squirmed in her chair and pulled her skirt down over her knees. I wonder, I wonder! thought the blonde. Then she turned her thoughts to gloomy considerations of a certain young stripper.

The revolving door disgorged two figures; the poorly lit lobby was illuminated by the white glow from two tennis outfits, and—speak of the devil, the blonde thought. The charming, charmingly charmed little Zuzka. By then the latter was rushing across the lobby in her painfully short white skirt, dragging behind her the somewhat embarrassed husband of Mrs. Lundquist.

He was well trained. He gave no indication that they had crossed paths before, and indeed had had a very good look at each other. In fact, he placed his athletic arm around the dancer's shoulders with the same ingenuousness he had displayed at noon, and the smile he turned on the singer seemed made for the purpose of display.

"This is Sören Lundquist," chirped the enchanted young girl. "And this is my friend and colleague Eve Adam."

The fair-haired young man raised one eyebrow, as if he were in a close-up shot. "Congratulations, Miss Adam," he said in velvety voice. "You must have had imaginative parents. Such an interesting combination of names—"

"How observant!" The girl's voice was like ice cubes tossed in a glass. "Would you believe that only about one and a half persons out of every two notices that combination? Men, that is. Ladies generally ignore it."

The young man maintained his practiced presence of mind, and once again showed his teeth, slightly clenched this time. The dancer took his arm.

The blonde's eye fell on something beyond the tanned ear that hugged the young man's head. There in the corner of the lobby, standing under a brass platter, was the little porter, his face contorted into what looked like an antique mask of jealousy.

She looked back to the other girl, so deeply infatuated. Ah, Zuzka, she thought, I suppose I'm going to have to ask what you meant when you said you were even *nice* to the porter at the beginning. I bet you even got it on with him, you wicked girl!

In his corner, the porter buffed a brass kettle until it glowed with heat. The young couple started up the stairs, and then the young man turned back to the porter and, in a voice reeking with the arrogance of his class, barked, "Boy! Run and get me some shaving cream, and bring it up to my room!"

Oh, God! said the blonde to herself.

Behind her the door to the dining room gave a creak, and she turned to see a dignified old lady walk through, placing a lorgnette to her eyes. Observing the white-clad couple, the old lady pursed her thin purple lips and made a low-voiced remark to the woman beside her, who was dressed like a professional companion. Then she looked around. An old man in an afternoon suit jumped out of an upholstered chair under a potted palm and scurried across the lobby to grab the old lady's hand: "Good afternoon, Countess! Just in time for a little game of bridge!"

Countess Wallenstein gave one more glance through her lorgnette at the indecent white skirt, and then took the proffered arm.

Bridge, is it? the blonde thought, and wondered how the other game would turn out; she glanced at the staircase, but Zuzka and her admirer had already vanished. Next she remembered the lady she had temporarily sedated, and asked herself how long those pills worked. Then, for no apparent reason, she thought of the pleasant but massive Mr. MacMac, who intended to settle accounts with some bastard that night, and a shiver went up her spine. She thought back to the girl in the tennis skirt, whose extensive knowledge of Sören Lundquist was probably limited to his perfumed sheets, and another shiver ran up her spine. Oh God, she thought, how is all this going to turn out? She was possessed by an uncertain but clearly nasty premonition.

. . .

The exterior of the Moulin Rouge Cabaret lit up the northern evening with a neon windmill, a copy of the famous one in the heart of Paris. The windmill's revolving purple arms played a pleasant kaleidoscope of colors on the blonde's face.

She squeezed past a group of bar-hoppers standing by the entrance examining the photos of a half-dressed dancer with dimples in her cheeks, and walked by her own photo, quite a bit more decent though still rather revealing. She disappeared inside and climbed down the spiral staircase towards the dressing room, stopping at a little telephone table to flip through the telephone book and dial a number.

"I want to speak with Mr. MacMac. He's a guest in your establishment."

Silence for a while, then the distant buzz of a crowded restaurant.

Then she heard the familiar voice of the large man with the American accent. "Is that you, babe?"

"Yes, it's me."

"Is the coast clear? You sure?"

The girl shivered again, but she was morbidly curious, and that nasty quality got the better of her.

"Yes," she replied and immediately regretted it. Eve, you beast, she thought, what if you're sending this nice man into a trap? How do *you* know whether the coast is clear or wrapped in smog? But it was too late to check out the meterological situation.

The nice man said menacingly, "Okay. It's half past eight now, I ought to be at the Moulin Rouge by nine."

"Wh-where should I wait?"

"At the bar. We'll have a whiskey to celebrate. Bye, doll! Take care!"

Mr. MacMac hung up.

No, thought the blonde, you take care. Her conscience was beginning to bother her. She entered the dressing room. Zuzka was there, lounging in an armchair, her dreamy eyes drilling a hole in the ceiling to the lounge. Around eleven her perfidious playboy would arrive there, ready to partake publicly of a vision that the blonde was convinced he'd seen all too much of in private. She decided to take action. . . .

Less than ten minutes later Zuzka went tearing out of the dressing room, and her eyes, no longer dreamy, were flashing bolts of lightning.

"The pig! I'll rip him to shreds!"

The blonde watched her friend zip up the stairs like a white spiral. I had to tell her, she thought, and shrugged her shoulders. It was for her own good. They still haven't got a pill for a broken heart. She shut the door and sat down in front of the mirror. She looked at her round face and fluffed up her hair. Well, that's that, kid, she said to herself. It's over and done with. It would have been even worse if you'd found out later.

. . .

By nine the blonde was sitting at the bar, curious, a little scared, once again examining her inexplicably successful good looks in the mirror behind the bar. She was just fending off the third attempt at a pass on the part of a tipsy salesman from Stockholm when the massive Mr. MacMac burst in and looked around wildly.

Something was wrong. As she froze on her bar stool Mr. MacMac spied her, strode over to her, and sagged heavily onto the next stool, flopping his obstetrician's case beside him.

"Scotch?" she asked uncertainly.

"I haven't time," panted Mr. MacMac. "I've got a train for Stockholm at half past nine, and I'm gone!"

He gave her a hard look, almost accusing, she thought. He glanced at the clock and ordered a Scotch anyway, then turned to the flustered singer. "You aren't trying to put one over on me, are you, babe?"

"Who, me?" she marveled, shakily.

"Who else? Because Peterson certainly wouldn't!"

Mr. MacMac nervously raised his glass, took a deep swig, and ordered another drink.

"Look, I only did it on account of Petersen, understand? He told me about the jam you were in, and he said you were a great girl—you struck it rich, true, but everybody said you deserved it because you were always great. That's why I took this on. Any friend of Petersen's is a friend of mine. So here it is!" He put his hand into his pocket and pulled out an oblong bag made of colored plastic. The blonde took it from him uneasily, hesitated for a moment, and then put in her purse.

"But if you're trying to put one over on me—"

"Me, Mr. MacMac?"

"You said the coast was clear, didn't you?"

The blonde's knees began to tremble under her sequinned skirt. But she said boldly, "It was, too!"

The huge man grabbed her hand. "Are you pulling my leg? Was it really? Was he really down here? Did you see him sitting here with your own two eyes?"

"Y-yes. But—but—"

He was looking in her eyes. "He left, did he?"

"Y-yes. W-we—"

"You got into a hassle? Is that what happened?"

"Y-yes—"

"And he got mad at you, and while you were phoning me he split?"

"That's it!"

Mr. MacMac downed his second drink and said philosophically, "Well, a woman's just a woman. But you should have controlled yourself. You should have kept him here. Knowing what you knew, I mean."

"I g-guess—"

"The fact is, I was a little late. Maybe that was lucky for me. If I'd got there before him, he might have—him or the other guy— *Damn!* This stinks!"

"Wh-Why? What happened?" quavered the blonde.

Mr. MacMac gave her a dour look. He appraised her one last time, and decided he could trust her.

"Stiff!" he hissed.

The blonde felt the stool wobble under her. "Wh-what do you mean?"

"Nixed. Croaked. Deceased. Is that clear enough?"

"But that w-wasn't what I—"

"Just what did you call Petersen for, babe?"

"I . . . I . . . ." The blonde couldn't get past the personal pronoun. Meanwhile the massive Mr. MacMac continued exercising his brain, talking more or less to himself.

"When I get up there, I cut a hole in the window—climb inside—the safe is child's play, just like I figured, a cinch—I'm through in ten seconds. Then I turn around and head for the door—"

"You shouldn't have killed him!" wailed the blonde. Mr. MacMac raised his eyebrows in surprise and stared at her.

"Have you gone crazy?"

"That's not what I wanted! Really, I didn't mean for you to kill anyone!"

Mr. MacMac gave the girl a long look, as she grew paler by the second. Finally he said wearily, "Keep a grip on yourself, doll. I didn't kill him. He was dead already. When I turned away from the safe and went to leave, he was there on the floor, half under the bed—that's why I didn't notice him at first. Was I ever surprised! Somebody hit him over the noggin so hard his face looked like a jigsaw puzzle!" As he went on remembering, he grew more and more upset. "So I step over him, go to the terrace door, and it's bolted shut. I slide the bolt open—"

Mr. MacMac sat up with a jerk. "Hold it!" he choked. "Hold it! That's impossible!"

The girl started, and grabbed the counter as the legs of her bar stool did a little dance on the marble floor.

"Wh-what now?"

But Mr. MacMac didn't pay any attention to her, he just continued his monologue. "The window was locked on the inside, so I had to cut a hole in it from the outside. The door to the terrace was bolted shut on the inside too. I know that for a fact because I had to slide the bolt. The door to the hall was locked and the key was in the lock on the inside, I tried it as soon as I got in the room. Shit, how did he get out of there?"

"He who?" squeaked the girl.

Mr. MacMac, gentlemen though he was, snapped at her, "Are you stupid or what, babe? The killer, of course!"

It took her breath away. The monumental Mr. MacMac rubbed his forehead, but he didn't come up with anything new. He tossed down the end of his drink, and an ice cube fell out of the glass and shattered on the marble floor.

"I'm getting the hell out of here," declared Mr. MacMac. "There's something rotten going on and I don't like it! Bye-bye, doll, take care! You got what you asked for. I'm off!"

He tossed a bank note on the bar, picked up his obstetrician's case from the floor, and was as good as his word. I just hope, thought the girl, that he didn't leave that plaid cap of his at the scene of the crime.

She stabilized her position on the bar stool with a shot of stomach bitters, and her normal pallor began to replace the pale green cast of her skin. A second and third shot brought her completely back down to earth. When he brought her the fourth, the bartender remarked, "Forget about him! He was too old for you anyway. A gorilla like him and a nice girl like you!" She just shook her head and did nothing to set him straight.

Suddenly she thought of something. She reached into her purse and took out the plastic bag. It contained a tiny cassette recorder. She stuck it back in her purse, slid down off the bar stool, and hurried back to her dressing room. Moments later she was sitting stunned in front of the mirror, but for once she wasn't looking into it; she was listening to a miserable, passionate female voice issuing from the tape recorder on the dressing table:

"Sören! Sören darling! I love you, I really do love you! But Oscar is terribly jealous! He senses something, I can tell. We have to stop seeing each other . . . at least for a while . . . darling . . . and we're not going to argue tonight, are we? Please, darling! It's our last night together . . . for a while, anyway . . . so let it be another beautiful one! Darling! I love you so awfully much! Kiss me. . . .Kiss me. . . . Oh! . . . Oh! . . ."

The voice lapsed into heavy breathing, and then the kind of unarticulated exclamations you might find on those records produced by the Pornophone company, and sold next to magazines with pictures suitable for gynecology textbooks. Ah, yes. The blonde was just looking at herself in the mirror, and noting that she was still a little green around the edges, when the door behind her opened and another greenish girl staggered in.

. . .

"Calm down, for heaven's sake! And tell me what happened. The hall door was locked, he didn't answer when you banged on it, and the chambermaid saw you banging on it—some smart move!— then you ran down to the lobby, out of the hotel, and up the outside staircase to the terrace, where you bumped into the Lundquist woman."

"Th-that's it! It was her!" Zuzka's teeth were chattering. "She was dragging a big trunk and she was all—bug-eyed. I'm sure she's the one who did it! You said yourself she had the urge—"

The singer shook her head. "Forget it. What matters is that you walked in through the terrace door, right? And left your fingerprints on the door handle, right?"

"That's right," sobbed Zuzka. "And then . . ." She fell silent, and the singer wondered what else was about to come out.

"When I was running away, down the stairs from the terrace— you can imagine what I looked like at that point, even worse than the Lundquist woman—Lund saw me. You know, the porter—"

"The one you were *nice* to?" the singer interrupted her.

"Him? Oh, come on! But he was walking with some old coot— they were helping that Countess Wallenstein up the stairs—you know, the one with the lorgnette. She lives in a suite off the terrace, too—"

"Better and better!" said the singer. "Now just listen, and add it up: the chambermaid will tell about you banging on the locked door, and you were probably yelling too, right?"

"Right," admitted Zuzka.

"Wonderful. Then Mrs. Lundquist will tell about you running up the stairs, and the countess about your flight down—and she'll have two witnesses. They'll find your fingerprints on the handle of the open door to the terrace. They'll find out you slept with Sören—to put it nicely. Furthermore that Sören was married. So they'll figure that you found out, and then you're up shit creek, kid."

"Oh, my God!" wailed the dancer.

"The question is how to get out of it. It won't be easy." She glanced at the tape recorder. "Actually, it'll be damned difficult. The only witness who could help you out is gone—"

"Who's that?"

The blonde sighed. "If I only knew. He said he was MacMac. But that's just what he called himself."

• • •

It was the chambermaid who officially discovered the murder. At nine o'clock she remembered that she had forgotten to deliver a pair of pressed trousers to the gentleman in the suite off the terrace. It seemed odd that he hadn't pestered her about them; he was one of those fussy guests. But when she brought them, he didn't answer her knock. It occurred to her, she said, that he might have been ill and passed out. It didn't sound very believable coming from her, and Niels C. Kölln, the young homicide detective who had been assigned the case as his first murder, recalled his criminal psychology textbook and decided she had more likely imagined some hanky-panky, and had gone to have a peek through the terrace door. Not that it made any sense to him—he was the product of a strict Calvinist upbringing, and while he'd learned about certain functions of the human body in sex education class, he hadn't entirely believed the professor. In fact, he hadn't believed any of it until a certain young man found himself in a situation labeled *penis captivus* by the sex education professor; the young man had called the police, but being bashful he had reported a murder instead. That had been a week ago, and for the young Calvinist detective it had been a belated awakening to an essentially healthy interest—so much so that he was almost sorry this new call to the homicide division was legitimate. Anyway, the chambermaid, overcome by fears for the health of the fussy guest, had set out on the path taken some ten minutes earlier by Zuzka: down the hall, out of the hotel, and up the outside staircase to the terrace. She had found the terrace door open and inside, beside the bed, she had discovered the guest who had been struck a mortal blow on the head.

Detective Niels C. Kölln added it all up just as the blonde had predicted, made the arrest, and found himself entranced. He had never in his life noticed that some young women had dimples in their cheeks. All the same, a telegram was quickly dispatched to Stockholm to detain the witness Mrs. Lundquist. She was on her way there by the same express train that bore the gentleman who called himself MacMac, but there was no mention of him in the telegram.

The detective sat silent in the room where the playboy had succumbed, unable to think of anything else to ask the blonde witness. He was thinking about the suspect—not in the context of the crime, they way he should have been, but in the context of what that sex professor had lectured about. His deductions were interrupted by the witness.

"Is it all right if I ask *you* something?"

The detective started. He nodded.

"When you first arrived, was the door to the hall really locked?"

"Yes. The door was locked and the key was in the lock, on the inside. The murderer came in through the terrace door."

"Ah," said the singer, getting up from her chair. "Can I go now?"

"Certainly. If you think of anything important—"

"I probably won't. But . . ." She paused. "But you might want to find out why, if the terrace door was open, the murderer cut that hole in the window over there." She pointed a silver fingernail at the evidence in question. The girl was calling the detective's attention to it to distract him from all the clues pointing to the accused. The truth was that a pair of dimples had long since convinced him of the dancer's innocence—but that was something the singer had no way of knowing.

. . .

She left, and the detective, a little crestfallen that he hadn't noticed the hole in the window himself, turned to examine the professional job done by the gentleman who called himself MacMac. Even though he was distracted by an indisposition that had no place in his line of work, he finally worked out that the window had been cut because the door had been bolted shut. It wasn't until after the deed had been done that the murderer had slid the bolt and fled through the door.

"Yes, but what was the man in the room doing while the one outside was working on the window with a glass cutter?" asked the blonde when, later on, he confided his deductions to her in the hotel lobby. "Those tools make a terribly squeaky noise. I know that from a girl I met in—" She gulped, and hesitated for a moment. "Anyway, I know they make an awful racket. The guy inside would have to be deaf, or a very sound sleeper—"

Niels C. Kölln, caught in another mental lapse, said nothing. The singer fell silent, thinking. The hotel lobby was as quiet as a church, for the specter of death had driven all the guests to their rooms, and the press hadn't arrived yet. In one corner a wide-eyed busboy was polishing a brass chalice while getting an eyeful of the blonde's miniskirted thighs. Somewhere a clock ticked loudly. The reception clerk was adding up a column of figures.

The busboy's gaze was so persistent that the blonde finally noticed. She pulled down her skirt.

Suddenly her eyes opened wide and she stared.

At the busboy.

She opened her mouth and sighed, "Good God! Komarno!" And she ran after the busboy.

The busboy fled.

· · ·

What the young detective lacked in deductive capacity, he made up for with legwork. In a little while the busboy was facing Niels C. Kölln and the blonde, trying to recollect his alibi.

It wasn't particularly air-tight. The previous evening, when he followed the instructions of Lund, the porter, and delivered shaving cream to the guest in the suite off the terrace, he had been given a pair of trousers that he turned over to the chambermaid for pressing. After that the porter thought up another job for him: polishing shoes in the corridor leading to the basement door. The porter had gone down to the basement to reset the oil furnace—that had taken him about ten minutes, and the busboy had stayed there cleaning shoes for about another hour. Then Mr. Lund had ordered him to the kitchen to help wash dishes, but he had never finished that because the chambermaid had come tearing in with the news that one of the guests had been killed.

The busboy fell silent and the blonde turned to the detective. "It's clear now, isn't it?"

"What is?"

"Everything. Don't you see?"

Niels C. Kölln didn't see, but rather than making him humble, this annoyed him.

"No," he snapped. "I'm not clairvoyant!"

"Neither am I," said the blonde modestly. "But when I'm bored, I read mysteries."

.   .   .

They were just turning towards the corridor leading to the basement when the phone rang at the reception desk. The clerk picked it up and then said, loudly enough that they could hear, "You want Mr. Lundquist?" He waved to the detective. "Just a moment." This time the detective's mind was on his job, and he reached for the receiver.

"Hello?"

The blonde moved her head closer so that she too could hear the thin, frightened, distant female voice. It was a voice she had heard before.

"Sören? Is that Sören?"

"Mm-hm," mumbled the detective.

"Sören! I couldn't make it! Believe me! I'm calling from the hospital. Please, wait a few more days. I'll come as soon as I can. For God's sake, I beg you!"

But now the young detective acted like an authority figure in a Victorian mystery. He cleared his throat with an affected "ahem" and demanded, "What hospital are you calling from, miss?"

The blonde slapped her forehead with the palm of her hand. They listened. The receiver was silent, and then they heard a click.

"Oh, you!" wailed the girl.

The detective blushed purple. "That was a mistake," he mumbled.

"You bet it was," said the blonde. "But never mind, she doesn't have anything to do with the murder. Where's that little busboy got to?"

The contrite Niels C. Kölln didn't ask why she was so sure of the innocence of the caller. He was rapidly arriving at the conviction that either he was an idiot, or the singer's brain was almost as perfect as that of his professor of logic at the police academy. He respected men equipped with such organs, but women similarly equipped terrified him. He felt an intense yearning for the company of the suspect with the dimples, and prayed she wasn't the murderer.

They followed the busboy to the basement door.

"Is this the only way in?" asked the blonde.

"Yes, miss," said the busboy, who was still unsure about the adequacy of his alibi.

> This is, of course, a Mystery of the Locked Room—but by now you should be able to deduce the *who* and *why*, and especially the *how* of it.

They opened the door and went down to the basement, an ancient stone-walled crypt. In the middle stood the oil furnace, and along the walls was a variety of objects that the hotel administration had stored there in case they ever came in handy. They looked around. The walls, made of large stone blocks, were smooth and damp.

"Well?" said the detective defiantly, collecting his courage.

The girl picked up an old broom handle and walked around the basement, tapping the walls. Niels C. Kölln didn't understand but he let it pass without comment; he had lost faith in his comments. The busboy watched her with his mouth open.

One very large block sounded hollow. The blonde smiled. She

seemed to be sniffing at the stone, but in fact she was examining the cracks—and she was pleased with what she found. For the two observers witnessed an extraordinary phenomenon.

The little hand with the silver fingernails pressed on the edge of the massive stone block. There was a creak, and the block turned on a vertical axis—it was in fact just a thin plate of stone, fortified on the inside with a metal construction and resting on two metal pegs. Beyond it was a large black opening leading somewhere inside the building.

. . .

"No, wait," she said. The girl was not only curious and clever, but also sensitive to feelings of others, and she realized that the detective was ill at ease. She decided that before bringing out the final proof of her roommate's innocence, she would introduce him to the mysteries of the case. She told him quickly about her meeting with Mr. MacMac, and about the mysterious tape. "I haven't any idea who MacMac is," she continued, "nor do I know who the woman on the tape is. But that tape must be very valuable to her, and the guy who was iced—"

"Was what?" he asked uncertainly.

"The one that got murdered," the blonde corrected herself, "knew very well it was valuable to her, and offered to sell it to her. I guess she was supposed to bring the money here to Hit-SongSea. . . ."

"Hitzungsee," the detective chided the girl, pleased that there was at least one thing he knew better than she. She immediately stripped him of that illusion.

"Zuzka calls it HitSongSea. Don't you like that?"

"But the correct pronunica . . ." the detective began, but he ended, "but I like that. It's fun. Hit Song Sea . . ."

"But she couldn't get her hands on the money. So she thought of an old friend, somebody called Petersen. You know how I told you MacMac said she'd 'struck it rich'? That indicates that at one point she wasn't all that well off, and she hung around with people like that too."

"We know a Petersen, I wonder if it's the same one," said the detective. "Possession of stolen property, smuggling, passing tips to burglars—"

"See how it all comes together? And because that unknown woman was a 'great girl,' Mr. Petersen sent her a pro. The trouble was, the pro had never met her personally, so they had to set up a recognition signal. But the pro didn't care much about literature, and figured one book was as good as another."

A light dawned for the detective. "And the girl, she was the one on the phone?"

"See how clever you are," said the blonde, a little impudently. "Something happened to her on the way to HitSongSea, and she logically concluded that since Mr. MacMac wouldn't have done anything without meeting her, she still had Lundquist's blackmail to deal with. That's why she called, to at least try to talk him into waiting a while. She has no idea she can take it easy now. She won't relax until she reads in the paper tomorrow that Lundquist has kicked the bucket."

The detective grinned. His self-confidence was gradually returning. "That won't help!"

"Why not?"

"Because she won't know what happened to the tape."

"That's true," said the blonde, and added magnanimously, "You really are clever!"

Pleased, Kölln continued to follow his logic out loud: "Unless of course MacMac looks her up through Petersen in Stockholm. Then she'll feel safe."

The blonde looked at him sadly, because besides being smart she was also kind-hearted. "Hardly," she said. "Mr. MacMac has no idea who in the world I am. So let's have a look at this secret passageway, all right?"

A blushing Niels C. Kölln followed her meekly.

· · ·

He traded places with her to climb the ladder, though, assuming she'd prefer it that way. (Once again he was mistaken; the blond hadn't had a Calvinist upbringing.) They went up the ladder, with the detective shining his flashlight ahead. About ten meters up, the shaft ended with a door in the side. It was closed with a hasp.

The detective looked beneath him uncertainly, but in the pale reflection of his flashlight he saw a face alive with irrepressible curiosity.

"Hurry up! Come on!"

So he hastily fumbled with the hasp and opened the door. Behind it hung some sort of fabric. By feel, he determined that it was stretched on a wooden frame.

"The entrance is covered with a painting," he whispered to the girl beneath him.

"So take it down!"

With both hands, the detective lifted the fame and raised it off the hook. Carefully he lowered it to the floor, and shone his flashlight inside the room.

Then he almost slipped off the ladder. A terrified screech sounded from the darkness, and in the cone of light cast by the flashlight the detective spied the wrinkled face of Countess Wallenstein snuggled up against the ruddy cheek of the old bridge player. The two of them were in bed, obviously without the benefit of nightclothes.

. . .

"No, no, no!" raged the blonde when they were back in the basement, and the detective tacitly enjoyed her failure, even though his Calvinist conscience bother him about it. "That's the only possibility! I read about it in a mystery story, and the author was a specialist in this—his name was Carr or Dickson or something. The Mystery of the Locked Room has a finite number of solutions and a secret passage is the *only* one that fits this particular murder!"

Spurred by the blonde's lack of success, the detective felt his lost deductive capacities reviving. "Maybe it wasn't a locked room at all."

"What about the key in the lock? And the hole cut in the window? And the bolt MacMac had to slide open?" shrieked the singer.

"Here's what I mean: when MacMac was cutting a hole in the

window, the room was locked. Because the murderer was still inside!"

"What do you mean?"

"The murderer must have been somebody known to the victim, so he let him inside. Then, to protect himself from surprises, the murderer locked the door to the hall and shot the bolt on the terrace door. After the deed was done, the murderer suddenly heard someone cutting the window open from the terrace, and just hid under the bed. When MacMac was gone, he simply left by the terrace door."

Kölln fell silent and glanced at the blonde. She didn't say anything. He asked her, "What do you think of that hypothesis?"

She sat there, her cheeks turning darker and darker. Then she blew her stack completely. She grabbed a jug off pile of junk and heaved it against the wall opposite, and it smashed into a thousand pieces. Two empty wine bottles followed. The detective reached out to prevent any further destruction of hotel property, but she had already snatched up a small stone ball, a remnant from some cornice or capital, and hurled it with all her might.

The ball hit the stone wall with a hollow thud.

The girl suddenly pulled herself together, and the detective's self-confidence evaporated once more.

.   .   .

The second secret passage led them to their objective, the suite where Sören Lundquist had succumbed miserably, and the psychopathic porter was arrested that very night. His motive had in fact been identical with that of the the security guard in Komarno, described to the blonde by a certain sentimental lieutenant: faced by a more successful seducer, he had been overwhelmed by sexual rage.

The girl was relieved to discover that Zuzka's being "nice" to the porter was courteous rather than physical. The murder was front-page news in the Stockholm press, but the blonde was soon caught up again in the everyday work of lounge singing. Evening after evening, she would stand at the microphone and, in her

melodic alto, convey to the world eternal truths about the eternal,
if banal, problems of life:

> Tragedy, tragedy!
> Here's my catastrophe!
> Tragedy, tragedy!
> My man's gone from me. . . .

On her left a perpetually sex-starved Swede blew on his tenor
saxophone, on her right a perpetually tipsy Dane blew on his
trumpet, behind her a perpetually stoned black American strummed
his amplified bass and a despondent man without a country, perpetually inclined to somber blues, fingered his electric organ. In
that musical group, a microcosm of the century, the singer also
operated the percussion instruments: with her fashionable little
pump she worked the pedal on the high-hat cymbals; with the
brushes in her delicate hand she tickled the little drum; now and
then she struck the large cymbal; and she sang:

> Stop the sun, stop the moon,
> Or I'll go crazy soon!
> Stop the whole month of June!
> Stop the band, stop this tune!
> My man's gone!

That season, it was fashionable to have a setup like that. Besides,
she got an additional ten percent for it—and to top it off, the
owner of the bar saved ninety percent of a regular drummer's
wage. And the blonde sang:

> Stop the trains everywhere!
> Stop the planes in the air!
> Stop the clouds on the go!
> Stop each loud radio!
> I demand, stop the show!
> My man's gone!

Evening after evening the brunette with the dimples in her cheeks exhibited her body, decently, but completely, to the paying audience. (Back home at Pragokoncert, the state-owned talent agency, this was posted as a dance program in national costume, and the bonus for total nudity went right into the brunette's pocket.) And almost every evening, the performance *sans* national costume was also observed by detective Niels C. Kölln.

The girl at the microphone didn't miss a thing. And she sang:

> Comedy, comedy!
> I suppose the joke's on me.
> Misery, misery!
> Where can my man be?

And she kept right on waiting.

. . .

Finally her waiting was over. Less than two weeks later she came down to the hotel lobby one morning, and there sat an elderly gentlemen and an attractive young lady with her head wrapped in a huge white sphere.

"May I join you?" asked the singer, and sat down without waiting for their reply. She took out a pack of cigarettes and then began digging in her purse like a dachshund. The elderly gentleman caught on and offered her a light with a gold lighter.

"You're awfully kind," caroled the singer, and with well-feigned concern she turned to the young woman in the white turban. "What happened? A car accident?"

The elderly gentleman responded willingly, with an abundance of information: "Yes, a bad one, too. Kastrin should still be in the hospital. But she took it into her head that she had to recuperate from the shock here in Hitzungsee. As if this were a place where they treat bad nerves. They only treat digestive disturbances here, don't they? It doesn't even seem particularly peaceful here."

"No, it isn't," the singer assured him. "Did you read about the murder here a week ago? Or has it been more than a week? Right here in this hotel. Some blackmailer. Apparently they found a tape cassette on him, and if it had got into the wrong hands it would really have messed up somebody's life—what's the matter?"

The young woman with the bandaged hand collapsed in her chair.

"Good God, Kastrin!" groaned her husband. Then he turned to the blonde. "You shouldn't talk about such terrible things in front of her, miss!"

"Oscar," whispered the lady, "would you please go up to the room and get my pills for me?"

"Certainly, my dear!"

The elderly gentleman leaped to his feet and skittered up the stairs like a mountain goat. The two young women were left alone.

"Please," asked the convalescent, "don't you know who has the—the—"

The blonde smiled.

"Yes, I do know," she said, opening her purse again and taking out the cassette. She handed it to the lady and got up.

"Burn it," she said. "There are fireplaces in the rooms, and they work. And give my best to Mr. Petersen. Tell him for me that Mr. MacMac is to be trusted, he's just a little weak when it comes to literature."

She turned and started across the lobby towards the exit, where the light of a lovely northern morning was pouring in. But just then the revolving door ejected a young couple in tennis outfits. In spite of the camouflage, she had no trouble recognizing the detective—and she didn't have to rack her brains to know that painfully short skirt. She groaned, and ducked behind a potted palm. When the two tennis players had disappeared up the staircase, she went over to the reception desk and spoke to the clerk.

"Send a bottle of Scotch and some ice up to my room, would you?"

"Two glasses?" leered the reception clerk.

She demolished him with a look. "One glass," she said. She turned to go, and a knowing smirk crept over the clerk's face, but he hastily recovered when she stopped and glanced back at him.

"But maybe you'd better make it two bottles," she said.

SIN NUMBER 3

The Man Eve Didn't Know from Adam

Laura and I are lying on a hillside in the pleasant shade of some Italian trees called stone pines, with a sensational view of one of the tiniest countries in the world, San Marino. Laura is babbling away in Czech, with all kinds of Italian words thrown in, and I am happier than I ever was in Prague. It's a great day. I'm a long way from jail, across several borders. Jail is nothing but the pluperfect past, and now the Mediterranean sun blazes overhead, the sky is blue, and my gig in the Orient Bar in Rimini doesn't begin until eleven o'clock tonight. Laura, who isn't really Laura but Lubomira Vosahlova, a schoolmate from our good old bishop's lyceum in Hradec—we were the only two day girls in our class, both of us from devout families, and we inspired all kinds of restless dreams in the boys who were there cramming Greek, most of them future clergymen—that selfsame Lubomira is sitting here telling me malicious tales about her husband the wholesaler, who isn't really her husband. She was married once, she's divorced, and tramps like her aren't allowed to remarry in Italy. In some ways they're even more pious here than they were at the lyceum. So they're living together, Laura and the wholesaler, living in sin, and it was in sin that she gave birth to his seven children—seven because the first six were girls, who were somehow not considered progeny by the wholesaler; he just had to have an heir.

Below us a gray road winds in and out between the trees and bushes, with little pastel-colored cars driving down it. . . . My eyes are heavy, Laura's babbling is putting me to sleep, she's turned into an all-around Italian. . . . That husband of hers isn't even really the wholesaler he makes out to be when he visits Prague to show off his social standing, mainly in the form of diamond necklaces displayed on Laura's generous décolletage. The truth is that Giulio owns a tiny little gold mine, a shop where he sells cans of ocean air and souvenirs made of seashells, the kind that must give the purchasers goosebumps every time they think of Rimini for years after.

But there must be a market for all that, because the shop brings in millions of lire; Laura's diamonds are genuine, and the little red sports car on the path nearby belongs to her, a pleasant souvenir of her most recent labor and the birth—finally—of their son.

Laura's beside herself with joy that Pragokoncert has delivered me straight to Rimini. She's mixing me up with the fairy-tale willow tree, she talks and talks, although I suspect that the reason she keeps taking me out of town for picnics like this is that she doesn't want Rimini's high society to see her in the company of a canary from the Orient Bar, namely me. She rattles on in Czech as rapid as her Italian, while my eyes droop and I feel like sleeping. Down on the road, a girl emerges from behind a bush; she's wearing shorts and has a knapsack on her back with a flag on it— it's too far away to see what kind of flag—a hitchhiker, she takes long strides along the side of the road, the sun lighting her rusty hair with a copper glow. Then she stops, turns around, and sticks out her thumb. There's the sound of brakes, and a small open car the color of raspberries pulls up. The driver is a man all dressed in white—of course he stopped, considering the legs on that girl. She runs around the front of the car, hops inside, and they take off as if they'd been shot out of a cannon. At that point I doze off, and there under the stone pines, in the fresh air that Laura's

Giulio sells in cans to dumb Americans, I sleep the sleep of the weary.

.   .   .

I hadn't the vaguest idea how much time had passed when Laura woke me up. The sun didn't seem to have moved at all. We gathered up what was left of our lavish picnic, got in the sports car, bounced down the path between the bushes to the road, and there Laura put her foot to the floor. The transmission made an unhealthy sound, but we took off at 140 KPH over the gray road, stone pines and hedges zipping past. Whenever I glanced to my left I saw Laura, her gorgeous classical profile held high, her raven hair fluttering in the wind like a black torch against a background of unfocused green.

.   .   .

We didn't get very far, though. As Laura was taking a sharp curve on two wheels, past the Chapel of St. Christopher, a white police jeep appeared up ahead. Behind it was a group of policemen, and one of them raised a paddle to stop us. Laura barely stopped in time.

"What happened?" She asked, eyes wide and thirsty for a bloody sight.

But the young cop in the freshly pressed uniform just boosted himself up on the hood, pointed his paddle to a side road among the stone pines, and directed us, "This way, please."

So we turned, and in a while we came to a little parking lot in front of an alfresco restaurant; there in a row, as if they were on display, stood five sporty little convertibles, all raspberry red. Beside each of them was a man dressed all in white, and beside each man were two policemen, and they were all carrying on what seemed to be a frenzied conversation. Apparently they weren't very pleased about something. But what on earth could be going on?

.   .   .

I was enlightened by a captain named Hercule Potarot—maybe an attempt at cleverness on the part of parents with a taste for murder mysteries. He stared at our car and at the self-important young cop on our hood who had guided us in. As soon as Laura stopped, Captain Potarot yelled at him, "Idiot! Why are you bothering ladies? What kind of an ass are you, anyway?

I had no trouble understanding. He spoke literate Italian, even if his vocabulary was a little folksy. He made a bow towards Laura and apologized for his language. Laura smiled and turned her audacious décolletage towards the captain.

The young policeman stammered, "I was just following orders to stop any red sports car traveling in the direction of San Ma—"

"Great God in heaven!" The captain struck his palm against his brow. "Use your head, man! Can a lady commit a sex crime against another lady?"

That was how I finally found out why those anxious gentlemen in white were standing there. Laura appeared to suppress a scream as she turned on her seat, opened the car door, and, in keeping with her social standing, passed out right into Captain Potarot's arms.

· · ·

Once Laura was recovered and seated at an outdoor table, it turned out that she and the captain knew each other, and fairly well at that. At least, her sidelong glances didn't look like a first-time performance, and the captain seemed all too willing to let us in on what was happening.

"It happened at kilometer 77," he began. "I'd come out on my motorcycle to visit a friend who has a cottage there. As I was walking back from his place, along the path towards the road, I suddenly heard a desperate scream for help from the bushes by the edge of the road. I rushed over but I was too late. The woman was dead, strangled, her clothes partly ripped off, but I'd apparently disturbed the culprit before he had time to complete his vile crime. When I looked around, I saw a fellow all in white disappearing into the bushes." The captain sighed with an emotion that was probably as genuine as Laura's faint. "As fate would have it, I only saw his back. So it could have been any one of these five characters!" He waved a hand towards the five arguing gentlemen, and his glance cast the same contempt on all of them, disdaining any presumption of innocence, although at best only one of them could be guilty. "And what's worse," he said, furrowing his brow, "I didn't even get a good look at the villain's car. It was hidden by the underbrush. All I had a chance to notice was that it was raspberry red, and almost certainly a sports convertible."

He looked over at the spirited discussion group. "But whether it was a Maserati," he said, "a Porsche, a Jaguar, an Austin, or an Alfa-Romeo—who knows?" He raised his arms to the heavens, and I thought he would actually wring his hands, but he didn't— he just let them drop helplessly to his sides. "We don't have anything to hold on to. It had to be one of those suspects over there, because I ran to my friend's bungalow and got to a phone in time to have the road closed at kilometer 120, where we have a highway police post." He gave an exasperated frown in the direction of the wealthy men he had branded as suspects. "There's no side road between kilometer 77 and kilometer 120, and no more than four minutes elapsed between the time I saw him start his car and the time our men closed the road. To go—" the captain spread his fingers on his left hand and counted something on them, "forty-three kilometers in four minutes, he'd have to do—" and he counted some more, "six hundred and sixty kilometers an hour. That would be an absolute world record. No, no, it was one of those degenerates there, for sure!" He pounded his fist on the table and the men, who had now been degraded to degenerates, stopped their discussion for a moment and glanced at us. Then he added that we, of course, could continue on our way, as the affair didn't concern us.

But Laura pursed her lips and made cow's eyes at the captain: "Please, Hercule, couldn't we at least see the victim?"

"Ah, that's not something for a lady," scowled the captain. "It's not a pretty sight."

"But maybe we could be of some help," pleaded Laura.

"How could you, *signora?*" sighed the captain tragically. "You couldn't even have known her. She isn't from around here, and she wouldn't have been staying at a resort hotel. She was a foreigner, probably a student. And I'd feel terrible if you fainted again."

A foreigner. A student. Something shifted in my head. I looked up through the crowns of the stone pines towards the sun—it was glaring down, and the trees cast a pleasant shadow on the orange-roofed restaurant, the gentlemen in white who were arguing again, the captain with his yellowish eyeballs, and Laura, who looked as if she'd been poured into her skimpy dress, so that the captain must have hoped, at least fleetingly, that the seams would burst.

"*Signore capitano,*" I addressed the captain with my somewhat awkward Italian, "did the girl have a sack, a . . . knapsack on her?"

He immediately grew serious, listening carefully. "A knapsack? Not *on* her—but *beside* her," he replied cleverly. "How did you know?"

"I have seen such a foreigner," I explained earnestly. "In short pants, wearing a knapsack with a small flag—"

"What kind of flag?" he interrupted me.

"Some flag, I don't know. It was too far. But the girl stopped a red car with a man in white. She ran around the front of the car and got in."

"Thank you, God, thank you!" the captain addressed the heavens. Then he turned to the white-clad company and yelled in a bloodthirsty tone, "Now you'll see, you scoundrels! An eyewitness!" He shook a fist at them, and showed me his teeth, saying, "Would you kindly describe the man in the red car?"

"I cannot describe him," I said, straining to speak properly.

The captain howled, "For God's sake, why not? A man is larger than a little flag, isn't he?"

"He is larger," I agreed, "but I was looking at the girl in short pants. I was watching the girl walk around the car and get in."

The captain's glowing smile dimmed a little. "The girl? Why does the *signorina* watch the girl? Why not the man?" He flicked his yellow eyes over the lovely Laura, made a sharp assessment of my own face, with the barroom rings under my eyes that I could never quite get rid of, and seemed to be nurturing a suspicion.

But I cut him short. "Because the man was inside the car," I pointed out. "Not much to watch."

He didn't give up his piquant suspicion, but a new thought

came to him. His pearly white teeth flashed again, looking as if they should be on an advertising billboard. "That's all right, then," he declared. "The man was inside the car. But you did see the whole car, didn't you?"

"Yes. A red car without a top."

"What type? What make?" The captain pointed to the five luxury sports cars parked in front of the restaurant. I looked them over, but of course it didn't help at all.

"I don't know," I said. "I don't know cars."

The captain dropped into a chair and once more slapped his forehead. "Why are you punishing me, God!" he wailed. "You send me an eyewitness and she can't tell cars apart!" He brooded for a moment, then opened his eyes wide and proclaimed, "But that's all right too. The *signorina* saw the whole car, the *signorina* will recognize it when she sees it again!" And he dragged me by the hand over to his own little sports car exhibition.

But as I'd predicted, it didn't help. I examined the little luxury vehicles one after another, but it was all for nothing.

The captain was stymied. He flopped onto a bench in front of the restaurant and began to curse the God he'd been invoking up to that moment. I looked around, and realized that while I'd been looking over the cars, Laura had been looking over the drivers. At a glance they were as alike as their vehicles—slick, tan, black-haired playboys, mass produced, two of them just slightly differentiated by virtue of moustaches.

I looked back at the captain. He was just getting up—slowly, as if hypnotized. He slunk over to Laura, who still couldn't take her eyes off those five fellows in white, one of whom was a sex murderer. From beside her, the captain spoke in a fulsome tone. "The *signora* saw the man in white too? And the *signora* is a wonderful woman, a hundred-percent woman. The *signora* wasn't watching the woman in short pants. The *signora* noticed the man! Am I right? What did he look like?"

The captain's flattery evoked an expression of profound responsibility on Laura's classical features, and I knew that meant trouble. Laura was going to start inventing things.

"Well, I don't know . . ." She squirmed. "After all, it was pretty far away. . . ."

"Ah, but the *signora* has wonderful eyes," the captain egged her on. "Wonderful eyes! The *signora* will surely recall what he looked like. Attention!" he yelled out of the blue, and, disregarding their protests, ordered the five playboys to line up there and then. He bowed to Laura and, with a sweep of his arm, indicated that the gentlemen were at her disposal.

Laura followed through beautifully. She walked around each one of them, fluttering her large eyes; she approached and retreated, taking about a thousand hours. Finally she walked off to one side, where the captain had been rocking on his heels the whole time and glowing with anticipation, and they put their heads together. They talked softly, occasionally flashing a glance in the direction of the five agitated men with sweat running down their foreheads. Finally the captain put an end to the production with a loud "Mm-hm!", straightened his jacket, and marched past the gleaming white row. And again, and yet again; he was a master at prolonging the agony. At last he stopped in front of one of them, as black-haired and smooth as all the others—it was absolutely impossible that anyone at a distance could have picked him out from the rest. The captain paused, poised like a predator—and made a wild leap at the man's neighbor, who had just begun to breath a sign of relief.

"Got you, you beast! I knew it was you all the time! Admit it!" The selected playboy's name was Filippo Terra, and I wondered why Laura had chosen him. He was maybe a tad handsomer than the others, a little slicker.

But I soon had to apologize for my suspicions, at least in my mind. It turned out that Potarot knew Terra, both personally and from police files, in which he was listed as having raped a certain young lady. The case was dubious as rapes go; Terra maintained that it had in fact been a seduction, but the police had acted like gentlemen and had stood behind the young lady. So Terra had a problem, and Laura had apparently hit the bull's eye.

Then something happened that seemed like the final sealing of the playboy's fate. On the captain's order, the policemen started to search Terra's car, and one of them found something there, something very tiny, and handed it to the captain. He took one look at it and his eyes lit up.

"So you won't confess, you scum?"

"I will not!" insisted Terra.

"And how do you explain how this got into your car?" The captain held up their little find. It was just a chewing-gum wrapper, but the fellow turned pale.

"I bought it—I mean, the chewing-gum—"

"Where?"

"In . . . in . . ." He turned to an absolute jelly. "In a gum machine at Piccini's. . . ."

The captain scowled and read the wrapper: " 'Made in Denmark.' All right, we'll call Piccini and find out if he carries Danish chewing gum."

Terra finally caved in. "No, don't bother to call there. . . . I—I gave that girl a ride, I admit that much. And she offered me a piece of gum. But I let her out at kilometer 68, because I was going to visit my buddy at Geletto. I swear! She went on down the road towards San—"

"What buddy?" the captain interrupted him sharply.

But here the playboy couldn't come up with anything useful. "Yes, well," he whispered, "he wasn't home, he can't confirm it for me. But I swear by the Virgin—"

"Why not?" The captain was glowering. "Go ahead and swear. Perjury won't make much difference if you're going down for a sex crime."

Unlike Laura's, the faint the playboy fell into was entirely genuine.

.   .   .

And I felt sorry for him. As he slid slowly down to the ground, banging his head on the fender of his beautiful little car, I suddenly had a funny feeling. "Laura, you bitch," I said to the heroine of the day, in Czech. "You thought it all up, didn't you? You picked him because he appealed to you more than the others."

"I beg your pardon!" Laura was offended, but she softened a

little. "I'm not saying he's the one. I'm just saying it seems to me that it could possibly be him, maybe."

But I suddenly knew for a fact, not that it wasn't Terra, but that there was something I was aware of—or should be aware of—that would finger the murderer. If only I could think what it was!

I walked over to the five cars and strolled past them. I read the manufacturers' names: Maserati, Porsche, Jaguar, Alfa-Romeo, Austin. Then I examined the plush interiors; created not for driving but for increased sex appeal, they were all done in black leather, as if the manufacturers had got together and agreed on it. So you couldn't tell them apart by their upholstery either. I looked at the steering wheels; two of them, in the Maserati and the Jaguar, were made out of wood, apparently some rare variety. The Alfa was Terra's, and there was a tennis racket on the right-hand seat, beside the driver's seat. The rest of the cars had steering wheels made out of some kind of plastic—maybe even a rare variety, but if I couldn't make out the flag on the knapsack, how could I have noticed what kind of steering wheel the murderer's hands were wrapped around? I walked past the back of the cars and stared at the chrome-plated tail pipes, racks, auto-club stickers, Playboy Club stickers—it didn't help. Nothing helped. Yet I knew for sure and certain, that somewhere in the very back of my mind, I had the definitive clue.

Then I wondered just what kind of car Laura was driving. I went and had a look. It was another Jaguar, also raspberry red with a black leather interior, and a steering wheel of some rare wood. But I couldn't tell if the car I had seen had been a Jaguar too. What could I say about it? It was red like a raspberry, didn't have a top, and had a steering wheel and four wheels. All very valuable details, Eve, and that's the truth.

I did one more turn around those luxury consumer products, out of sheer desperation. Nothing, nothing at all. And then, all of a sudden, a little spark seemed to smoulder amid the sawdust collected inside my head.

"Mr. Potarot!" I called to the captain, who had ordered some Chianti by now and was treating my clever girlfriend with it, feeding her olives on the side. "Mr. Potarot! It wasn't Mr. Terra! You can let him go!"

"Really now!" Potarot shook his head and asked sarcastically, "And who was it, then? Who was the man in white inside the car?"

"Not Mr. Terra," I said coolly. "I remember that I did notice one thing about the man in white, after all. He had a moustache on his nose." I was lying, but I knew what I was doing. I knew that it wasn't the playboy Filippo Terra.

> Though the identity of the murderer is not clear, you should know—if you have not overlooked two obvious clues—why Eve is so certain about Terra. But what is the sin against Father Knox?

"You don't say!" The captain clapped his hands together. "The man in white had a moustache on his nose!" He slammed his fist merrily on the table, with such force that the straw-encased bottle jumped and spattered red wine down Laura's neckline. I had mixed up my prepositions again—and the captain showed no mercy. "Than it couldn't have been any of those present!" he laughed, "because none of them has a moustache *on* his nose!"

I tried to recover my dignity. "If Signora Laura can tell at a distance of eighty meters that one man is who he is, I can tell if one man *isn't.*"

"But Signor Terra admits he had the Danish girl in his car!" He was still laughing to beat hell, and glancing over at Lubomira for her approval.

"But Signor Terra insists he dropped her and left her walking down the road."

"Signor Terra has no proof."

"You don't either," I said. "I suggest a . . . a reconstruction of the events. With all the men in white. We will recognize the murderer by his car."

The captain started to put me down again with his weighty sarcasm, but suddenly a light went on in his eyes. "Excellent, *signorina*. Why not?" he said mildly. "Experience in criminology shows us that the culprit often falls apart at the scene!"

• • •

And so it happens that Laura and I are once again sitting on the grass. There are still traces of our picnic here. But the sun has moved perceptibly westward, the shadows on the road have lengthened, and Captain Potarot is with us this time, outdoing himself with sarcasm. "Ah, the *signorina* is so daring!" he jokes. "The *signorina* can't tell a Porsche from an Alfa-Romeo, the *signorina* doesn't know anything about automobile technology, yet she dares to recognize the murderer by his car!"

"Go ahead!" I urge him icily. "Maybe today will show that you are the one ignorant about automobile technology, *signore capitano!*"

But the captain simply laughs, claps once, and raises his hand. A tiny policeman down on the road also raises a hand, and somewhere beyond the stone pines an engine roars. Down in the gap between the trees, where the Danish girl with the knapsack stood a few hours ago, a barefoot volunteer dressed in black now stands. Beside me, Laura is ostentatiously silent.

"First," declares the captain, after the fashion of announcers at the Targa Florio, "we have Giovanni Pelotta driving an Austin." As he speaks, a tiny car the color of raspberries appears in the gap between the trees, a fellow in white behind the wheel; the barefoot girl climbs in, and the car takes off and vanishes.

"What does the *signorina* think?" asks the captain, fairly dripping with sarcasm. "Did the driver have a moustache on his nose or not?"

"I couldn't tell," I say. The only thing the exercise has confirmed for me is the fact that you couldn't recognize your own lover at that distance, much less notice a moustache. "I can tell this, though. *Signor capitano* would do better to notice other things."

But the captain, intoxicated in part with Chianti, in part with Laura, but mostly with his male conceit, ignores my remark and continues his announcements: "Second, we have Sergio Volante driving a Porsche!"

The whole performance is repeated and Potarot asks after the moustache again, but this time I ignore him. Pignolo follows in the Maserati, and Sylvestri in the Jaguar, and Potarot doesn't notice a thing. He is in an excellent humor. He announces Filippo Terra in the Alfa, and courteously passes Laura his binoculars. Terra picks up the barefoot girl and the Alfa disappears beyond the stone pines. The performance ends. Nobody has fallen apart at the scene.

"The *signorina*, who has an excellent grasp of automobile technology"—the captain is outdoing himself, and casting glances at Laura that plead for her admiration, which she is withholding— "the signorina can now of course tell us who the murderer is."

"The *signorina* certainly can," I reply slowly. "Can Captain Potarot?" I ask, rhyming his name with "hot-to-trot."

"Potarow!" he corrects me. "Of course I can!" For lack of a table, he slams his fist into his own knee. "It is Filippo Terra in the Alfa-Romeo."

"No," I declare. "It is Sylvestri in the Jaguar."

Pot-a-rot aims a look of exaggerated surprise at me, and a self-assured, coquettish glance at Laura. "The *signorina* can of course prove what she is saying?"

"Of course," I say coolly. "Look, Mister Pot-a-rot—"

He corrects me again with a scowl, implying that I am really stupid, and Laura, who knows me, gives me an evil look too.

"Look, Mister Pot-a-rot," I repeat adamantly, "you can't tell anything this far away. No moustache, no flag, no face, not even your own brother's. *You* can tell a car, maybe, but not me. But I can certainly see *movements* from this far. And they show the murderer."

"Movements?" Potarot asks theatrically. "But the murderer was inside the car. He wasn't displaying much movement."

"He wasn't displaying any movement. The *victim* was moving. It's absolutely logical. Do you remember what I told you? The girl stopped the car, ran around the front, and sat beside."

"Sat beside *what?*" he asks, mocking my grammar again.

"Sat *herself* beside," I snap. "Well?"

"Well, what?" He scowls, and it escapes him entirely.

I'm silent for a while, and then I ask, "Can they drive around again?"

Pot-a-rot is still in excellent humor. "Anything for the *signorina!*" he whoops, and issues the necessary orders. And so the playboys drive past again, the barefoot volunteer climbs in each time, and the Porsche, the Maserati, the Alfa, and the Austin vanish in turn behind the stone pines.

Then the last car drives up, the Jaguar. The girl runs around the front, climbs inside, and the Jaguar takes off.

Now Pot-a-rot is visibly disturbed. He looks over at me, his forehead damp with perspiration. He stares at me and asks, "How was it you described it, again?"

"You heard right. She *ran around the front of the car* to sit beside the driver."

Whereupon Captain Potarot does something that raises him considerably in my esteem. He gets up from the grass, tightens his belt, brushes off his trousers, bows deeply in front of me, and declares humbly, "*Signorina,* please forgive me my uncouth behavior. I am contrite before your powers of observation."

. . .

Afterwards, when we had driven down to the road where five little red cars were parked one behind the other, it finally dawned on Laura, too. We stopped at the head of the row of cars. Four playboys sat in single file. Only one was out of line, the one with the Jaguar—Sylvestri, the son of some industrialist, who'd brought his luxury bait for attractive female hitchhikers straight from England. And because he'd wanted to have something entirely different, he'd bought the English version of that splendid little car, in which the driver sits on the right.

. . .

That evening, the headwaiter at the Orient Bar gave me four letters. They contained a lot of flowery gratitude and—more interesting—a variety of proposals. Not a single proposal of marriage, but two of them were proposing a date in Rome, one a date in

Venice, and one went so far as to offer a month's cruise on a private yacht on the Atlantic. I stuck the letters in a drawer in my dressing room, and some unknown person stole them from there that very same night.

Laura came around. She even went so far as to express admiration for my little mind. "However can you be so smart, Evie?" she gushed. "Is my memory failing me, or do I recall your having to repeat math every year but one?"

"The year I didn't was the year we had that young Jesuit teaching it instead of Father Silhan," I said. "What was his name? He was crazy about me, and I took advantage of it. But you're right—only this doesn't have anything to do with math. It's simply that when I look at something, I see what I'm looking at. Details, you know? Almost every woman knows how to do that."

"Maybe so." Laura looked down at the sketch she'd had to make for herself so she'd understand. "I must be one of the exceptions."

· · ·

As for those letters, the person or persons unknown who stole them may have done me a favor. There's no trusting playboys in red sports cars. Besides, who wants to spend a month on a private yacht? Nuts!

SIN NUMBER 4

A Question of Alibis

The big grandfather clock opposite the reception desk in the Majestic Hotel had just struck half past seven when a black-haired-gentleman emerged from the revolving door. He was of medium build, dressed in a double-breasted gray suit, with a moustache and huge dark glasses covering his eyes.

The gentleman looked around, stepped up to the counter, and spoke to the starchy reception clerk in English: "Has Mr. Jensen from Uppsala arrived yet?"

"Yes, sir. He's in his room. Room 327."

The stranger asked for a house phone, and the clerk directed him to the opposite side of the lobby, where three booths—old-fashioned cabinets of solid wood—stood side by side. The gentleman turned, strode vigorously across the lobby, and disappeared into one of the booths. A little red light went on above it, showing that it was in use.

It was pretty busy in the lobby just then, and the reception clerk had his hands full, so he didn't pay any more attention to the Englishman. Later on, he was unable to say what the stranger had done after that first enquiry.

• • •

The palm-decked corner of the third-floor corridor was dimly lit by the pale rectangle of a television screen. On it, four politicians of the social-democratic persuasion were discussing the advantages of violent revolution. Old Mrs. Ericson, who disliked violence, looked at the clock above the television. It was two minutes to nine. She patiently returned her gaze to the tube, but just then the door to the room opposite the TV corner gave a creak and distracted her from the well-tailored gentlemen on the screen. By the time she turned around to look, the door was merely half-open. Nonetheless, Mrs. Ericson didn't turn back to the revolution; she knew the room was occupied by her old acquaintance Mr. Jensen, and she was reluctant to miss the opportunity to exchange a friendly word or two. She didn't have long to wait. The door creaked again and opened wide, and Mr. Jensen appeared. He stepped out into the corridor, shut the door behind him, and met the old lady's eyes. Mrs. Ericson smiled and nodded. Mr. Jensen gave a polite bow and started towards the elevator. Old Mrs. Ericson had the feeling there was something she wanted to ask him, but she couldn't remember what. Then she stopped thinking about it, because the politicians on the screen had been replaced by the opening credits of a film. Mrs. Ericson sat back comfortably in the armchair; her favorite horror movie was coming on.

· · ·

The gentleman in the dark glasses appeared in the lobby again just as the grandfather clock struck nine. He approached the desk clerk and asked, in English, for a railway timetable. The clerk handed him the volume, but didn't pay any further attention to him this time either. When he looked up from his work a little later, he saw the revolving door swallowing the Englishman. Beyond was the Scandinavian night, and darkness.

A little while later Mr. Jensen came out of the darkness around the corner from the hotel, and into the light of the neon sign over the hotel's bar entrance. He walked past the doorman, whose epaulettes glittered with neon reflections, and the doorman greeted him politely. Mr. Jensen, who was not usually accompanied by his wife when he traveled to Stockholm, was a frequent guest of this particular establishment, and the source of generous tips. Now he nodded to the man in uniform and stumbled a little as he walked in the door.

. . .

There was a sprinkle of lukewarm applause, the blonde singer took a bow, and the dance floor gradually began to empty. The club was crowded. The saxophone player with the showy moustache put his hand on the singer's bare shoulder, but she knocked it off briskly and headed across the dance floor to the bar. She was wearing a short, sequinned dress, and in the half-light a pair of widely spaced gray eyes shone out of her pale face—the face of a professional night bird.

At the bar, she sat down on a high stool and unabashedly turned those glowing eyes on the males in the area.

A man appeared in the doorway—about forty-five, dressed in a gray suit, bald-headed, with bags under his eyes. He stopped for a moment, the neon sign outside painting him a hellish crimson. Then he noticed the girl and walked over to her, as if irresistibly drawn by the snazzy sequins. But he didn't walk in a straight line. His gait suggested he'd just come from the wet side of town; he sat down on the stool beside the singer at a tilt, and failed to straighten up. The gray eyes sized him up expertly.

"My name's Jensen, miss," he hiccuped. "What d'you want to drink? Order anything you want, as much as you want. I'm picking up the tab. Because tonight, I'm going to be murdered."

"How unpleasant!" said the girl. "And who's going to do such a nasty thing?"

The inebriated gentleman hailed the bartender loudly, and the blonde asked for a gin fizz. The gentleman himself ordered a bourbon. He leaned over towards her, enveloping her in the smell of peppermints, and confided, "That nasty thing will be done by a fellow I trusted for years." He grew angry. "That bastard! I know he's after my wife! She told me so herself! She's scared of him but he's mad about her. Or perhaps he's mad, period."

"Is he?" said the singer. "But how come you know he's going to do you in tonight?"

"He warned me this morning," Mr. Jensen explained. "Over the phone."

"How unkind of him!" The girl took a pack of cigarettes out of her sequinned handbag, decorated her face with one, hesitated, and offered one to the gentleman who was about to be murdered: "Have a coffin nail?"

"No, thank you," he said. "Or—why not? I'm dying today anyway."

He took a cigarette and stuck it awkwardly into the middle of his mouth. The girl waited for him to come up with a lighter, but he didn't seem so inclined, so she struck a match, lit her own, and leaned over to give him a light.

The gentleman took a puff and started coughing. He took the cigarette out of his mouth and looked at it in disgust.

"Damn, what kind of garbage is this? Seaweed, or what?"

"You've probably never smoked anything like it," grinned the girl. "It's called a Partyzanka, and it's Czech."

Mr. Jensen shook his head, examined the girl's amiable expression, and carefully put the cigarette back between his lips. Its glowing ember was doubly reflected in the girl's gray eyes as he began to envelop them both in a veil of dense white smoke—smoke that hadn't passed through his lungs.

. . .

A taxi pulled up in front of the Majestic's bar, and the neon glow illuminating the doorman also lit the face of the square-built man who emerged from the cab. He was wearing a double-breasted gray suit, and when he straightened up he must have been close to two meters tall. He had heavy black eyebrows that made him look angry. He checked his wristwatch and compared it with the clock that shone like a full moon from the church steeple across the street; it was twenty past nine. He strode energetically into the bar.

Meanwhile the singer had glanced down at her companion's

wristwatch and then up at the band on stage. The saxophone player was gesticulating, indicating that she should quit loafing and get to work. As the band started a heavy-handed foxtrot, the inebriated Mr. Jensen babbled, "So, how about us getting together, then? Tomorrow morning at Bränd Tomten, you know where that is?"

"But you're going to be murdered tonight," the blonde reminded him sweetly, sliding down off the bar stool and smoothing her palms over her sequinned hips. Mr. Jensen looked hungrily at her bosom.

"Oh, that's right," he said. "I almost forgot about that—with you."

She smiled, "Well, have fun here for a while, before you kick off," she said, and started towards the stage. Soon she was offering that same pleasant and entirely professional smile to the swaying crowd below her, singing invitingly:

> Put your cheek on my cheek,
> Close your eyes, lift your hand . . .

The square-built man with the heavy eyebrows was standing in the outside doorway, looking around with a scowl. Mr. Jensen pulled his lecherous gaze away from the vision on stage, turned on his bar stool, and squinted into the finger-marked mirror behind the bottles.

Then he must have felt ill, because he hiccuped again, slipped off the stool like a sack of potatoes, and hurried out into the hall that led to the lobby and the washrooms.

• • •

Count Dracula, impaled on a wooden stake, gave one last inhuman bellow and dissolved into a putrid puddle, in front of thousands of grateful spectators. Old Mrs. Ericson sighed and raised her gaze from the screen. For the second time that evening her eyes met those of Mr. Jensen, who was just coming from the elevator, his bald head shining in the dimly lit hallway. Mrs. Ericson still felt she wanted to ask him something, but again couldn't remember what. The man smiled and nodded, and Mrs. Ericson returned the nod and the smile. Then he disappeared into the room, with another creak of the door, and Mrs. Ericson reluctantly turned her attention back to the television. A quartet of long-haired young men was giving vent to some high-decibel hell. Glumly the old woman pushed a button, making the noisy troubadours vanish. She yawned, rose heavily, glanced at room 327, shook her head, and shuffled back to her own room.

As she slowly undid the buttons on her gray mohair cardigan, she was still wondering what she'd wanted to ask Mr. Jensen. What could it have been?

. . .

Down in the bar, the square-built gentleman examined his manicured fingernails and then looked probingly around the room. He took a sip of the abomination called dealcoholized champagne and concentrated his frown on the stage.

A singer in sequins was performing at the microphone. The saxophone player singing a duet with her placed his hands around her waist—or somewhat lower—as if he were obeying her plea: "Put your hands on my hips. . . ." She gave his hand a sharp but inconspicuous slap, and continued, "Put a kiss on my lips!"

The saxophone player decided he didn't dare.

The scowling man was watching the captivating blonde with interest when the waiter spoke in his ear.

"I beg your pardon—Mr. Cyrus?"

"Yes?"

"You are requested to kindly go to Mr. Jensen's room. He doesn't feel well. It's room 327. You go out through here to the lobby, where the elevators are." The waiter pointed to the exit leading to the washrooms.

The man gave a bleak nod. When the waiter left, he finished what was left of the repulsive beverage and took one more look at the singer.

"It's a shake, it's a shake," she sang, shifting her tiny feet in their silver slippers back and forth in a dance step. The saxophone player joined her in a duet for the last lines, once more resting his hands on her sequinned curves.

"It's a hippy, hippy shake!" they sang in harmony, as the square-built man watched the mesmerizing pattern of her high-heeled slippers.

"—a hip-py shake!" The girl hit a high note and her spike heel buried itself in the saxophone player's patent leather shoe. He yelped unmusically and stopped singing, so the blonde's melodious alto was the only voice holding the final note.

The square-built gentleman gave three brief claps. Then he rose and left the bar.

The lobby was full of people in costumes and masks, and there was music sounding from the Palm Lounge, where the Kiwanis Club was holding a masquerade party. The clerk was adding up a column of figures behind the reception desk. The square-built man emerged from the door marked *Bar,* hesitated, and then entered one of the wooden phone booths at the end of the lobby; in a moment the light above the booth went on.

The reception clerk gave the grandfather clock a tired glance. It showed twenty minutes to ten; he still had a long, tiresome night ahead of him.

. . .

Of course, old Mrs. Ericson said to herself, that's what it was! The dentist! Mr. Jensen said he worked *completely* painlessly. Well, it's not too late—she glanced at her watch. It was twenty to ten. Surely Mr. Jensen wouldn't be asleep yet.

She did up the mohair cardigan again, shuffled down the corridor to room 327, and knocked on the door. There was no answer. She knocked again. Nothing. Somewhere in the hotel, a clock was pleasantly chiming a quarter to ten. Mrs. Ericson tried the handle but the door wouldn't open. Then she noticed a yellow thread of light escaping through the keyhole into the half-lit hallway. She tried knocking one more time, and called softly into the keyhole, "Mr. Jensen!"

No answer. The old lady looked around cautiously and then, instead of her lips, placed her eye to the keyhole.

She saw Mr. Jensen. She pursed her wrinkled lips as if she were about to whistle at him. Then she straightened up with surprising vitality, and ran towards the elevator.

. . .

"Are you sure?" the desk clerk asked, looking distrustfully at the old lady.

She nodded. "I'm perfectly sure! You'd better come with me."

The clerk took the passkey from under the counter and opened the partition to let himself out. He motioned the old lady to lead the way and they both walked over to the elevator. Being experienced in the ways of hotels, the clerk glanced once again at the clock. It was ten minutes to ten. Just then the red light went out above one of the telephone booths, as the square-built gentleman emerged and headed towards the elevator as well.

They all arrived there at once. The two men let the lady precede them, and then the clerk deferred to the guest.

"What floor?" he asked, inside the elevator.

"Three," said the guest in a funereal voice.

The clerk pushed the button, and the elevator rose silently to the upper floors of the Majestic.

On the third floor, they followed the same order of precedence, and the three of them proceeded down the hallway in single file. It turned out that they were all headed to the same place; they stopped in front of room 327.

They looked at one another.

"Please . . .," the guest said to old Mrs. Ericson.

"I'd rather . . ." Mrs. Ericson gave the reception clerk a pleading look.

The clerk touched his necktie and said, "Allow me."

He turned the handle, but the door was locked. A thin yellow finger of light reached out into the hall through the keyhole. The clerk took the passkey out of his pocket, unlocked the door, and opened it wide.

All three of them saw Mr. Jensen.

Somebody had indeed done a nasty thing to him, just as he'd predicted.

He was lying on his stomach on the rug, with a bloody wound gaping in his left temple.

. . .

Detective Niels C. Kölln, who arrived at the scene of the crime at half past ten, gazed almost benignly at the terrible sight. It was his first murder since his transfer from Hitzungsee to Stockholm, and it was very important to him that he do himself proud. Moreover, he had been married less than a year, and he still wanted to impress his wife.

The gentleman lying before him on the green carpet had yellow, nicotine-stained fingers, and was clutching a lace tablecloth that had apparently covered the little round coffee table between the two armchairs. It seemed that there had also been a bottle of Jack Daniels and two glasses on the table, but as Mr. Jensen had fallen he must have caught the lace cloth and pulled it off, along with the testimony to the good time he'd been having with whoever gave him such a nasty pat on the head. The bottle and the two glasses lay beside the dead man, along with a bloodied marble paperweight. On his wrist the corpse had a watch, its crystal smashed. It had stopped at 8:57. The detective smirked contemptuously when he noticed it. What an old trick that was for establishing an alibi!

"So you spoke with him around eight o'clock?" he asked the square-built man with the scowling eyebrows.

"That I did. By telephone from my hotel. I'm at the Esplanade. We agreed that I would meet him here at the bar at half past nine; we were confirming an appointment we'd made a week ago. We wanted to have a brief meeting together before we attended a late dinner at Mr. Lundstrom's."

"You flew in from Copenhagen yesterday, and he arrived from Uppsala tonight by evening train. And was the dinner meeting with Mr. Lundstrom also arranged a week ago?"

"That's right. I'm the director of Mr. Jensen's enterprises. I've been checking up on our Copenhagen branch. The meeting with Mr. Lundstrom was to concern an important merger."

"It seems you were actually the last person to speak with the victim, Mr. Cyrus," said Kölln. "Mrs. Ericson saw him later on, but she didn't speak with him."

"If you'll allow me," said the reception clerk, "the waiter down in the bar told me that later on—that is, after Mr. Cyrus—their singer was talking with Mr. Jensen."

"A singer?" asked the detective, with an unaccountable feeling of unease.

"She just started here today," said the clerk. "She's some sort of foreigner. Her name's Eve Adam, or something like that. Do you want me to send for her?"

The detective was taken aback. According to the lastest word he'd had from his wife, the singer was supposed to be in Italy. But singers are wandering birds—and fine-feathered ones at that, he thought. "Oh well—may as well send for her," he said, resigned.

. . .

The singer displayed exuberant joy at seeing him again. He, on the other hand, was very businesslike, and that bewildered her. Whatever could I have done to him? she wondered. Nothing bad that I recall. Or is Zuzka getting on his nerves already? It sure didn't take long, if she is!

But the explanation for the detective's coolness lay elsewhere. It was partly that he was still jealous on account of the case in Hitzungsee. But it was mainly that he'd made an unpleasant discovery: he'd realized that the singer was the ideal his wife modeled her speech and behavior on. And although the blonde wasn't out of line with his own ideal of women in general, his image of a wife was defined by an old German motto: *Kirche, Küche, Kinder.*

The detective kept his interrogation down to the minimum, and acted like a total stranger to the singer—he didn't even invite her home. But he hadn't counted on the girl's native vengefulness, one of her innumerable worthy attributes.

When he finally got home, shortly after two o'clock in the morning, his wife and the blonde were sitting in the company of three bottles, two of them empty and the third open. And it showed. The detective gave the singer a cool hello, and turned sternly to his wife.

"Susan! You know that in your condition, alcohol is—"

"Belt up, Sherlock, and come have a belt," the singer said. Her tone was friendly, but the detective returned evil for good.

"You, Miss Adam, ought to be ashamed of yourself! You knew about my wife's condition, and instead of seeing to it that she—"

"You're calling me 'Miss'?" said the blonde. "Zuzka, he's 'missing' me!" And she added in Czech, "I'll try calling him 'Mister.' Or can you do that in Swedish? I get so confused. . . ."

"In Swedish you can do anything," the detective's wife hic-cuped in her mother tongue. "Especially talk stupid."

"Speak Swedish!" the detective barked, and then he turned on the singer. "And don't write my wife so many letters! Because of you she is neglecting her new language, and when we go out with my friends she sounds like an idiot. The only Swedish she remembers is the words she gets from you. When she opens her mouth, you'd think she came from a house of ill repute."

"So it's all right for you to appreciate her body," the singer retorted, "but in the company of your witless friends you want her to act like virtue personified. Right?"

"My dear young lady, by marrying Susan I helped her remove herself from a dubious environment that you, on the other hand, seem to enjoy—"

"Me enjoy?" exclaimed the singer, rolling her eyes to the ceiling. "You big dumb Swede, what do you know about life? And you call yourself a detective? If it weren't for me, you'd still be back in HitSongSea, arresting strippers, you pompous ass!"

"You . . !" The detective choked as he searched for the right word. His upbringing hadn't equipped him with an adequate vocabulary, and the only word he could think of was one he'd picked up from his wife. "You, Miss Adam, are a—"

"And don't call me 'Miss,' damn it!"

"You, Miss Adam, are a—" and he used a word that even his wife only used in the privacy of her home.

In return he got a slap in the face that spun him right around, and he felt as if he were being counted out in the ring at the police academy gym.

. . .

The following evening, after a day of fruitless investigation, the detective was beset by pangs of conscience—partly because of his ingratitude for HitSongSea, and partly on account of the expression he'd used—and so he went to the bar to fortify himself with the mixed drink called a Windfall.

As he took his first sip, he felt someone tap him timidly on the shoulder. He turned to look. Behind him stood the singer, a bit the worse for wear, but the better for some intoxicating perfume and her overwhelmingly splendid (if somewhat worn) sequinned gown.

"Niels," she chirped, in a voice he hadn't ever heard from her before, "I have to apologize. You're absolutely right. Now that Zuzka's expecting, I shouldn't have—"

The detective waved a hand in dismissal. "I should apologize to you!"

"Forgive me!"

"You forgive me!"

There was no way this bilateral desire for forgiveness could result in anything but a reconciliation. They sealed it with a couple of Windfalls, and because the singer, although humble and conciliatory, retained all her curiosity, the detective started on another Windfall, entrusting her with the modest but still confidential results of his investigation to date.

"We do have a suspect," he began, gloomily. "It's Mr. Cyrus. We heard from Uppsala that a certain Mrs. Svensen had seen him with Mr. Jensen's wife about two weeks ago in the Northern Lights Hotel, which is a place people go with that sort of purpose in mind. It's true they didn't stay the night, but that was apparently because they had a fight, after which Mrs. Jensen left abruptly. Mr. Cyrus has an explanation but it sounds pretty phony. He says Mrs. Jensen asked him to meet her at the Northern Lights to discuss urgent personal matters—something her husband musn't know. At the hotel she accused Mr. Cyrus of cheating her husband in business matters, then had a hysterical fit and ran away. He says he decided to talk to Mr. Jensen about his wife's state of nerves, but it never came to that; an emergency forced him to leave for Copenhagen immediately. The trouble with this story is that Mrs. Jensen is quite famous for her unemotional nature. Nobody in Uppsala remembers her ever being in hysterics. There were scenes, but it was always Mr. Jensen who fell apart. Anyway, what happened at the Northern Lights Hotel gave rise to rumors. Actually, there's a lot of gossip going around in Uppsala. For instance, the day before the murder, Mr. Jensen spent the whole afternoon looking for his wife, and he couldn't find her anywhere. She didn't come home until evening, supposedly after a walk in the woods. And Mr. Cyrus was back in Stockholm from Copenhagen that day, and it's a comfortable afternoon's drive from Uppsala to Stockholm and back." Niels sighed. "But what's the use? Cyrus has an alibi."

"What alibi? He was in the phone booth at the time of the murder, and—"

"—and the phone booth exits not only into the lobby, but also into the Palm Lounge. I know," admitted the detective, taking a little diagram out of his pocket and spreading it out on the bar.

"There was a masquerade party going on in the Palm Lounge," he said. "Mr. Cyrus could have had a little mask in his pocket, put it on his nose, left the receiver off the hook to make sure the red light stayed on above the booth, gone through the lounge to the kitchen corridor and turned left into the service elevator, and ridden it up to the third floor. He would have arrived there at about the time Mrs. Ericson turned off the TV and went to her room. It would have taken only a few seconds to do the deed, especially since Mr. Jensen was drunk."

"But Jensen was *expecting* someone to come and do him in. He would have been careful," the singer objected, a thoughtful wrinkle forming on her much-creamed, smooth forehead. "He would have defended himself, wouldn't he? Was there any sign of a struggle or anything?"

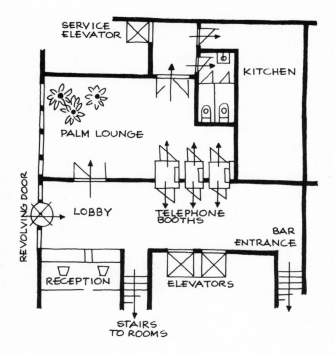

The detective shook his head. "No, there wasn't. If only I had the Englishman! He was with Jensen for almost an hour and a half, between half past seven and nine, but heaven knows what they did together—aside from drinking almost a whole bottle of Jack Daniels." He sighed. "Be that as it may, Cyrus was in the phone booth at the critical moment. It's true nobody could actually see him in there, but his alibi is supported by the person on the end—"

"But that could have been prearranged," the singer interrupted him. "If he had Mrs. Jensen as an accomplice—"

"It couldn't. I mean, it *could* have been prearranged, if . . ." He paused and considered for a moment. "If the person he was talking to weren't who he is."

"Ah, you mean some Party memb—I mean a government official?" asked the girl measuring the situation against her own experience. "Somebody like that? Somebody whose truthfulness you can't doubt even though he's obviously lying?"

The detective sipped his Windfall, and glanced down at the bar to a little puddle of his drink. He made a wet circle out of it with his finger.

"No. Cyrus said he dialed the number of his friend Sjöberg, but someone else answered."

"Mrs. Sjöberg?"

"No. A man who picked it up and just said 'Hello?' So Cyrus said, 'Hi there, Uve, you old drunk!' And the man said, 'I beg your pardon?' in an offended tone of voice."

"Wrong number," said the singer, adding the ears and whiskers of a cat to the ring of Windfall on the bar.

"Right. Cyrus asked politely, 'Excuse me, but am I speaking to Uve?' and the man on the other end just said, 'Wrong number!' and hung up. Then Cyrus dialed again, and let it ring twelve times, but nobody answered. Sjöberg wasn't home. And that's the truth, we checked."

"But the first part is no alibi, and neither is the second." The girl drew two squinty eyes in the cat's face. "He could have known Sjöberg wasn't home. And as for dialing a wrong number, anybody could say that."

"Except that we found the wrong number."

"You what? In an automatic switching system?"

"Sometimes all you need is a little logical thinking." The detective wriggled on his bar stool and set out to dazzle the blonde, who had always made him feel inferior, with his deductions. "Cyrus maintains that he was dialing carefully. The number he was calling was 372951. If he was in fact dialing carefully, we can hypothesize that he misdialed only one number, and that by only one digit. That gives us exactly eleven possibilities."

Niels turned the diagram over and wrote on the reverse:

26184 . . . . possible mistakes
372951 . . . . Sjöberg's number
483062 . . . . possible mistakes

"So we made up a list of the eleven wrong numbers he might have got. It was no problem finding out who had those telephone numbers in the city of Stockholm. In half an hour, we had him. It was a Mr. Wahlsund, and he confirmed everything . . ."

The detective noticed that the wrinkle on the blonde's forehead had deepened. She noticed that he'd noticed her wrinkle, and immediately stopped thinking.

"Niels," she said, "we're being stupid."

"Why?" the detective asked, alarmed.

"Think about it. I've got to go sing."

> Now you have everything you need to
> deduce *how* the murder was committed,
> if not by whom—and of course the sin
> against Father Knox is more or less evi-
> dent. But no guessing!

When she rang the bell at the Köllns' front door at half past three in the morning, the detective let her in immediately in spite of the un-Calvinist hour. It turned out he hadn't gone to sleep yet. He led her into the kitchen, where a scowling Zuzka joined them, offering to make the singer a cup of coffee.

"Ask her to make me some too," Niels said mournfully. The blonde grasped the situation immediately.

"Zuzka, love, your hubby would like it if you'd make him some coffee too!" Then she turned to Niels. "What was your fight about?"

Niels said, in an injured tone, "She promised me that, now she's expecting a child, she'd quit smoking!"

"Tell him," said Zuzka, "That I *did*! I only had *one,* tonight."

"One! Tonight!" groaned Niels. "Look at her fingers, Eve!"

The singer took the delicate hand of the reformed stripper in her own. The index and middle fingers showed the marks of a passionate smoker.

"It's just that it hasn't faded yet," insisted Zuzka. "A couple of months isn't long enough. After all, I'd smoked since I was ten years old."

But the blonde wasn't listening. The wrinkle formed again on her brow, and this time it remained there undisturbed.

"Tell her," said Niels, "not to forget that I have specialized training. I know what color fingers are supposed to be after two months of not smoking!" And he glanced at the blonde, as if he expected her support. Instead she said, in Delphic tones, "You see, Niels? See how it all comes together?"

Once again the detective had a disturbing sense of professional incompetence.

"What comes together?"

"Her smoker's fingers. And the Partyzankas."

"What?"

"Oh, nothing. Here, give me a piece of paper." The singer sat down at the table, took a fat fountain pen out of her sequinned purse, and started writing. There was a picture of a bathing beauty on the pen. As she wrote, the bathing beauty's various pieces of apparel disappeared, until she was revealed in the altogether. The girl didn't pay any attention, and the righteous detective didn't even notice: he was too involved with what was being written:

7:30	Englishman enters lobby, phones from booth, clerk loses track of him.
About 8:00	Cyrus phones Jensen to confirm date in bar.
About 9:00	Jensen leaves his room and is seen by Mrs. Ericson. Jensen does NOT seem drunk.
Shortly after 9:00	Jensen enters bar through street door. He IS drunk.
Before 9:30	Cyrus enters bar from street, and immediately after that, Jensen leaves bar for lobby.
Shortly after 9:30	Mrs. Ericson sees Jensen entering his room.
About 9:35	Jensen phones bar, asking Cyrus to come up to his room. Cyrus leaves bar, but stops off in phone booth, where he remains for ten minutes.
9:40	Mrs. Ericson leaves television and goes to her room.
Shortly after 9:45	Mrs. Ericson returns to door of Jensen's room and sees dead man through keyhole.

| 9:50 | Cyrus emerges from telephone booth, joins Mrs. Ericson and desk clerk in elevator. |
| About 9:55 | All three discover the murdered Jensen in his room. The watch on his wrist, which broke when he fell, reads 8:57 |

Detective Kölln placed his finger on the end of the last line and said, "This, of course, is an old trick for establishing an alibi."

"—that!" said the blonde, using one of the expressions that had given Zuzka a bad name among his friends. "And take a look at this!" She indicated the entry:

| About 9:00 | Jensen leaves his room and is seen by Mrs. Ericson. Jensen does NOT seem drunk. |

"Mrs. Ericson had been sitting there for about an hour by then," she said. "She was watching some politicians. If the Englishman was up to see Jensen, he must have left before eight o'clock, because Mrs. Ericson was never too engrossed in the politicians to see or hear anything, and she was there until half past nine. And the Englishman was down at the reception desk shortly after nine. But if the Englishman left Jensen before eight, where was he until nine?"

"Ah," said Niels.

"And here," she pointed again:

Shortly after 9:00 Jensen enters bar through street door. He IS drunk.

"Wherever did Jensen get that drunk?" asked the singer. "In the elevator? Because when he walked past old lady Ericson, he wasn't staggering. And why did he come into the bar from the street instead of from the lobby?"

Silence fell. The detective was perspiring with embarrassment, and avoiding the enquiring gaze of the singer, who was staring into his eyes. He looked around the room, and what he saw pleased him, because it gave him a chance to draw attention away from his professional lapse.

"What are you doing with those?" he squawked. "Will you leave them alone!"

The singer turned to see Zuzka standing at the kitchen table with Niels's briefcase in front of her, holding two large photographs. Eve hurried on with what she had been saying.

"And I figured something else out—thanks to your observation. Niels—" she said beguilingly, getting up and taking Zuzka by her stained fingers. "The dead Jensen had fingers like this. But alive, he choked on a Partyzanka, as if it were the first time in his life he'd ever had a cigarette in his mouth. You can't imagine the careful way he stuck it in his mouth, to be sure he didn't burn himself."

At that point, however, the detective wasn't listening; he was confiscating the photographs, mumbling something about confidential material. To the singer, it sounded pretty absurd.

"But I've seen those two people!" Zuzka was defending her curiosity. "The pictures were sticking out and I recognized the people, that's why I pulled them out for you!"

The detective stopped short. He gave his wife a searching look, then looked at the pictures and slowly placed them on the table.

"I know I've seen them!" she replied.

"Are you sure you're not mistaken? Where did you see them?"

The blonde peered over the detective's shoulder. One photo was of an unpleasant-looking beauty in the prime of life, and the other was of Mr. Jensen.

"I'm absolutely certain!" Zuzka said resolutely. "The day before the murder, at the café on the Håkonsgatan. This old battle-axe had a goblet full of ice cream too close to the edge of the table, and as I passed them—being a tad broader than usual—I knocked it over. She made a real scene. I definitely couldn't forget her."

The detective stared thoughtfully at his wife. The singer said, "It's perfectly obvious. The day before the murder this gentleman was in Uppsala, where he spent the whole afternoon looking for his wife, who didn't get home until late that evening."

"That was just gossip," Zuzka said, insulted.

"I don't think so. Right, Niels?"

"I think you're right," sighed the detective, and the look he gave the blonde was so admiring that Zuzka noticed—and the blonde, in turn, noticed her noticing.

"Don't worry," she said in their mother tongue. "Your little ninny's only admiring my mind, not my anatomy."

"I should hope so. Especially now that my anatomy is mostly tummy," said Zuzka, her hand resting on her belly, which did look rather like a soccer ball. Then she reverted to her little ninny's mother tongue. "But I don't know what you two are talking about."

"Look," her husband explained. "The Englishman came out of Mr. Jensen's room two minutes before nine. Mrs. Ericson saw him—"

"But it was Mr. Jensen she saw!"

"No," he explained. "That was a *double*."

.   .   .

"I don't know how come—" Niels shook his head, "but whenever Eve gets involved, we end up with the nuttiest cases."

"I don't understand it myself," said the blonde. "When I get back to my homeland, maybe I'll enlist in the security police."

"Oh, yeah, they'd take *you*," Zuzka grimaced. "Maybe the secret police. But no, they wouldn't either—you talk too much."

"Me? Talk?" the blonde marveled. "I'm the most close-mouthed lounge singer in the world!" And she added, in Czech, "Otherwise I'd have talked some guy into a permanent slot in my life, wouldn't I?"

"You've got to work with your anatomy," responded the former stripper. "Look at the catch I made, and I don't know how to talk Swedish right, even yet."

They both looked at the catch she'd made. Niels grew uneasy whenever they spoke in Czech in front of him, so he asked, "Do you recall, Zuzka, that before Mrs. Ericson saw Jensen, the door creaked twice? That's because the murderer panicked. He opened the door, saw Mrs. Ericson there, and drew back. Then he took off his wig, dark glasses, and moustache, and came out of the room as Mr. Jensen. It probably occurred to him that it might seem odd to her that the Englishman was alone in Jensen's room, because later on she could have figured out that Jensen must not have been in the room, if she hadn't seen him leave but later saw him come back." He stopped, because it seemed a little too complex even for him. But there was a certain logic to it. "He simply panicked. Then in the elevator he put the wig, glasses, and moustache back on, so he walked through the lobby as the Englishman again. Outside, he took the whole disguise off again in the dark, and went around the corner. That's when the doorman saw him as Mr. Jensen. Inside the bar, Eve spoke with him. He was pretending to be drunk, so we'd think later on that he'd drunk the whole bottle of whisky with someone in his room. And he told Eve all about the fellow he'd 'trusted for years.'"

"But Cyrus wasn't after his wife, and the only one who had it in for Jensen was his wife." The singer picked up the thread of the detective's deduction. "She'd invited the dupe Cyrus to the Northern Lights Hotel deliberately. She knew they'd be seen by the gossips of Uppsala, and she wanted to start a rumor. The day before the murder, she had a date in Stockholm with the double. I don't know where she recruited him, but his amazing likeness to her husband probably gave her the idea. As we know, she's a tough cookie, no tantrums, no emotions. She sounded out the double, found he had no objection to money—not even money with a little blood sticking to it—so she promised him a share of what she'd inherit when her husband was dead. Even cut in half, it would be a tidy sum. Maybe she did him some other favors too, if you know what I mean. She'd had enough of old Jensen; all she needed was his money, which he was apparently pretty tight with. In Stockholm, she told the murderer about the meeting with Cyrus that her old man had planned for the following day—meanwhile he was looking for her all over Uppsala—and she set it up so it would all be blamed on Cyrus. But they didn't expect Mrs. Ericson to find the corpse. It was supposed to be Cyrus, and then, of course, he'd have been up to his ears in it. The unknown Englishman wouldn't have been found, but that wouldn't have mattered, because he'd have had a perfect alibi: there'd be witnesses who'd seen Jensen alive in the bar long after he'd left the hotel."

"You can never determine the exact time of death, right down to the minute," said Niels. "But if there were a large discrepancy, it would come out. That's why the double waited until almost nine before he killed Jensen."

"Yes, they needed the corpse to be relatively fresh," said the singer. "And when the killer saw Cyrus coming into the bar, he rushed upstairs, where he was seen by Mrs. Ericson, but as Jensen. That upset his plans a little—he hadn't counted on her still hanging around there. But fortunately she got fed up with the music and left, so he phoned right down to the bar for Cyrus, and left. Maybe in a different wig and glasses, I don't know. But that wouldn't have been a problem any more. If a person *wants* to disappear in a fancy hotel like that, it isn't hard. At the beginning, as the Englishman, he wanted to attract attention. That was also why he was so interested in the railway schedule."

The light on the coffee maker went on, catching the blonde's attention.

"Eve," said Niels humbly, "you really are observant, I've got to give you that."

"Me? And what about your better half? If it weren't for her powers of observation, I don't know how we'd prove this—this phantasmagoria against the Jensen bitch, in a court of law."

Niels smiled and tenderly lifted his wife's hand to his lips. He inadvertently kissed her fingers right on the brown nicotine stains.

The blonde observed all this, then looked at her own nicotine-stained fingers. "And even with your better half's powers of observation," she said, "in the end it may prove to be just that: a phantasmagoria that can't be substantiated. But what the hell! I'm just an amateur. You're the professional. It's up to you to square this circle. I mean—to prove it all in a court of law." She kept looking at her brownish fingers as if she were thinking of some way to make them lily-white again. Another circle to be squared. Niels said nothing.

"Isn't it? Up to you, I mean," she insisted.

She looked up at the detective. It was obvious he wasn't listening. Zuzka was looking deep into his eyes, and it seemed to the singer that it wasn't a performance this time. His second kiss landed on a more propitious spot: the dimple just right of the funny little mouth.

The girl in the sequinned gown watched and seemed to grow sad. For a while she was silent. Niels kissed the other dimple. The singer crossed her legs. The detective's lips started for his wife's but they never connected—the family idyll was interrupted by the blonde's impatient voice.

"Well, how about that coffee?"

SIN NUMBER **5**

Why So Many Shamuses?

There were seven interesting murders in the Saturday *Evening Echo,* and the night before there'd been a cop in The Pink Jungle. I guess "cop" isn't exactly the right word; when you call somebody a cop back home in Prague you risk getting punched in the nose, and anyway this was a private one, a shamus, and that's no great insult here in New York. A rich Jewish guy who used to come to The Pink Jungle when I first started singing here, but unfortunately stopped before I could get to know him better, once told me the word "shamus" came from the Yiddish name for the sexton of a synagogue. But the shamus I'm talking about didn't look like any sexton. He was tall, muscular, good-looking, with gray eyes—straight out of a detective story. Besides, in English it doesn't mean sexton; that same guy told me some mystery writer named Hammett put the word in the English language when he couldn't think of a better name for the sort of person who makes a living out of the private investigation of crime—of a certain sort, mostly. It's not a bad word, "shamus."

Heaven knows I could tell he was a detective. When he kept pressuring me to tell him later on, what I said was the truth: I just knew. Back in Prague I could always tell when somebody was a cop, but there I never spoke to them. This fellow, though—as soon as I set eyes on him leaning against the bar, the left side of his tuxedo jacket bulging a little from his pistol, whisky on the rocks on the bar in front of him, his gray eyes sweeping back and forth across the room as if he was bored to tears, I said to him, "Hi, shamus!"

He started as if he'd grabbed hold of a doorknob—at least my doorknob at the Granada Hotel, where every time you touch the knob you get an electric shock, and they send a maintenance man every day because I keep complaining but he can't figure it out. The maintenance man is actually a Czech like me, he used to own a florist's shop in Prague before the Communists took over in 1948, but over here he pretends it was an electrical repair shop. And he begged me not to rat on him, which of course I won't, only it means that every time I reach for my doorknob I have to wear gloves, even when it's June in Manhattan and half a dozen breadwinners are collapsing of heatstroke every day.

Anyway, that's the way the detective jumped. Then he proceeded to deny it, but I can tell when somebody's lying. He was very good-looking, and he began to trust me when I told him I could probably tell because he looked like Paul Newman playing Harper in the film of the same name. He didn't really look a bit like him, but my poor powers of observation didn't seem to bother him at all, so we began to joke around and I said it must be a pretty dangerous profession to have in New York and McGrogan— that was his name—said it wasn't really, and it was mainly boring. Why? Well, because shamuses aren't allowed to do that much. It's only in books that they're always dealing with corpses; in the real world, in New York as everywhere else, it's mostly bored wives who are getting a little too much fun out of life, and as soon as a detective does stumble on a corpse he has to quick run and report it to the police. "Well, that's nice," I said, "I'm glad your job is such a bowl of cherries," and I glanced at the bulge in McGrogan's tuxedo jacket, but he pretended not to notice and smiled an artificially masculine smile, like Paul Newman as Harper, and I added,

"As long as it pays well." Then the masculine smile faded and he sighed, shook the ice in his glass, and replied wearily, "This is the only jingling I ever hear in my business. And that's mostly because I can chalk it up to expenses and put it on the client's bill. I don't have money jingling in my pockets the way some people do."

I looked into his eyes and there were pink dots floating there, reflections of the little pink lamps on the tables in The Pink Jungle. I glanced around the joint—they say that occasionally even Rockefeller drops in; I don't know if they mean the old one or the younger one or the youngest one of all, it wouldn't surprise me if the whole lot of them enjoyed the artistic dancing we promote here—and my eye fell on a blonde presiding over a table of four gents in tuxes; she looked like a mannequin in the window of a costume jewelry store, except that what she was wearing wasn't costume jewelry at all, and not a single one of the men around her was built like McGrogan; not even Johnny Starrett, her hubby's brother, and if you're wondering how I know all this, it isn't because I'm especially curious, it's just that I have this strange talent, maybe telepathic, for finding things out about gentlemen in a real hurry, and I never even know how it happens. Anyway, Johnny Starrett didn't have the chest McGrogan had, all things considered, nor did Leary, who sure acted like an intimate friend of the family, and not even old Henrickson, who probably had his hand in too, the way he had with at least five other women I knew of, and he'd like to have with me as well, maybe to make up a lucky seven. Not even Rocky Mellow had as photogenic an anatomy, although he once played Tarzan in a TV serial, and rumor has it that he also played in some of those films they call "underground" but he didn't do too well because he wasn't well enough hung. And if you don't know what I'm talking about, don't ask.

Anyway, when I consider McGrogan's tux—which must have been purchased by somebody a good deal fatter than McGrogan in the ready-to-wear store where it originated, before it was finally hocked and wound up in a rental shop where McGrogan rented it—and when I compare its cut with the tailored sonnets decking the bellies of the guys around the blonde with the diamonds, I turn back to McGrogan and say sweetly, "By *some* people do you mean *those* people over *there?*" I mean about what he said, not having money jingling in his pockets like some people. But he shakes his head and looks off into a corner and says, "No, they're not in the same line of work as I am. There's nothing strange about their having money. I meant people like me." And he keeps staring into the corner, so I ask him, "Oh, you're not alone here?" "People like me are never alone in a dive like this," he replies, and he adds, "That is, if you can call him a person like me." "Why not?" I ask. "Because this one's a disgrace to our line of work." "A disgrace? Isn't he good at his job?" I ask. "He's good all right, too good," replies the shamus. "But he misuses it. He finds things out, even about his own clients, and then he makes them pay." "Aha," I say, "that's how he gets his money." "Exactly," says the shamus, placing his hand on the bulge under his arm. "It's on account of guys like him that I get to carry a lump here, for safety's sake, instead of a wad here," and he sticks his hand into his pocket, which jingles a little, just a penny-ante tinkle. "And which one is he, this colleague of yours?" I say. "Not that I'm curious or anything, I'm just interested, that's all." The shamus stares off into the pink darkness of the corner; something is glowing like a copper kettle there, sort of ginger-rusty, but the face is turned away. The shamus pulls his hand out of his pocket and grasps his glass, and I say sweetly, "So why do you come to The Pink Jungle to jingle your ice cubes? Why not go someplace where you could get the same drink for what you pay here for just the ice?"

McGrogan gives me a strange, lopsided sort of look and says, "What if you think about it a little?" I'm sort of insulted, but because I'm by nature a thoughtful person, I don't take offense; I go ahead and think about it. Unfortunately I don't get anywhere. Meanwhile I watch his glance as it touches on the foxy blonde, whereupon he slides elegantly off the bar stool and says, "Well, now I can go home. Bye-bye, baby!" He reminds me of a certain MacMac, except that MacMac was in the opposite line of work. He raises two fingers to where the brim of his hat should be—the hat he probably left with Maude, our cross-eyed hatcheck girl, because we are in fact a very high-class joint—and shifts his shoulders a little inside his slightly outsize tux, and walks out of The Pink Jungle with long, sexy strides.

Well, that was the last sentence I ever heard him speak. At least three of the murders described in the Saturday *Evening Echo* were more interesting than that of Dick McGrogan, but it must be obvious why his was the one I was most interested in.

· · ·

The next day, Sunday, there was another shamus among the murder victims, named McBride, and again it wasn't the most interesting murder—he was discovered on a couch in his office with an ordinary bullet hole in his head—but it was the one I was most interested in. True, I didn't know him from The Pink Jungle, though his picture did look a little familiar to me; according to the news item, he was a redhead, and I recalled that rusty head in the corner where McGrogan had been staring. But it was more because he was the second murdered shamus in New York in as many days, and Irish, too.

Of course, New York has fourteen million inhabitants, or something like that, including I don't know how many detectives, and certainly even more Irishmen. So it could perfectly well have been a coincidence.

· · ·

With the third one, O'Malley, it didn't seem like a coincidence anymore. Not that I could get that across to a certain handsome police inspector by the name of O'Raglan, when I tried to convince him of some connection between the three. "Get on with you," he says, "is it the number three you're all worked up about? Something mystical to it, is there?" He makes a face at me, and I get mad. "All right," I say "but there are at least two peculiar things: all three of them were shamuses, and all three were Irish. Call it woman's intuition if you want—but that seems a little odd to me."

And O'Raglan makes that face again. "Look here, angel face," he says, and I want to snap at him that I'm not anybody's angel face—I'm kind of proud of my Bardot features, and anyway I'm an important witness—but he doesn't let me get a word in, he just keeps talking. "In the last three days," he says, "there were seventeen murders in the city of New York. Three detectives, you say. But there were also three real estate agents, seven housewives, and nine people killed with a blunt instrument, so why don't we give up our criminology textbooks and turn to numerology instead? Furthermore, two of the detectives were murdered by a blow to the head and one of them, McBride, was shot, so there goes your precious symmetry, my girl. And as for them all being Irish—in New York, wherever there's crime, there are Irishmen. And they're almost always on the right side of the law. Don't forget," he adds proudly, "the name's O'Raglan."

"Fine—maybe I'll get to read about *you* in the evening paper tomorrow," I snap. I'm still steaming about the way he makes fun of me, but I don't get to ask any more about the three shamuses. O'Raglan starts questioning me about an entirely different murder, this one concerning, of all people, the bejeweled blonde from Friday night, Connie Starrett, and one of the men in the tailor-made tuxes—Leary, the one I guessed to be an intimate friend of the family. Now, you can't tell me there's no connection here. And he was quizzing me because Seller, the head waiter at The Pink Jungle, had told him that late Friday evening I was invited to sit at their table. Connie Starrett said she wanted to talk to me, so when I had a break old Henrickson, a regular at the bar whom I knew a little from there and elsewhere, came over and asked me to join them.

That Connie was a real dimwit. She noticed I sang with a foreign accent—how observant!—and decided she had to find out more about me. She went for me like a textbook lesbian, but I saw right through her; the fashion in New York is to be the opposite of what you seem, and if she was a lesbian, I'm Muhammad Ali. That's what I told O'Raglan, and I listed the gents by name, because I always pay attention to names—they sometimes turn out to be important, and I have a good memory for them: Johnny Starrett, brother-in-law to the blonde, who leered down her powdered front in an entirely unbrotherly way; Leary, the one who was to die by her side later on; old Henrickson, who was leering too, but for him it was nothing unusual—he'd goggled down my neckline, and every other décolletage within reach; and finally Rocky Mellow, the star who thinks checking out necklines goes with his career—his TV career, that is, not the underground one he isn't well enough equipped for.

Naturally, because I was interested, I really played up to the tedious O'Raglan. It didn't work at the beginning, he only wanted to find things out, and totally ignored the fact that I wanted the same thing. But finally, when he was leaving, he did tell me something that maybe he shouldn't have.

True, I knew a lot from the newspapers. The murders took place on Saturday between 10 P.M. and 2 A.M., when they were discovered by Connie's husband, Pete Starrett. Both victims died of gunshot wounds but no gun was found, and it all happened in the second-floor parlor in the Starretts' home in Orchard Lane, the wealthy residential area on the Atlantic shore. According to the newspapers, Starrett had returned unexpectedly from a business trip to Philadelphia, so it looked for all the world like a common little marital triangle, resolved in the standard way. And Starrett topped it all off by declaring he was missing the revolver he kept hidden in his desk drawer on the ground floor.

That last item wasn't in the papers, it's O'Raglan who tells me; and by this time we're on a first-name basis—or rather, I'm calling him Zeke, and he's trying out a repertoire of pet names on me.

"Now, listen, Zeke," I say, "those three Irish detectives might have been a coincidence, but when somebody blows away two people in a house where a gun's missing the same day, that's too much for me." I pout fetchingly, and bat my eyes until my false eyelashes almost come unglued. It works. For the first time this evening, O'Raglan softens a little, and after a final struggle with his police training and his better judgment he says, "Okay, darlin', chalk one up for you. Pete Starrett never used his pistol except for target practice at his country estate. We checked the target out there and there were only two bullets in it—he'd only managed to hit it twice." He adds wryly, "You'll be pleased to hear that the bullets from the target and the ones from the bodies of Connie Starrett and Marty Leary came from one and the same weapon. But that's all there is to it—just another trite little triangle. So don't be letting your 'intuition' run away with you, love!" And he gets up and leaves, just like that.

"Is that so?" I shout at his departing back. "How about taking a look at the bullet in McBride's corpse. Just in case it matches up too!"

. . .

Cocky as he was, he did take a look. I could tell the next day, when he arrived at The Pink Jungle looking sheepish—if you can imagine a tall, good-looking sheep—and drew me over to the bar saying, "Listen, duck, I owe you an apology. There must be something to your intuition after all." "You mean the sudden leap in the mortality of private eyes isn't a coincidence?" I ask. "No, not that," he says, shaking his cute crew cut, "but at least one of those deaths is tied in with the Orchard Lane murders. That's proved beyond any doubt now." "You don't say," I remark, turning on the old eyes again. "And just how was it proved? Did someone confess to something? Come on, O'Ragsy . . ." "No, nobody confessed," he says. "This is better than a confession. It's been confirmed by ballistic evidence."

"Aha!" I say. "And McBride was the only shamus to die of a bullet wound, right?" Rags nods. "You got it, sweetheart," he says. "The bullets in Starrett's target, the ones in Connie and Leary, and the one in McBride—all that lead comes from one and the same weapon, the one that vanished from Pete Starrett's desk drawer."

. . .

That's a lot of bullets and a lot of corpses, I think to myself—but then, they do things in a big way here in the States. Rags and I are perched on bar stools like a couple of lovebirds; he's jingling his ice cubes like the late McGrogan did on that Friday night, and I'm licking the sugar off the rim of the gin fizz he's generously ordered for me. And we're thinking. But it's obvious Rags is almost as interested in me as he is in his tangled murder case, so it doesn't surprise me that he's not the vigilant police officer he started out as.

"Let's say," he muses into the darkness, pink dots reflecting in his dark eyes, "let's say it's like this: Connie Starrett was easy to look at, and easy in the virtue department, too. She was a stripper before she nailed her husband. Pete Starrett was an elderly millionaire. Easy-looking ladies of easy virtue occasionally have company they don't know about, especially when they happen to belong to elderly millionaires. In Connie's case it was Tom McBride. What do you say, snooks?" "Oh," I say, "you've really got a head on your shoulders, Zeke!" And he preens a bit and goes on, "So when Pete Starrett shot Connie and Leary out of jealousy, he also had to get rid of McBride, so the detective wouldn't let the cat out of the bag. Of course, Starrett's still denying he had his wife tailed by anybody, let alone McBride."

He gives me a bright, victorious look. Without removing the admiration from my eyes, I say wickedly, "Okay, honey . . . but if Pete Starrett's your murderer, why did he admit his gun was missing, when he could perfectly well have kept it to himself? Nobody would have known about it, except maybe Connie or his valet. And valets are known for their loyalty, aren't they? His brother Johnny might have known, but he'd hardly blow the whistle on his own brother, especially where an easy-virtued lady was concerned, would he?" Rags's pleased expression fades and he turns visibly sour, so I decide to cheer him up by telling him what I've kept back about McGrogan: that he was in The Pink Jungle Friday evening, when Connie was here with her entourage.

Rags seems to revive, but he starts grumbling about coincidence again. "No, no!" I shake my head to make my curls bob prettily. "Shamuses don't go to overpriced bars like this just for the hell of it. McGrogan was in The Pink Jungle on business. Somebody hired him to keep an eye on somebody, and he was enjoying the booze because he could chalk it up to expenses." "Maybe so," Rags concedes, "but this joint has a seating capacity the size of a small railroad station. McGrogan could have been watching anybody." "But don't forget my intuition, Zeke!" I say, making eyes at that amiable goon and restraining a sudden urge to run my hands over his crew cut. I work my eyelashes a little harder and add, "I'll tell you one more thing, Ragsy. I'll tell you what McGrogan said to me just before he left. He said, 'Well, now I can go home. Bye-bye.' Why could he suddenly go home? Obviously because his job was done for the evening, he didn't have to tail the person any more."

"Connie Starrett," says Rags, and he continues, as if to himself, "and he was hired by . . ." He stops for a moment, and then muses, "By Pete Starrett? The fact is, he's a jealous man—and the Starrett woman was kind of fast." He reddens puritanically at the idea, but I destroy his theory with a single blow.

"Wrong, Zeke. Pete Starrett never hired McGrogan. Why not? Because when McGrogan went home Friday it meant he didn't have to keep an eye on the person any more. Let's say it was Connie—we don't have any proof of that, but let's assume it anyway, since she was the most watchable of the whole group. Anyway, why didn't he have to watch her any more that night?" Rags opens his mouth, but nothing comes out; on the contrary, he dumps his whole double Scotch in it, ice cubes and all. And chokes.

"Don't you see? It's perfectly clear, Zeke! He didn't have to watch her any more because his *client* was there. The client could do his own watching from then on, and the shamus could pack it in for the night and go home." I feel a pang of pity for poor McGrogan, who apparently gave his life to keep an easy lady from being an easy lay. "And who was it who hired McGrogan? Not Pete Starrett—because Pete Starrett wasn't here Friday night."

I heave a sigh for the dear departed shamus, and beside me Rags sighs too. His is a sigh of admiration, though, and it pleases me—even if, for once, the admiration isn't directed at my anatomy.

. . .

On the stage of The Pink Jungle, Bubbles Marlene, our local stripper, is beginning her performance. She works systematically, and a little like a wind-up doll. No wonder—she's been doing this number, "Before the Bath," for three years now. She's toured the

States with it, and she's getting ready for a Scandinavian tour as well. She isn't really looking forward to it. She has a husband here in New York who works at the head office of Alcoholics Anonymous and who comes to pick her up night after night in a beat-up old Chevy. As for Bubbles, she spends the breaks between performances knitting him sweaters with rather drunken designs on them, talking about nothing but his digestion—he ruined it back in his heavy drinking days, so his conversion to abstinence wasn't entirely a matter of ideals—and how hard it is to cook for him. But on stage, illuminated by green, pink, and blue gels that our lighting man, Tony, flicks across the spotlight, she bounces her stupendous bosom with just enough energy to show all the bald-headed men at the darkened little tables exactly how firm those two wonders of the world are. Not that it will do the bald-headed men any good, because Bubbles is a textbook example of a faithful wife. She winds up her performance the way she always does, by sticking her wonderful, round white behind out at the audience, to a collective bald-headed sigh, and then Tony turns off the spotlight.

Rags doesn't join in the sigh, and it seems he hasn't even noticed her appeal to his baser nature. After a moment he does sigh, though, and he says, "The most obvious thing about the whole case is the motive. The least obvious is the letters." He jingles his ice. Because Bubbles, stripped to the buff, has retired backstage, the pink lamps on the tables are turning on again. "What letters? And what motive?" I ask. Rags replies, "The letters that Pete and Johnny Starrett and old Henrickson received, and that Rocky Mellow didn't. It's really strange." He goes on to explain.

All the letters arrived Saturday afternoon, by special delivery. They were all typed, and they were all signed *Connie*. The police handwriting expert thinks the signatures are forgeries, although it's just possible they're genuine. The typing was definitely done on Connie Starrett's typewriter, and the text seems aimed at getting the three to go and enjoy the great outdoors. Her husband, who was in Philadelphia on business, was instructed to go to his country estate in Thatchy Heights, the one where he used to do target practice, on Saturday night, and wait there for Connie, who was to arrive between ten and midnight: *I have to talk to you, it's very urgent. If you don't come, I don't know what will happen.* Pete Starrett insists he had no idea what she meant, but he dropped everything and rushed there; when nobody had arrived by midnight, he drove on home to New York.

Johnny Starrett was also instructed to go to his cottage somewhere in the woods of upstate New York: *My husband is terribly and unfairly suspicious of me. You have to help me, Johnny! Please come!* Again, Pete says he can't imagine where she got such an idea—"Although I doubt he's telling the truth about that," remarks Rags—but Johnny dropped everything too, and hurried to his cottage.

Henrickson's letter was explicitly vague: *Bill, come to Cedar Grove immediately, and wait for me until I arrive.* Still, it was enough to make Henrickson drive to Cedar Grove. At first he tried to keep the letter to himself, but because he was known as a skirt-chaser and a barfly who hated to be by himself except in his bath—occasionally—he couldn't give any satisfactory explanation of his solitary vigil in the dark woods, and he finally had to admit to the letter.

"It's all so clear," says Rags, "and it's a total mess. Not the motive: that's obviously jealousy. You see, we say there are only six motives for murder: jealousy, personal gain, revenge, fear of disclosure, psychological abnormality, and tactical murder committed to obscure another murder—but that last only happens in murder mysteries, I've never heard of it in real life. So we can eliminate that, as well as psychological abnormality—in this case there's too much obvious premeditation, and besides, the corpses weren't mutilated. Fear of disclosure? If that were it, then Connie couldn't be one of the victims, because she had the most to fear from any sort of disclosure."

"What about personal gain?" I ask, but he shakes his head. "That's out of the question, Connie didn't have any property of her own. She was one of those clever little poor girls who marries not for love but for money. So all we're left with is revenge—which is a possibility as long as you realize that in this case the revenge was out of jealousy. And we're back to where we started."

No we're not, because Louis Bijou and his Howitzer Hummers, which is the pompous name of our band, launch noisily into "The Sad Rhythm of Love," and I have to go to work. And as I lay on my sultriest voice, I watch the sweaty undulations on the dance floor among the artificial palm trees—frilly white shirts covering millionaire paunches, girls in tight miniskirts—some for hire, some already bought and paid for—wiggling to their own private rhythms, certainly not to the conga beat of "The Sad Rhythm of Love." And I watch the stuffed monkeys hung from the rope vines all over the room, their glass eyes taking in this perfumed Sodom and Gomorrah. And something dawns on me that I have to rush over to tell Rags as soon as I've taken my bow to a wave of lukewarm applause, and even before Louis Bijou has finished beating the conga drum with his ebony hands.

"Listen," I say to Rags, who's ordered a new drink in the meantime, and who's still applauding, all by himself. "What about McBride? What about that mysterious other shamus somebody must have hired too, since McBride got shot with Pete Starrett's pistol? Even if Starrett does deny being his client?"

"Smart girl," mumbles Rags "I was just thinking of him, that I was. You see now, McBride was a perfectionist. He had neat files for his clients, each client in a separate envelope and all the relevant material in the same envelope. The trouble is, there are no names on the envelopes, just ciphers. The code to what each of them means must be somewhere else. Probably in a safe-deposit box somewhere. Except . . ." Rags fades off into a trance.

"Except what, Ragsy? Don't keep me in suspense!" I nudge up closer and work the old eyes again.

"Except that in one envelope we found a picture . . . here, take a look." He takes a photograph out of his pocket. It's a little out of focus, but clear enough to show that dimwit Connie and the dirty old man Henrickson sitting on a park bench somewhere. To the right of them a cute little white kid is playing with an even cuter little black kid, to the left some dude in a cap with a plaid visor is lighting a cigarette with a fancy lighter, but the two on the bench are oblivious of all this: they're deep in each other's eyes, and they're even holding hands. "Goddamn it!" I say, and the pious Rags winces a little. He points out, "That's old Henrickson, the one who dropped everything and came running. Suspicious, wouldn't you say? Anyway, one thing's clear. Henrickson and Connie were scr—" he reddens and quickly corrects himself, "were having an affair. And if Connie and Leary had something going too, then the murderer could just as well have been Henrickson. Because not one of them has an alibi; all three of them followed the instructions in the letters and went to their cottages, and all three of the cottages are way out in the middle of woods and lakes, so there are no witnesses to anyone arriving or leaving, or even to say there were lights on. We've just got their word, and of course we don't have to believe it . . ."

I stare at the three ice cubes in Rags's glass and muse, "Three cottages, three letters, three dead detectives . . . Three Irishmen . . ." "Give the mystical numbers a rest, pudding," Rags groans. "Besides, you said three letters, but there was a fourth fellow, Rocky Mellow, and he never got a letter. And we have witnesses who swear he was all over Connie in the last little while, more than anybody. And—let me finish!" He's noticed that I've got the tip of my tongue between my teeth to repeat, "Three . . ." "And the photograph shows Henrickson and Connie, which can mean just one thing: the person who searched McBride's office and sent McBride to the land of his Irish forefathers couldn't have been Henrickson. After all, he wouldn't have left the photo as his calling card. So it wasn't Henrickson who put those three bullets into those three bodies." "Smart," I say, and wink at Rags. Just a little too smart, I think.

Our local Jimmy Durante impersonator is outdoing himself on the stage, and the bald-headed men sitting under the plastic trees and stuffed monkeys are splitting their sides laughing. "Anyway, it all still points to Pete Starrett," Rags says sadly. "He hired McBride, who reported back to him that Connie was fooling around with Leary. Starrett's jealous, and he's a conniver. He organized the whole thing with the help of those forged notes, did in the two lovebirds, and then, realizing McBride might get scared and shoot his mouth off, he killed McBride too, and took everything incriminating out of his file. He probably meant to take the whole file, but then decided to leave the one picture because it pointed a finger at that old lecher Henrickson—which, by the by, may have been news to Starrett. Ah well," he sighs, this time sounding really glum, "tomorrow we'll pick up poor Starrett, and what do you bet it comes out he was McBride's client?"

"Maybe," I say. "But have you forgotten that Starrett's the one who told us about the missing gun, lover?" Rags turns red around the collar again. I suddenly have the feeling that there's an explanation hanging in the air somewhere, a crazy, weird, unlikely-sounding explanation that will in fact turn out to be the right one. "And what about Starrett's brother? And Rocky Mellow?" "His brother," Rags informs me, "also has one of those flimsy alibis, being alone in a deserted cottage. His wife is sick, has been for a long time. She hosts some kind of spiritualist circle at her bedside, and apparently couldn't care less where her husband spends his Saturday nights—or any other nights, for that matter. Johnny Starrett doesn't deny that he's fond of Connie—he even admits he envied his brother such a gorgeous young wife, which is one reason he dropped everything, just like old Henrickson, and rushed off when she begged him to. As for Mellow, he's the only one of the four who were here with Connie that night who has anything resembling a decent alibi. He spent Saturday evening tippling with a couple of friends in his Park Avenue apartment, and by eleven all three had succeeded in drinking themselves unconscious. They didn't come around till about noon Sunday." "Pooh!" I scowl. "An alibi like that—" Rags interrupts me: "Right—an alibi like that isn't worth beans. All he needs to do is pretend to be drunk out of his mind, and when the others are out cold, nip over to Orchard Lane, do the dirty—there and at McBride's office—and get back to Park Avenue to fake a granddaddy of a hangover. But why, darlin'? What's Mellow's motive?"

I feel like saying, who cares? But Louis and his Howitzer Hummers have replaced our Jimmy Durante imitator and it's time for me to go crank out another three syncopated observations on the nature of love. And while I'm on stage, looking down on the glass dance floor with its pink lighting shining through from below (this is, after all, The Pink Jungle), I get another idea, a really nutty one this time.

Back on the bar stool, I say to O'Raglan, "Listen, think what you like, but I say this is a case for Pythagoras." "I don't know any shamus by that name," Rags huffs, "and if you think I'm so thick I need help with a murder in a plain old love triangle—" "Aw, come on, don't get mad," I chirp, turning up the charm. "Take another look at it: three cottages, three letters, three bullets, three corpses. I can't help it, Mellow just doesn't seem to fit in. And then there are the three shamuses, and all three of them Irish. . . . Look here, let me show you graphically," I say, and it's just as if I were back in drafting class under Father Silhan—where, of course, I seldom managed to demonstrate anything graphically. "Graphically?" growls Rags, "Like this," I say, and I have the strange feeling that everything's cockeyed but coming out right.

I reach behind Mack the bartender's ear, where he keeps a pencil, turn over the coaster—pink, of course—and carefully draw the geometry:

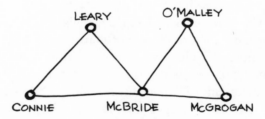

I take a look at what I've drawn, and say under my breath, "Now, if there isn't something mystical about all these threes, I swear I'll do a striptease myself, right here, and that's a promise." Unfortunately Rags hears me. He looks at my drawing, and looks some more, and then puts on a leer. "In that case, I'll soon see

everything the good Lord gave you, toots," he says, but he turns a bit pink at his own lechery. He changes the subject. "To hell with that feminine mystique of yours," he says, and takes the pencil stub out of my hand, and does a drawing of his own:

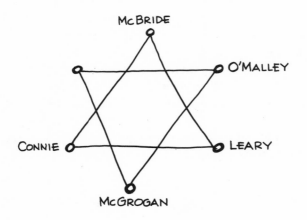

"Well, I'll be—" he hoots. "Now, that's mystical. Maybe we should consult a rabbi."

I don't take it as lightly as Rags does; something in my head keeps saying it's almost right, it's just a little off, this Star of David doesn't work. "We're missing one," I say. "What do you mean, missing one?" "One corpse," and I add a question mark at the unoccupied point. "This has six points, and we only have five bodies." "You never know," says Rags hopefully, "another one might turn up."

"Besides, the mystery is right here," and I indicate the point connecting my two original triangles, the point labeled "McBride." "My mind keeps coming back to this. It's the connector for the two threesomes. Of the three shamuses, two were killed with a blunt instrument, and only one with a bullet—and that one was shot with a bullet from the same gun as these two," and I indicate the Connie and Leary corners.

"Look, precious," says Rags, "it's all very nice, but these two, O'Malley and McGrogan, don't have anything to do with it. In

New York there's an average of twelve murders every—" and suddenly his eyes bulge, he gasps, "Oh, hell!" and takes a swig of his drink. "You shouldn't have done this to me, baby; I already had you stripped to the buff in my mind—" he forgets to blush this time, so he must be starting to take my triangles seriously—"and then you come up with this! He was struck with a blunt instrument too!" "Who was?" I ask. "McBride! First he was hit with a blunt instrument, then he was shot with Starrett's gun! You're right, he really is the connecting link!"

He tosses down his entire drink, and the rest of his ice catches in his throat; he chokes so badly that Mack has to grab him off his bar stool and shake him until the ice melts in his throat. Meanwhile I'm just sitting there, poring over the drawings and confirming the mystical link.

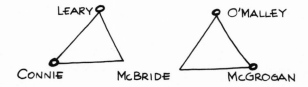

Three bullets in three corpses, three Irish detectives struck by a blunt instrument, and one of them with one of the bullets in his body. It all hangs by that one bullet, I can feel it but I don't know why.

By now Rags's ice has melted and he's back on the bar stool beside me. "Zeke, honey," I say, "did McBride have a car?" "Sure he did, you can't be a private dick in New York without a car. We have it impounded now." So I tell him, "Listen, you know what? Take a really close look at it. Take an especially good look at—" "But why?" Rags wants to know. Maybe I'll have to draw him another picture. I say patiently, "You found him in his office, didn't you?" "That's right." "And he was struck and then shot? With the same gun as Connie and Leary, the same night, on the other side of the city?" "That's right." "Then listen to me, Ragsy—

give his car a real going-over, especially—"

Louis Bijou gives a loud drum roll, his black musicians blow on their saxophones, and Bubbles Marlene hops onto the stage dressed—as only I and the regulars at The Pink Jungle know—in fifteen filmy nylon shifts, one over another, which she will remove one by one until she's wearing nothing but a gilded replica of a very shrunken fig leaf. I decide angrily that if Rags gets to hold me to my promise, my fig leaf will have to be at least three times as big, otherwise I won't keep my word—even though that's unheard of in America. I turn back to my detective with the cute crew cut, and explain just what my logic is, and what they should be examining on that automobile.

.   .   .

That night there I am on stage, doing a striptease, with nothing on but the spotlight with its colored filters and the gilded fig leaf. Somehow I don't really mind, even though Rags is gawking from the front table, with the usual congregation of baldies behind him. In my dream I say to myself, "Evie dear, a dream like this means you've been virtuous too long—" whereupon The Pink Jungle vibrates with the harsh cry of a telephone, and I reach my naked hand out into the pink darkness and hear Rags squawking as if his voice is changing, "There's a chestnut leaf down there!" I look down at myself and he's right, it's not a fig leaf, it's a lovely orange-red autumn leaf like the ones that fell off the chestnut trees along the castle road in Hradec, on the way to our favorite necking spot, the whole road was beautifully rust-colored in the autumn and if it wasn't very warm that time of year, well, no girl ever went there by herself. . . . But Rags is still squawking, "It's caught in the tread!" "Caught *where?*" "In the tire. The chestnut leaf. That means McBride must have been in Orchard Lane that night, there are chestnut trees there. And there's more, babe, we also know that—"

"Wait a minute! Where are you, Ragsy?" I'm completely awake by now. "I'm down in the lobby," he says. "And I also know—" "Wait, you can tell me in person," I say. "I'll be right down, lover, just keep your shirt on."

I leap out of bed, right onto the nail that always climbs out of the floor by morning, although I pound it in every night with the heel of my shoe. There's no getting around it, the Hotel Granada is haunted.

For that matter, New York is a pretty odd place in and of itself.

. . .

But I should know better than to get up so abruptly anyway. No sooner have I lifted my weight from the bed than it starts vibrating like crazy. It has a coin-operated machine attached to it, which I discovered my first night here. I hadn't found a television in the hotel, though where I come from they say every hotel room in America has a television and a Bible. For that matter, there wasn't even a Bible—there was the Book of Mormon instead, because the owner is a member of that denomination. But there was this slot for a quarter right next to my bed, and above it a message "Do You Want To Rest Your Body?" Who wouldn't, in New York? "Insert 25¢ and See How It Feels to Be in Paradise!" Well, I can't resist inserting anything in any slot, if there's a message instructing me to—once, in a public toilet in Grand Central Station, I put a dime in a slot that promised "Spiritual Encouragement," and what fell out was a medallion with the Lord's Prayer—anyway, I lay down on that wide, soft American bed, put a quarter in the slot, and waited to see how it would transport me to Paradise. It began to tremble a little, to vibrate, and I said to myself, yes, well, it really isn't half bad, actually sort of pleasant. I found myself getting into the feeling of Paradise. But it went on and on. After five minutes I was growing uneasy. By the time a half hour had gone by, I was saying to myself that this was a little bit too much—if Paradise vibrated like that, it would certainly get on my nerves over the course of eternity. I climbed off the bed and tried to do something with it, but of course I couldn't. Another quarter of an hour elapsed, and I called down to ask the management to send me up a man, but they misunderstood my English and told me icily that they didn't provide that kind of service. I finally managed to explain, and a man arrived, unlocked the mechanism, and took out the quarters, but he couldn't stop the bed's shaking either. We got talking, though, and I learned that he was Czech, and heard all about the florist's shop he used to have in Prague.

Of course, I know now that the Granada is haunted by dark forces, and nothing surprises me. I hobble over to the window and open the green drapes, thumbing my nose as usual at the group of Babbitts in the skyscraper across the street who every morning press their collective noses to the windows of the Sewer Toy Company, although I don't know what they get out of it; as soon as I've opened the drapes I disappear behind a curtain in the corner, where there's a sink, a shower, and my wardrobe, and I emerge more fully dressed than I am at The Pink Jungle. They're probably hoping the curtain will fall down some day at the right moment; for that matter, maybe it's not too much to ask of the gremlins haunting the Granada. Behind the curtain, I turn on the cold-water tap, which as a rule runs hot but today produces something that looks like weak coffee and smells like moldy pipes; luckily the hot-water tap has decided to run fairly clear. Meanwhile the radio goes on all by itself, but with yesterday's news—I told you the place was haunted. Everything else here is crooked and cock-eyed, so why not the case of the three shamuses? I'm thinking about this as I get ready, so I forget to put on a glove, and when I touch the doorknob I get a shock of at least 220 volts; the current in New York may only be 110, but the ghosts take care of the rest. Then I spend another quarter of an hour in the elevator—it gets stuck between floors and they have to crank it down by hand, only the handle breaks on them—and I finally make it down to where Rags is waiting impatiently in the lobby, which looks like a seraglio crossed with a twenties' movie house—just like something out of a Sinclair Lewis novel.

· · ·

When I get downstairs, I see something that's rare even here in the U.S.A., first thing in the morning: Rags is swigging away at a tall drink. And he's got it all worked out.

"Orchard Lane is bordered with chestnut trees—McBride's car traveled there that night, or at least was parked there, and the murderer noticed him. He was sitting in the car reading the paper, and when somebody sits in a parked car at night in Orchard Lane, reading a newspaper by the light of a street lamp, he might just as well hang a sign on his hood saying 'Private Eye.' Let's say it went something like this: McBride tails Connie to the house in Orchard Lane, where he sits waiting and reading his paper. He registers the arrival of Leary, but misses the arrival of the murderer, or maybe notices it but doesn't see any need to hide because, let's say, it's his client. Or else McBride doesn't see him arriving because the murderer knows he'll be waiting there watching the house. Anyway, the murderer hits him over the head with a blunt instrument, ties him up inside the car, then takes care of the two in the house. Then it occurs to him that McBride might have something to incriminate him. So he drives off in the shamus's car to his office, does in fact find photos, and destroys the negatives and prints but leaves one to turn our suspicions in an interesting direction. Then he takes the unconscious shamus, still tied up, and puts him on the couch and shoots him with Pete Starrett's gun. And there's nothing to say all of that couldn't have been done by Pete Starrett himself."

"No, no." I shake my head. "It all could have happened the way you say, Zeke, except that the murderer knew the photo pointed to Henrickson, while the gun indicated Starrett. So it had to be some—"

"Some third person," Rags interrupts me with a sigh. The waiter brings me a glass of orange juice; my stomach growls the way it always does in the morning, but I drink it down—so much for breakfast. I've gained over a kilo since I came to America, I don't know how; probably those rotten ghosts. "A third person," Rags is mumbling, "always that number three." I'm drawing pictures again, only this time just in my head. "A third person! Rocky Mellow, the one with the inebriated alibi, right?"

But Rags shakes his head. "Thinking is rarely a strong point in the female sex; you women go more by intuition," he philosophizes. What he's saying doesn't really upset me, because I've heard it from every philosopher with a fly on his trousers. I notice he's stopped using pet names for me, too, now that I'm one of "you women." But I say humbly, "You're probably right. But what have I overlooked?"

He throws a photo on the table in front of me. "Take a look at this." It's an enlargement of a man's hand holding a cigarette lighter. The ring finger is missing. "What is it, Zeke?" I ask, and Rags replies, "Do you remember the picture of Connie and Henrickson? Well, this is a blow-up of the smoker on their left." "He's missing a finger," I remark. "And who's missing the ring finger on his right hand?" he asks, and answers himself, "Our friend Tim O'Malley! So we're back to threes again," he concludes sadly. "Good God!" I exclaim. My uncomfortable of vision of having to do a striptease suddenly vanishes. I grab his napkin, pull a pencil out of my purse, and scribble a new picture on the napkin:

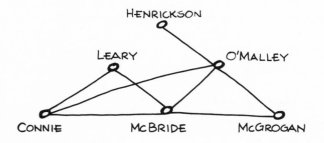

Rags stares at it, "Damn it, baby, you're off your rocker!" "No, I'm not," I snap, and my brain is working, a little cockeyed but hard. "And I'm not going to give you the pleasure of seeing me in my birthday suit, either. You see how it all fits in? With new connecting links turning up? O'Malley—Henrickson; O'Malley—Connie; all we're missing is a sixth corpse, and we'll be able to fit it into the Star of David after all. And the sixth corpse is Henrickson." "But he's still alive," says Rags. "He won't be for long. And we have a new link here, O'Malley—Connie, so to make this work

there has to be a link between Leary and McGrogan! And also
. . ." I stare at my drawing, my head buzzing, while Rags shakes
his crew cut. "If there's one between Henrickson and O'Malley,
there has to be one between Leary and Henrickson."

Rags sighs, "You're nuts, cutie. Forget all that, and notice the
cigarette lighter." I look at the lighter, but it doesn't say anything
to me. "It's not just a cigarette lighter," Rags says. "It's a micro-
camera—the kind spies use. And O'Malley's using it to take a picture of the couple on the park bench."

"Wait a minute. . . that means . . . O'Malley's snapping the two
on the bench, and at the same time he turns up on McBride's
picture. Did McBride realize he was taking his colleague's picture
as well? God only knows. But the murderer probably didn't—you
can't make out O'Malley's face on the regular-size picture."

For a moment I'm deep in thought. "Was he a redhead?" I ask.
"Yes, he was," says Rags, and in my mind's eye I see the handsome shamus McGrogan staring into the depths of The Pink Jungle, and it comes back to me, glowing like a copper kettle in the
corner among the pink lamps—a carrot-topped head. "Tell me,
Zekey, has O'Malley ever been in trouble? I mean, with you, with
the police? Maybe for extracting money from someone because if
they didn't pay up, a third person would find something out about
them and that the third person hadn't ought to know?"

"I don't know," says Rags, "but I can find out. Look here,
though," and he points to the picture, "you can't tell he's missing
a finger, or that the lighter's actually a camera until you blow up
the picture. And his hat covers his red hair, and casts a shadow
on his face. And where does it say that only husbands can be
jealous? O'Malley could have been hired by Leary, who got suspicious of the old goat Henrickson and wanted O'Malley to keep
an eye on Connie for him and—damn! Henrickson *should* be dead
then, he's the one holding hands with Connie." I get a feeling
down my spine, as if I'm taking part in a Black Mass, and I say,
"Maybe he will be. You ought to put a guard on him. Unless," I
muse, "unless O'Malley was in fact hired by Henrickson—but that's

nonsense!" "No, no, it isn't nonsense, babe!" Rags jumps in. "I'll put another connection into that triangle of yours, even though it spoils my chances of ever . . . Look here: Leary and McGrogan!" he exclaims, and he draws in the line, making a picture just perfect for exhibition in a witches' gallery:

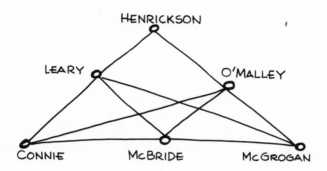

"McGrogan," says Rags, "was hired by Pete Starrett, and Leary's shamus O'Malley found out somehow that McGrogan was on his, Leary's, trail. So Leary, who was getting set to kill Henrickson, first did away with McGrogan, to keep him from figuring any-thing out, but before he could carry out his main intention and murder Connie and old Henrickson, Henrickson got the word from McBride—you said McBride could have been a blackmailer, I'll look into that; it would explain why he took a picture of his own client *in flagrante* so to speak—anyway, Henrickson beat Leary to the punch. . . . It's really pretty complicated—"

"That it is," I say, because I think O'Malley was the blackmailer, not McBride. All of a sudden Rags yells, "Damn!" and the owner of the Granada, the devout Mormon, who just happens to be passing by, gives him a dirty look. "Wrong! All wrong!" groans Rags, pulling a fat red pencil out of his vest pocket. "We've got to fill in some more connections in our diabolical geometry, and those, baby, will change everything!" Then he traces what he has in mind on the napkin:

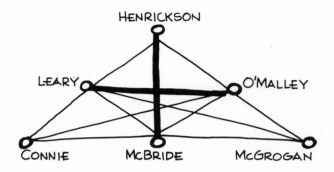

He gapes at it like a tropical fish, opening and closing his mouth, not saying a thing. Finally he sighs, "And now, instead of a Jewish star, we have a good old Catholic cross." He calls to the waiter for another drink. "Henrickson hired McBride. Leary hired O'Malley—because McBride's Irish and redheaded, too!" He glances at me to see how I am reacting to his theory.

The mysticism has collapsed like a house of cards—and that's just what our drawing on the napkins looks like. And the evil spirits of the Granada are probably no more than mechanical defects, the kind you can count on when a hotel's electrical system is maintained by an ex-florist. Because if it had been Henrickson, he wouldn't have left his picture in McBride's file; we'd thought of that earlier but had forgotten it in the excitement. And if it was this mystical triangle and not a perfectly normal marital one, Henrickson would be dead by now.

Just as I'm chewing on the notion of having to do the striptease after all, an undernourished bellhop comes through the lobby yelling at the top of his lungs, "Call for Mr. O'Raglan! Call for Mr. O'Raglan!" The detective gets up, his feet tangle into a pretzel under him, and the skinny bellhop has to prop him up and point him at the telephone booth. In spite of my concern for my waistline, I order another juice. Before I finish it, Rags is back, as pale as the vampire Nosferatu. He pulls out his fat red pencil and, his face immobile, silently draws the following:

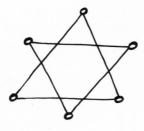

Then he says, "Not only that, but Pete Starrett's confessed." "To the murders?" I ask mechanically. "No," growls Rags, "just to hiring McBride to tail Connie, because she was an easy—" "An easy lay," I finish his sentence for him, and even in his inebriation a pinkness creeps up around his ears. He pulls out a silver Parker and shakily adds names to the picture:

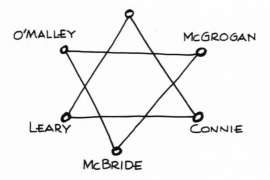

Finally he moves to the uppermost point of the star, and with exaggerated care prints in: *Henrickson.*

"Really?" The word catches in my throat. He nods.

I think to myself, now we have all six corpses, and I don't know whether we need a rabbi, or a priest for an exorcism. At least it seems there won't be any striptease, after all.

· · ·

I had to take Rags home from the Granada by taxicab—he'd over-done it—and I had to call in sick for him to the Homicide Bureau.

He was just sober enough to tell me they'd found Henrickson in Central Park, dead of a blow to the head with a blunt instrument. Someone at Homicide had been quick to check out the remaining members of Connie's entourage for alibis, and the only one who had one was Pete, because he was in custody under the watchful eyes of the cops. Both Johnny Starrett and Rocky Mellow said they'd spent the night alone at home, in bed.

Rags's place was on the north edge of Greenwich Village, so I started walking up Broadway towards midtown, hoping the wind that's always blowing on that strange street would straighten out the mess inside my head, and blow away the spirits of the Granada and all the other nonmaterial beings there. I was beginning to feel a little anxious about it all. I tottered along in my high heels, passed the usual metropolitan types who seem to have nothing on their minds but bed—almost like me—until I finally wound up on Thirty-fourth Street, where the salesgirls from Macy's were just getting out. The wind had really swept out my brain—so thoroughly, in fact, that all that was left was a perfectly ordinary late afternoon, and it seemed absolutely impossible that anyone in this soberly mad town could commit murders for the seven deadly sins, as in Ellery Queen, or according to children's nursery rhymes, as in Agatha Christie, let alone go around murdering according to mystical geometrical symbols. I dropped into a Chock Full o'Nuts, a pleasant New York coffee shop with redheaded black waitresses, and platinum blonde ones with complexions like floured pancakes. I asked a black girl in a white cap and a tight-fitting yellow uniform for a cup of coffee and an order of Grandma's Bumbleberry Pie, because that's me, nothing for breakfast but juice, and then make a pig of myself on pie. I had two pieces, then another. Americans turn up their noses at plain old pie, worshipping European pastries instead, but I can't resist it. The service here is exemplary: the girl takes a piece of pie in her pink-varnished fingertips, gets whipped cream on her fingers and wipes them on her slender hip, slaps the pie on a plate she's just removed from a sterile wrapper, takes a grubby dollar bill from me with those selfsame fingers, tosses a gleaming grin at the chocolate-colored dude at the end of the counter (making me sigh with envy), and, ignoring me, starts to fix a ham sandwich with her fingers of whipped cream, dollar bills, and heaven knows what else, for a lady beside me who's wearing a small pink garden of geraniums on her head.

I set about thinking again, and it's got me totally confused. So there were two of them tailing Connie, the poor little playgirl: O'Malley, who was hired by either Henrickson or Leary, and McBride, who was hired by Pete Starrett. Isn't there a possibility that Pete also hired O'Malley, just to keep McBride honest? There is indeed, my dear Watson, I answer myself, and I recall once again that good-looking shamus and the copper-colored head in the corner. I pound my forehead to try to settle things back down in my mind. It's perfectly clear, Evie, it's a fact—or almost a fact—that there was somebody redheaded at The Pink Jungle that night. It could have been McBride, but it could have been O'Malley. And Pete Starrett hired McBride, and then he hired O'Malley to keep tabs on McBride—he could afford it. And when he'd put bullets in the bodies of McBride, Leary, and Connie, O'Malley came to put the squeeze on him. So he knocked him off too.

Except that Starrett couldn't have killed Henrickson, because he was being watched by the cops—and nobody will convince me that Henrickson just went out for a stroll in Central Park and was mugged to death. And why did Starrett admit to owning that gun? Maybe because the best defense is a good offense? Because the best hiding place is out in the open where everyone can see? Nonsense, Evie. Good thing Rags can't hear you. I glance at my watch—it's seven o'clock. I slip off the stool, shove aside the tubercular chest of some sexually unemployed New Yorker who's offering me his services, and set out towards The Pink Jungle.

· · ·

Bubbles Marlene is sitting in the dressing room, knitting a sweater design called Tale of the Orient and describing how to make chop suey, a recipe she memorized from a book called *Chinese Cooking* in between acts. It's her birthday today, and her husband went to one of those little shops on Forty-second Street and bought her a sexy negligee with lacy borders and openings in unusual places, which the husband thinks is a clever joke—and so, apparently, does Bubbles.

I undress, put on my robe, sit down in front of the mirror, and start to put on my makeup. Halfway through, I pause, deep in thought. The spooks of the Granada are working in my head again. McBride and O'Malley are undoubtedly connected somehow with the departure of the late lamented Connie and Leary. There's even proof of that: there's the bullet and the picture. The only thing there isn't any definite proof of is how the third shamus, McGrogan, ties in with the corpses from Orchard Lane.

Or is there? Think, Evie. I urge my weary little head to go over that Friday night at the Pink Jungle once again. Could Starrett have decided to cover his behind not only with O'Malley but with a third shamus? Three again?

No, he couldn't. Because McGrogan's client was in The Pink Jungle, and Starrett wasn't. And you're right back where you started, bright-eyes. Maybe that male cliché about women and logical thought is true.

· · ·

As soon as I get up on stage, I spy Rags at the front table. Apparently revived by coffee and benzedrine, he looks terrific. The pink lights of the club blend with his greenish complexion to make an orangey turquoise, so he looks a little like the obsidian mask of an ancient pharaoh. He blinks at me, observed with a morally critical eye by a corpulent lady at the next table; she's with a small man who looks as though he might be a rich real estate broker from the sticks, in New York for a good time, who somehow forgot to leave his wife at home. Anyway, Rags can't take his eyes off me, and the lady is watching him in turn. Louis Bijou hits the drums, Sticky Lips Charlie, the trumpet man, pokes a mute in his horn and begins "The Rocking Blues," and I start swinging my pelvis in rhythm—partly because it's in my contract, on account of the baldies, but mainly so Rags will have something worth staring at. I sing, "If you don't want me, honey, cast me in the deep blue sea." The lady pricks up her ears and appears to condemn even that innocent little line, and I continue, "I say, if you don't want me any more, honey"—I see Rags shaking his head, as if such a thought hadn't crossed his mind—" . . . cast me in the deep blue sea. So the whales and all the little fishes," I sing, but there is something ". . . can make a fuss over me . . . " suddenly— I can't prove a thing, but something is coming to me. And there on the stage of The Pink Jungle, I completely forget to take a bow—I just stand there, gaping at the microphone as if it were the Holy Grail, until Louis Bijou drags me behind the backdrop and starts lecturing me paternally in Harlem tones, telling me LSD is a terrible thing and I'm too young for that kind of vice, which proves that even Papa Louis Bijou has been fooled by my skillful hand with makeup.

Then I find myself in my dressing room, and Rags bursts in too—Bubbles gives a little scream because she's just straightening her fig leaf, and leaps behind the screen in the corner—and I squeal, "Oh, Rags, baby!" and throw my arms around his neck. "Run and ask . . . ", and when he obeys and runs to ask, and Bubbles comes out from behind the screen with her fig leaf in place, I suddenly feel terribly depressed after all that excitement. Because mysticism is definitely out of it, and I can look forward to a fig leaf myself. But then, what the hell, maybe Rags won't insist on holding me to my word—for I have every intention of setting up a private performance for him this very night, at the Granada.

·   ·   ·

So I wait for him on my big bed, dressed in the negligee I got that spring in Stockholm from a certain Petersen, but I don't intend to tell Rags about him. Across the street the windows of the Sewer Toy Company shine into the night, but there are no Babbitts pressing their noses to the glass, just cleaning women mopping the floors.

Time passes, flies by, as the July stars twinkle over New York City in the parching breeze. Finally, at two, the phone rings. "Can I come up, baby?" Rags asks, though he really doesn't have to ask, and I'm overcome by a sudden, sinful feeling of elation to think that my very chaste existence—in keeping with the integrity of a citizen of my socialist homeland, as called for in my passport—will once again be brightened by a small immoral intermezzo. Besides, I'm looking forward to finding out whether it all happened the way it came to me, on the stage of The Pink Jungle—although at this particular moment, it's not crime that's uppermost in my mind.

I stretch out seductively, turn on the bedside light, and wait. The long, silent seventeenth-floor corridor of the Granada resounds with Rags's hurried strides, and then a soft knock. "Come in, honey!" I say in my sultry voice. But instead of slipping inside discreetly, he hollers *"Damn!"* at the top of his lungs so loudly that in the room above mine Miss Donelle, who's afraid of burglars, falls right out of bed.

Of course . . . I forgot to tell him to wear gloves. My poor sweet Rags got a jolt of 220 volts, courtesy of the nefarious spirits of the Granada Hotel.

. . .

As for the murders, the motive was in fact jealousy. As Rags himself said, where does it say only husbands can be jealous? So who was it? It's perfectly obvious, I knew it from the beginning. It's just that, when it comes to murder, somehow . . .

> And you've surely worked it out too—
> but not, I hope, the way Eve did.

Of course, it was *Johnny* Starrett who had all those murders on his conscience. Who else? He was the one who hired McGrogan to keep an eye on Connie, pretending he was acting on the instructions of his embarrassed brother. He was the one who found out from the unfortunate shamus that Connie was stepping out on both him and his brother, with Leary. But McGrogan's broad shoulders and beautiful gray eyes didn't make any impression on Johnny, and he killed the shamus to keep their business relationship a secret. Then, in his brother's house, where his presence didn't surprise anyone, he typed the letters on Connie's typewriter—one of them to himself, and none to Mellow, to complicate things even more. He also typed two other letters—the first to Connie, to get her to stay home that night, and the second to Leary, to get him to go and see her and bring the letter with him—but of course he destroyed those letters when he'd done the pair of them in. Johnny noticed McBride in Orchard Lane on his way in, and knowing what he must be doing there—because Pete had confided in his brother—he crept up to him and knocked him out and tied him up. Then he went inside and shot the two of them with a gun he'd stolen from his brother's desk drawer, and proceeded to drive McBride, in McBride's own car, to McBride's own office, where he discovered that the man was really serious about his job. He had a report prepared for Pete Starrett that included him, Johnny. So Johnny used his brother's pistol for the third time that evening, on McBride, whom he'd dragged in from the car unconscious and dumped on the office couch. Then he destroyed the photos and reports in the file, except for the one picture that showed old Henrickson playing patty-cake with Connie.

That was where he made his one mistake that murderers always make. He didn't recognize the bystander with the cigarette lighter as O'Malley, and he didn't know the lighter was a spy-style camera; he should have spent less time running after women and more time going to the movies..

So imagine his surprise the day after the murders, when O'Malley comes to him with his blackmail scheme. Because—surely you've figured out what I realized when I watched the morally outraged wife at The Pink Jungle—the third shamus, O'Malley, was also following Connie, not for Pete, not for Johnny, but for Johnny's *wife*, Rachel, the indisposed spirtualist. It turns out she cared more about where her husband spent his evenings than she let on.

To make a long story short, rich people like the Starretts can afford the services of private detectives, so on account of the amorous activities of one former stripper, three shamuses found employment, and all three of them laid down their lives in search of the precious truth about what she was up to. *O tempora, o mores!* as our history professor, Father Dostalek, once exclaimed when Lubomira and I showed up for school in slacks. O'Malley wasn't satisfied with payment for services, so he decided to go in for a little extortion. But by then Johnny had four murders on his conscience, so a fifth one didn't particularly matter. And number six was no trouble at all—Henrickson, the dirty old man with all the money, also knew a thing or two about Connie, and Johnny, and Leary; Henrickson didn't have to waste his time making a living, so he used it to put two and two together, and came to Johnny to urge him to turn himself in. It seems the old lecher was in fact a devout Presbyterian, which is not uncommon—the more devout you are, the more you enjoy sinning. Which I can confirm from my own experience, God forgive me.

As I said, if you've got five murders under your belt, a sixth doesn't count for much. So the immoral old Henrickson wound up dead too. God in heaven! Six dead bodies over one bleached little slut with nothing but sawdust for brains—and as for endowment, the good Lord could have made three of her out of Bubbles Marlene, with another whole Connie left over as a free sample.

But that's the way it goes in this world: vanity, vanity, all is vanity. Rags finished telling me about his nighttime visit to the home of Rachel Starrett—that's where I sent him when I threw my arms around his neck in my dressing room, after everything fell into place for me on stage. He took off his jacket, unbuttoned his vest, and, try as I might, I couldn't care any more about not finding anything mystical in the case. Then Rags told me about the third degree they'd put Johnny Starrett through, and—as he removed his necktie and unbuttoned the waistband of his trousers, because he said it was too tight—he also told me about Johnny's collapse and confession. By then—why deny it?—he was beside me, and I was yearning for the end of my period of celibacy. At last he was through talking; he took me in his arms and whispered lovingly, "Oh, baby, baby! It's a sweet head you've got on your shoulders, damned if it isn't. How did all that come out of this lovely round little head?" But his hands were on something else, equally round, but far from my head.

The spirits of the Granada are ever vigilant, though. When Rags stretched out to assert his masculinity, his elbow jostled a certain machine. The mattress began to tremble under us, more and more. It wouldn't stop, and it struck me as funny, though I don't know why. I started to snicker, and then to giggle, and finally I broke up entirely. The bed hurled itself back and forth until we both tumbled onto the floor, I on one side of the bed, Rags on the other, and even then I couldn't stop laughing. But Rags took it personally, and yanked on his clothes and stormed out.

I called him on the phone the next morning, feeling a little guilty about my fit of giggles, and he told me he couldn't stand cynical women. Then he turned right around and told me that he was going to hold me to my word.

So here I am walking up and down Forty-second Street, where Bubbles' husband bought her that naughty negligee, trying to find a fig leaf. Trying to find a bigger fig leaf.

All the ones they have are *awfully* small.

SIN NUMBER 6

Miscarriage of Justice

The blonde in the miniskirt pressed her nose up against the shiny glass of the display window in the Orvilleton airport, looking at all the fool's gold in the souvenir shop window.

"Look here, Bob! This is the same alarm clock you bought the other day at Woolworth's. It plays 'Summertime' too. Except you paid $7.50 for it there, and it only costs $6.30 here."

"Really?" asked a plump lady, although the young woman hadn't been speaking to her but to the tall, good-looking man with the interesting salt-and-pepper hair sitting in a plastic chair a little farther on. He apparently hadn't heard her. "Really, Bob!" said the plump lady, looking into the window herself. "Isn't that just like you! Why buy something cheaply when you can buy it expensively, right? We didn't need an alarm clock anyway. You've got one inside your head."

It was dark outside the airport. The plump lady walked over to the panoramic waiting-room window and stared out at the town shimmering in the night of upstate New York. Bob with the gray hair looked nervously at his watch and lit a cigarette. The young woman turned away from the display window and rested her gray-eyed glance on him. He didn't notice, or he pretended not to, so she caught the interested look of a businessman with a cigar, aroused him with a flash of her pearly teeth, then turned away to sit down. There were three plastic chairs along the wall, a red one, a blue one, and a white one; the handsome Bob was sitting in the red one. The young woman hesitated over the adjacent blue one, but finally decided for the color of innocence. A freckle-faced girl in blue jeans, who had been watching inconspicuously from a distance, placed a wad of pink bubble gum in her mouth and proceeded to blow a bubble, which grew bigger and bigger.

. . .

Then something happened in town, and the plump lady gave a shriek, while the travelers all rushed over to the window. Even the businessman with the cigar succumbed to the temptation to observe someone else's misfortune, smiled apologetically at the young woman, and joined the crowd. The girl in the blue jeans removed a bubble almost two feet wide from her mouth, stuck it onto the seat of the blue chair, and pushed her way through to the window. The only ones left sitting were the young woman in the miniskirt and the handsome man, who discarded his freshly lit cigarette and sat on, immersed in what appeared to be entirely private thoughts. The young woman looked at him across the pink bubble. He didn't show any interest, he only displayed a certain absence of mind. The young woman crossed her legs and looked offended.

The freckle-faced girl came running back. "It's a fire! And I'll bet it's our house!"

The man in the red seat seemed to accept her news with equanimity, even indifference. The young woman, on the other hand, launched herself into the crowd of businessmen at the window. She shoved the man with the cigar aside so brusquely that he lost his balance and, backing up, sat down abruptly on the big bubble in the blue chair.

"Oh, shit!" said the girl in the blue jeans.

An announcement came over the speaker system, and the handsome man in the red chair sat up. The announcer said that the

Mohawk flight for Buffalo and Chicago hadn't yet left New York's LaGuardia Airport, due to inclement weather conditions. The man in the red chair muttered through his teeth, "Oh, shit!"

The businessman, busy peeling pink shreds off his trousers, gave him a shocked look.

The young woman in the miniskirt drew away from the other spectators at the window and announced to the gray-haired man, "It's true, Bob! There's a fire, and it seems to me it's at your place!"

· · ·

It turned out that she was right. A little while later, an announcement came over the speaker system saying that if there was a Mr. Cornhill there, he would do well to return home, as there had been a fire at his house. That upset the gray-haired man a little, but not as much as the announcement about his flight had. The plump lady, however, fell into an immediate panic. The businessmen were so concerned with the loss of property, albeit apparently well insured, that no one noticed the remark of the girl in the blue jeans: "Come on, Mom," she told her distraught mother, "it's the best thing that could happen to us."

At that moment, the speaker system announced that the Mohawk flight from New York to Chicago was being canceled due to continuing inclement weather conditions.

· · ·

Something just didn't seem right to the insurance adjustor. That's why he didn't even wait for the smoke to clear before he was on the phone asking his company for an expert. Something didn't seem right to the expert, either. A telephone call disturbed the slumber of Sergeant O'Mackey, who was on duty that evening at the East Precinct. Ten minutes later, he was standing in the partially scorched ground floor, musing, "You mean, on account of the insurance? Sure, Bob's having money troubles, that's common knowledge, but . . ." The sergeant examined the policies the insurance man was showing him. They were impressive evidence of the gray-haired man's touching solicitude for his family. Fire insurance, life insurance for his wife, his daughter, his mother, insurance against burglary and insurance against accidents. Certainly, thought O'Mackey, he wouldn't be the first homeowner to try to resolve his money troubles that way. But earlier that evening, at the precinct house, the sergeant had been reading the evening paper, full of reports of the actions of the Weathermen and such, and he thought of something that made him stop and consider. The idea appealed to him, and he recalled another article in the same context, in another publication. "Nope, it wasn't the insurance! But then, it would . . .

· · ·

"I told you, Bob, you should have kept your mouth shut," O'Mackey reproached his friend, when the two of them were alone. "When those guys write that someone had better compose his last will, that someone is well advised to pay attention, just in case. You were lucky you weren't home."

"How come . . . why. . . ?"

"Because this has a distinctive trademark. This isn't the way people commit insurance fraud."

"I don't understand you." The handsome man looked at him anxiously, and seemed uneasy.

"You didn't have to testify against them, back then," said O'Mackey. "Not that it wasn't a matter of honor. But the boys in Chicago would have given all the evidence necessary, and sometimes it's better not to be all that red-hot to do your civic duty."

"What are you babbling about, Jim?"

"Wasn't your name in that underground rag of theirs? 'We will kill all the perjurers and traitors!' And at the top of the list was Bob Cornhill—"

"For God's sake, Jim, are you trying to say my house was set on fire by—"

"Who said anything about setting a fire?" snorted O'Mackey. "They planted a bomb!"

· · ·

The police worked fast, and well before dawn they had a suspect in custody. True, there was no evidence that he had anything to do with the Brotherhood—but he was black, and they'd picked him up in The Paradise Bar wearing a fashionable Afro wig. He wasn't there as a customer; he was a dishwasher, and when they came for him he was just splitting a bottle of champagne with the singer, who was on her break and had confiscated the almost full bottle from the table of a customer who'd already passed out. The singer wasn't black, she was blonde—but as soon as the cops discovered where she lived they brought her along, without even giving her time to change from her sequins into the little girl's skirt she'd been wearing when she arrived at work, a little late, the previous evening.

The black man in the wig now sat in the slightly smoke-damaged kitchen, and vehemently denied everything.

"As God is my witness, Sergeant, I'd never—I'm a Christian! I'm an usher at the First Baptist Church, and my brother—"

"What about that wig?" asked O'Mackey.

"I'm bald, Sergeant. My Cindy doesn't like skinheads."

And what were you doing last night here at the Cornhills'? Don't deny it! We have a witness. You were hanging around here, ringing the bell, pounding on the door—"

The eyes of the black Baptist sparkled with an emotion that was less than Christian. He paused a moment before he spoke, in restrained tones. "Cornhill owes me money for some gardening I did. He told me to come for it yesterday evening. And when I got here, he wasn't home—again."

"How much does he owe you?"

"Seventeen-fifty."

"And for seventeen-fifty you set a bomb in his house, you lunatic?" asked the sergeant. The black man stared, dumbfounded. The sergeant continued, "The bomb supplied by your spiritual brothers? And I *don't* mean the Baptists."

There was a knock at the door, and the insurance expert walked into the kitchen. The sergeant sent the black man away, and he and the expert talked for quite a while. O'Mackey appeared to grow dejected at first, but in the end he regained his good humor.

"It still makes sense! Where was it we picked him up? At The Paradise, where he was whooping it up with that night owl!"

He strode over to the door and called loudly, "Eve Adam!"

Then he thought of something, and snickered. The young woman walked in wearing a sequinned dress as brief above as it was below. The sergeant took a good look at the snow-white slopes bordering the pleasant valley, and made his witty remark: "Well, tell me, just what kind of sin were you up to, there in The Paradise?"

An angry furrow appeared on the girl's forehead. She protested virtuously, "I beg your pardon! Once in a while Mr. Turpin and I have a drink together in the kitchen, and he corrects my pronunciation. That's all there is between us."

"Corrects your pronunciation? Ben Turpin?"

"Nowadays 'big-city blues' are all the rage. You can't get away with singing them with a European accent, not in the States. And Ben's from Chicago."

O'Mackey gave a satisfied smile, opened the door, and hollered, "Turpin!"

The black man in the frizzy wig obediently appeared in the doorway.

"The lady here says you're from Chicago," said the sergeant. "And you swore to me you'd never been there in all your life."

"I'm not from Chicago, I'm from Cicero," the alleged revolutionary said rebelliously. "There's a difference, don't you know? There are a lot of Czechs in Cicero—and the lady's a Czech, so we sort of . . . got together. . . . " His self-confidence seemed gradually to be petering out, and the sergeant waited until it was entirely gone.

"So that's how it is. Hmm," he said, and with his glance measured first the well-built Baptist and then the even better built singer. The contrast of black and white was impressive. O'Mackey's glance stayed with the white curvaceous one.

"What are you gaping at?" the singer piped up, a little impudently. "I'm telling you that outside the kitchen, I never so much as spoke to Ben. He—"

"When did he give you the bomb?" O'Mackey asked tersely.

Improbable as the sergeant's hunch might seem, the singer's studied cool vanished and her response was extremely suspicious.

"Wh-wh-what bomb?"

At first O'Mackey wanted to keep at her, but then he fell silent, observing an interesting natural phenomenon: the snowy slopes of that pleasant valley were coloring like a rosy evening sky. The singer forced herself back to her cocky self-confidence. "What bomb, for heaven's sake? What kind of nonsense is that?" But the sunset was still growing deeper, like the clouds over snowy hillsides at dusk.

"A time bomb," O'Mackey said. "They're very popular nowadays. They started with them in France. In Montreal they plant them in libraries in English-language universities. In Ireland they put them in coffee shops where Protestant ladies meet. And the members of his Brotherhood—" he nodded in the direction of the Baptist, "they toss them into our police stations. Usually the mechanism is imported from Eastern Europe. And that's where you're from."

"So what?" the singer protested. "In the first place, I am from *Central* Europe, and in the second place, all they do there is drink too much."

"But what about the comrades there—"

"I'm a Catholic, myself. I even wanted to study theology. If it hadn't been for those com—"

"Baloney!" O'Mackey made a face. "You can't kid me, I was raised in Ireland! A Catholic girl study theology! Anyway—" and he pointed a finger at the exposed slopes of the valley.

"The neckline goes with my profession," the singer snapped at him. "And I don't understand—"

"Neither do I," said O'Mackey. "The explosion centered on your room, Miss Adam. Your windows were shut, and the explosion blew them out. But your blinds were drawn, and they stayed that way. And your door was locked. So can you explain to me who could have thrown a bomb in there, and how?"

Then he left the singer to consider this mystery of her own locked room, and went next door to interrogate Sharon Cornhill. His associate sat silently between the singer and the Baptist, and saw to it that they didn't exchange any signals. But the two of them—the black Baptist suspected of being a Brother, and the white Catholic suspected of being an agent—sat aloof in opposite corners of the kitchen.

. . .

Mrs. Cornhill's hands were shaking, but she tried to keep her voice calm. "Yes, Bob and I let her have the room for nothing, because my mother is her grandmother's sister. I suppose that makes me her great-aunt. I thought she ought to be paying us some rent all the same—it's not as if we're so well off that we don't need every dollar—but my husband wouldn't hear of it. That's him all over. You never saw anyone more kind-hearted than Bob."

"Maybe so," said O'Mackey, "but couldn't the fact that he didn't charge her any rent mean that . . . " He hesitated.

"I don't know what you're talking about," Sharon Cornhill declared, like a character from the most Victorian of novels. The girl in the blue jeans, sitting off to one side on a soot-marked chair, smirked, and her mother noticed it.

"Yes, kind-hearted," she repeated emphatically. "Besides, Bob has an exceptionally well-developed sense of family. He'd give his right arm for even the most distant relative. If someone in the family meets with misfortune, it's just as if it were Bob himself."

The girl in the blue jeans gave another smirk. "*That's* a fact. Evie cut herself on the electric carving knife a couple of days ago, and he fussed over her as if she was going to bleed to death."

"Bob's very good with his hands," said her mother archly. "So he feels for people who aren't as handy as he is, Sheila."

"Especially when they're young people of the opposite sex."

"You're quite wrong, Sheila," said Sharon Cornhill loftily. "Your father was brought up in the old American tradition of respect for women, and he treats all women the same. Just think of your grandmother. Remember how upset he was yesterday afternoon, when they announced the snowstorm in Illinois, until he heard she'd landed safely in Chicago. He waited so long for her call that we were almost late for his flight to Buffalo."

For a third time the girl gave a smirk, a very cynical one at that.

. . .

"Look, don't listen to Mom," she told the sergeant afterwards. "In things like this she's as blind as a newborn kitten. But ask him about his business trip to Buffalo, where he had to fly *tonight,* all of a sudden. If he had to go, why didn't he fly with Grandma this afternoon? Her flight had a stop in Buffalo. Why didn't he? I'll tell you why. Because Grandma isn't like Mom. She sees right through him. He'd never be able to explain to her why he had to *fly* to Buffalo, when we're so short of money and it's only three hours' drive. Mom trusts him totally, but not Grandma. That's why he didn't remember he had to fly out until after Grandma had left."

The girl was very excited. Her freckles almost disappeared in the flush that spilled over her cheeks.

"Why do you think he had to fly to Buffalo?" O'Mackey asked drily. He was hard-pressed to understand that kind of extravagance. The girl sniffed.

"Her name is Drugan," she said. "Her husband is a traveling salesman for evaporated milk. I know all about it. But that's not the point. The point is that he also has something going with Eve, and Grandma knows but she's still pretending she doesn't. That's why he sent her off to Chicago so early, even though Christmas isn't until—"

"Now then," the sergeant scolded her, "you could talk a little more nicely about it."

"What, about him cheating on his wife? Why? There's nothing nice about it, is there? Especially when she's a sucker like Mom."

"You might control your language a bit," O'Mackey insisted. "Besides, do you realize that accusing your own father of this is . . . is . . . "

"A matter of grave consequence, is that what you want to say? Of course I realize it," said Sheila, blowing a big bubble and carefully sticking it to her knee. "But I'm *sure.* It's not just that they're forever whispering together, like when she cut her finger. Not just on account of that. I know because of something I found."

"What?"

Sheila took the bubble off her knee, blew it a little larger, and handed it to O'Mackey. "Want it?"

"Cut it out," said the sergeant, and he pushed away the hand with the bubble, which popped.

"Know what I found?" said Sheila. "I found Dad's cigarette case. Under Eve's bed."

The sergeant leaped on a clue of such significance like a hungry tiger, though it might have nothing to do with the bomb. He failed to notice the unusual gleam in the girl's impudent eyes, a gleam that suggested more than just the usual moisture. "Mom was in New York that week," said Sheila, "and I came home early, and when I was unlocking the door I heard footsteps upstairs. Like running, fast, you know? And through the window I saw a man's shadow flash past, and then I heard the back steps to the garden creaking. I went to the kitchen and poured a glass of milk, and who should come in from the garden but Dad, in his shirt-sleeves, babbling something about feeling sick in the store and coming home to lie down." The girl's freckles were entirely lost against her flush. "So why wasn't he lying down, if he came home to lie down? Why was he traipsing down the stairs to the garden?"

At that point a couple of rather childish tears welled up in her eyes—this time the sergeant noticed—and slid down either side of her nose, where she licked them up.

"But that's still no proof that your father—"

"And what about his cigarette case? See, then Ben Turpin walked into the kitchen—"

The sergeant started. This was beginning to tie in with the case. "Turpin?"

"That's right, Turpin. He was working in our garden that week. Dad does things around the house, but he only does the kind of things that don't give you backaches. So Ben comes into the kitchen and asks me if I know if Eve—of course, he said Miss Adam—is still at home. I tell him I'll go take a look, so I run upstairs, open the door, and the first thing I see is her unmade bed—she spends most of the day in bed, because she works nights—and right there under the bed is Dad's cigarette case. The one Mom gave him for his birthday. Suddenly it all figured, that crazy running around upstairs, his feeling sick and coming in from the garden in his shirt-sleeves, even though it was pretty cold out." The girl fell silent and wiped away the tears with the back of her hand. "Oh, shit!" she said. "I couldn't care less. But it isn't fair to Mom."

· · ·

It was really morning by now; the sun was up, and Bob Cornhill's silvery temples seemed to gleam in the early light. It occurred to the sergeant that Cornhill resembled Clark Gable, and he thought to himself that, while the cigarette case in the singer's bedroom was inexcusable, from her point of view it might be entirely understandable.

But Bob Cornhill resolutely denied any relationship but a strictly avuncular one with his exotic niece. Then O'Mackey brought up the evidence of the cigarette case, a little self-consciously.

"A cigarette case?" wondered Cornhill, and then he burst out laughing. "So that's how it is!"

"What?"

"That's why she's such a defender of spiritual brothers!"

"Who, damn it?"

"Eve. Our Evie," Cornhill laughed. "In Europe, I understand, black men are supposed to be quite popular. I mean with women, if you get my drift."

"Now, just a minute. First explain the cigarette case to me. We'll get back to spiritual brothers in a minute."

"That's where we are," Bob said with a smile. "I lent my cigarette case to Ben Turpin."

O'Mackey was stunned. "Bob, we've known each other long enough for you to . . . I mean, really . . . you lent a valuable cigarette case to Turpin?"

Cornhill's face grew serious. "It's a little awkward. I owed him some money, and he started to threaten me. That he'd spread the word—you understand. So I gave it to him as a sort of collateral."

The sergeant got up thoughtfully. Suddenly, remarkable connections were forming between things. He asked Bob Cornhill to wait in the next room, and he walked over to the door and yelled, "Send in that rascal Turpin!"

. . .

The Baptist objected vehemently. "Hey, man, how could you think anything so stupid?"

"What's stupid about it? She's an attractive woman, and she works in nightclubs—people like that aren't prejudiced—"

"But I am!" howled Turpin. "White women don't appeal to me."

"Don't lie to me!"

"They don't! They're all . . . blotchy. I've tried it with them, but I couldn't—I just wilted. . . . "

"Wilted? What are you trying to tell me, Ben! You? And with the Adam girl? Besides," he added, almost taking it as a personal affront, "she isn't blotchy at all."

"You've never seen her undressed," Ben blurted. "Here on her back—" he indicated a spot quite low on his rump, "she has three big fre—"

"Aha!" exclaimed O'Mackey, and the Baptist realized he'd said too much. "Where did you see her with her clothes off, then?"

"At The Paradise! You've got to believe me—the girls there dress and undress behind a curtain, I swear it. You can go take a look yourself!"

But the sergeant's response was typical of a policeman, and explosive. "Don't try to squirm out of it, it's all perfectly clear to me. Chicago! That Brotherhood of yours! That foreign white tramp—such a pretty one! And Bob testified in court against your people of his own free will. You put your mark on him in that rag of yours, didn't you? So quit lying and tell me how that cigarette case got under her bed!"

It took a while before Turpin understood just what he was being accused of. Then he replied, quite simply, "I gave him back the cigarette case the very next day. He gave me the money he owed me, so I returned it to him!" He thought for a moment, and then added, "Which I shouldn't have done. He didn't pay me the next time either, and he still owes me for it."

. . .

Bob Cornhill flatly denied that he'd ever paid Ben Turpin and got his cigarette case back. Now it was one man's word against another—and despite his prejudices Sergeant O'Mackey didn't leap to any conclusions. But he did have second thoughts about the veracity of the Cornhills' impudent daughter. He vaguely recollected something from his criminology course called the Oedipus complex, and he spoke to her in paternal tones. "Look, kid, you're jealous of your dad, aren't you? Dad made a few jokes with his niece, and you turned around and invented this ugly story about him."

"Invented? Me?"

"Your Dad gave the cigarette case to Ben Turpin, to hold for him, because he owed him some money."

Sheila stared at him, her eyes full of disbelief which gradually changed to astonishment. Inside her little head, with its waist-length, perfectly straight fine hair, things began to fall into place, and the gleam in her eyes was one of anticipated victory. She stuck a hand into the hip pocket of her blue jeans and pulled out a silver cigarette case. "So it was Ben—sure! He works at The Paradise too, doesn't he? And that day he was working in our garden . . ."

The detective was unnerved by the sight of the cigarette case. Sheila was apparently telling the truth. But that didn't resolve the problem of a black man's word against that of a white man. The sergeant decided he'd have to determine the exact times in question.

. . .

Bob Cornhill wrinkled his brow, but he couldn't remember. Was it Thursday? Or maybe Wednesday?

Ben Turpin, on the other hand, had the events firmly fixed. "Wednesday," he stated, with absolute certainty. "I gave it back to you Thursday morning.

Bob Cornhill laughed helplessly. "But you didn't give it back to me."

Ben Turpin frowned. He looked at the sergeant. "Mister O'Mackey," he said, almost spitefully, "couldn't you find out just when that reliable witness of yours came across the cigarette case under Miss Adam's bed?"

But recalling the time had already proven to be beyond the powers of Miss Sheila, for whom even important events blended into an uncertain mist. Nor could Cornhill's two employees, who sold shoes in the failing shop on Main Street, recall what day of the week the boss hadn't been in the store four weeks ago. What they did agree on was that the boss was frequently out of the store. And now Bob Cornhill was insisting on flying to Buffalo on the urgent business matter he'd been unable to take care of the day before, due to the inclement weather, and because the detective had no reason to hold him, he decided to use good old-fashioned police methods and lean on the singer.

. . .

"All right, miss, out with it," he said, confronting her. "Ben Turpin has confessed."

By now the singer had sent for her regular clothes, the child's skirt and the high-necked white sweater, and she'd armed herself with cockiness again. "What do I care?"

"He confessed about the two of you."

The singer hesitated uncertainly, but immediately went on the offensive. "If you mean the bottle in the kitchen, I never stole it, if that's what you think. The customer gave it to me because he was too far gone to drink any more. That's the honest truth. You can ask—"

"Don't play stupid with me," O'Mackey interrupted her. "Look here, I'm on to you. I've had a lot of your kind pass through my hands. You don't give a darn what a man is, black, white, or even blue, as long as he . . . And even Ben Turpin . . . " He stopped and corrected himself. "Not that I consider it wrong from the human point of view. I'm not a racist. Though as a Catholic, from the religious viewpoint—"

He didn't notice the blonde turning red until her unexpected passion exploded. "You sanctimonious Irishman! I'm on to you, too. A lot of your kind have passed through my . . . Like in New York, a certain O'Raglan! A Catholic, like you! And a redhead, too!" She was raging the way people do when someone tells the truth about them. "And you? All I need to do is look at you, and see your eyes always glued where they've no right to be!"

"You watch what you say," growled O'Mackey. "You'd do better to explain how this cigarette case got under your bed, if you're so damned pure!"

He wasn't expecting the immediate results he got. The singer stared wide-eyed at the silver item as if she were afraid of it. Although she immediately denied any knowledge of how the thing had allegedly found its way under her bed, her initial response was enough to convict her in the detective's eyes.

Just then the telephone rang. Somehow, the fire had missed the telephone wiring.

O'Mackey grabbed the receiver. "Yes?"

"Bob?" said a female voice, old and distant.

"Just a minute," said the sergeant. He put down the receiver and looked at the phone, assessing the technical situation, and then went next door into the kitchen. There on the wall hung another telephone. The detective picked up the receiver: "Hello?"

"Is that Bob?" asked the same elderly voice. The sergeant turned and without a word handed the receiver to Cornhill, who was squirming on his chair under the eye of a policeman. Then he rushed back to the singer, but instead of continuing his interrogation he picked up the receiver and listened in.

"Bob," said the voice, "you're going to be terribly annoyed with me, but imagine what I did! I must have left that perfume behind!"

"What?"

It seemed to the detective that Bob sounded alarmed.

"Please don't be angry with me, but when I got here the box wasn't in my suitcase. And it couldn't have got lost during the trip because the case was locked, I locked it myself, and the perfume box was right on top, just where you put it, in that lovely fancy wrapping paper. Now don't let it upset you, Bob. You know what? I'll buy Mildred some here in Chicago. There's plenty of time till Christmas. You know, just between you and me, I know you like sandalwood on women but your Aunt Mildred, she prefers floral, like lily of the valley—"

"That's okay," said Bob Cornhill, "get her lily of the valley. Worse things have happened."

"Oh, thank you, dear. But you know, I just can't understand it, I locked that suitcase myself and it was right there! Then Evie borrowed the key when I was in the bathroom and put in the record for Freddie, and the record's there all right. And when she brought the key back to the bathroom, she asked what was in the pretty box, so it must have been there then. And I tested the locks, too." The old lady fell silent. "I don't know. Am I getting that senile, could I have taken it out? Bob, would you run up and take a look in my room . . . ?" She fell silent again. After a long pause, Bob Cornhill said, "Don't worry about it, Mother. I'll have a look around. Things here are—"

"I can well imagine. Things are always topsy-turvy before Christmas—"

The sergeant stopped listening. He hung up the receiver and looked at the angry blonde in the child's skirt. Then he stepped over to her, bent down, and sniffed at her sweater. "Sandalwood," he said.

"I beg your pardon?" she snapped at him.

"Your perfume. It's sandalwood," said the sergeant.

And the blonde flushed a little.

> Now, of course, you know who committed what crime—and what sin Eve committed in this tale. But take care not to rely on your instinct—it may be unreliable!

The detective turned and went to sit down. For a long time he didn't say a word. He was thinking. But he did notice how the young woman's exposed knees began to tremble.

"All right," he said, with unprecedented civility, "admit it. It was Bob, of course. He gave you the perfume. He likes the smell of sandalwood on a woman."

If he'd been more observant, he would have noticed that the pretty knees gradually stopped trembling. The singer dropped her lashes—very conspicuously—and chirped, "You're right."

"And he did something mean to you, right?" Something really nasty. So you took a—a—I don't know, he has all sorts of bullets and shotgun shells around, everybody knows he's a passionate hunter. And it's all the rage these days, you can find instructions on how to build one in practically any newspaper. All you need is an ordinary alarm clock—"

"Who, me?" The blond raised her conspicuous eyelashes again. "I haven't the remotest idea about things like that."

"It isn't complicated. Even a woman—"

"Wait a minute!" she interrupted him. It seemed to the sergeant that her pretty face had stiffened. "That's why Bob had to fly to Buffalo so urgently. That's why he insisted we all go with him to the airport—so nobody would be home when . . . and that's why he bought the alarm clock, expensive as it was. . . . "

The detective gave her a sharp glance, and her fingertips flew girlishly to cover her mouth. The sergeant recalled the insurance man's traditional theory, without the political fantasy that he, O'Mackey, had brought in with the hypothesis about Turpin's Brotherhood. Good Lord, could it be that simple? He thought of the trial of the Brotherhood in Chicago, of Bob's key testimony, of the list of "traitors" who were to meet their comeuppance because, according to the Brotherhood, they'd perjured themselves. And anyway, wouldn't a bomb be a safer way to resolve financial pressures than the more conventional methods familiar to insurance companies?

O'Mackey had his prejudices, but he wasn't a dyed-in-the-wool racist. He began to wonder whether the Brotherhood might have been right—not about the revenge, but about the perjury. Because if they were . . . a light began to dawn. If that was true, then everything changed.

He glanced at the singer. She crossed one beautiful leg over the other, and the detective asked gently, "But he did do something mean to you, didn't he? To make you turn on him like this?"

The blonde once again dropped her lashes—which the detective never guessed were artificial—and after a long moment raised them again. There was a lot, indeed, that O'Mackey never guessed.

"Yes, he did. Very mean. You know, you understand these things."

"I understand," said Sergeant O'Mackey with a discerning smile.

If the truth be known, you don't understand a damn thing, the blonde thought to herself.

. . .

Bob Cornhill was sentenced to fifteen years, for arson of an especially dangerous variety. Before they transferred him to the state penitentiary, he was visited in jail by his mother, his wife, his daughter (on the urging of his wife), and finally also by his niece.

She sat with him in his cell, and from time to time the guard peered in through the peephole. It seemed to him that the two of them were behaving oddly, but he couldn't see anything specific that was out of line, and of course he couldn't hear what they were saying.

"I've got it all written up, Bob, and I've left it with a good friend. If you get out of here early and something happens to me, the friend will open it and—"

"Eve," said Bob Cornhill hoarsely, "how could you even think I'd ever—"

The young woman looked at him mournfully, almost reproachfully. "All things considered, I can think just about anything of you, ducky."

He cringed and held his tongue. After a long moment, he dared to speak up again. "But it was quite a risk for you to take. All you had to do was set it wrong and it could have gone off while you were in bed."

"What do you mean, risk?" said the young woman. "I thought I'd defused it. It's just that I'm not good with technical things, not the way you are." She paused. "I'm not at all like you, do you understand me? Not in anything."

"I know," he replied, guiltily.

"So you're going to do the time for arson instead of me." She said it without a shadow of regret, but all the same, Bob Cornhill did something unexpected. He dropped to his knees, grabbed her hand, and in a fit of gratitude began kissing her bronze-colored fingernails.

"Evie, you saved my life!"

The blonde got up irritably and tried to yank her hand away. Her eyes, which up till then had just looked sad, or maybe unfeeling, filled with something like revulsion. She yanked her hand again, but Cornhill was holding onto it like a leech.

The guard, who had just looked inside again, grew indignant and abruptly opened the cell door. "Look here, Cornhill, cool it! And visiting time's over! Let's go, miss."

Bob Cornhill collapsed on the floor in tears as the blonde strode haughtily out of the cell, flashing those gorgeous legs that her childish skirt did nothing to conceal.

The Mathematicians of Grizzly Drive

I've discovered that here in America, when you want to illustrate an embarrassing predicament, you tell the apocryphal tale of the gentleman who turned up at a formal affair dressed in a sports jacket. But that's nothing compared to the time I found myself in one of those shops on Forty-second Street that sells magazines for men. I had no idea it wasn't a place for a girl to be, not even if she's a lesbian, and they do carry merchandise of that sort too. Anyway, the reason I went is that after a long silence I finally got a letter from two pals of mine, Brucie and Georgie, and they hinted they'd heard that in the States you could buy special magazines for their particular fraternity. I was just so overcome with homesickness for their little cubbyhole in Prague's Lesser Quarter that I grabbed the next subway train to Forty-second Street, and chose the largest shop in that long line of flashy neon signs. I was a bit startled to see two little black girls pressing their noses to the display window and giggling like crazy at what they saw: row upon row of magazines, each with one or two extremely underdressed women sprawled across the cover. But when I took a better look, I couldn't blame them. True, the world goes wild over the female form, but first of all, only one out of a thousand is beautiful—I'll admit mine happens to be one of them, and I'm not alone in saying so—and second, even that one is only beautiful if it's beautifully posed. If it's in some idiotic position like standing on its head—which these shameless models would no doubt have done if they'd known how—good-bye beauty. Those two little girls were perfectly right to laugh their heads off, at least until an older woman came up and whacked them one.

I stepped inside the supermarket. And that's what it was—racks and racks of immodest ladies, catering to every possible taste and perversion. But I headed straight for an island of immodest gentlemen. As I stood there picking and choosing among the bare bodies, my sixth sense suddenly told me someone was examining my own—fully dressed—body with the same concentration, but with a different motive. I glanced around through my eyelashes, and nearly died on the spot: a nose like that could only be a figment of Rostand's imagination. In fact, the pock-faced young man staring at my legs looked like something out of Disneyland. He had a nose like a rocket ship, only red and shiny, and on either side were squinty eyes with invisible lashes, because the poor fellow had hair so light it was almost white. Heaven help his parents—you'd hardly think such a creature would be a progeny of love.

Uneasy as all this made me, I glanced the other way, to discover another stare—and while this one didn't have such a unique proboscis, he resembled nothing so much as a murderer of small girls. I broke out in a fine sweat and grabbed one of the homo-magazines at random (I later received a thank-you note filled with such steamy gratitude that it came unglued en route), and turned around to pay. But the nondescript little fellow behind the cash register, on a high pedestal so he could make sure nobody made off with any of his topless wonders, was staring at me too—not lustfully, just incredulously. He was apparently accustomed to seeing just about anything here except a live, fully clothed female. I took a deep breath, made a contemptuous face the way I did when someone who was obviously broke was annoying me at The Pink Jungle, walked over to the cash register, paid, and proceeded to the exit like Queen Elizabeth—or maybe Queen Victoria. The two little black girls were back giggling by the window again, but when they spied me the laughter died on their lips and they turned and zipped down Forty-second Street, the tin butterfly barrettes on their little pigtails flashing as they ran.

This experience sort of prejudiced me against nude photographs, although in principle I have nothing against them. But two weeks later, in San Francisco, in the bar called The Sailor's Dream, a *Playboy* photographer offered me a couple of thousand bucks for two pages and a centerfold. At first I was disdainful—partly because there was another fellow sitting at the table who appealed to me—and said, "Thanks but no thanks." To be honest, it was also because it occurred to me that you can always find a copy of *Playboy* in Prague if you look hard enough, and that centerfold would surely wind up in competent (or maybe incompetent) hands, and I'd end up accused of bringing disgrace to the socialist homeland that had sent me out to earn foreign currency—there's always plenty of disgrace, though never enough foreign currency—and while in many ways I am a disgrace to my homeland, it isn't because of the way I use my body, but just try and tell them that. So I said, "Thanks but no thanks, Mr. Arbuckle, I'm a singer, not just a body to gawk at." The other fellow at the table, the one who appealed to me, said, "Good for you. For a build like yours, an absurd sum like that is an insult, especially coming from a magazine as financially secure as *Playboy*. I'd give you that much for a single private showing!" And he laughed so hard his diamond tiepin fell right into his Manhattan, and gleamed there like a firefly. I answered smartly, "A private showing always costs more than a public one, mister." Just between you and me and the gatepost, it turned out later that I was right—it was a damn sight more expensive.

Then I had to get up and sing, because Boozy Buckshot—who was one of the laddies himself, and black, and very nice to women—had strummed a few strings, a little out of tune, as usual. I could see past the microphone, even through the murk of darkness and cigarette smoke, that the fellow who appealed to me was undressing me with his eyes. He looked like a widower, or a bachelor who'd stayed single by choice rather than out of diffidence. Not that I'm the sort who makes forays into enemy territory to rob some affluent citizen there of his so-called freedom. But a woman doesn't get any younger, so we've all got to keep our eyes open—and if I have to put up with male companionship, I prefer an unattached male, and one who's at least somewhat prosperous. Anyway, he seemed to enjoy the idea of me without the little I was wearing, so I was a bit miffed when he and the photographer disappeared after my performance.

It never crossed my mind to associate him with the card the usually empty-handed mailman brought me two days later, according to which a Mr. Marcus Twisten requested the honor of Miss Eve Adam's company at a cocktail party at his residence at 1275 Grizzly Drive in Berkeley. I brooded over it for an entire day and night. Why was I being invited to a party by a Twisten? I didn't know anybody named Twisten, much less Marcus. But I'd been in the land of opportunity long enough to be crazy about cocktails, and also to know that, although a bottle of Scotch that costs 330 crowns in Prague only comes to $6.50 here, a poor nightclub singer can't afford more than one a week. So I overcame my girlish shyness of strange men, put on a nearly new cocktail dress that didn't waste a lot of fabric either above or below, climbed into my 1958 Pontiac, which cost me $200 and actually runs, and drove out—first past Fisherman's Wharf, then across that beautiful long bridge like a silver-plated brontosaurus, across the bay to Berkeley, up a winding road with a view, to the steep hill where Grizzly Drive is. My little buggy couldn't quite make it up that stretch, so I thought I'd have to walk the last half mile in my spike heels—which I'd have done gladly for the free drinks—but about fifty feet along the road I was offered a ride by a man who, it turned out, was also on his way up for the gratis cocktails. From him I found out that Marcus Twisten was the chairman of the Mathematics Department of the young and famous Berkeley campus of the University of California—which still didn't tell me why he was inviting me, of all people, for cocktails.

Professor Twisten's residence was spread across the top of Grizzly Peak, its colored windows overlooking the fairytale bay and the stone nest that is San Francisco, with fluffs of fog floating around the skyscrapers like little angels. As I was sauntering seductively toward the front door, my gallant chauffeur walking chivalrously behind me (never taking his eyes off my rear, of course), something emerged from the bougainvillaea on my left. It was a nose— the same unmistakable nose I'd seen on Forty-second Street—and behind it the same man, squinty eyes and all, but dressed in a tuxedo this time. When he saw me, those squinty eyes widened a little and the color of his super-nose spread all over his face; he was startled, as was I. He muttered something like "Hello!", even though we hadn't been introduced in that body shop on Forty-second Street, and with a broad gesture he held the door for me.

Inside, one mystery was resolved: the man who disentangled himself from the cluster of bored guests to greet me was in fact the man from The Sailor's Dream, the one who'd more or less offered me over two thousand for a private view; that reinforced my somewhat weakened self-esteem.

When you get right down to it, cocktail parties must have been invented by the good Lord as a punishment for alcoholism. You have to stand there on display, you have to chitchat with people you don't care about over things you're not interested in, and all that for a few shots of free booze and all the ice cubes you can use. So when Marcus (later known to me as Markie) went to get me some whisky, I had to stand and listen to some uneasy scholar's obligatory "Is this your first time in California?"—as if he cared—and watch his obligatory amazement when I said it was, as if a nice girl like me couldn't ever be in California for the first time.

In fact, the only even mildly interesting person there, aside from our host, was a blue-eyed demon named Venca Q. Fajrunt, a mathematician who'd emigrated illegally from Prague some time ago and who laughed like a horse neighing, all the time. Because I'd arrived at the party a little late, and he'd already pestered the

other ladies present, he directed all his pestering at me—especially
when he discovered I too was from Czechoslovakia. In order to
get rid of him, I made a date with him—as a fellow countryman—
and he went off to tell a cluster of offended but flattered ladies
how he regularly crossed into Nevada to visit the brothels.

Meanwhile Marcus came trundling up with a drink of spirits
guaranteed to have been bottled in Scotland, and kept me all to
himself, which is a faux pas at a party like that where you needn't
say anything intelligent or entertaining, but you absolutely have
to drop from six to twenty words, on any subject at all, to everybody present.

Marcus, on the other hand, was quite entertaining; I enjoy
hearing my appearance described in metaphors, even when they're
not original, and his sources ranged from King Solomon to that
detective writer, Chandler. He stood head and shoulders above
the other tuxedos in the room, who were babbling about cars
and the weather, and making terribly interesting observations such
as the fact that when you fly from Frisco to Sydney you arrive a
day younger because you've crossed the international dateline; or
maybe it's a day older, I forget.

While Markie was entertaining me with his artful flattery, I
noticed a girl in the corner behind a potted palm, spectacles on
her nose like Franz Schubert, her skirt just below her knees, a
regular museum piece—miniskirts were going out of style, true,
but what was coming in was maxis. She had her hair pulled back
into a little bun that looked like she'd inherited it from her great-
grandmother, and she held a glass of orange juice in her hand. I
wouldn't have paid any attention to her if she'd been by herself,
but beside her, with his back to me, stood that living tribute to
the human nose, a glass of orange juice in his hand too, and I
heard the walking schnozzola clear his throat and say, "I think
this orange juice is better than the kind we produce where I come
from. Is it native or imported?" The young maiden aunt answered,
"I really wouldn't know. I could ask my uncle, if you like." "It's
not all that important," he assured her. I was so taken by this
performance of pointless conversation that I turned to my host

and said, "Professor Twisten—" "Call me Marcus," he interrupted, and I continued, "Marcus, then, this may be rude, but I don't know that tall thin man with the Indian nose." "You mean the one whose nose is a living exhibit for the Los Angeles Otorhinolaryngology Institute?" chuckled Marcus. "He's . . . wait, I'll introduce you." He pulled me over and said, "Bill . . ." The man with the nose turned to face me and blushed, and Marcus proceeded, "Bill, I'd like you to meet this young lady. In a certain sense, you two belong together. Miss Eve Adam—meet Mr. Snake." Marcus burst into laughter, and I thought to myself, Markie-boy, the humorous possibilities of my name have been exploited by something like a thousand gentlemen—not even counting the boys in high school—and your joke is hardly one of the funniest.

But Marcus was still snickering. "Miss Adam is a singer," he went on. "And this is my niece, Miss Ann Bradstreet. She's boarding here with me." "It's a pleasure," said the mouse, "are you with the San Francisco Opera?" I don't know why, maybe it was the spectacles and the pimples and the schoolgirl uniform, but I replied, "Oh, no. I sing in a sailors' dive on Fisherman's Wharf." The Viper pursed his lips, while the girl turned red and spun away from me as if I were transparent, and said to a pregnant lady behind her, "Mrs. Wallace, what do you think of my uncle's bougainvillaea?"

To hell with that noise. I turned back to the man who would soon become Markie-darling and said, "You've got a charming niece, Marcus." He nearly choked on his maraschino cherry.

• • •

"She's an awful girl," Markie says to me later, when we're standing by the picture window in his study with San Francisco Bay spread out beneath us. Because the bay reaches out in an arc into the far distance, the lights blend to form a gleaming lasso ending in a big electrical bouquet of warm gold interspersed with a few pale yellow gems, with here and there the red and green jewels of traffic lights. Somewhere in all that is The Sailor's Dream, where I have a gig starting at ten. I don't feel like it at all. "She's terrible," Markie goes on. "A good head for mathematics, but otherwise—a fine example of the value of an orthodox religious upbringing. Her father, my brother-in-law, is a mathematician too—he has a few patents in computers—but do you know what he uses his computers for? A more precise calculation of the number of years elapsed since the creation of the world." "And how many years is it?" I ask, because things like that were neglected at the bishop's lyceum, and he makes a face. "According to him, 4,723 years—and seven months. He feels that's an improvement on the eighteenth-century estimates of Bishop Dumbwood, which indicated seventy-three years less—but without computers, of course. It seems you have to add up the ages of all those famous elders in the Old Testament, and make all sorts of comparisons, and things have a way of not agreeing. And then, nobody knows how old Adam was when God did the plastic surgery on him that started all the trouble."

"So what you're saying is that your good old brother-in-law is a little . . . ," and I tap my forehead. Marcus nods. "It's congenital, it ties in with the genes for mathematics. He belongs to the sect of Mather's Fundamentalists. In case you didn't know, Cotton Mather was a Puritan clergyman who specialized in Salem witches. I'm sure these fundamentalists would replace sex with that plastic surgery from Genesis, if they could." Markie gives a lecherous glance towards my apples of temptation. "And the result is this little niece of mine. I don't even think she's a woman. I've never seen her in a bathing suit, but sometimes I think she doesn't have a belly button."

"What do you mean?" I ask naively.

"I wonder if maybe my brother-in-law succeeded in copying that operation, with the help of computers and white magic. I'll have to count his ribs one of these times!" He laughs and adds, "It may have something to do with her talent at mathematics, but she doesn't seem to have any normal female qualities. She's as reliable as clockwork, but she has no idea of moods, she doesn't giggle or cry, she doesn't listen to love songs—just Bach, and only his fugues, at that—she arrives everywhere right on time, and she does precisely what she's told. Once I told her I had a new mistress, just to see what she'd do, and do you know what happened?" "She wouldn't care," I say, "if she's not a woman, the way you say." "Wouldn't care? She passed out! Fainted dead away. As she was falling she cracked her head on the aquarium, and I was afraid it might affect her mathematical mind. Not her; when she came to she said, 'X is the absolute value of the integral of minus y. All that over two.' Then she stiffened, looked at me, and declared, 'Five: Thou shalt not commit adultery.' And what do you think? She was out cold again! I don't know what I'm going to do with her."

He sighs, and adds, "Maybe she was also affected by a shock she had in school in Switzerland, where they sent her to learn French—not so much to expand her horizons, but because Calvin used to preach in Geneva, and they thought she might absorb some of the holiness of the place. There was one girl among the pupils who—wait!" he exclaims, "she was from somewhere near where you're from, Ruritania or Transdanubia or whatever all those little countries are called—where Dracula lived, where they assassinated Reinhard Himmler, where they brew Pilsener Urquell. I think it's governed by a Catholic priest named Tito . . . or maybe they hanged him." After this meticulous description of my homeland, I stop him: "Now, just a minute! Which parts of that are you certain of?"

"Well, my specialty is the theory of numbers, so I may be a little weak in geography; but I know they brew beer there because my cousin, a combat chaplain for General Patton's Third Army, was in on the liberation of the brewery, and he said it's an ancient land of some sort, and they speak Latin there." "Latin?" I ask, surprised. "That's right, Latin. When my cousin stopped his jeep on the square in the town where they brew Pilsener, a priest walked out of the building right across from the church and called out, '*Salve fratre!*' Not that my Latin is all that good, but my cousin told the story so many times that everybody in our family learned it. '*Salve fratre!*' says the priest, '*Ego sum sacerdos Catolicus Romanus!*' And then a Nazi machine gun started firing from the steeple, so my cousin dragged the priest under a Sherman tank for cover, and as they lay there on the ground the priest kept talking Latin, and using words for machine gun and tank that my cousin had never learned in the seminary in Sacramento. Later the priest took him through the brewery, and it's a fact that he couldn't understand the people working there, but I guess ordinary people spoke in some *lingua vulgata*, which makes sense, the simple people using common Latin while the intelligentsia use Church Latin."

Then he asks, "Listen, Eve, are you really from that country?" He gives me a look, and I nod and reply, "Yes—and I know the town you mean." "So you must speak Latin too, right?" "Sure," I say, "would you prefer to continue our conversation in the language of Horace?" "No," he says, "I just speak American and a little English, almost no Latin. But say something so I can hear what it sounds like." And I do: *"Ranam dissecui et preparavi eam in tabula in qua erat machina electrica—"* "Is that *vulgata?*" "Probably," I say. "It sounds nice," he says, "but it's very different from American, maybe it's closer to English. Anyway, back to my niece, Annie. It seems there was a girl at that boarding school from your country—"

"Do you know what her name was?" I ask, interrupting him, because I'm getting a funny little suspicion. That husband of hers, the reason she couldn't marry the father of her seven children— actually nine now, because he wanted an extra heir or two just in case, but the other two turned out to be more girls—I'm talking about Lubomira, as you've probably guessed—anyway, she latched onto that husband right after she split from Czechoslovakia to Switzerland, where she got herself into some rich Protestant girls' school as a poor refugee. That's where it all started—back home she'd been a perfectly decent, well-behaved day girl. "Oh, I don't remember her name," says Marcus.

"Was it Lubomira?" I suggest. He thought. "Could be. She caused a scandal later on, because she eloped through a window with a Spaniard or Greek . . . or an Italian . . . or was it an Arab? Anyway, there was our Annie, buttoned up to the chin in a new blouse bought at the Mather sect's shop back in Salem, walking into the room where all the new girls were being introduced to each other, and that girl I was talking about pointed a finger at her and started tittering, until our Annie thought maybe her blouse was unbuttoned. But it wasn't." So what was it Lubomira found so amusing?" I ask. "That blouse," he says, "or at least the pattern printed on it. Annie wrote to her mother about it, and her mother told all the relatives, and finally the Mather shop had to take all those blouses off the shelves." "What was the pattern, for heaven's sake?" I ask—not that I'm all that curious, but he never seems to be able to get to the point. "I don't know if it's familiar to you— American folklore has nothing like it—but in Transdanubian folklore it's supposed to be a very common design, dating back to the seventeenth century or something. It was apparently used among simple people as an expression of love. Farm boys would bake gingerbread hearts and draw the design on with colored frosting and give them to their sweethearts, and if the girl ate it they were considered to be engaged."

Now, I'm not all that well versed in folklore, but something like this wouldn't have escaped me. I suspect this bit of folk history came straight from Lubomira's imagination, which was fairly well developed, at least in certain areas. "What was the design, then? Describe it, Marcus!" I say, and he answers, "A rhombus." "You mean a diamond shape?" I ask. "That's right," says Marcus, "but with a line down the middle." Of course! That's our Lubomira! "My, I never saw anything like that," I lie, in an astonished tone of voice, but clearly it was that bitch Lubomira who shocked the living daylights out of Annie, by informing her that the pattern printed on her pious blouse was a grossly obscene sign for certain female parts—a symbol familiar to anyone, from small boys up, who had ever frequented public washrooms in her native land.

Once I've figured this out, my interest turns elsewhere. "What about Mr. Snake? He really seems to be interested in Miss Bradstreet." "Who, him?" Marcus grins. "He's nothing but a walking, talking illustration of Adler's famous inferiority complex. He's a mathematician too. He's been after her for the past two years, but the furthest he's ever got from math towards sex was last week on her birthday. He asked her where she was born, and when he said the word 'born' he blushed. It's hopeless. If he were to set eyes on a woman in the buff, he'd run to get her a bathrobe."

Well, I could sure tell Markie a thing or two, like about the shop where I'd encountered the Viper not three weeks before. He hadn't been running for any bathrobe then. But, as I said, I had to go to work.

. . .

Otherwise, I thought to myself on the way down the hill—my Pontiac had caught its second wind and taken its place in the smelly ranks of cars crossing the bridge at fifty cents a crack—otherwise I could have told him the story of how, when they wouldn't let me study theology, I took a room with a Catholic lawyer's family; they had to sublet because their apartment was bigger than they were allowed, and also because after the so-called victory of the people their income had declined, since the father had to retrain from lawyer to machinist, and he wasn't all that good at it. Originally he hadn't wanted a girl tenant—his instincts were sharp—but his wife was a school chum of my mom or something, and I had an advantage in that I'd been a student at the bishop's lyceum, so I finally got it.

The lawyer had an adolescent son who adolesced himself into a crush on me, but he was so shy that he hid it even from me. There was a beautiful big bathroom in the apartment, and I never used to lock the door; it was an absolutely moral household, and besides, they always knew I was in there by the sound of water splashing, and anyway I'd always tell them when I was going to take a shower. But one day when I was in there the door flew open and the kid came tearing in, red as a tomato, and before I could scream he threw himself at me right there under the shower—in a double-breasted sports jacket—and proceeded to cover my body with torrid kisses, like someone out of a novel, only my foot slipped and as I was falling I grabbed hold of the hot water tap and it turned off. I landed in the tub with the boy tumbling in after me, and the water sluicing down on us turned icy cold and brought him to his senses; he turned pale, stammered something, scrambled out of the tub, and fled. I never told on him, but a couple of weeks later, when he'd calmed down a little, I took him aside and he admitted he'd been spying on me through the keyhole for six months—which of course I'd known all along.

As I was saying, I drove past Fisherman's Wharf, watching swarms of tourists seeking yet another monotonous form of entertainment, and thought to myself that I could have told Marcus about all that, and about how the youth turned out to be a perfectly wonderful pal—so great, in fact, that six months later he threw me over and knocked up a certain Jana Honzlova, a singer with the State Song and Dance Ensemble. But she took care of it.

Anyway, I said to myself as I walked into the dressing room and surprised Boozy Buckshot lighting up a joint, anyway, look out for Mr. Bill Boa Constrictor, he just might explode some day in little Annie Bradstreet's fundamentalist bathroom.

. . .

It wasn't snobbishness that made me consider learning to play bridge. Someone had told me it was like chess only easier, and since the only thing I'd ever used cards for was to tell fortunes, I told myself that maybe here in America I should learn something new. By then Markie-boy and I were pretty close, and he said, "Why not? Bridge is a fine mathematical game. It's true you have trouble adding and subtracting, and your multiplication's worse—still, it isn't *only* a mathematical game. . . . Come over tomorrow. I'll invite Shad Snyders and Raymond Daly, they're both known on the Berkeley campus for their bridge."

That's how I come to find myself in front of 1275 Grizzly Drive one fine summer evening—my little Pontiac had got used to the Berkeley hills by now. As I'm crossing in front of the bougainvillaea, I recognize the cracked voice of the Viper: "Isn't it a nice evening? One of the nicest all day." I stick my head inside the bougainvillaea and discover that he's just addressed this improbable statement to Ann Bradstreet, who's sitting two arm's lengths away from him, at the far end of the pink bench behind the bougainvillaea. You're not making much progress, I think to myself, but at least you're determined. And I walk inside the house.

The first to arrive for our little bridge party is Professor Shad Snyders, whose field is applied mathematics. That's obvious right away: "I thought," he says, placing a large flat box on the bridge table, "that if we got tired of playing bridge later on, we might play a little roulette. What do you think, Marcus?" Despite his impeccable reputation in the sphere of number theory, Markie is always inclined towards games of ill repute, and he says, "Excellent! Let's start right away—the three of us can't play bridge anyway, so until Daly comes let's pass the time with roulette." "Feel free," I say. "You're the well-paid lackeys of the American establishment, with your lucrative industrial patents and all, whereas I was driven to America by poverty, in search of bread and Coca-Cola." Whereupon the two of them exhibit extraordinary chivalry, declaring that I'll take part in the winnings but that they'll cover my losses between them—which I think Snyders, at least, came to regret before the evening was out. So instead of a mathematical card game we spin that ingeniously simple contrivance for unmasking mathematical probability, and within an hour I have enough to replace my Pontiac.

At that point the door chimes sound, announcing the arrival of Raymond Daly, professor of Middle English literature, famous for having found a puzzle in some old poem about a peer and a ploughman—an anagram or something that attacked the British social system of the day. The solution of the anagram or whatever was so complicated that they had to use number theory on it, or something like that—mind you, at the time the poem was written people didn't know how to calculate anything more advanced than equations with one unknown, but of course that didn't diminish Daly's fame.

Something about Daly bothers me from the very beginning, but I can't place it. He joins the game enthusiastically—not bridge, I never did learn to play bridge in California—and after he's lost his first hundred (by then Snyders is down $170, and his chagrin is beginning to show) and we take a refreshment break, I realize that it's his name that's familiar: it combines the names of two famous California writers.

"Say," I ask, turning to Daly, "don't you write detective stories on the side?" Daly chokes on his canapé, spattering crabmeat and mayonnaise all the way to my waist, and says, "How did you know?" "Your name," I say; "But I write under a pseudonym," Daly objects, amazed. "Of course," I say: "Raymond as in Chandler—in Czechoslovakia he's one of the most popular American authors, thanks to a certain writer named Kopanec who promised himself he wouldn't quit until all of Chandler's novels were published in Czech. And of course there was a certain American named Carroll John Daly who founded the so-called hard-boiled school of detective fiction." I say this so knowledgeably that Daly's mouth falls open and he marvels, "I thought you were a nightclub singer—" "And?" I say aggressively. "I did finish high school, and besides, Kopanec is a good friend of mine, and a secret admirer."

Raymond Daly takes me by the hands and says, "Come over here with me," and he draws me out the door towards the bougainvillaea. From the concealed bench comes the hiss of the Serpent: "Back home in New England, it's probably a bit cooler this time of year." And Ann's reply: "I don't think—" But I stop listening at that point, because Daly is talking excitedly. "Please don't tell anybody about me, I keep it a secret; it may be all the rage now, pop culture—one of my colleagues even wrote a monograph about Edgar Wallace—but who knows, things could get snobbish again, so I write under the name Ernest W. F. Fitzgerald. I enjoy it so much. Every so often . . . " He gazes past the bougainvillaea to San Francisco Bay, and out to the Golden Gate Bridge in the sunset, and clenches his fists. "Sometimes at parties . . . the dumb conversation . . . I'd like to punch some noses, you know?" He reaches out his well-formed fist to the tip of my own little nose. "I know," I say, "but I just drink and ignore it." Daly keeps musing: "Or the banks—you wait for your paycheck from one month to the next, and all you really need is a pistol, a reliable accomplice, and—" he reaches out that fist again, this time with a finger stuck out like a gun barrel, " 'Give me all your money, teller!' " Then he wilts, adding, "But those are just pipedreams. In real life I'm analyzing T. S. Eliot. Would you believe, the poem 'The Love

Song of J. Alfred Prufrock' conceals an obscene anecdote about Gertrude Stein? Or maybe Mary Pickford, I'm not entirely certain which yet." Being not all that familiar with T. S. Eliot, I want to change the subject, but just then we hear Markie's impatient voice; he's eager to be fleeced again, so we go back inside.

We find Ann there. "Uncle Marcus," she chirps, the consummate obedient Mather Fundamentalist niece, "Bill has invited me to go see him play Bobby Fischer in a simultaneous chess match tomorrow morning. I told him I have to work on my dissertation, but maybe I could take a couple of hours off, I'd make it up in the afternoon. What do you think?" Marcus pats her on the cheek and murmurs, "Go ahead, Annie, you need some fun too, go watch Bobby Fischer play Bill in a simultaneous chess match." Annie doesn't catch his tone of voice at all, but after she leaves he says, "Hold me back or I don't know what I'll do. That silly fool thinks she's living in a convent here, and I'm the mother superior. Some day I'm going to blow up."

Thanks to the gallantry of those present, I'm up on the game, Markie's running fifty-fifty, and Shad Snyders is gradually winning back what he lost at the outset. But for Ernest W. F. Fitzgerald the night's a catastrophe. It's almost ten o'clock—fortunately this is my night off at The Sailor's Dream—when Ernest W. F. heads for the washroom, sweating, his hands shaking. "It seems to be getting to him," I say, and Shad glances after him to make sure he's out of hearing and whispers, "I'll tell you something about Raymond: he leads a double life." "I know," I say, and Shad asks, "Did you sing at Lake Tahoe too?" "No, I didn't sing," I reply, confused. A few days later, Markie drove me up to that delightful little town in the Sierra Nevada, and couldn't drag me away; I was totally taken by the poisonous magic of the slot machines. I was so gone on them that I only remember poor Markie using his belt to tie me up, and getting two croupiers to carry me out to the car. A few miles from the California border, he called my attention to the Kit Kat Klub brothel—it so happened that they were just tossing Venca Q. Fajrunt out of there, yelling something at him about paying as you go. . . . "No, I've never sung at Lake Tahoe," I repeat; "Did Mr. Daly lecture there or something?" Shad shakes his head. "No, but a week ago he lost three thousand playing blackjack there. Which is nothing to sneeze at, for an assistant professor of English literature." At that point Ernest W. F. returns to lose another fifty-three dollars, making it an even three hundred.

We quit about midnight, and just then Ann comes in with her Snake, saying she needs to get a good night's sleep before the chess game. "Me too," says Marcus, "I'm off to Santa Barbara tomorrow morning. I have a lecture there in the afternoon on the theory of relativity. It's been all the rage among ladies' clubs for the past thirty years; the ladies keep hoping it will sink in, even if they've barely mastered the times tables, and I let them believe it—partly because the clubs pay well, but mainly because some of the members are young things. . . . " I sneak a peek at Ann in case she faints, but she's being distracted by the Viper, who's pressing a letter into her hand and stammering, "Here . . . I wrote . . . it's an answer to what we . . . ," and by now his hair's almost catching fire from the red glow on his face, so he turns and runs out of the room without even saying good-bye. Quite a guy. Marcus just has time to call after him, "Bill, phone me about that article!" before the Viper is swallowed up by the starry night.

Shad Snyders' Chevy takes off down Grizzly Drive first, and behind it the subdued Ernest W. F. Fitzgerald, a.k.a. Raymond Daly, and finally, with Markie's passionate kiss still burning on my neck, me. It's a pleasant drive through a pleasant California night. At the end of Grizzly Drive, Ernest W. F. turns left towards El Cerrito and I head on across the brontosaurus bridge to the edge of Chinatown, where I've sublet a little cubbyhole from a certain Mrs. Wong Li, widow of an importer of Chinese incense.

. . .

The next day the weather is fine except for a little rain shower right after lunch, and since my tomcat Markie isn't home I spend the day playing golf with his assistant; the truth is, I suspect Markie's planning a birthday surprise for me—for his birthday—and I want it all to work out. That's also why, faithful sweetheart that

I am, I phone him first thing the following morning—I can barely survive a whole day away from my darling. Marcus picks up the phone, and he sounds nervous, a rare state for him. He says, "Look, Evie, if you've got strong nerves, come on up. Otherwise don't bother." Which intrigues me, so I hop in my Pontiac and climb Grizzly Peak in record time. But when I burst into the living room, dying of curiosity, there's a strange actor sitting there, dressed in what could be a costume from seventeenth-century Switzerland: he's all in black, with high black lace-up boots, and out on the hat rack in the hallway is a broad-brimmed black hat like the ones Orthodox rabbis wear. He looks as if he's failed the Last Judgment.

"This is Ebenezer Bradstreet, my brother-in-law," Markie says gravely, "and this is Miss Adam, a nightclub singer." I guess he says this out of malice, because the Swiss burgher, whose gaze has already stumbled uncomfortably over my miniskirt, immediately turns to ice and looks away from me, as if I'm some kind of diabolical temptation—which I am, but not all *that* evil, there are far worse sins in the world than the violation of that old commandment. Anyway, he looks away from me, and from then on he talks right through me and acts as if I'm not there.

"Ebenezer arrived by the morning flight from Salem, Massachusetts, and it was the first time in his life he'd ever flown. So you can see it's something really serious." Marcus adds, very solemnly, "Yesterday somebody kidnapped his daughter, I mean Ann, and phoned him to demand ransom." The burgher clears his throat and says, "He wants ten thousand dollars by tomorrow night." I think to myself that they don't value Ann all that highly—not that her body would be worth any more than that, but according to Marcus she's something on the order of a female Einstein, so at ten thousand that brain of hers should be a regular bargain. "Of course, I am perfectly prepared to pay the ransom," the burgher adds, "but I am opposed to calling in the police, as my brother-in-law suggests. It could jeopardize Ann's life. Kidnappers are very disagreeable people, or so I was told by the Reverend Nathaniel

Wigglesworth, who has it from the newspapers."

"If you don't want to, then we won't," Marcus says. "We have Eve here now, and she's told me how she saved the reputation of a perfidious lady in a place called HitSongSea, in Sweden or somewhere like that. If it's true, it was a job worthy of a detective. Evie may not know long division, but she has a fine grasp of elementary logic. She also has splendid powers of observation, although that doesn't surprise me—women see a lot, and while they usually don't know how to put it all together, she does. To make a long story short, Evie is our own private little FBI, so we'll turn her loose on this problem like a bloodhound, and see what she can do." I can tell that all this hasn't made much of an impression on Ebenezer; he's still looking right through me. But my main interest now is in seeing the scene of the crime.

Actually, it's not entirely clear whether it is the scene of the crime. But before I got here, Marcus came up with a theory of sorts himself. He hadn't discovered that the house door was bolted shut from the inside until the cab brought Ebenezer in from Oakland airport that morning, and it was only after Ebenezer told him what had happened that he went up to Ann's bedroom and discovered she not only wasn't there, but apparently hadn't slept there the previous night—which agreed with Ebenezer's statement that the kidnapper called him the previous evening at 6:05 California time, or just after the price of long-distance calls goes down, which shows how hard up the kidnapper must be. Anyway, my clever little lover assumes the door was bolted since midnight of the night before last, when he bolted it himself after the bridge-roulette party, because in the morning, when he left for Santa Barbara, he went straight into the garage through the side door, which he found still open when he returned from Santa Barbara that night. Naturally he didn't go to check on his niece that late at night; he assumed she was upstairs in her virginal boudoir. As for old Ebenezer, he was so distraught over the bad news and the upsetting struggle to arrange a flight to California that it never occurred to him to call Marcus: he probably didn't even know you could telephone from Salem to California. So it was that at nine that morning, when the burgher rang at the front door, Markie-baby was still enjoying untroubled dreams.

For clarity's sake, I draw a little map:

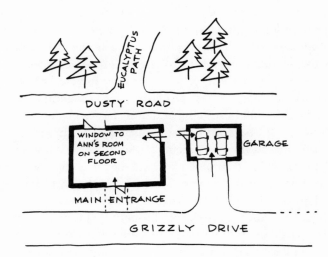

"Okay," I say, looking at the map, "but Ann went to watch the chess match yesterday morning. She would have bolted the front door again when she got home." "Baloney," says Marcus, "she didn't go to any chess match. I've found out that much already. Bill Snake will be here shortly."

Before the Snake comes, I sniff through Ann's room, which Marcus refers to as the scene of the crime because it's probably where she was kidnapped from. In the corner is a narrow bed, and it's not turned down. By the window, looking out onto the eucalyptus grove, stands a broad desk with piles and piles of papers on it, covered with equations that are vaguely familiar to me from my days at the bishop's lyceum, all written with a fastidious hand, and interspersed with incomprehensible sketches of the sort I remember the melancholy Father Silhan drawing in chalk on the blackboard.

As I stare at all these figures, I hear the chimes of heaven downstairs. By the time I get there, Marcus is already at the door; he opens it and there stands the Worm, white as a sheet, babbling. I have to lead him by the hand to an armchair, and there he begins, in a tremulous voice: "She was always so punctual . . . so I phoned her at exactly five past ten, and on the signal—we'd arranged a signal, you know, so the phone wouldn't disturb her when she was working . . . ," says he incoherently, and I think to myself, sounds like at least a little progress, and he goes on, "Then the chess match started, but I got away for a minute, to the phone, at a quarter past eleven . . . but nobody answered . . . and then I had to play until one, and I tried one more time later in the afternoon . . . and still no answer."

"What kind of a signal, and what were you doing afterwards, until midnight?" I ask the Viper sharply, and he mumbles, "I was . . . at home . . . working, and things . . . I went up to the Faculty Club before six, I had something to give to Professor Wolfsheim there . . . and I stayed for about half an hour . . . and after that I went for a walk—" "Alone?" I interrupt him. "Alone," he nods, uncertainly. "And as for the signal, it's like this: dial, let it ring once, hang up, and dial again. We only arranged it last night," he adds, but I'm not interested anymore.

Looky here, I say to myself, no alibi from one o'clock on. Could he have improved on my shower experience with a violent abduction? Could he maybe have done poor virginal Annie in, in a fit of passion, somewhere in the woods? And what about the ransom call to Ebenezer? An attempt to cover it up? It wouldn't be the first time.

Now stop that! I can feel myself falling victim to the passion of the hunt, like that time with O'Raglan. Who was it who lost three thousand bucks at Lake Tahoe not long ago, and three hundred more right here at this table the night before last? And who was so spoiled by hard-boiled detective mysteries that he seriously thought about doing his banking behind a gun barrel, pointing it at the teller so she could see the bullet all ready to pop out at her? Ha! Or what about Shad Snyders, infamous gamesman? He emerged none the worse for wear that night, but heaven knows how many quarters he's tossed into the one-armed bandits at Lake Tahoe, not to mention roulette and blackjack. And all three of these gentlemen knew that Ann would be at home alone that morning, and that my tomcat Markie wouldn't be home until late at night. Okay, Evie, you've got to check their alibis.

We let the terrified Viper go for the present, leave Ebenezer to his prayers, and pile into Markie's luxury Caddy and head out to El Cerrito. On the way, Marcus says to me, "Speaking of phone calls, that reminds me. In the morning, when I'd just finished in the bathroom, the phone rang as I was walking past. I picked it up but all I heard was someone hanging up. But no sooner did I walk away than it rang again, and it was Bill Snake calling with some bibliographical data I'd asked him for the night before. That was about nine. I left around half past." By this time we've arrived in El Cerrito, in front of the home of Raymond Daly.

Daly's floating like a corpse in his green swimming pool, his eyes closed, and when he opens them it seems to me that we've startled him. Marcus speaks to him as though it's all a big joke: "Okay, Ray, quit kidding and tell us where you've stashed the girl." But Daly gives a perfect performance of innocence, and then comes up with an almost perfect alibi. From nine in the morning on, he was in his study at the university, having consultations with his students; from ten to twelve he had a seminar on *Sir*

Gawain and the Green Knight; then for lunch he went to Ye Olde Tavern in El Cerrito, arriving a little late because he had to change a flat tire (a tiny gap in the alibi) but he was at Ye Olde Tavern by a few minutes before one, had lunch with Dr. Bickley and stayed with him until a quarter past three, then drove back to the university, where he continued with his consultations—his mania for consultations is becoming a little obtrusive from where I sit— and by six he was at dinner in the Faculty Club, where he stayed playing whist until 10:30, when they tossed them out of the club. That's the way Daly relates it to us, in a nice orderly manner, on the shore of his little green swimming pool; as we drive off I look back to see him reimmersing his body in the warm water with its litter of drowned butterflies.

Shad Snyders isn't floating in a pool, he's spending his weekend working in the garden. When he's described his uninteresting professional activities—the morning spent without witnesses (another noticeable gap), a noon lunch with a friend at the club, a return there before six following an afternoon spent teaching the long-haired hopes of America's future—when he's described all this, he asks why we want to know. So Marcus tells him, and Shad says, "That's odd. I called Ann just before I went to the club for lunch—I'd promised her some data for her dissertation—and she was still home then." "She answered the phone?" Marcus asks, surprised. "She did," says Shad, "she was home all right."

This is really strange. Either Shad is pulling our legs, or else the Viper is. "Which would put Annie's disappearance either in the morning or in the afternoon, take your pick, since we don't have a lie detector handy," muses Marcus on the way to the club. We want to stop off there just to be on the safe side, and it turns out to be a good idea; in the book of long distance calls—which is kept on an honor system—Marcus finds the notation "6:00 P.M.— Long Distance to Salem Mass.—Prof. Snyders."

We drive through the warm afternoon, back up Grizzly Peak, and Markie is so deep in thought that he forgets to place his hand where he usually puts it when we drive, just above my knee—in fact, if it weren't for my miniskirt I could say it was under my skirt. He says, "Okay, either Bill is lying or else Snyders is. But one thing seems fairly clear: the kidnapper has to be one of the three. Whoever it was had to know about my trip to Santa Barbara; and there were no signs of a struggle in Annie's room, which means she left of her own free will, unsuspecting." "But it could have been something else entirely," I suggest. "What if she went to run an errand somewhere and a stranger nabbed her outside the house?" "Come on, Sherlock," says Marcus, "there's nowhere on Grizzly Peak to go run an errand, and even if there were, the front door would have been either open or locked, but not bolted from the inside, right? And if she went to town to run this errand, she could only have done it by car, and her MG is still sitting in the garage. The only other possibility is that she went out the back door into the eucalyptus grove, but why would she do that? She makes a point of working indoors; the raccoon activity and the twittering of birds in the trees disturb her concentration."

But I still have something on my mind. As soon as the Cadillac slips quietly into the garage beside the chaste little black MG Ann received when she got her MA, I say, "Excuse me!" and run out the garage door, but I don't go straight across into the house. Instead I run around the back, across the dusty road that no one ever drives on, and stop at the edge of the eucalyptus grove, where an old raccoon is sitting, mauling a stolen hot dog.

And what do you know? In front of me is the dusty back road, and Ann's window looking out into the wood. If someone stood here and whistled at her, and she was sitting working equations at her desk, she'd have no trouble seeing him and, quick like a bunny, hopping down and out the back door into his arms. But that couldn't be our Annie, I say to myself skeptically—not our holy virgin of the integrals, who probably came into being by means of one of those famous rib operations.

Or else . . . I think back to that buddy of mine, the one who knocked up Jana Honzlova. Nobody would have suspected him of anything like that either—not even the secret police. So why not Annie? Out the back door so no one would see . . . and into the grove towards a meadow?

I feel that dumb wrinkle forming between my eyebrows—not a sign that I'm getting old, as some aging beauties like to claim I am, but something I've had since birth; my head was squeezed by the forceps. Anyway, let's say the Viper's lying. Then everything begins to fall into place. The Viper phoned at nine with the signal, but Marcus took the call so the Viper disguised it with his bibliographical data. Then Marcus left. Let's say the Viper phoned again after that, to tell her not to come to the chess match, that he'd whistle under her window that afternoon. He told us she hadn't answered the phone, but that could have been a clumsy attempt to make it look as if she'd disappeared while he was up to his eyeballs playing chess. Still, he couldn't have known Shad would phone her before noon—unless Shad was inventing all this because, for alibi reasons, he needed to show she was there in the morning too.

Then I think of the ransom, and the long-distance call to Salem. Of course, anyone in the club could have been responsible for the notation in the book. As a matter of fact, it probably points away from Shad, because nobody's stupid enough to sign his own name when he's in the process of committing a crime.

I start back to the house, and then stop. Wait! Wouldn't the Viper have checked up on Annie if, as he claimed, she hadn't answered the phone that morning? If she was so all-fired punctual and reliable, it must have made him wonder when she didn't show up. So why didn't he drive over?

Why not? Of course! Suddenly it's clear to me why the Viper—obviously surprised she hadn't shown up—would have decided to spend the afternoon at home "working, and things." If he's telling the truth there can be only one reason, from the psychological point of view, and that's a reason I'm very familiar with; I've often made my pals feel that way, myself. Lots of times I've pretended to take offense, when some youth was too pushy for my taste and I decided a little futile yearning wouldn't do him any harm. I refuse to see him for a few days, and some of them feel they have to respect this and keep out of my sight. I'm always pretending—but Ann would have been perfectly serious.

With this hypothesis in mind, I rush into the living room, where Ebenezer is still on his knees, praying, and Marcus is disturbing him by insisting we call the police. It's all very clear to me now. It means neither the Viper nor Shad was lying to us, for the simple reason that the calls the offended Annie wouldn't take were the ones signalled by the Snake, not non-signal calls like the one from Shad—if you can follow this negative trail of logic. I run upstairs to her boudoir and start going through her papers, in search of the love letter I saw the Viper passing her that night, just before he fled out under the starry sky. But I can't find it. The only things I find are like $\frac{ab}{1} + \frac{1}{ab} = ab^2 + 7$, stuff like that, all too boring for a detective—nothing else.

Then I notice the wastepaper basket, a classic item in any detective's repertoire, and I start burrowing into the balled-up papers; what if the love letter he wrote had something shyly forward in it, and the chaste and virginal Ann was upset and refused to take his calls? And what if he felt he had to keep out of her sight? I dig through those papers like a cat that's just peed, but all I find is equations—until at last my patience is rewarded. Finally, that interesting epistle.

Actually, it's an envelope, made of fancy vellum with a return address printed on the flap: "William Q. Snake, 1352 Bancroft Ave., Berkeley, Calif." And it's empty. I keep on looking, uncrumpling the papers until I've seen them all, but there's nothing there except the Queen of the Sciences—nothing the least bit erotic.

I glance back at the mess on the desk, and something strikes me. Among all the sheets of foolscap is one page the same size and shape, but of fancy vellum. And only then do I notice that it has a monogram: WQS. On the paper is a neatly printed equation:

$$(4|x| + 2|y| - 4)\,(\,|\,|y| - 1\,| + |y| - 1 + |x|)$$

and above it, in somebody's handwriting, presumably the Viper's: *Graphically, Ann, the Solution expresses it all.*

Under it are some letters and numbers in a more delicate hand, apparently Annie's, working at the equation until she found the—

Solution! Just a minute . . . "graphically"—but I don't see any graph, he must mean . . . symbolically. That the equation is symbolic of some problem and its solution. But what problem? As I recall from the melancholy Father Silhan, an equation is not a solution, but something to *solve*. The outcome is the Solution . . . but the Solution of what? And what does the Solution express?

At that point the door creaks, and Marcus says, "I talked him into it. We're going to call the cops about Shad."

> And now you know who abducted Ann Bradstreet—because you know who was telling the truth, and where and why. Or at least you know which commandment was violated. No guessing, of course— that would be most inappropriate in the sphere of mathematics.

"Hold off a minute," I say, and pass him that incomprehensible mathematical love letter. "Take a look at this. What does it say to you?"

Marcus takes a look and his eyebrows go up; he gets drawn into the mathematics of it so that he forgets I'm there. He sits down on Ann's chair, grabs Ann's pencil, and follows her calculations as if he were correcting a homework assignment.

Then he scowls horribly and turns to me. "Annie wrote this?" he asks. "So it seems," I say. "I believe that about as much as Ebenezer believes in Darwin," he says. "Annie wouldn't have thought up something like this." "Who says she thought it up?" I ask. "She got it from WQS, Bill Snake—look at the monogram. She only worked on solving it."

Marcus scowls again, and so he won't get drawn back into it I babble, "I have a theory, want to hear it? Ann got offended at Bill for something, so she didn't take his calls even with his signal, I mean especially with his signal, because then she knew it was—"

All of a sudden, Marcus bursts out laughing—so hard, in fact, that his tiepin flies off and skitters across the floor—although laughter seems terribly inappropriate in view of the tragic circumstances. "Evie! You're a genius after all! You figured it out! The equation calls for absolute values, but you still solved it, all by your lonesome!"

"I've got to tell you, Markie, you're overestimating me," I say. "I can't figure this out, not at all, understand?" I say this in a wounded tone, and he puts his arm around my shoulders and says gently, "Evie, my love, I'm going to give you a lesson in algebra; a little education won't hurt you, even if you don't need it. I'm afraid it will be rather like in Santa Barbara yesterday, when I was trying to explain the space-time continuum to the ladies' club." I sit down, a little snootily, on Ann's bed and he proceeds like a real professor.

"Look," he says, "let's take this equation of ours:

$$(4|x| + 2|y| - 4)\,(\big|\,|y| - 1\big| + |y| - 1 + |x|) = 0$$

On the left side there's an algebraic expression—"

"What?" I ask. "You're talking to a complete simpleton, so please express yourself accordingly." "All right, my dear simpleton," says Markie, "on the left-hand side of the equation there are all sorts of x's and y's and numbers, and on the right-hand side there's a zero. Zero, as you may know, means nothing." "Let me think a minute," I say, thinking, and then I agree, "I understand, zero is nothing." "Correct," says Markie, and proceeds: "If we replace the x and the y with any two numbers, we can calculate the entire left-hand side of the equation, and by determining whether or not the left-hand side actually does equal zero we can decide whether or not the two numbers are a correct solution to the equation."

"Solution!" I exclaim. "And are they?"

"Just a minute," he says. "I never said which two numbers. Because the solution to the equation can be a number of numbers. And all of them together are the solution of this particular application of this specific equation that we're looking for." "Well, keep on looking," I urge him, since I'm dying, not of curiosity—I'm not the least bit curious—but of interest. And he continues his lecture: "It says here, 'graphically' "—and I interrupt, "Does that mean symbolically?" and he replies, "Well, symbolically too, but graphically, you understand?" I nod, so as not to seem a total idiot, and he says, "All right, let's take a look at how all the solutions of our equation can be expressed graphically. In order to do that, I'll draw two lines, a horizontal and a vertical." And Marcus draws:

"Each line is called an axis, if you recall your elementary geometry," he says. If the truth be known, all I recall from elementary geometry is the melancholy eyes of Father Silhan, but I nod anyway. "We take each axis and label it with a scale of numbers, with zero at the intersection point." He puts his finger on the spot that I vaguely recall is called an intersection point. "Then we number the vertical axis upward and downward from the intersection, the way a thermometer is numbered, 1, 2, 3, and so forth, and also down from zero, -1, -2, -3, and so forth. We number the horizontal axis so that positive numbers are to the right of the zero and negative numbers are on the left. If I were to explain it this way to my students they'd think I was confusing them with kindergarten pupils, but—" "Thanks a lot," I say. "No offense," says Marcus, "but pay attention. We have to insert two separate numbers in our equation, one for x and one for y. Let's say that every pair of numbers we use—because there could be a lot of them—represents a point, I mean a dot, on a plane. . . . " I'm beginning to not understand again, and he can tell by the blank look in my eyes, so he takes a pencil and says, "Okay, we find the number for x on the horizontal axis, which we call the x axis, and we draw a vertical line through it. On the vertical axis, called the *y* axis, we find the number of *y*, and draw a horizontal line through it. The point where those two lines meet is the point I was speaking of. So, for example, if we make *x* equal to two and *y* equal to, for a change, minus three . . . " And he creates the following picture of the result:

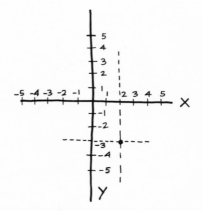

"There's one point for every solution," Marcus continues. "But because I told you that our equation has a lot of solutions, and all of them together make up the Solution with a capital S that is referred to in the letter, they must be represented by a whole lot of points which all together will constitute a *graph*, to *graph*ically illustrate our equation. Of course, before we can draw this graph we have to learn how to calculate the expression, I mean that series of *x*'s and *y*'s and numbers, lines, and symbols on the left-hand side of our equation. You probably wouldn't know what this means," he says, writing |*x*|, "sweetheart of mine, right?" "I will when you tell me," I reply. "Why shouldn't I tell you?" he asks, his left hand unbuttoning the top of my blouse. He gets his hand unceremoniously slapped, so he buttons it up again, while his other hand is scribbling. "This particular expression—" he indicates the |*x*|, "represents the absolute value of *x*, and it means the number as it stands, regardless of its sign, whether it is plus or minus. In other words, the absolute value of five is five, and the absolute value of minus seven is simply seven. So now we can begin." He hands me a pencil, as if he expects me to do the calculations. "Cut it out!" I say, and refuse the pencil. "Oh, women!" he exclaims, and he writes it down again:

$$(4|x| + 2|y| - 4) \, (|\,|y| - 1| + |y| - 1 + |x|) = 0$$

"First, if we've been paying close attention," he proceeds, "we will have noticed that in this equation we never find an x or y standing alone, but always between vertical lines, representing absolute values. This leads to one favorable mathematical consequence. If one of the solutions is, for example, x equals minus three and y equals five," and he puts down $(-3,5)$, "then other solutions will be—" and he writes $(3,5)$, $(-3,-5)$, $(3,-5)$. "And why is that?" I don't answer because I haven't the faintest idea, and he answers his own question: "Because we are only using the absolute values, so the original numbers can be either sign! You have to understand that for every point that represents a solution, there will be three more corresponding points which we can arrive at by simply changing the signs, or by mirroring the points around the axes. If we take our original example," and he draws:

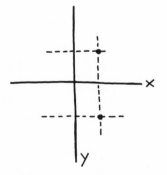

"Now if you would kindly lend me your mirror," says Marcus, and I pull one out of my pocket, polish it on my derriere, and pass it to him. He takes it and stands it on end along the vertical line, and with the reflection even simpletons can see the following:

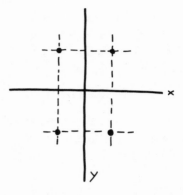

Now he takes the pencil and shades in the upper right quarter of the picture:

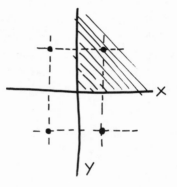

Then he says, "That will simplify our task because, as you can see, all we need do is determine the section of the graph that represents positive numbers or zero—or, to put it in more scholarly terms, the non-negative numbers, which would be located in the shaded sector. Then we can carry the results over to the other three sections by reflection."

I wonder for a moment what all this has to do with Ann Bradstreet, and where that poor unfortunate soul's body is lying at the moment, bound and gagged and miserable—and what about the Swiss burgher downstairs, praying and trembling, thinking my dear professor has called the cops from up here, and expecting their imminent arrival? But Markie has forgotten all about calling the police, and he proceeds with his lecture: "So we can just write x for $|x|$ and y for $|y|$, which I hope is perfectly clear to you, Evie." Which it is, almost, and besides, in the humility of my stupidity I'm willing to rely on his wisdom. "And so we replace the original confusion of lines and numbers and what we have left is simply:

$$(4x + 2y - 4)\,(|y - 1| + y - 1 + x) = 0$$

And what values are solutions to that equation?" he asks. "That is to say, what values plugged into the left side will make it equal to zero? All right now, what we have is actually two groups of numbers in parentheses, multiplied together—that is to say, two factors. And what is needed for the product of two factors to equal zero? Give me an answer, Miss Adam!"

Of course, Miss Adam doesn't have an answer. All Miss Adam does is roll her eyes, and Markie again answers his own question: "In order for the product of two factors to equal zero, one of the two factors must equal zero. So our equation is really a pair of equations:

$$4x + 2y - 4 = 0$$

and

$$|y - 1| + y - 1 + x = 0$$

and we will obtain a graph of this pair of equations by combining the graphs of each of them."

"I'm not interested in this anymore," I protest. "Let's try to figure out who kidnapped your niece, instead." "Oh, I know that already," replies Marcus, "and so will you as soon as you see the solution to this problem. It will confirm a certain hypothesis of yours, and once that is proven we will be able to deduce, from the movements of the three suspects, who is holding Annie and whether it's for love or for money." And so, with considerable effort, I exert all my powers of concentration. "As far as the first equation is concerned," he continues, speeding up, "let us accept the proven fact that it is the equation of a straight line. Proof of this is given in high school mathematics for the formula $ax + by - c = 0$. A straight line is determined by two points. Two solutions to the equation in question $4x + 2y - 4 = 0$, are $(1,0)$ and $(0,2)$, because:

$$(4 \times 1) + (2 \times 0) - 4 + 0 \text{ because } 4 + 0 - 4 = 0$$

and

$$(4 \times 0) + (2 \times 2) - 4 = 0 \text{ because } 0 + 4 - 4 = 0$$

and the corresponding line, if you follow me, looks like this:

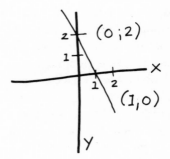

I am almost following him. He goes on to say, "We will only concern ourselves with the section of the line in this quadrant. And do you know why? Because it corresponds to the non-negative values we want. But we still have the other equation to solve, $|y - 1| + y - 1 + x = 0$. That will open—"

What opens is the door, and in walks the Swiss burgher, asking, "When can we expect the police to arrive? I've been thinking, and I wonder if it wouldn't be—" "Take it easy, Ebenezer," says Markie, "I haven't called them yet. Miss Adam here is an FBI agent." I look at him in astonishment, but right away I see what he's trying to do. "You see, Ebenezer," he says, "her nightclub singing is just a cover. She isn't a mere night-bird, or worse—she's the federal agency's most capable homicide agent, and she's working in that dive because she's hot on the trail of a famous international gangster, whose name I'd better not mention. Sergeant Adam has already solved the case of the kidnapping, and before the sun sets tonight, Ebenezer, you will once again embrace your daughter—that is, if you two do that sort of thing." But the burgher, overwhelmed by paternal feelings, doesn't catch the implication. "All that's left is a minor calculation," says Marcus, picking up a pencil.

"Now, where were we? Ah, yes. Here let us note the expression $|y-1|+y-1$. It is evident that this expression is equal to zero when $y-1$ is negative or equal to zero, and is positive where $y-1$ is positive." I notice that the burgher is looking at me almost respectfully, apparently even excusing my miniskirt as a necessary disguise. Straining my brain, I reply, "I think I understand." "Then let us proceed," says Marcus. "Remember that the expression $|y-1|+y-1$ is always non-negative, and equals zero only when $y-1$ is negative or equal to zero. When we started drawing our graph," and Marcus indicates the sketch:

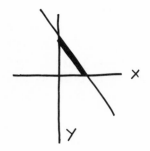

"we limited ourselves to values of x and y that are not negative; so clearly $|y-1|+y-1+x$ will equal zero only when x is equal to zero, y is not negative and $y-1$ is negative or equal to zero. Graphically expressed, in our equation y can only be something between zero and one, inclusive." "Inclusive of what?" I ask, and Marcus hastens to explain, "Of zero and one. And now," he says solemnly, taking a clean sheet of paper, "now we are almost at our Solution with a capital S." He grabs the pencil—Ann seems to have chewed on it in some exponential orgasm—and draws as he talks: "The graph of the second equation is a vertical line along the y axis, its extreme ends at (0,0) and at (0,1). Like this:

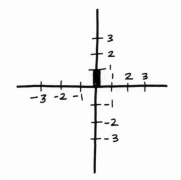

"And since this lets all the other suspects off the hook," he says, with a diabolical grin, "let's go pick up Daly now, okay?"

I stare at what he's drawn as he goes over that one-inch-long line, and it seems to me that all that unhealthy thinking has damaged my brain. "Just a minute, Markie," I say, "I really don't know why. I mean, not that Daly isn't damned suspicious, on the basis of normal deduction. But how can you say that this lets the other two off the hook?"

"Just use your head," he replies. The burgher walks over to the desk and stares over my shoulder at our equations. "Use your head," Marcus repeats. "What is it that William the Serpent wrote to Saint Ann about this problem?" I dig among the papers on the desk, and find the page: *Graphically, Ann, the Solution expresses it all.* But the Solution of what? The abduction?

The Swiss burgher grumbles behind me and picks up the chewed-on pencil, and I remember that he too is a mathematician, albeit a biblical one. He starts talking, more to me than to himself: "Graphically—because the two equations are part of the original equation—we can place both on the same graph—graphically expressed, it will look something like this:

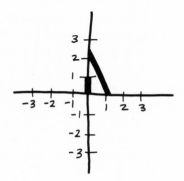

The burgher takes a long look at what he's drawn, and there's a diabolically lecherous grin on Marcus's face as he picks up the thread of the explanation: "If you recall, Evie, I said at the beginning that there are actually four sets of values that fit this equation. Because there are four solutions we can arrive at the graphic expression, not by painstaking drafting, but simply by mirroring along the axes. Since my good brother-in-law has already put one quadrant of it on paper for us, all we need now are the reflections along the *x* and *y* axes. Here, lend me your mirror one more time." Which I do, whereupon he looks around the room, seizes a rectangular mirror from Ann's dresser, and places both along the two axes of the drawing. Together the lines make up a certain geometrical figure which I've claimed not to recognize, but which of course I do. A light bulb goes on in my head—in *this* kind of geometry I'm something of an expert—and I say, "The filthy pig! Let's go!" "For the FBI?" asks the Swiss burgher. "No," I reply, "for Ernest W.F.F.R. Daly. And while we're at it, for your daughter." Once again the image flashes through my mind of how that youth in the double-breasted sports jacket leapt into the shower with me. True, the Viper didn't leap into a shower, but he too lost control.

It also dawns on me that Lubomira wasn't the one who veiled the meaning of that popular symbol with a lot of hoopla about folklore—not Lubomira! That little bitch would have served it up in its full anatomic vulgarity, and that must by why it was such a terrible shock to the girl. But Ann herself would have heard about folk customs like gingerbread hearts decorated with icing, and when she told her mother about the blouse she must have sanitized it for maternal consumption. Then her embellished version, still quite shocking to the sensibilities of Mather's Fundamentalists, spread through the family down to Marcus, and from there to the ears of the Viper. Poor boy! He wanted to use a quaint old Transdanubian custom to propose marriage to the maiden of his choice, while the maiden—haunted by dirty-minded Lubomira's obscenities, and probably having forgotten her own sanitized version—was so offended she probably passed out again; she certainly wasn't going to answer any phone calls from such a horrible young man!

The Swiss burgher frowns down at what he's drawn, then picks up my shiny little tool of worldly vanity and places it along the y axis, and he takes his daughter's mirror and places it along the x axis. He frowns some more, knotting his eyebrows, and says, "A rhombus limited by the points plus one, plus two, minus one, minus two. . . ." He shakes his head and declares, "I don't understand. Could it be some sort of prearranged sign?" He's apparently forgotten all about the blouse incident.

. . .

We left the burgher to his rhombus, and drove down to El Cerrito to call on the floater in the little green pool. He wasn't floating any more. A victim of his own conscience, he was just typing a confession on his Smith-Corona portable; on the desk beside him lay a revolver straight out of Dashiell Hammett, heaven knows where he got it. When we walked in without knocking, he went to use it—not on us, on himself. But Marcus smacked the gun out of his hand—as if he were the hard-boiled detective fan, rather than Daly—and it flew across the room in a wide arc. After that the three of us drove out to get Ann, who was lying in a dead faint in a cabin in the woods; it belonged to one of Daly's students, who'd been promised that if he helped with the abduction, Daly would help him with his dissertation, which he, Daly, would be grading himself. Marcus resolved the whole thing by punching

Daly in the face. As for the accomplice, who was half dead with fear, Markie agreed to let the whole thing go if he could have access to the cabin to meet selected female students of mathematics; of course, the arrangements for all that were made after I left town, because he wouldn't have dared while I was still around. His assistant wrote me about it. The cops never did find out about the incident, and it was presented to Shad and the Viper as a practical joke.

Anyway, we loaded the revived Annie into the car, leaving the two criminals to stew in their own uncertainties; on the way home we stopped off to pick up the gun, and we arrived at 1275 Grizzly Drive just in time for a family dinner. The reunion of father and daughter was touching—he actually pressed a kiss on her forehead. Later that evening the Viper arrived outside the house, crept under Ann's window, peered in for a while, and was then bold enough to come to the door—but she saw him approaching and whispered something to her father, who strode to the door and flung it open, grabbed the Viper by the collar, and with a fundamentalist kick sent him flying way into the middle of Grizzly Drive. The next day, when the burgher was making his farewells, he told me that he'd be forever grateful to me, and that I'd get a reward— which I never did.

. . .

To be perfectly truthful, that's what annoys me most about Marcus, even more than the fact that he finally left me for a certain Chinese student of number theory named Priscilla Fu. A fine den of iniquity, 1275 Grizzly Drive! That fundamentalist kick had as salutary an effect on the Viper as the shower had on that beau of mine who moved on to Jana Honzlova, except that Ann Bradstreet didn't know how to take care of it. The Viper fled to Australia, but the burgher boarded a plane for the second time in his life, flew halfway around the world, and dragged him back by the scruff of his neck, all the way from Brisbane. The wedding was solemn, very fundamentalist, except that the bride wasn't dressed in white—Cotton Mather's disciples are nothing if not truthful.

But of course, that's not what I meant about iniquity. The point is that I arrived at the wedding in my new mink coat, which Marcus gave me when he already knew he was going to ditch me for that student, so while he bitched about how much he'd spent on me—for which he was bountifully rewarded—it was in fact to assuage his own guilt. At the wedding Ann, having turned painfully worldly—I'd got so used to her virtuous behavior that she seemed almost sinful now—ran her fingers through my mink and said, "Gorgeous! Is that what you got for the ten thousand?" "What ten thousand?" I asked. Well, she seemed startled. "Aren't we supposed to mention it? But after all, its practically in the family, so to speak," she said wickedly. "I mean the ten thousand dollars Daddy sent Marcus to give to you; he thought you'd be offended if he gave it to you in person, and besides, the FBI might consider it a bribe, and you could end up getting in trouble, after all you did for me."

That night, I made an awful scene. I had every right to be furious—the mink was gorgeous, but it couldn't have cost a penny over six thousand, if that. I'd never have expected Marcus to stoop so low. Anyway, the swine moved on to that girl from Hong Kong—and left me feeling sweet and sour.

SIN NUMBER 8

An Atlantic Romance

After taking a Yellow Cab around Robin Hood's barn to get to
the Cunard Line pier, Mr. Right presumed he'd lost Deborah Bell
for good. She was the reason he was fleeing to Europe—she was
his mistress, and she was an altar-happy widow. And that wasn't
all of it: Deborah Bell also had a five-year-old son who was conspicuous in his resemblance to Mr. Right. He and Mrs. Bell had
met six years earlier, when the late Mr. Bell was still alive. But ever
since that well-heeled manufacturer of cardboard cartons had passed
away a year ago, Mr. Right had felt increasingly apprehensive.
The feeling had culminated on this winter day, with his panicky
ride from Fifth Avenue via the Bronx and Queens to the West
Side of Manhattan, where the taxi finally dropped him at his des-
tination. Passengers lined up to board the transoceanic liner *Queen
Elizabeth* were stamping their feet in the frosty afternoon, and Mr.
Right was glad to join them. The last time he'd spotted Mrs. Bell
had been somewhere near Coney Island, leaning out of a taxicab
in a gorgeous mink coat, looking for him but luckily in the wrong
direction. After that she'd vanished into the maze of Babylon on
the Hudson; Mr. Right sighed with relief at the thought. And—

as often happens in this vale of tears—no sooner had he heaved this sigh but his attention was caught by another mink coat, equally gorgeous, enveloping another woman, considerably more gorgeous than Mrs. Bell. Since Mr. Right had nothing against women, just against marrying them, he looked her over with an expert eye and promptly moved into pursuit mode.

His brown velvet gaze rested on what stuck out of the high mink collar. Thanks to his expensive inclinations, Mr. Right knew his way around luxuries, and he could estimate the value of the fur at no less than $6,000. What he saw above it was a well-shaped, frost-nipped nose, a round Slavic face with large, widely spaced gray eyes, and thick blonde hair; and below it a pair of legs that would count as handsome in anyone's books, in a pair of alligator pumps. To the seasoned Mr. Right the whole picture added up to an allowance of $500 a week, but he didn't falter.

The gray eyes of the costly young woman encountered Mr. Right's velvet gaze and drifted off immediately in the direction of the flags atop the steamship, but soon returned. After several such detours they finally met his gaze, to the delight of Mr. Right. The young woman raised her head in the fur collar, displaying a pair of full, rosy lips—which increased the amount of the estimated allowance in Mr. Right's mind, but he remained unshaken—and with a gleaming smile he went on the offensive.

But his attack had to be aborted because of—a mink coat: not the one enclosing the strange young woman, but a familiar one just emerging from a taxicab. Mr. Right hesitated for a moment, and then expertly melted into the crowd.

The attractive stranger's lips retreated inside the fur collar, and the gray eyes moved back towards the gangplanks, which were just being lowered. In his flight from Mrs. Bell, Mr. Right failed to notice that the young woman headed towards the tourist-class entrance. In any case, the presence of a mink coat in tourist class would have been entirely out of keeping with his experience.

•   •   •

A steward bearing a letter on a tray approached a table in the tourist-class dining room; he looked at the letter, then at the place card on the table, back to the letter on the tray, and finally at the man sitting beside the card.

"Mr.—ahem—Silly?" he asked, uncertainly.

"Give it here," growled the gentleman, whose waxed moustache and erect bearing revealed one of His Majesty's retired officers. He took the letter and turned to his tablemates—a gentleman, and two young women, one gray-eyed and one black-eyed, both with round faces, widely spaced eyes, and high cheekbones that suggested Slavic descent. The other member of the party resembled Mr. Moto; he wore tortoiseshell glasses and was obviously of Japanese blood.

"It's that damned name of mine, ladies!" the colonel said lightly, curling his moustache. "I'm sometimes tempted to curse my dear departed father, although of course it wasn't his fault. You can't choose your name; your name is your destiny, so to speak."

"It could be a lot worse," interjected the gray-eyed young woman. "I knew a fellow back home in Hradec whose name was Adolf Hitler, and he was a terribly nice person. He was a medical man, a specialist in venereal diseases. But the Germans didn't care for that and they put him in concentration camp. So it isn't all that awful to be called Silly."

"But the joke, Miss Adams," the colonel interrupted her gently, "is that my name *isn't* Silly. My name is Sally, and that's bad enough."

The blonde young woman squinted at the typed place card in front of him:

Col. J. A. SILLY

"That's what I'm trying to explain," said the colonel. "People often misread my name. Typists often mistype it. So I am often turned from a Sally into a Silly."

Everyone at the table laughed.

"You can imagine how many opportunities it gave my troops to make stupid jokes, can't you? Even my real name was enough to set them off. A man like me, with a woman's first name for a surname—" and the colonel reached for his moustache again, "gives people who see themselves as witty too much cause for jocularity. As an officer I was a stern task-master, I made no bones about it. I demanded discipline and obedience. That's why my men began to call me 'Sally, the old—' " He cleared his throat. "Forgive me, ladies. It's not a word one uses in mixed company. Then one time, while typing up an order, my clerk made a typographical error and put my name down as Colonel Silly. From that day forward I was Old Silly, to the entire regiment. But I must say my troops never disliked me. They'd have followed my anywhere, even into the flames of hell—and sometimes they did."

The colonel stopped talking, and silence fell over the table. The old soldier's faded eyes discreetly touched on one of the girls' place cards, and he continued on the topic. "For that matter, your own name is also interesting, Miss Adams. I'd be willing to wager that if there weren't an 's' on the end, my troops would have found ways to make a joke out of that—"

The gray-eyed girl looked at her place card. It said:

Miss Eve ADAMS

"Look at that, it's got a mistake too," she said. "There shouldn't by any 's' on the end. So your soldiers would have split their sides, I suppose. A lot of people have pointed out to me that my name borders on the indecent."

"Indecent?" wondered the black-eyed young woman. Unlike the blonde, she pronounced the Queen's English almost perfectly. She wore a very simple dress, in contrast to large gold seashell-shaped clips in her ears. "Why indecent? It sounds lovely to me. So . . . biblical. . . ."

"But the only thing most people think of when they hear about about Adam and Eve is the so-called original sin—and everybody knows the apple is only a metaphor for what they really did," the young woman explained wearily. "Every jerk comes up with—"

"Of course, names don't really mean anything," the colonel said quickly. "For example, in spite of my surname I trust that I'm not in any way feminine, nor am I particularly silly. The same goes for this lady here," he added, picking up the card belonging to the other girl. "Miss Abigail Wrong," he read pensively, and then accompanied a chivalrous bit of wit by a discreetly admiring glance: "There certainly isn't anything wrong with Miss Wrong, that I can see."

The black-eyed girl started to say something, but the blonde got in first. "Well, honestly, the names here are all pretty funny, one way or another. That can't be a coincidence!" She looked over at the place card of the Japanese gentleman and stifled a giggle. It read:

Mr. Toshiko FUKURI

"Ah, you laugh at my name too," said Mr. Fukuri mildly. He sat immobile, his hands folded on the tablecloth, looking a little like a Buddha. "But this is an old Japanese name, it has no funny meaning at home."

The blonde looked down at her own name again; her face was pink. "And anyway names don't always suit their owners. As the colonel says, there's nothing wrong with Miss Wrong."

The black-eyed girl again started to say something, but instead burst out laughing, and reached for her right earring.

"You're mistaken. Unfortunately, there is something wrong with me," she said, and removed the gold seashell from her right ear. The company at the table saw that she was missing the lobe of that ear.

"That's why I wear these earrings," she explained, quickly replacing the ornate clip. "I've been without it ever since I was little. It happened in the war."

"I understand," the colonel said solemnly. "In the London blitz, right?"

"Something like that. I was very young, so I don't remember exactly."

"Damned war," declared the colonel. "It's marked each of us one way or another. Me, for example—if the ladies will allow me?" He gave a questioning look from one girl to the other, and they nodded assent.

The colonel pushed his chair away from the table gravely and pulled up his trouser leg, revealing a pale military shin with a crater-like scar on it. "Happened in Burma. Now and then the wound opens up again, and takes a long time to stop bothering me." When the ladies had looked their fill, he dropped his trouser leg again.

"Terrible," said Miss Wrong.

"It could be worse," remarked the other girl. "One fellow I know had his left index finger shot off in the war, and he was a professional violinist—" She stopped abruptly, her eyes wide.

Mr. Fukuri had uncovered his right hand, which until then had been hidden inside his left, and stretched it out in front of him. There was an ugly gap where his index finger should have been.

"Oh, my!" exclaimed the girl. "Were—were you a violinist too?"

"No," smiled the Japanese. "Just a professional officer in the Japanese Imperial Army." He turned courteously to the British colonel. "I fear, sir, that we were what is referred to as enemies."

"Nothing of the sort, my friend," Colonel Sally assured him, waving a hand. "We were both professional soldiers. That has nothing to do with personal relationships. I fought as a young officer back in the First World War, and I can assure you that between the wars I counted several Austrian officers among my best friends. I encountered one of them after the Second World War, when I acted as liaison in a prisoner-of-war camp in Bavaria. I used to supply him with tobacco. A damned fine chap! No, one of the greatest misfortunes of our times is the fact that passions, I mean political passions, become involved in military service. When I was a young man, the army was a career. We were able to respect a professional opponent. Today?" He gave a contemptuous wave of his hand. "Nobody would have believed it in my day. They commit brutalities—why, even officers do, and even against *prisoners of war,* sir! Utterly disgraceful!" His moustache bristled. "Where did you see action, sir? Not in Burma, by any chance?"

"There too," replied the gentleman. "But I spent most of the war in Singapore."

"Ah, Singapore!" sighed the colonel, but then he came back to earth. "Forgive me, ladies. I almost succumbed to the reminiscences of an old soldier." He laughed. "It's damned odd, that. We all have unusual names, we've all been physically marked by the war—except for you, Miss Adam, you escaped unscathed, I hope?"

The gray-eyed girl was startled. "Unscathed? I wasn't marked physically, not much. Although—I don't know. They had something called an Institute for Racial Research—I mean the Germans. One time all the high-school girls in Hradec got called in—including us two day girls at the bishop's lyceum—and we had to report to this institute, and they took pictures of us from all sorts of angles, naked, I mean, and they measured our physical dimensions—"

"Ahem—really?" asked the colonel.

"It's the truth!" said the girl. "I think they said it was to find out if the Slavic race was any different from the Teutonic one, or something. Only some of those bastards sold the photographs in bars—there was an awful scandal over it. The Right Reverend Father Nebesky, the headmaster of the bishop's lyceum, filed a protest with the Gestapo. It seems photos of me and Lubomira came into the possession of a certain waiter, who told the Right Reverend Father about it in the confessional, so the Right Reverend Father went to the Gestapo with the pictures and they kept him there. He survived, but he caught TB. So you see, I wasn't marked physically. Not by the war, not until later. That was—"

Once again she didn't finish what she'd started to say, because a ship's officer walked into the dining room and announced in a loud voice that the tourist-class swimming pool had just opened.

• • •

The two young women met at the pool the following day before lunch. The blonde was anxious to experience everything her tourist-class ticket entitled her to, and she finally won over her more reserved companion, with whom she shared not only a table but also a cabin.

Side by side they entered the heated enclosure, the blonde in a bathing suit that could be called a mini-bikini, Abigail in a high-necked black one. But when they saw the pool, they were a little disappointed. The Cunard Line advertisements had shown it surrounded by partying crowds of passengers of both sexes, but this pool was hardly wide enough to hold the one fat gentleman who was trying to shed some weight in it. When the girls slipped into the green waves and surfaced, they could barely squeeze past this rotund swimmer as he did the crawl, and as they passed him he unwittingly kicked the blonde in the kidneys. So they retreated carefully to a corner of the pool, holding onto the edge, occasionally splashing water at each other and trying to be playful, as they'd seen people doing on the posters. But the weight-watcher made it a little difficult. All they were really doing was waiting until he got tired of swimming back and forth.

He finally did. When he emerged heavily from the little pool to clump off to the changing room, the water level—which had been up to their chins—suddenly dropped, all but revealing the blonde's nearly bare charms.

"Let's race—there and back!" suggested Abigail and counted to three. They both pushed off, but she was considerably the stronger of the two; she beat her blonde friend by half a length, spun around with a professional underwater salto, and swam back with healthy strokes towards the opposite side of the pool, where the changing rooms were.

The blonde swam leisurely to the end, turned, and swam back, her hairdo held carefully above the water. But just as Abigail was reaching the other end, the door to the men's changing room flew open and a man with a fiery scar across his belly lunged through it, giving a wild yell and throwing himself into the pool over Abigail's dark head.

It frightened her so much that she began to flounder, her head under water.

By the time the blonde pulled her out of the pool, with the help of the wild man—who turned out to be Mr. Fukuri—her face was greenish and she was almost unconscious. They helped her to her cabin, where the ship's doctor gave her a thorough examination, and administered a shot of a sedative, so that by evening she was perfectly fine.

The next day, though, she didn't make it to the dining room for lunch. For that matter, a lot of passengers didn't make it. About two hours before lunch the ship ran into an ugly winter storm, and so, instead of steaks, most of the travelers were downing motion-sickness pills.

The only people in the dining room were several English old maids who were clearly accustomed to difficult crossings of the Atlantic, the fat man, who was ignoring the storm and making up for what he'd lost swimming, and two pale stewards. At the last moment the gray-eyed young woman arrived too, reluctant to forgo any benefit her ticket entitled her to. Firm in their belief in the curative effects of fresh ocean air, the stewards had thrown open the portholes in the dining room, and so, to ward off the cold, the girl sat there in her mink coat.

. . .

As for Mr. Right, after he had succeeded in avoiding his mistress's embrace he had slipped down to the ship's bar, where he'd fortified himself with a double bourbon and, without stopping to take a breath, had launched a systematic search for the lovely young woman in the mink coat.

Almost three days had passed since then, and the ship had crossed nearly half the distance between the two continents, but Mr. Right's search had been fruitless. Still, he wasn't one to give up. He'd been through the entire first-class area, had studied all the passenger lists, and had had the stewards point out to him all the ladies with Slavic-sounding names. He did the same in cabin-class, and finally, mainly because he believed in being thorough and wanted to feel he'd done everything in his power, on the third day he headed down to third class, euphemistically renamed tourist class. There his disbelieving eyes spied a mink coat in an almost empty dining room, and in it a young woman who surpassed the image that had stuck in his memory. She sat alone at a table for four, staring—unhappily, thought Mr. Right—at a big steak on the plate before her, as if she was trying to make up her mind to do something.

The practiced Mr. Right first approached her from behind and read the place card beside her plate. He rejoiced—destiny itself had given him an ideal opening gambit.

He went around to the other side of the dining hall, slowed down, and—with strides as elegant as the tossing of the ship would permit—walked up to the girl from the front, with a radiant smile. The young woman took a deep breath, speared a huge bite of steak, put it in her mouth, and turned pale.

Mr. Right came straight to her table. "Good morning, Miss Wrong, I'm Mr. Right," he quipped. "There must be more to that than mere coincidence don't you think?"

The blonde swallowed the immense bite and turned green. "What?" she asked faintly.

"Well," said Mr. Right, "may I join you?" He sat down easily, without waiting for a response. "Wrong . . . Right . . . an ideal combination, am I right?"

The girl glanced down at all the steak left on her plate, once again seemed to struggle with some inner resolve, and replied, more tersely than she intended, "You're wrong."

"No," he retorted wittily, "I'm Right."

She shook her head. "My name isn't Wrong, that's the other girl, the one who usually sits here," and she indicated the empty chair beside her. "She doesn't feel well so she stayed in bed. My place is over there." She pointed with her chin, putting another bite on her fork and stuffing it into her mouth.

Mr. Right, a little disappointed but in no way put off, picked up the place card she'd indicated and discovered that destiny was still on his side. It read:

Miss Eve ADAMS

"Ooh," he crooned, "such a charming name! It's truly *charged* with—do you know what?"

The blonde made a determined effort to swallow, which forced her to retreat to her glass of beer. When she'd emptied the glass, she finally answered shakily, "I'm sure I haven't the slightest idea."

Experienced though he was, Mr. Right didn't register the sarcasm, or else he misread it as normal Slavic intonation.

"Let me tell you," he said with a smile. "Your name is charged with—the sin of Eden!"

The girl looked him over with her gray eyes. "You know, you're not exactly the first to notice that. I'd say somewhere around a thousand guys, all of them terribly clever—" At that moment her face was suffused with green; she stiffened, stood up, staggered, said without the slightest trace of an accent, "Excuse me!" and stumbled towards the door. She left her mink coat behind on the chair.

Still undaunted, Mr. Right picked up the fur and slowly walked down the corridor towards the washrooms. A year earlier, when the blonde had crossed the Atlantic in the opposite direction, she had dreamed of wealthy, handsome men in the land across the sea. Her dreams had come bountifully true, but unfortunately not quite the way she'd imagined. Now all she had left of them was her mink coat. That's why, when she first came back out into the corridor—restored to her normal bar-room pallor—and saw Mr. Right holding her precious fur, she was determined not to pursue her dreams any further. But seasickness and the approaching European shores did a lot to weaken her resolve, and the Scotch—the very best, $32 a bottle—that the knowledgeable Mr. Right ordered for her in the first class lounge fatally influenced her decision. And so she accepted his invitation to dinner.

When the time came, she was a little worried; her snazzy sequinned dress just wasn't right with a genuine mink coat. But then she thought, to hell with him! Is it me he likes, or my mink? She stood tall and strode into the first class dining hall, her sequins catching the light and flashing it in all directions. She was pleased to note that the intimate lighting did just as much for the faded glamour of her dress as the dazzling stage lighting had done in various bars around the world.

Try as he might, Mr. Right was unable to get them a table for two. The ocean had calmed in the course of the afternoon, the pills had done their work, and after their noontime fast all the passengers were eager for dinner. Mr. Right and his fair-haired acquisition had to share a table with an elderly couple of the Orthodox Jewish persuasion.

Mr. Right ordered something—the blonde couldn't hear what—and when the stewards brought it she gazed at it in astonishment. It looked like a Christmas tree, with chrome-plated branches holding tidbits of every kind of meat (Mr. Right really knew how to make an impression): chicken and turkey legs, and whole quail, and beneath this, set out in alabaster baskets, various voluptuous seafoods in red and pink shells. The blonde, who came from a country not known for its gastronomic restraint, was taken aback not so much by the volume as by the lavish presentation—it smacked of the opulence of ancient Rome. Pleased with the effect of the goodie tree, Mr. Right nodded to the steward, who raised his white-glove hand and sprinkled the tree with French cognac. The Orthodox gentleman, who had been regarding the tree with envy, mournfully breathed in this five-star fragrance. It made the girl's head spin, but before she could say a word a second steward stuck a silver tinderbox and the tree caught fire. It burned with a clear flame, and by its light the steward served the Orthodox couple some flat cans containing an indescribable mush. This was too much for the bearded Orthodox gentleman, who growled to his wife, in Czech, "Hana, I can't stand it! Danm it, why does he have to treat his floozie to this banquet at *our* table?"

While Mr. Right looked mystified, his companion said in amazement, in her native tongue, "Gosh, are you Czech too?" Then, her temper rising in a flash, she snapped, "And who are you calling a floozie, fungus-face?"

The old man turned pale, then flushed and spoke long and ardently. Mr. Right had the impression he was apologizing, but the blonde was obviously not mollified. Mr. Right tried several times to determine what they were talking about, but they ignored him. Eventually the blonde allowed herself to be appeased, but not before she had defended herself vociferously. "All right, maybe my dress isn't suitable for this environment, but I make an honest living. No sugar daddy is paying my way, and I'm nobody's floozie—"

"Certainly not, of course not please forgive me!"

"I'm a singer, a poor girl sent out by Pragokoncert, and can't I have a good time now and then if some jerk with money turns up and offers me a Christmas tree full of tidbits in the vain hope that he'll get something in return? Which he won't, let me tell you, Mister—"

"Stein."

"Mr. Stein, believe you me! I'm not that kind of a girl—" The blonde was in the kind of fury that always possessed her when she heard something about herself that wasn't entirely untrue.

For the fifth time Mr. Right tried to interrupt her, and this time he succeeded. "This lady and gentleman are Czech too?"

"Originally," replied Mr. Stein. "Now we are citizens of Israel," he explained, looking mournfully down at his mush.

The blonde, her fury now entirely spent, noticed his despondency. "Listen, Mr. Stein, don't you want to join us here?" she asked in English. "What you've got there looks like something out of a concentration camp, and there's enough food for twenty here."

"Unfortunately, miss," said Mr. Stein, glancing at the next table, where a family dressed in dinner jackets and evening gowns were gloomily eating the contents of similar cans, "my religion does not permit it, even when I'm traveling. But you see, the ship's kosher cook is sick today, which is why they are serving us these cans." He gave a sour smile. "As for your description, it is very apt; it reminds me of concentration camps too."

"Oh, were you in a concentration camp?" asked Mr. Right, with the discourteous interest of one who has never been in any such danger.

Mr. Stein nodded.

"That's awful," Mr. Right continued ingenuously. "It's hard to believe the things people who were there say hap—"

"Shall we dig in?" the blonde interrupted him.

Mr. Right forgot for a moment what he'd been about to say, and nodded at her with a smile. She deftly plucked off a charred quail, two chicken legs and three frogs' legs, a large chunk of pork, and a bunch of shrimp. Mr. Right speared a lobster tail, placed it on the plate in front of him, and, recalling what he'd wanted to say, proceeded. "It's almost incredible sometimes. Did you read about that murder last week?" He sliced open the lobster tail savagely, and ate with relish as he talked: "A girl of twenty-five shot a man of about fifty. It came out during the investigation that the fellow had been a concentration-camp guard during the war, and that he'd killed her father there. So twenty years later she—what do you think of that?"

Mr. Stein nodded. "I don't know. Maybe it is brutal of me, but—I understand." He glanced over at his wife and then went on. "If I were in her place, I wouldn't be able to wait for justice either, I would take it into my own hands."

"You're thinking of the war, I can understand that," said Mr. Right. "But now, in peacetime, when things like that don't happen any more," he went on, not noticing the skeptical smile that appeared on his companion's face, "it's hard to justify. All I'm saying is that we mustn't under any circumstances allow wartime methods to become peacetime rules!" He heard wisdom in what he was saying—which surprised even him—and was inspired to add, "I don't like talking about it, but the fact is that I could look for revenge myself. But . . ." He seemed to have entirely forgotten the presence of the blonde, and his less than honorable intentions. He continued, a different Mr. Right. "But what I would do is make the fellow face a proper court of law. Taking the law into one's own hands casts a person back to a time mankind has already transcended. That's not justice—forgive me, but that's nothing but brute vengeance."

"There are times of peace and there are times of war," said Mr. Stein softly. "In peaceful times—at least in your country—no one can do anything so terrible to you that it gives you the right to take the law into your own hands. But during the war—and in another country—"

"This *was* during the war," Mr. Right interrupted him, *"and* in a damned different country. But I still wouldn't be able to kill him. Though I'll admit I find myself taking a very close look at every older Japanese man I meet."

The girl in the sequinned dress choked—no wonder, for she was clearing the tree for both herself and Mr. Right, who seemed to have forgotten even his half-eaten lobster tail.. When she got her breath back, she asked, "Why Japanese?"

"Because it was a Japanese who shot my sister," Mr. Right replied gravely. "An imperial officer. During the occupation of Singapore."

"Oh, dear," piped up Mrs. Stein, "you were affected by the war too. . . ."

"That I was. And her husband wasn't even a soldier, not even a Westerner; but he was involved in what *they* thought was anti-Japanese activity. They shot both of them. As for their child," he said, his voice rising in sarcasm, "they only beat *her* unconscious. Fortunately my sister's Chinese maid took the girl in, and after the war she gave her to a family of British missionaries to raise. We never did find her. So you see, I might also have the right to get even. But I'd never do it. At least, I don't think I would. That's what proper war-crimes tribunals are for."

At that point he realized that the blonde was staring at him in amazement. He remembered that the war was long over, and that now he could revel in the joys of peacetime. He turned back into the old Mr. Right, and said in worldly tones, "But enough of that! Water over the dam, water under the bridge! Let's be glad we're more fortunate than some, may they rest in peace. Come on, let's have a drink."

The girl watched the viscous burgundy flowing into the cut-glass goblets, and asked quickly, "Did that Japanese officer have a missing index finger on the right hand?"

The bottle of burgundy clinked against the crystal. The worldly Mr. Right was taken aback. "How did you know?"

"And on his stomach did he—did he have a scar, across his whole belly—like a hara-kiri or something?"

"How—how could you know all that?" Mr. Right asked suspiciously. "That's just how my sister's maid described him—but where did *you* . . . ?"

The girl in the sequins pushed her plate away and said faintly, "I'm not hungry any more."

. . .

When Mr. Right had heard Eve's story, he resolved to postpone his original, not entirely honorable, intentions for the evening. It was clear that the erstwhile Singapore killer and Mr. Fukuri were one and the same person. In even the most legalistic society, those four corresponding items—the missing finger, the scar, the time, and the place—would have sufficed for a warrant to be issued. On his way from the first-class dining salon to the third-class dining room, Mr. Right kept repeating that all he had in mind was criminal prosecution.

In tourist-class, however, dinner was already over, since it hadn't been delayed by flaming Christmas trees. "Mr. Fukuri? All the guests from your table have retired to the lounge to play bingo, miss," said the waiter.

When they arrived in the lounge, the bingo game was in full swing. The ship's third officer was turning the wheel of fortune, and the enthusiastic English old maids, with comical paper-cone hats on their purple-tinted hair, were rashly betting halfpennies. But although the fair-haired girl and Mr. Right covered the room from stem to stern, they found neither the gentleman with the tortoiseshell glasses nor the girl with the gold shells in her ears, not to mention the stiff old man with the white moustache.

To Mr. Right the past, terrible but elapsed, was always less significant than the present, no matter how frivolous; the importance of finding Mr. Fukuri was decreasing in his mind in proportion to his awareness of the blonde's presence, and the approaching end of the voyage.

"In any case," he said as they were leaving the lounge, "he can't get away from me on a ship. I'll come by tomorrow at breakfast time. Now—" he inhaled deeply the odor of oil vapor that penetrated into tourist-class from the engine room, "do you smell the fresh air? That's the ocean for you! Let's go for a stroll on the promenade deck. It'll be lovely there."

The blonde was, in the final analysis, only a blonde, and the idea of strolling on the first-class promenade deck beside a man who seemed more and more eligible was not to be sneezed at. But to get to first-class they had to pass the tourist-class cabins, so she said conscientiously, "Wait just a minute, please. I'll pop into our cabin and see if Abigail's there. Maybe she knows where he went."

Abigail was indeed in the cabin. She was lying on the lower berth, solemnly reading a big book with gold-leaf title reflected the light of the bed lamp. Cotton Mather: *Wonders of the Invisible World,* read the blonde, and was surprised that her cabin mate hadn't mentioned being interested in microbiology.

"Have you seen Fukuri anywhere?" she asked.

Abigail placed the book on the bedspread. "Yes, he walked me to my cabin and said he was going to play bingo with Silly—Sally, I mean."

"That's strange, they're not there now. Neither of them."

"Maybe they went to the bar?"

"Probably. Well, good night." The blonde glanced in the mirror, fluffed up her bangs, and left.

· · ·

First they spent a brief romantic spell on the promenade deck (it was too cold and windy there), and then an equally brief but very promising interlude in the first-class bar. Mr. Right resorted to all the tactical tricks garnered in a long and successful career, and was just about to perform his ultimate maneuver, which he was certain would lead to her unconditional surrender, when an awful fate descended on him. Sometime in the course of the evening he'd consumed a spoiled oyster. Now, in spite of his precautions of preventive medication, his poor, weakened gall bladder flared up with such urgency that he was obliged to excuse himself in mortification and drag himself off to his superfluously impressive suite. The blonde was accompanied to her cabin by a very over-tipped busboy.

She was a little annoyed. Still, she comforted herself with the knowledge that the ship would be sailing the ocean for another two nights—and that during one (or maybe both) of those nights she would probably sin. She thought of her resolution with respect to her dreams again, and updated it with the decision that if Mr. Right played a role in them, she wouldn't be satisfied with a mere fur coat. At least, not just a mink.

At half past eleven, when she snapped her wristwatch around the bedpost of the upper berth and clambered up, dressed in her superfluously seductive little teddy, she had no idea she'd be saved from such a sin; another, even more awful fate was in the cards for the experienced Mr. Right.

· · ·

Three of them met at the breakfast table: the wan-looking Abigail, the rosy-cheeked, well-rested blonde, and Colonel Sally, with his moustache drooping and marked bags under his eyes.

"Too much rye whisky," he explained to the two ladies. "I'm not what I used to be. In the good old days, I used to drink two or even three bottles in a night and be up on the drill field, bright and chipper, at seven in the morning."

Mr. Fukuri did not turn up for breakfast. The colonel was surprised. "Wherever can he be? When I awoke this morning, he was out of the cabin already, but I never noticed him get up. And last night—"he chuckled, "well, I don't know about last night. He sleeps in the upper bunk, and to tell the truth, when I got in from the lounge towards dawn I was, if you'll forgive the expression, a little under the weather."

· · ·

The blonde girl spent the afternoon strolling around the tourist-class deck. Then she browsed in the magazines in the ship's library, and finally she decided to blow two dollars on a White Lady in the tourist-class bar. All her waiting was of no avail, however; Mr. Right was apparently still confined to his bed by his gall bladder.

Then a sailor came into the bar with some disturbing news, a welcome diversion for the bored tourists. Apparently the second officer had found a pair of tortoiseshell eyeglasses in the wire mesh of the railing on the upper deck, at half past ten the previous night. By daylight, in the same mesh, the officer had found a white shirt fabric and a cufflink. That was enough to make him suspicious. The glasses and the cufflink were shown to a number of the tourist-class passengers, and Colonel Sally recognized them as being the property of Mr. Fukuri. After half an hour of feverish searching, the captain announced that the gentleman had disappeared. Simple deduction indicated that he must have fallen into the Atlantic the night before, under the influence of alcohol.

Soon the whole bar was agog with the sensation, and the White Lady tasted bitter on the lips of the blonde in the mink coat. A certain dream of hers had just disintegrated, as once again she lost faith in a man's word. Hadn't Mr. Right sworn he would never take the law into his own . . . What's the matter with me, she asked herself bitterly. What makes me attract murderers like some heroine in a detective serial? I won't tell on him—no, she decided, I won't. But I could never—not with a murderer, no . . . that's too much.

At that moment the murderer she was thinking of, his gall bladder mightily improved, walked into the bar, looked around, and beamed at her. In a flash he was sitting beside her on a bar stool.

"Here you have me, Eve. Hale and hearty and ready . . ."

His words froze on his lips, his smile faded, as the gray eyes looked at him gravely with an expression that even the experienced Mr. Right was unable to interpret. The blonde didn't explain anything; she just gave him that long, mournful, inexplicable look, and slipped off the bar stool.

"Good-bye, Mr. Right." And she turned and walked out of the bar.

Mr. Right looked at her retreating back and her lovely legs with his mouth hanging open. He didn't understand: nothing like this had happened to him in his entire life, in spite of all his experience. He turned to the bartender and ordered a double bourbon. He was confused, and puzzled.

For God's sake—can an ordinary gall-bladder attack upset a woman so much? True, I shouldn't have eaten that oyster, but . . . it couldn't have shocked her *that* much, could it?

He stopped short, watching the doorway. Another young woman had just walked through it, wearing wide pants and larger-than-life pale pink eyeglasses. The fashionable T-shirt covering her well-formed chest bore a chartreuse message: LOVE ME, YOU FOOL! She carried a huge handbag with the name JOYCE on it, in gold rivets.

The experienced Mr. Right let his velvet-brown gaze linger on the pink glasses.

. . .

In the meantime the blonde had arrived in her cabin, which was empty, and plopped herself down on her trunk. She was overcome by a feeling of utter hopelessness. Her promising Mr. Right had committed this awful deed, while feigning a gall-bladder attack, and in direct violation of his word. No criminal prosecution . . . a murder for a murder . . . the law taken very firmly into his own hands.

With unseeing eyes she stared at the narrow tourist-class berths, the rumpled bedspreads, the wristwatch she'd snapped around the bedpost over the sleeping Abigail's head and forgotten to put on in the morning, her own delicate gold mules with pink feather trim—a souvenir of a dream that hadn't come true somewhere in Texas, the black suitcase beneath the lower berth with Abigail's white business card tucked into the luggage tag. . . . But all she could see was Mr. Right, the murderer. She shook her head, focusing her gray eyes on reality. . . .

All of a sudden she took pity on Mr. Right. She jumped up, opened the door, and fell directly into the arms of Colonel Sally in dress uniform, impaling her nose on a pointed medal on his chest.

"Oho!" exclaimed the colonel, "what's your hurry, little lady? I came to ask you if you'd care for a game of bridge."

"I don't play bridge, thank you," snapped the girl, feeling her nose with a fingertip. She found a drop of blood on her finger, and it annoyed her.

"Thanks a lot, Mr. Silly!" she said, turning on her heel and slamming the door. The colonel shrugged his shoulders in irritation and marched off towards the smoking lounge.

Behind the door, the girl stopped short.

Something occurred to her.

Something quite odd.

> Now you know who killed Mr. Fukuri—
> and you've also discovered the entirely
> innocent sin against Father Knox.

But a glance in the mirror distracted, her, as she wondered if the sharp point of the colonel's medal could have been tainted with some sort of oriental poison; her normally delicate little nose was swelling badly. She attacked it with sandalwood and cold cream, and even as she did so her thoughts kept returning to her idea. That odd recollection of the names. Of Colonel Sally, called Silly, and the typist had mistyped it that way too. Of Mr. Fukuri, his name an invitation for off-color jokes. Of her own name, so inspiring to Mr. Right, but with the extra "s" typed on the end. Of Miss Abigail Wrong with her missing earlobe, blushing like a missionary's daughter in her high-necked bathing suit. She reached out to the lower berth for the big black book about microbiology. But the author's name . . . Cotton Mather . . . now where . . . ? Good God! Of course! A certain equation, a certain fundamentalist wedding . . . She opened the book, and on the first page was a quotation from the Bible: not microbiology but theology. Then she looked again at the card on the young lady's black suitcase; she stopped short, looked again: MISS AGIBAIL WONG!

Thoughts rushed through her attractive head like a hurricane. Mr. Right's sister and her husband, who wasn't even a Westerner, both shot in Singapore because he was suspected of opposing the Japanese. The Chinese maid who gave the Eurasian child to some family of British missionaries. The girl with the wide-set black eyes and broad, high cheekbones—there are people in the world with faces even broader than the Slavs'. . . .

Perhaps she ought to feel sad about Mr. Fukuri getting what he deserved. But at least it hadn't been Mr. Right, and that opened the most agreeable prospects. She looked again at her nose. Although it had stopped swelling, it hadn't returned to its normal size. But she decided that, in the final analysis, one's nose was not a deciding factor where love was concerned.

. . .

She ran out on the promenade deck. There, by the railing, stood Miss Wong, her big, black eyes focused out to sea.

The blonde stopped, unsure for a moment what to do. She decided the best thing to do was nothing at all. She left the girl to her thoughts and joyfully set out in the direction of the bar.

Then she stopped for a second time. Her eager face fell, and the swollen nose protruded visibly. For standing behind a white lifeboat, somewhat (but only somewhat) hidden from the eyes of the promenading passengers, stood Mr. Right, passionately exchanging kisses with a young woman who had dropped her handbag and removed her pink eyeglasses for the exercise. Spelled out on the handbag was the name JOYCE.

The blonde said something out loud in a foreign language. A sickly professor of phonetics who happened to be standing nearby captured the sounds in his ever-ready little notebook, using the Jones International Phonetic Alphabet. According to his records, what she said was:

To pe: tele pra: tse!

SIN NUMBER 9

Just Between Us Girls

"Are you ready?" asked the girl with the black hair and the dimples, glancing from her newspaper to the two lads sitting beside her on the floor amid a clutch of embroidered cushions. The newspaper was French, and the lads were dressed in blue-and-white striped tights, the ones popular in the West because they cling to the body as tightly as the peel clings to an apple. They weren't in the West, though, but in the Lesser Quarter in Prague. The room they were sitting in was decorated with oriental throw rugs, a painter's easel with an immaculate canvas, wormwood statues of saints (the kind enterprising villagers steal from deserted chapels to sell to rich tourists), and mystical paintings of strangely intertwined nude men flying among the clouds. The subdued light was from a copper lamp with perforations in the shape of a Chinese dragon. In the middle of the room, on two rococo armchairs pushed together to form something like a fancy carved cradle, in a cloud of pale-blue lace, slept a rosy, golden-haired baby.

The girl repeated, "Are you really ready for this?" and she handed the lads the newspaper she'd brought with her from Paris that very day. They both stared open-mouthed at the large front-page picture of the same dimpled girl, and sighed, "Oh, wow! Zuzka!"

Above the picture, an inch-high headline screamed: *"L'EPOUSE D'UN POLICIER SUEDE L'HEROINE DU CAS DE NEUILLY!"*

"Oh, Zuzka," said one of them, "when your hubby sees this he'll burst with pride."

"Not on your life, Brucie," said the girl. "He'll just be nasty. In the first place, he gets jealous when anybody but him does any detecting, especially a woman; and besides, he ordered me not to see Evie any more, after she stole a march on him, twice actually, once in HitSongSea, which I told you about, and another time in Stockholm, which maybe I'll tell you about some day. When he finds out I snuck off to Paris to see Evie, when all he said I could do was go to Prague to show off little Pernille to my mom, he's going to kill me!"

"Look, Georgie," said the lad called Brucie, ignoring her imminent danger and turning to his mate. "Look here! It's Evie!" He indicated a smaller picture farther on in the news story. It showed a group of wide-eyed young women in dressing gowns, including a slender blonde with beautiful if rather startled eyes. Beside her stood Zuzka, also in a dressing gown, with her arm around her waist.

"You're right, it *is* Evie!" declared Georgie. "And how is she, after her trip around the world? Is she still out to nab a husband?"

"She sure is," Zuzka assured him. "Evie never changes. But every time, the swine just fools around with her and then takes off. In Paris Evie had this dark guy—"

"I knew it! Look what she sent us from America!" Brucie exclaimed, fishing a magazine out of a little filigree bookshelf and passed it to her. "All black, every one. Her world travel is giving her exotic tastes!"

The girl leafed through the magazine, and sighed, "Oh, look at those bodies! But I didn't mean Evie's Jean was a black man, I just meant he was olive-skinned, an Italian type. Acutally I barely caught a glimpse of him, just long enough for him to check me out with these magical gypsy eyes, and then he and Evie vanished into the bedroom next door. In a moment she popped out again and said she was sorry, but of course I understood, didn't I, her Jean coming home unexpectedly after being away quite a while. So of course I understood, I left them to their lovemaking and grabbed a taxi back to the hotel where I'd originally registered, before Evie invited me to Neuilly because Jean was on a business trip. And that was the first and last time I saw the dreamboat, because two days later he took off again."

"They must have spent a couple of passionate nights, if he'd been gone a while."

"I'll bet they did. Especially the second one, because the next morning Evie looked as if she hadn't slept a wink. I mean the morning after the second night, not after the first one; that first morning she looked more like Pernille." Zuzka turned a gentle glance on the rosy baby in the pale-blue cloud, who opened her eyes, as blue as a winter sky, and for a moment looked like a picture-book Scandinavian infant. Pernille blinked, the two lads said in unison, "Peek-a-boo!" and the baby gave an angelic smile, closed her eyes, and floated away to the Land of Nod. "It's a fact," Zuzka insisted. "After that first night she was fresh and rosy and radiant with love, typical Evie. That afternoon she took me to visit somebody called Joyce, a bit of a playgirl—British, her French was really funny—and she had a place in Neuilly too, near Jean's. She'd just returned from London the night before, and she phoned Evie in the morning. Evie and Joyce had met on the *Queen Elizabeth,* the two of them beat up some creep called Mr. Right one night and threw him into the swimming pool in his tuxedo. Anyway, there were three other really neat girls at Joyce's place: Laura, Ginette, and Danielle, all dancers from the dive where Evie was singing, topless dancers—"

"Just like you in HitSongSea, right?" asked Georgie innocently.

"I beg your pardon!" huffed Zuzka. "I was there to do folk dances. For Pragokoncert!" And she continued, "So there we sat, Evie and me, and Joyce, and Ginette, Laura, and Danielle, a real hen party. We criticized the boyfriends of girls who weren't there, and praised our own—naturally I talked about Niels. And Evie— just like a teenager, she's incurable—she raved about that Jean of hers. But it turned out that all she knew about him was his big black eyes, his coal-black hair, and his olive complexion—and that he travels a lot on business. That was all!"

"That's typical," says Brucie. "It wouldn't be the first time she got burned, all because she's just too trusting. What do you bet the little fool was hoping this Jean would marry her? And he's obviously some kind of con artist."

"You know Evie," said Zuzka, "hopelessly sentimental. That was clear to everyone from the way she raved about the guy; one of the girls, Ginette, even warned her about it. She told her the story of a certain Mireille, a topless dancer who wasn't there that afternoon. Mireille was a simple country girl from somewhere in Brittany, not very educated, her spelling was terrible and she couldn't keep her tenses straight. She met a fellow called Gideon Markham in London and spent a week of passion with him there, so much so that she talked herself into believing Gideon Markham was in love with her, and after that week, when he had to return to Rome on urgent business—he was one of those American expatriates with a home base in Rome—Mireille thought how pleased and surprised he'd be if she dropped in on him there. So she took all her savings and flew to Rome, and looked up his address in the phone book. When she got there, she thought she must have made a mistake, because what she found was a harem. But it was no mistake. Gideon was just sitting down to supper, like the Lord Jesus with his twelve disciples, only Gideon had twelve concubines. Actually, he welcomed her quite graciously, inviting her to move in too; I guess if there's space and food for twelve concubines, it shouldn't be too hard to find a slice of bread and a corner of the bed for a thirteenth. But Mireille was sort of naive, and rather than stoop to polygamy she just left. She'd spent all her savings on the airfare, so she had to sell her body to get a ticket back to London, but she didn't care, just as long as she saved her pride."

"If I'd been in her shoes, I'd have drowned myself," said Brucie.

"She wasn't *that* naive," Zuzka squelched him. "From London she returned to Paris and found herself a new lover, a monogamous one, and soon she was back in seventh heaven with him. Ginette wouldn't say who he was, though, because Mireille was afraid it would get around about her having a lover, because she was such a proper country girl and so proud of her virtue. Back home in Brittany she'd spread the word that she was in Paris studying ballet, and all the while she was showing off her boobs at the Beige et Blue."

"Shame, Zuzka," Brucie chided her, and she corrected herself: "All right, showing off her breasts, then. Anyway, the only one who knew who the lover was was Ginette, and she refused to tell us because she'd promised Mireille. That night we all went to the Beige et Bleu, and the girls showed themselves off until midnight and Evie sang like a nightingale in love, but right after the program she disappeared. The rest of us stayed around and got drunk together. But believe me, the next afternoon, when we got together at Evie's, I mean Jean's, place, none of us looked more hung over than she did. Washed out, rings under her eyes, her hair a mess—"

"He must have been quite a guy!" remarked Brucie, wistfully.

"That's exactly what I was thinking," Zuzka agreed. "And I wondered why Evie had dragged us all out of bed by phone so early in the morning. I mean, it wasn't even half past noon yet, but she insisted on us girls coming over, because Jean was gone on business again and we could have another gabfest. I thought maybe she was so beside herself with happiness that she couldn't bear to be alone. By the time I arrived at about three, Ginette and Joyce and Evie were already there, along with two dancers from The Olympia, Louise and Lucy. They all looked a sight, each more dragged out than the next, and as I said, Evie looked the worst of them all. She was just pouring them wine, some terribly old vintage—the label said Châteauneuf-du-Pape—and I wondered if Jean knew his ladylove was treating a bunch of her girlfriends to a bottle he'd probably stashed away for somebody really special. The thought just flitted through my mind, though, because Louise was telling a sensational story: It seems that the day before, the singer Jean Topaz had returned to Paris from a tour; he was known as Cool Jean and he was famous for his virtue. He was supposed to have sworn a vow of chastity when he was very young, and he never sang anything but pious chansons, which of course made all the girls chase after him three times as much as they would have otherwise. Anyway, Louise's news was that she'd discovered that the whole story was nothing but a cheap publicity ploy. She told us how he was rehearsing at The Olympia that morning, and put his book—a prayer book, of course—on a chair, and she noticed something sticking out of it and out of sheer curiosity she took a peek while he was on stage. It turned out to be a totally, obscenely passionate love letter—and to top it off, the spelling was awful and all the tenses were screwed up."

"Mireille!" exclaimed Georgie. "That one who sold herself for airfare to London!"

"Don't get ahead of me!" said Zuzka. "I'm telling you a mystery story, so quit interrupting. Joyce, the playgirl, remarked that she was really disappointed in Cool Jean, partly because he wasn't the saint he claimed to be, and partly because it was with such an ignorant cluck. But Lucy said Cool Jean hadn't disappointed her and couldn't, because she'd always assumed his virtue was just a kind of trademark, and for that matter it would be a crime for a body like that to go to waste, and she'd forgive a body like that almost anything. I asked for some detail about this body, because I didn't know Cool Jean at all, not even from a picture, so Lucy—she has a talent for poetry, she moonlights by writing for a literary magazine—anyway, she began to describe that body, a dark Italian type, black hair, white teeth, heavenly blue eyes, and a divine voice—and while she was talking I recalled another identical description of a body that Evie had laid on us at Joyce's the previous evening. And then I recalled the body itself, which I'd glimpsed in the doorway that time, and that body was also called Jean—"

"So the illiterate letter was from Evie!" Georgie piped up. "Good heavens! Cool Jean and Evie's Jean are one and the same body, right?"

"Will you two quit butting in?" Zuzka was getting annoyed.

"Anyway, Lucy was really gone on Cool Jean, so someone suggested we drink to his health, and the five of us must have toasted him with eight rounds of Châteauneuf-du-Pape—I said to myself that the other Jean, if he wasn't really the same one, would have a fit—till we were all pretty much in the bag. And by the time Danielle and Laura arrived around seven o'clock, we were all half in love with Cool Jean ourselves, shouting 'Long live Cool Jean!' Except for Evie, who was melancholy drunk. Laura said, 'Cool Jean? What a coincidence! My brother was just telling us—he's a taxi driver and he drove us here—that last night, at two o'clock in the morning, he picked up Cool Jean just around the corner from here and drove him home someplace in the Latin Quarter. So Danielle and I were wondering what he could have been doing in this neighborhood that late, when there aren't any churches here— 'And this isn't where uneducated working girls live, or country bumpkins either,' the inebriated Ginette interrupted her.

"Just then the doorbell rang and Louise—she's a real character, a barrel of laughs—she yelled, 'Oh, Jean!' and we all rushed out into the hallway. When Evie opened the door, who do you think fell into her arms?"

"Cool Jean!" cried Brucie. "And in front of God and all of you, he ripped Evie's clothes off and—"

"What are you, crazy or something? It was Mireille. You know, the one from Brittany, who worked her way from Rome to London. She was in tears because that mysterious lover of hers had beaten her up and thrown her out. And it had to be true, because one eye was all puffy and one of her teeth was so loose it wiggled. Louise said he must have been raging like a jealous Sicilian, and Evie, who was pretty far gone by then, dropped a gorgeous cut-glass goblet and said, 'Men are a bunch of bastards, let's drink to that, and gorge ourselves! Follow me!' We started out with Jean's refrigerator, Evie's Jean, that is. It was huge, the kind they have at the Grand Hotel Ritz, and it was full of goodies, so we helped ourselves and fed Mireille some Boursin cheese to help her get over her sorrow. Next Joyce found a barrel of fresh oysters packed in wet seaweed in the bathroom, about two hundred of them, so we all stuffed ourselves till the kitchen was knee-deep in oyster shells. Then Evie dug up a case of champagne somewhere, so we topped off all that Châteauneuf-du-Pape with about seventeen bottles of champagne, and smashed at least another seventeen against the furniture because we decided we were mad at men, the bastards, and then Ginette demolished the Venetian mirror in the dining room, and finally we made kindling out of all the antiques and everything. By the time we went to sleep, the place looked like a luxury bordello hit by a band of robbers."

A baby's cry sounded from the improvised cradle, and the three of them turned to look. The rosy little golden-haired creature had turned a shade darker—nearly red—and proceeded to communicate in the international language of infants.

Zuzka said, "Pernille shit herself again, Georgie. Would you, please? You know it turns my stomach."

She lit a cigarette with yellowed fingers and watched the two lads expertly changing Pernille, patting baby oil on her and powdering her. She held her nose when Georgie picked up the dirty disposable diaper and hurried off to the toilet with it, and took a long drag on her cigarette. As soon as Pernille had been changed and rocked and lulled back to sleep, she continued.

"We made an incredible mess of the place, and then we simply went to sleep. Evie and I slept in Jean's bed, remarkably wide even for a bachelor's, and Joyce took the couch in the den next door. Mireille, Lucy, Louise, and Ginette stayed in the dining room because the carpet there was so deep you could lie in it as if it were grass. Laura and Danielle slept in the guest room. As I was dozing off, all kinds of things ran through my head—like what if Evie's Jean and Cool Jean were really and truly one and the same Jean, because both of them had arrived in Paris the same day, the day before yesterday, and both were dark-skinned Italian types, and at two o'clock in the morning Jean had taken that cab from there to the Latin Quarter where he was supposed to live, where church people went to interview him. It could be that this was just his secret pied-à-terre. . . . Besides, everything else fit: Evie's French isn't good so her spelling wouldn't be all that great—elementary, Watson, I said to myself. And then my mind filled up with memories of how I helped Evie solve that terribly difficult case of the doubles in Stockholm, back when I was first expecting Pernille. But by then I was just about asleep."

Georgie sighed. "Being abroad has really been a bad influence on our Evie."

"Wait a minute, you haven't heard anything yet. Later that night—"

"Ah!" breathed Brucie.

"Later that night," Zuzka continued, "someone in the next room suddenly gave a horrible scream. It woke me up and I reached for Evie, but she wasn't anywhere in the big bed. By then I could hear voices all over the apartment, and lights were going on, so I jumped out of bed too. Next door in the den stood Evie, trembling like a wet puppy, and on the couch lay Joyce, stabbed with an ice pick. By then all the girls were crowding in through the door. Lucy and Mireille both fainted. Evie said for somebody to call the police, so Ginette, Louise, Laura, and Danielle ran off again, and an idea started running around in my head, round and round till I got it, and Evie was saying, 'Who did it? For God's sake, who did it?' I left her there and went out in the hallway. The front door was locked and chained shut on the inside—the flat was on the fourth floor—and when I went back to Evie she was still saying, 'Who did it?'"

"Damn it, who *did* do it, then?" demanded Brucie, overcome by the suspense. Zuzka smiled mysteriously.

> By now you know everything, and you have identified—which sin? (No, not gluttony—Father Knox's rules, remember!)

"It was Cool Jean's girlfriend, of course. One of the two of them that destiny happened to bring together at Evie's pajama party. Joyce was one of them, but she had no idea there was another, and she paid the price for her ignorance. The other one, who stabbed Joyce with the ice pick, had cottoned on to her that day, and when she got really drunk it got to her. Now she's behind bars. With good behavior, she'll be there another ten years."

"But which one did it?" Brucie almost yelled. "All these women sound the same!" And he tried to count them off, one by one, on his fingers: "Evie, Laura, Lucy, you . . . Mireille, Ginette . . . Danielle . . . Louise . . ."

"It's not so complicated, just think it through," Zuzka urged him. "The day before, when we were at Joyce's flat, we found out that the day before that Evie's lover had arrived, and that his name was Jean, and he had an olive complexion and a beautiful body. The next afternoon, the day we got so drunk at night, Louise told us about the semiliterate letter, and Lucy admitted to all of us that she loved Cool Jean and she described him: olive-skinned, raven-haired, eyes like the sky, voice like a god. Then Laura and Danielle arrived and we found out from Laura that her brother had picked up Cool Jean at two o'clock that very same morning, somewhere nearby in Neuilly, and driven him home to the Latin Quarter, and Ginette piped up to say that ignorant working girls and country bumpkins didn't live in Neuilly, but just then poor beaten-up Mireille came, and after that Cool Jean never came up in the conversation. So figure it out for yourselves."

"Come on, Zuzka, do Georgie or I look like Sherlock Holmes or something?"

"I'm no Sherlock either," said Zuzka, "and I never was. But you don't have to be. It's as clear as crystal." Zuzka got up, walked over to the easel, and with a piece of charcoal wrote the following on the virgin canvas.

> *The day before: Evie, me, Laura, Ginette, Danielle*
> *In Neuilly at first: Evie, me, Ginette, Louise, Lucy*
> *Afterwards: me, Evie, Louise, Ginette, Lucy, Laura, Danielle*
> *Finally: Me, Evie, Louise, Ginette, Lucy, Laura, Danielle, Mireille.*

Then Zuzka gave the two lads a questioning look, but neither of them was especially gifted in logical deduction. So she lit a cigarette, and for a moment the smoke enveloped the dimples in her cheeks in a translucent shadow. "Louise and Lucy," she said, "who weren't at Joyce's the day before, didn't hear what Evie's lover looked like. Laura and Danielle did hear her description, and they knew Cool Jean, but they didn't hear about the misspelled lover letter. And Mireille didn't hear any of it. All right, now: As for people who might have written the letter in bad French, there were only three—excluding me, and I'd arrived in Paris for the first time in my life only two days earlier, and even with the best intentions in the world I couldn't have latched on to Cool Jean in that short a time. The three were Mireille, the country bumpkin; Evie, being Czech; and Joyce, because she was British." Zuzka took a baby's pacifier out of her purse and thrust it in Pernille's pink mouth.

"Come on, Zuzka, don't keep us in suspense!" wailed Brucie.

"What a pair of birdbrains!" Zuzka picked up the charcoal again and said, "The murderer had to have heard it all: What was said at Joyce's the day before, what Louise told us before Laura and Danielle arrived, and what Laura told us before Mireille came crying. Also, it had to be someone who knew who Mireille's lover was. In short, this is who it was." And with the charcoal, she circled one name that appeared on all the lists: *Ginette*.

"Ginette heard it all," she explained. "And she was the only one who knew who Mireille's lover was, so she knew Mireille wasn't Cool Jean's mistress. She figured out by deduction that it was Joyce: she'd make mistakes in French because she was British, and she lived in Neuilly. And Evie wasn't the one, because Evie's Jean had eyes like the devil, not like the sky."

Silence filled the room, but it was broken by Pernille, who began to wail again. Zuzka glanced at the clock.

"And that was what you told the police?" Brucie asked, his voice filled with awe. "That's what got you on the front page?"

"That was it! And that's also why I'm scared to go home, because Niels is going to clobber me."

"Hey," Georgie piped up, "what about Evie? And her Jean? Is she still carrying on with him?"

"No way," said Zuzka. "You see, those rings under her eyes weren't from passion. The second night, after she heard Mireille's tale of woe, she made her Jean confess that he was in fact Gideon Markham, the guy with the harem. He had pieds-à-terre in all the capitals of the Western world, including one in Karlovy Vary in Czechoslovakia. The authorities there knew about it, but they let him get away with it because he contributed hard currency to the constructive activity of the secret police. But since his experience with Mireille, he used pseudonyms. You can imagine that the whole thing was quite a disappointment for Evie."

"So she made a scene that night?"

"Not right away. That night she pretended to be broad-minded, but she decided to get even by consuming his stash of delicacies. And because there was a lot to consume, she invited us over to help. And help we did—successfully."

Pernille's cries were growing more insistent.

"So much for the case in Neuilly," said Zuzka. "And now turn your backs, kids, it's five o'clock and Pernille won't wait."

The two lads turned away obediently, and continued their cozy gossip facing a plump Baroque madonna holding an excessively chubby Christ child.

SIN NUMBER 10

The Third Tip of the Triangle

Lieutenant Boruvka stared gloomily out of his office window at the peeling façade of the old church across the way, where the statue of the crafty St. Sidonius crouched under a cap of snow, an icicle hanging from its nose. It seemed to the lieutenant that it was laughing at him again, as it had three years earlier—but that had been on a mild night in May, when his daughter Zuzana was only seventeen. This was a dismal February evening, and the ever-mournful lieutenant had a particular reason to be despondent. This morning Zuzana had casually announced that in about seven months the melancholy lieutenant would become a grandfather—without the benefit of being a father-in-law. According to Zuzana, the candidate for son-in-law was an idiot and a jerk, which she unfortunately discovered a little late, but not so late that she was stuck with him for good. The lieutenant exerted considerable effort to extract the jerk's identity from her but he was unsuccessful, and he didn't dare subject her to the third degree because he had some foggy notion about the physical frailty of a pregnant woman— even if she was only two months along, and was a phys-ed student and university champion in the hundred-meter breaststroke. Finally, following an amateurish attempt at a scene in which he played the old-fashioned dishonored father and Mrs. Boruvka the devastated mother—the drama foundered on his very modern love for his daughter, and on Mrs. Boruvka's even more modern matter-of-factness—the lieutenant had left for work. As soon as he'd arrived, he'd convinced the policewoman with the lovely chignon that she was feeling ill, and made her go home; today he was somehow irritated by her being at least eight months along. (Unlike the lieutenant, her surrogate father, who was her uncle and the famous author Kopanec, *did* have a proper son-in-law—and a brain surgeon, at that.) The lieutenant had spent his working hours pretending to do his regular job, and now he was just waiting for the day to be over. As he waited, he mused dismally on how shockingly eroticized the world was getting these days, something he opposed on a professional level, even if he personally succumbed to it from time to time, at least on a theoretical level. Take the sad case of his daughter . . . but somehow it didn't seem all *that* sad. He looked out again at the plaster saint. Moved by its knowing glance, he admitted to himself that the saddest aspect of Zuzana Boruvka's state was the fact that her youthful indiscretion would transform her still well-preserved father into a grandfather—almost a year before he turned fifty.

At that point the telephone rang, and an agitated voice said, "Please, could somebody come over here? There's been a . . . a sudden death."

"Where?" asked Lieutenant Boruvka churlishly. "And who's calling? And what do you mean by a sudden death?"

. . .

It turned out that the sudden death was the result of a small-caliber firearm. The deceased was an electrical engineer named Ludvik Arnold, and he'd met his end in his apartment, which consisted of a large room, a small kitchen, and a shower stall hidden by a screen covered with pictures of dancing water nymphs. The apartment was in the building above the archway on Loreta Square, and when the lieutenant arrived on the scene three people were waiting for him. The first was the daughter of the lieutenant's friend Obdrzalek (the manager of a National Enterprise Bookstore). Her name was Irena and the lieutenant knew her well; she was the same age as Zuzana, so he prepared himself for the worst. The second was a man of about thirty who introduced himself as Dr. Petr Bydzovsky, psychiatrist. The third was a young woman who had reportedly arrived just before the lieutenant; her name was Milena Pelent, and she was the wife of a certain Rudolf Pelent, also an engineer, and a colleague of the deceased. Alone with the lieutenant, she sniffled into a batiste hanky, as she perched on an elegant little art-nouveau armchair before a marble copy of a famous Greek statue (Doryphorus, the lieutenant thought, reaching back to his student days). He was feeling uneasy. For one thing, he was disturbed by the allure of the weeping woman; but on top of that, Doryphorus's classically proportionate sex organ dangled incongruously right above the witness's mussed platinum-blonde hair. In the back of his mind the grandfather-to-be was moralizing about the eroticized times, and reflecting that this sudden death was very likely just another variation on that ancient and tragic theme, the human inclination to be monopolistic in the sphere of sex. But in the forefront of his mind he was listening to what the sobbing beauty had to say:

"I wanted to ask Ludvik whether he'd found my necklace. I must have lost it here last night, at the party, and my husband will be very upset if I don't find it. It was a Christmas present from him, pearls and brilliants—"

"What kind of party was it?" asked the lieutenant wearily. "And who was here?"

"Me," said the young woman. "Ludvik, Petr, Lucy Ejemova— that's Ludvik's sister, she's a widow—then Mrs. Feher, my husband, and Irena Obdrzalek. Ludvik had just got back from a business trip—he'd been to India—so we were celebrating. . . ."

"Where do you all know each other from?" He was trying to interpret the logic behind this hierarchy: the dead man first, that was natural—the murder was uppermost in her mind. But it was interesting that her husband came almost last.

Mrs. Pelent continued; he noted that she was still very nervous.

"My husband is—was—Ludvik's colleague at the institute. Ludvik started there about six months ago—and we met Petr at Ludvik's—my husband really enjoyed coming over here, he's an engineer but he likes culture and things, and we don't have many friends who go in for that sort of stuff—except Ludvik, I mean. He could talk about paintings and statues." The lieutenant again registered the presence of the marble appendage, and scowled. "And Petr's an old friend of Ludvik's, I don't know where they know each other from. And Mrs. Feher . . . she lives upstairs here, she's a translator—from Hungarian, I think. As for the Obdrzalek girl, I've no idea. Ask her. She knew Ludvik from somewhere. . . ."

. . .

The lieutenant questioned the psychiatrist next. Petr Bydzovsky was a tanned, dark-haired, smooth-shaven man in a fashionable yellow sweater, and an unfashionable black eye.

"What happened to you?"

"She . . . told you about it, didn't she?" asked Bydzovsky.

"Who? And what?"

"Milena. Didn't she? It's embarrassing. Her husband did it, yesterday, here at the party. We got kind of drunk, and he just made up his mind that I was trying to seduce his wife."

"Were you?" asked the lieutenant. He usually posed his questions more tactfully, but he was not so delicate now, less because of his violence-infused line of duty than at this reminder of the eroticized times.

Bydzovsky winced. "Of course not. But she likes to confide in me, and he caught us at it a couple of times. You know how it is. A woman falls in love, unhappily, and she needs a listening post. She instinctively won't trust another woman, so she finds a man—preferably a friend of the object of her unfortunate affections. In this case she chose me. I mean, as the friend."

"And who was the . . . object?"

Bydzovsky looked down at the sharp creases in his trouser legs. Because he was considerably taller than Mrs. Pelent, it was only when he bent his head that the irritating symbol behind him reappeared in the lieutenant's line of sight—just for a moment, though, because the dark head was soon raised again, and Bydzovsky shifted his gaze from the razor-like creases back to the criminologist's eyes.

"Ludvik, of course. But he didn't care for her." The psychiatrist checked the state of his creases again. "Actually, Ludvik had a problem with her. She was crazy to get a divorce, but then that other one started running after him—" Petr Bydzovsky nodded towards the kitchen door. "She's the one who discovered his body. I was on my way home from the hospital; it was nice out, not too cold, and I like walking, it's good exercise. As I was passing under the archway—I live a little farther on, at Pohorelec—Irena comes tearing out of the front door and almost knocks me down. She's trembling all over and stammering that somebody's killed Ludvik."

.   .   .

The next one to sit in the uncomfortable armchair was Irena, the girl the lieutenant knew. She was wearing a green suit with a miniskirt, her hair was the color of copper, pulled back into a knot that was somehow familiar to the lieutenant, and her green eyes were rimmed with red. As she sat down, the criminologist got up and discreetly turned the marble statue around. After that, he paced back and forth a few times. The girl was silent, following him anxiously out of the corners of her eyes.

The lieutenant turned to her. "You loved him, Irena, didn't you?"

Her lips tightened. She swallowed. Then tears tumbled out of her eyes. "Yes," she said, very softly.

"And so what happened?"

For a while she battled the tears, until she finally regained control and started talking, almost in a whisper. "We . . . last night at the party we arranged that I'd come over today at five . . . and . . . the door was open. . . . He was lying there on the couch. . . . I just lost control and I ran outside . . . and I bumped into Petr out front . . . so I came back in with him. . . ."

She was interrupted by a creak of the door. The eager face of

Sergeant Malek appeared in the doorway. "Comrade lieutenant," he said in a professional tone, although he usually addressed his superior by his first name, Josef. At least, he had ever since certain tensions between them had been resolved, when the policewoman with the splendid chignon had chosen the brain surgeon. "Comrade lieutenant, the doctor's here."

"Would you go back to the other room for a minute, Irena?" the lieutenant said, and without really thinking about it he watched her pretty legs, very watchable in the miniskirt, until she disappeared through the door.

· · ·

The lieutenant looked over the photos with Dr. Seifert. They showed the face of a handsome, fair-haired man. The only ugly thing about him was the bloody hole in his temple.

"The shot was fired at close range, Josef," said old Dr. Seifert. "It would have to have been, because the weapon was only a .26-caliber."

"Really!" said the lieutenant. "But they don't make anything that size, do they?"

"They used to. Of course, that was a long time ago. You could still find them on the market before the war. Sometimes even jewelers used to sell them."

"Jewelers?"

Dr. Seifert nodded. "They used to decorate them with mother-of-pearl, and sometimes even precious stones. They called them ladies' revolvers; ladies were supposed to carry them in their handbags to protect themselves from being raped."

The lieutenant looked at the dead face in the photograph. He thought of his daughter's determined decision concerning the unidentified jerk, and of what he'd learned from the psychiatrist about Milena Pelent. He recalled the morality of the times, and asked himself bitterly when they would put a gentleman's revolver on the market—but he quickly chased that fantasy out of his head. Besides, with all the red tape, who'd be able to get one anyway? For that matter, how had anyone obtained even this little bourgeois minigun?

"It'll kill, all right," Dr. Seifert said over his shoulder, "but you have to get very close. Here, you see these burns?" He indicated the wound in the photo. "They're more typical of a suicide, where the victim holds the weapon right up against his temple."

"We've eliminated suicide," said Boruvka. "We didn't find the weapon."

At which point Sergeant Malek proved him wrong. He stuck his eager face in through the doorway again and, forgetting to sound professional, exclaimed, "Josef! The Obdrzalek girl had the gun! She tried to throw it in the trash when I wasn't looking!"

He held out his hand. On a clean purple handkerchief on his palm lay a sparkling little thing inlaid with rainbow mother-of-pearl.

. . .

This time the lieutenant paced the room for a good five minutes. Now and then he stopped and examined the old paintings in their carved frames, testimony to the dead engineer's passion as an art collector. He opened and shut the semicircular leaf of the antique secretary; he picked up a glass vase inlaid with the silver snakes of Medusa's hair and weighed it in his hand. The whole time he was silent. Perhaps he was thinking. The girl with the copper-colored hair no longer tried to repress her tears; they dripped down onto her short skirt, making dark streaks on it.

"Listen, Irena," the lieutenant said finally. "It's a stale old criminological cliché—but the truth is that it would be better for you—and for your dad," he added, a little illogically, "if you'd tell me everything, just the way it happened."

She raised her green eyes, so similar to the eyes of his own daughter, to look at him. The effect undid him.

"I didn't kill him, honest I didn't. I loved him. A lot. I could never have—"

"What about Mrs. Pelent?" he asked gently.

"She was after him, I knew about that. But Ludvik didn't care about her."

The tears overwhelmed her again. She turned and buried her face in an ornamental cushion, and Doryphorus's bare behind appeared above the knot of her copper hair. The lieutenant frowned. He walked around and picked up the statue, and carried it across the room. There he stood it beside a coffee table that looked like a figment of an opium dreamer's imagination.

The girl more or less recovered herself.

"Mr. Boruvka," she said urgently, "you can't believe that. You know me! I know it looks as if I made it all up. But it's true: Ludvik brought me the revolver from India—he even bragged about how he smuggled it through customs—and he gave it to me last night. He'd brought everybody a present. He was terrific at picking gifts for people. Well, but then we sort of . . . had a little argument . . . and I got a little, well, drunk. And to top it off, Petr got into a fight with Pelent. I mean, everything was a mess, and the revolver must have fallen out of my bag or something, or maybe when I took it out to dig for my cigarettes I forgot to put it back. Anyway, when I got home it wasn't in my purse. So the next morning I called Ludvik as soon as I got to work—"

"But you said you'd had an argument, didn't you?"

"We made up again afterwards. It was all silly. Silly of me, I mean. It just seemed to me that Ludvik was getting too chummy with that old Feher woman. I'd know for a long time that she had the hots for him. And Ludvik once admitted to me that he had a weakness for older women. But I think he was just saying that to make me mad. Besides, the Feher woman's really a lot older. So I got over it in a hurry, and we made up again and made that date for today. And what's more, the Feher woman got plastered that night too.

"Anyway, I called Ludvik from work this morning to see if he'd found the gun, and he promised he'd have a look; he said it was sure to be around somewhere, and to be here at five." She stopped, and fresh tearstains appeared on her lap. "But when I got here . . . he was stretched out there on the couch . . . the stupid revolver was on the carpet beside him so I picked it up, and it didn't dawn on me until later on, in the kitchen. . . . I wanted to get rid of it, I just panicked." She raised her red-rimmed cat's eyes to the lieutenant again. "Mr. Boruvka, I'm telling the truth, honest I am!"

"Hmm," growled the lieutenant. He had just discovered that by moving the statue he had revealed a painting of an over-endowed woman being attacked by a frenzied swan. He'd heard about something of the sort, but he couldn't quite place it. He sat down at the grotesque antique table, rested his forehead on his hand in such a way that the hand blocked his view of the lewd canvas, and said, "Hmm. Well, all right. But do you have any idea why Bydzovsky and Pelent were fighting?"

The girl shrugged. "No, I was pretty far gone by then. Petr said Pelent was jealous of him—he'd seen Petr with his wife in a coffeehouse a few times when she'd told him she was going somewhere else, and he'd decided Petr was having it off with her."

"And—ahem—was he?" asked the lieutenant, firmly convinced that one shouldn't talk about such things in front of one's children's peers. He remembered that he was on the road to becoming a grandfather . . . still, that didn't change his opinion. "Well, I'm not sure," said the girl. "But as far as I know, Petr's seeing Lucy Ejemova, Ludvik's sister, you know? At least, I've seen the two of them together. Several times. And when I've called him recently, she's always been the one who answered the phone."

"How well do you know her, Irena?"

"Pretty well. She was over at Ludvik's a lot in the past few weeks. Her husband died about three months ago, and they were talking about trying to trade in her flat and Ludvik's for a single bigger one that they could share, one they found in the Klamovsky mansion, because the people who live there are splitting up—"

"So the rumors that Bydzovsky is seeing the Pelent woman aren't true?"

"I don't know." She paused, but then something like hatred flashed in her eyes. "But I wouldn't bet on it. She couldn't keep away from Ludvik, either. Even though he was seeing me. She's an awful cravie—"

"A what?"

"A cravie," repeated the girl, and her offhand vocabulary made the lieutenant think of a certain almost forgotten singer he'd once helped out of an ugly jam. Although he'd hoped for more (without ever really admitting it), his only reward had been her friendship. Where was she now, he wondered.

"That's what an old friend of mine, Zuzka, used to call a certain kind of woman," explained Irena. "Meaning a woman like Mrs. Pelent, who craves it, you know? She can't be satisfied with just one man."

.   .   .

Could you call this one here a cravie too, the lieutenant wondered, a little while later. Under the painting of the naked bacchante and the lecherous bird (which he had now covered with a brocade throw, having finally remembered the myth) sat a thin woman whose gray hair had a purple tint to it, whose cheeks were conspicuously rosy, and whose lips were colored a bright carmine. It appeared to him that she'd reached the age when most women wore black cotton hose and sensible shoes, and spent their time crocheting for charity bazaars. This woman, on the other hand, was wearing a pale green minidress with a deep décolletage and setting off her age-spotted skin with an antique brooch depicting two naked bodies, male and female, their silver hands pulling at a purple gemstone. She sat with her legs crossed, wearing nylon stockings that couldn't conceal her clusters of varicose veins, and purple shoes with big buckles. Her left wrist was adorned with a bracelet shaped like a snake.

The lieutenant covered his eyes with his hand again, as if he were deep in thought. He asked, "So you didn't hear the gunshot, Mrs. Feher?" She shook her head. "No, I was working on my translation. Besides, I like to play Bach when I'm working. I didn't hear a thing."

"And how . . ." The lieutenant hesitated, and reformulated his question: "Did you know the victim well?"

"Very well," said the woman, recrossing her legs and making the lieutenant think nostalgically of ankle-length skirts. He looked at her face; it seemed to him to be marked by fairly intensive activity in certain spheres of life. He told himself that, in spite of her years, even this potential grandmother might well deserve the label Irena's friend had invented.

"Yes, I knew Ludvik very well," she repeated. "Poor fellow, he suffered a complex that many technical people have—the fear that they lack erudition in the humanities. He loved intellectual conversations. So of course—" she chuckled, in a voice evidently well tempered with distilled spirits, "I made myself available. He was very entertaining. And as for that *erudition* of his," she said significantly, although the lieutenant had no idea what the significance was, "it wasn't all that lacking."

Her slightly faded eyes latched onto the lieutenant's and he quickly turned the conversation elsewhere. "I understand there was a disagreement during the party last night between Dr. Bydzovsky and Mr. Pelent?"

"Disagreement? Better say a brawl. Petr threw himself at Rudy so hard it frightened me—"

"Why was that?"

"Because he might have hurt him."

"No, I meant why do you think they fought?"

She chuckled again, and he thought of the seven deadly sins, and the murky Gothic apse where once, long ago, he had confessed to the Reverend Father Meloun the sin of lust committed by feel. In those days high-school students rarely got any further than that with their girlfriends. . . . He gave his head a shake to escape the memory.

"It was jealousy, you know," she said.

"Jealousy? Oh yes, I know—Pelent's wife. But listen," he said uneasily. "I've heard that Bydzovsky was having an affair with the victim's sister—"

"With Lucy?" The woman gave the lieutenant an amused look. He felt she was leaving something unsaid, not because she was unwilling to tell him, but because she assumed he knew. And with an oddly inexplicable feeling of shame, he somehow didn't feel like asking. He just said awkwardly, "Well, they were—ahem—

seen. She was a frequent visitor of his."

He averted his eyes, and spotted an alabaster statuette of the god Hermes on the inlaid spinet.

"Well . . . ," the woman faltered, and the lieutenant had that feeling again. "Ludvik and Petr were good friends—*very* good friends—but that Petr should have wanted to take care of Lucy *that* way, you understand, after she lost her husband . . . I really don't think so. Of course, he . . . she . . . but . . . Why don't you just ask him?"

By then the lieutenant was certain the old woman knew more than she was telling. But that uneasy embarrassment kept him from pursuing it.

. . .

Yet he did ask the black-haired man in the yellow sweater, as she had suggested. The man was squirming a little, but then the lieutenant recognized that the armchair was very uncomfortable.

"I'm fond of Lucy, very fond. That's why . . ." He fell silent.

"Fond how?" the criminologist asked bluntly, as he would never have dared with a female suspect.

The man squirmed again.

"I don't know what you mean."

"I mean, do you have something going with her? Do you want to marry her? Or is she just your mistress?"

"No, not really," said Bydzovsky. "I simply . . . care for her. I might marry her. She's pretty. But that isn't what she's after. She needs someone to confide in. The death of her husband really shattered her, she's quite unstable. . . ."

"A lot of women pick you for their confidences, I'd say!"

"Well, yes. but that's not so amazing. After all, I am a psychiatrist—"

"Does Mrs. Feher confide in you too?"

"Her? No! Why should she?"

"I haven't the slightest idea," snapped the lieutenant. He got up and pushed aside a leaf of a ficus plant that partially concealed another painting in a gilded frame. Above the plant, the painting showed a kneeling monk with a ginger tonsure, and a rosary around his waist. His head was bowed, apparently in penance. But when the lieutenant moved the leaf, he saw that the repentant monk's gaze rested on a woman's head peering up out of a rocky pool. The painter had made the water so pure and transparent that it was evident to both the monk and the lieutenant that the woman was wearing nothing at all—but on a rock beside the pool lay the black habit and starched wimple of a nun. The lieutenant let the leaf drop back into place, and ran his eyes over the nude statue with its back to him, the impassioned swan, and the alabaster Hermes. He felt a wave of pity for his friend Obdrzalek. Then he opened the door and bellowed, "Is Pelent here yet?"

• • •

Pelent was. He took his seat in front of the exposed picture; the brocade throw had slipped off when the lieutenant bellowed, and he hadn't had a chance to replace it. Pelent had wavy chestnut hair and a wrinkled face. A blue polka-dot bow tie poked perkily out from under his white shirt collar, above an impeccably tailored suit of a light, opalescent fabric

"Suspicion?" Pelent shook his head. "It never occurred to me. And this argument . . . you know, I can't even remember."

"You don't say!"

"Oh, wait a minute, it's all coming back." The engineer was visibly racking his brain. "It was something I said to him. We were both . . . under the weather, let's say. . . . Yes, that's right. It was about Ludvik's sister and Bydzovsky." He paused. "I said something that upset Petr. I didn't mean anything by it, but he just up and exploded."

"What was it?"

Pelent hesitated. He hesitated a little too long.

"You know, as a psychiatrist he . . . he's treating her . . . and I made a critical remark about his methods. He's very touchy about that."

"And you're not touchy," the lieutenant interrupted him, "about your wife seeing Bydzovsky behind your back?"

The man in the opalescent suit bowed his head, and hesitated again. He didn't seem like a hesitant man, thought the criminologist, yet he kept hesitating. Finally Pelent made up his mind. "You apparently know anyway—it's pointless to pretend. She kept dragging me to these parties at Ludvik's because of what she called my love of art—but Bydzovsky was always at the parties too. Wherever Ludvik was, Petr was. Of course, I didn't care about Petr. Or about Ludvik's parties; I shared an office with Ludvik all week long. And as for my being all that interested in the arts, I'm not. But my wife . . . well, you're right, she was obsessed—"

"Why Bydzovsky?" The lieutenant remembered very well what the psychiatrist had told him about Pelent's wife, and that version was more in keeping with reality. "Or with Arnold?" he asked.

The man in the shimmering suit hesitated yet again, this time long and intensely. Finally he thought his way through to the core of the matter and said, "You know, if I hadn't surprised her with Bydzovsky a number of times . . . well, I wouldn't have know which one it was."

． ． ．

As soon as the door closed behind the elegant engineer, the lieutenant made one final attempt at putting up the brocade throw. Then—just when he thought he was through with distressing persons of the opposite sex—Malek stuck his head in and whispered, "Josef, they've brought that sister of his. Do you want her?"

The lieutenant gave the throw a final tweak and stepped back, but even as he set eyes on Lucy Ejemova, the brocade slid heavily to the floor. The girl didn't pay any attention, though. She stood before him like a lovely drawing in charcoal. She was dressed in mourning, black from head to foot, but the white face glowing above her widow's weeds was crowned with gold, like a medallion of an idealized and slightly morbid martyr. She was the image of the dead man: the same fair hair, the regular oval face, but a shade softer. When she sat down in the chair and put her hands on the armrests, the lieutenant noticed two wedding bands on her third finger, and saw that her hands were trembling. He stared at her as if she were a vision from a fairy tale.

She raised her gray eyes with their tiny black pupils to the lieutenant's round face, and quickly dropped them again. But that brief moment was enough to let him regain his equilibrium, and to consider that perhaps Pelent was right about Dr. Bydzovsky's methods of treatment. He pulled up an art-nouveau stool, sat, rose again (the perverse imagination of *fin-de-siècle* cabinetmaker had placed a pointed spike in the middle of the seat), sat again, and leaned over towards Lucy. Then, although it was something he never did during an interrogation, he took out a cigarette, put it in his mouth, and patted his pockets.

"I'm sorry, do you happen to have a light?"

The widow opened the black purse on her lap. At that moment his cigarette dropped clumsily out of his mouth and, in an awkward attempt to catch it, he knocked the purse out of her hands. It fell to the floor and its contents spilled out. After successfully pulling off his complicated maneuver, he wiped his forehead inconspicuously and quickly knelt down at the widow's feet. He forced himself not to look at her slender calves in their black nylons, and earnestly proceeded to collect her scattered possessions.

He found what he was looking for.

He picked up the vial carefully, read the label, and looked reproachfully at the grieving young woman—confirming that even though they were the focus of her beauty, there was definitely something wrong with her eyes.

"Do you take a lot of these?" he asked.

Her hands on the armrests were trembling again. "Not a lot," she said uncertainly. "But . . . I've been terribly nervous ever since my Jarmil died . . . we'd only been together three months—"

"Who prescribes them for you?" he asked darkly.

"Who? Nobody. I mean, a doctor. A physician—"

"At the medical center?"

"No, I . . ." And then the ethereally lovely young widow fainted right into the lieutenant's arms.

· · ·

The girl was stretched out on the same art-nouveau divan that until recently had been occupied by her dead brother, and was being given an injection by Dr. Siefert. The lieutenant turned to Dr. Bydzovsky, showed him the container of white pills, and challenged him sternly. "What do you know about this?"

Bydzovsky glanced over at Lucy and decided it would be foolish to deny it. "I didn't prescribe more than was safe," he said coldly.

"Why wasn't her family doctor prescribing them? Or maybe he was prescribing a safe dosage too? Maybe what she got from you was just to top it up, so to speak?"

Under the influence of the doctor's injection, the girl came to, and immediately guessed what they were talking about. "It wasn't his fault," she said miserably. "Lieutenant, he only—"

"Shut up, Lucy," Dr. Bydzovsky snapped, and turned angrily back to the lieutenant. "Look here, my records are in order. The medication is appropriate to her symptoms, and I prescribed the right dosage, out of friendship to her brother. Besides, in cases of a neuropsychosis like this, one of the most important things is the patient's confidence in the physician. I don't know whether she was getting more elsewhere, but her her family doctor wasn't prescribing it for her. Naturally, I kept him informed. But I advised her most emphatically—" and he turned to the girl in mourning, who had sat up and was pressing the palms of both hands to her temples, "to forget about Jarmil, which she didn't, and to remarry and have children as soon as possible. That's the best medicine for what ails *her*."

"Don't say that, Petr," cried the girl. "Please, not that."

. . .

He was alone again with the widow. It was dark already, and the art-nouveau lamp cast colored lights on her deathly face. It looks like a Tiffany lamp, thought the lieutenant.

"I don't want to marry again!" wailed the girl, while the lieutenant, helplessly enchanted, watched the curve of her bowed head, and her arm movements, reminiscent of a dancer. "I don't want to. I know that's hard to understand, but I just can't. Ludvik was the only one who understood me. He suggested we trade our two flats for one in the Klamovsky mansion, and I agreed. I wanted to be with him. To take care of him. Because nobody else understands . . . and now he's . . ."

She bent her white neck, and bowed her head to the white hands folded softly in her lap, looking for all the world like a *Jugendstil* painting. The gold crown of her hair quite dazzled the lieutenant.

. . .

Later he strode under the gas lamps of nightime Prague, searching his mind for particulars of a sphere of human existence quite remote from his life—a sphere about which he'd read a little, but which he didn't really understand.

When he got home, he had to face the agitated questions of his friend Obdrzalek. He was unable to convince the man that the arrest of his twenty-year-old daughter had been unavoidable, as all the evidence was against her. He tried to assure the poor man that he didn't believe she was guilty. But to his surprise the distressed bookseller admitted, indirectly, that he himself *did*, and he went on to deliver a weepy tirade against the depravity of the era—against miniskirts, striptease, and the Communism that he felt had brought them all about. It was after midnight when the despondent man finally left, exhausted, and went out into the cold winter night.

Later, in bed beside the calmly sleeping grandmother-to-be, the lieutenant watched the white February moon rise over the tile roofs, and felt overwhelmed by the utterly hopeless weight of the world. How long had it tormented him at moments like this? It must be since he'd begun to feel that he was in the last third of his life. He fell asleep. Monstrous shadows engulfed him, mateializing into girls in miniskirts; into Irena Obdrzalek, now suspected of murder; into the macabre widow; into the policewoman now eight months along—though this wasn't apparent in his dreams; into a certain sad dancer he'd once known; into his own daughter—and he was overcome with sadness, because he realized he was facing the end of something extremely beautiful. . . . And then a whole crowd of spirited young girls appeared on a sunny playing field, and they all seemed familiar to him—yes, they were the girls he had once taught to play basketball—and one of them had later turned up in the geography office, where private detective Jaroslav V. Klima eventually found that damning black garter button. . . .

In his sleep, the lieutenant shut his eyes more tightly, so as not to see the world of that strange fiftieth year of his, a year in which the approaching spring had the fragrance of old, almost forgotten yearnings; so that this mad world would disappear. And he felt a sudden longing for a figure from an old etching, a woman whose legs were concealed, an art-nouveau lady in a long, draping mantle all the way down to the floor. . . .

. . .

So the following afternoon in the Lesser Quarter Café, when he raised his eyes from reading Malek's report, he felt for a moment that he was still dreaming. The lady stood opposite him, and her elegant winter coat reached all the way to the floor, falling in graceful folds. The lieutenant stared at her as if he were hypnotized.

The lady said, "Don't you recognize me, lieutenant? That's a fine how-do-you-do!"

"For heaven's sake! It's you . . . Eve. . . !" and then he hastened to correct himself, "Miss Adam!"

"It's me, all right," she said. "One and the same. Unfortunately."

The lieutenant didn't register the somewhat cryptic adverb. "And what's that you're wearing?" he blurted. "It's beautiful."

She gave an amiable smile. "Do you like it?" She spun around on her heel, and the coat stood out in a lovely cone, revealing her small foot and slender instep. The lieutenant shivered, as his Victorian forebears must have done at a similar sight. "It's all the rage in the West now. The maxi. In this case, a maxicoat." The girl stopped, standing with her arms a little out from her body so the lieutenant could get a good look.

He got a good look, and everything that had been bothering him was forgotten in the presence of the radiant girl. In the two years since he'd seen her, she had stood up well—in fact she'd grown younger, or so it seemed to him. He said joyfully, "What a great surprise! Have a seat! Sit down, Eve—Miss Adam."

"Call me Eve, okay? 'Miss Adam' always reminds me of that jerk in Paradise who started all our troubles in the first place."

The lieutenant made no objection to her flawed interpretation of biblical history, and as she was beginning to undo her buttons, he jumped up gallantly to help her out of her maxicoat. Under it, she was wearing a very minimal miniskirt.

"It's really—elegant," he said, as he hung the long garment decorously on the hanger behind him. "It must have cost a lot of money." He couldn't think of anything else to say.

"Just wait till you see my mink coat! That'll blow you away!"

"Ahem," said the lieutenant, involuntarily glancing above the singer's knees. "I can see that you've, shall we say, done well for yourself. A mink coat—I've never actually seen one, but I understand mink isn't exactly inexpensive," he said, suddenly becoming a little awkward. "So I'm told, I mean. Though performers in the West must make quite a—"

"Well, the fact is," she interrupted him quickly, "I didn't buy it. It was a gift. From a friend. That is . . ." She gave him an uncertain glance, but he was watching her with such a look of devotion that she relaxed again. "That is, a friend of my late mother. Well, the friend's husband, that is. I mean, I hope you don't think I was making up to some creepy old millionaire!"

"Heaven forbid!" The detective's round face radiated real horror, but the blonde could see something else there too—sadness, a certain sorrow, and something else—and she felt the urge to cheer up her old friend. She felt a premonition—she was rather superstitious—as if they were bound by some common bond, not necessarily bound together, but to something they would share in the future, she had no idea what. As if they were both standing on the brink of a time that wouldn't bring more joy—not to her, but especially not to him, or for that matter to anyone else. And yet the lieutenant's round face still welcomed her with the breath of home; not the safest place in the world, but still home.

"I don't pretend to be a saint or anything. I'm not. But I'm not the other either, right? I'd be awfully unhappy if you though I was."

"I don't think anything of the kind, Eve. I always thought you—"

"Well," said the blonde, "I did have one gentleman friend over there, and he wasn't any boy scout, let me tell you. But he wasn't all that old, either. I'd say," she said flatteringly, "that he was maybe a year or two older than you—"

"Really?" asked the lieutenant hopefully, not registering her guile. He called a surprised waiter and ordered champagne. "Well, he wasn't all that young then, either," he added, but because he wasn't particularly anxious to hear the details, he changed the subject back. "And what about this fur coat?"

"Yes, well," said the blonde, "one time I went to visit that friend, I mean, my mom's schoolmate and her husband. Before they left Czechoslovakia, ahead of Hitler, they'd had a furrier's store in Prague. Later on he made a lot of money in America, and they were both so pleased I'd come, especially him, that when I go to leave he gives me a fur coat. To remember them by, he says."

The lieutenant was a little confused by all this, but he didn't doubt the ex-furrier's pleasure one bit.

"And to make my mother happy, he says. And I tell him my mother's dead, but he says, then it's to make my husband happy. 'But I haven't *got* a husband, unfortunately,' I say. 'But you will have!' he says. 'I'll never believe someone like you will stay single! You make me laugh!' But it looks like the laugh's on him now, right?"

The lieutenant waved a dismissing hand. Inexperienced with wines, he was drinking the champagne as if it were beer, and he was rapidly beginning to feel very good. "I agree, I totally agree! Not with you, of course, but with him!"

"Yes, well, we Czechs are always optimists, even when pessimism is clearly in order. I tried to tell him that I couldn't take the coat back to Czechoslovakia, that I'd probably be arrested at the border for giving the state a bad name. But he says, 'I'll tell you what you do. Take the express train out of the Gare de l'Est in Paris. That train takes almost twenty hours to get to the Czech frontier, and lots of Americans travel on it. You're young and attractive, twenty hours is plenty of time for you. Get to know the Americans, explain the situation, and get one of them to take the coat and pretend it's her own, and then give it back to you when you've crossed the border—' And here I am!"

The lieutenant had fortified his faith so successfully that he swallowed it all—just like the champagne, which had vanished without much help from the girl, so the lieutenant had to order some more.

· · ·

He gave no more thought to the unsolved case from Loreta Square until Dr. Bydzovsky walked into the coffeehouse with Lucy Ejemova. Then he called out, "Hello, there!" excitedly, as if he'd just encountered his best friends after ten years. "Come and join us! Come on, I'm not here on duty. I want you to meet Miss Eve Adam, but we mustn't call her that because it reminds her of nudists," he said, in a bit of a muddle. "And look what she brought from America!" He turned to the young widow, taking the fashionable coat off the hook and holding it up for her to see. "A super-coat!" he explained, victoriously. "Isn't that something? And you should see how good it looks on her!"

In spite of being in mourning, the widow was irresistibly drawn to the garment the lieutenant called a super-coat. Soon the two young women were side by side, poring over a fashion magazine the singer had pulled out of her bag. The policeman ordered more champagne.

· · ·

By the time Lucy and Dr. Bydzovsky left, the lieutenant was quite drunk. He wasn't entirely unaware that he'd established a closer relationship with the two than might be warranted from a professional point of view, but as soon as they vanished from his sight he called for more champagne.

The blonde saved him from total disaster. "From where I sit, you need Turkish coffee more than you need champagne. And so, I think, do I." She ordered two cups, and then two more, and finally another four, until the lieutenant sobered up a little.

Now he became gloomy and dismayed, and began worrying

about whether he'd shot off his mouth too much. "Talked too much," he corrected himself, because as the level of alcohol in his blood dropped he became conscious of his language in front of the blonde. She untruthfully assured him that he'd hardly spoken a word, and he more than made up for it in the half hour that followed. That was how she found out all the details of the labyrinth of relationships, varied but apparently for the most part erotic, surrounding the dead man and all the living, perhaps with the exception of the one between Dr. Bydzovsky and Lucy Ejemova, which fell more into the area of narcotics legislation. And of course about the sisterly love of Lucy Ejemova for her murdered brother.

The lieutenant was just describing this relationship to her, and showing her the picture of the murder victim, when the blonde raised her eyebrows. The dead man was posed arm in arm with a friend, smiling into the camera.

The blonde said, "This reminds me of something."

"Of what?"

"Don't you remember?" She turned the photograph towards him. "If you hadn't been so clever, there wouldn't have been any America for me; I'd still be behind bars.

The detective gave a pleased smile. The singer picked up another picture—one of the dead man and the widow—and held it up in front of him as well. The lieutenant tried to remember what it was that his erstwhile cleverness had to do with, but in the presence of those gray eyes he wasn't capable of memory or even thought.

"The two of them! The brother and sister! They looked as much alike as these two. And if it weren't for that Dr. Hejduk, they might perfectly well have committed—what is it you call it when a brother and sister. . . ."

The lieutenant finally caught on. Partly. "Incest, you mean," he said. "But there wasn't any danger of that here. Those other two didn't *know* they were brother and sister. These two did. And the rather . . . intense emotional attachment of Mrs. Ejemova to the victim is easy to explain," he continued pedantically. "She had just lost a young husband, after a marriage of only three months. You must understand, such a young woman, suddenly alone—"

"Oh, I understand," she nodded, but the lieutenant had the vague feeling that she was understanding things her own way. "That was the hardest thing in the clink, too—harder than the stale cheese. Mainly for the ones who were there for longer stints. I don't mean those two would have . . . But still, to want to share a flat with your own brother—I was happy when my brother moved out."

"Do you have a brother?"

"Yes, I have."

"I didn't know that. What does he do?"

"Not much of anything. I don't like talking about him."

"Don't be so modest. What does he do?"

"He embezzles," said the girl. "That is, he did." She put the two pictures back on the table in front of her, and made it very clear that she was concentrating on them. The lieutenant didn't voice any further interest in her brother.

"And who's the other one?" She indicated the man whose arm Ludvik Arnold was holding.

"Pelent. He's a engineer too, they worked in the same office." The lieutenant looked at the happy pair in the snapshot in front of the singer.

"There's something similar about them, too," mused the girl. The criminologist didn't see any resemblance between the handsome countenance of the murdered blond man and the wrinkled face of the husband of the woman who might have been the former's mistress. But maybe that was because he was seeing them both upside-down. "Maybe it's just that they're both so nattily dressed," said the singer. The lieutenant was startled. He hadn't noticed that the two men had that in common. He looked again, and it was the truth. Meanwhile the girl was reaching for the next picture. It was an official photo of the scene of the murder. "Hmm," she said. "A cultural inferiority complex, did you say?" She looked at the art-nouveau divan with the corpse, the marble Doryphorus that was also clearly visible in the shot, the mythological lady and the swan, and the Tiffany lamp. "It looks like a museum in there."

But then the detective brought a picture of the murder weapon out of his briefcase, and people were forgotten at the sight of the deadly little object. "How pretty it is!" squealed the girl. "It seems like a shame to shoot it, doesn't it? And you say he brought it from India for her? Really? What did he bring the others?"

"Similar things," said the lieutenant. "All Indian. Slippers for his sister, a book for the Pelents—*The Kama Sutra,* or something like that. It was pictures of statues—"

"I've seen it," said his companion. "It's really fab!"

"Fab?"

"Well, it's not for children. It shows, you know, various positions . . . in India they're supposed to have made a whole science out of it."

"Out of what?"

"*It.* Don't ask me! *You* know!"

"Oh, *that,*" nodded the lieutenant not wanting to appear ignorant, and he continued, "For Bydzovsky he brought some shoes. Boots, I mean, high ones—embroidered. Apparently they're all the rage in the West, too." A light suddenly dawned, and he realized what the book of statues must be about. "And for Mrs. Feher—well, actually something like *The Kama Sutra*—"

"You mean there *is* something else like that?" she asked with interest.

"I don't mean a book," said the lieutenant. "It's an inkstand. Sort of a reclining woman—I mean, a nude. On her back, you know, and her top—well, they both sort of open up. For black and red ink. It's in pretty bad taste," he added quickly, glancing at the blonde to see if he'd gone too far.

Perhaps he had. Because the blonde thought for a moment and got up, saying, "It's been nice, Mr. Boruvka. But I've got to run."

· · ·

Someone rang the doorbell. Dr. Bydzovsky, who was sitting in an old-fashioned easy chair listening to his stereo, frowned and got up. He went out to the vestibule, tightened the belt of his Chinese silk dressing gown, took the chain off the door, and opened it.

A girl in a floor-length navy-blue coat stood there, smiling at him pleasantly.

"Excuse me for troubling you," she said. "But I live nearby, in Brevnov, so it's on my way. I forgot to return your fountain pen, so I've brought it."

She held out a pen. Dr. Bydzovsky gave it a surprised look, and his face took on an expression of revulsion. She put the pen on her palm. In the warmth of her hand, the bathing beauty on the pen gradually began to shed her clothes.

"My fountain pen?" Dr. Bydzovsky asked. "I don't recall lending you—and something like this—I'd never own anything like that," he added, still looking disgusted.

"No? Then—could it have been Lieutenant Boruvka's?" the lady wondered.

"That's is *entirely* possible. A pen like this would probably appeal to him."

"That's true," said the lady, looking around. "My! It certainly is nice in here! May I come in?" Having invited herself, she immediately accepted the invitation, although Dr. Bydzovsky didn't seem particularly anxious to have her there. She spun around in the center of the room, her long coat again forming a beautiful cone. She was evidently enchanted by the decor.

"How terribly tasteful! Is this really Meissen?" She picked up a porcelain figurine, and Dr. Bydzovsky scowled. "And the carpet, real Persian, isn't it? May I take off my coat for a while?" The coat was off in a flash, tossed over the back of a loveseat, and the girl was transformed into a figure skater without skates, spinning on her axis on the Afghan rug. Her more than excellent legs shone like silk as she turned and turned. An objective observer might have suspected that she wasn't doing it to get a better look at the collection of floral still lifes on the walls, but rather so the irritated man in the Chinese dressing gown could have a good look at her. But he was clearly irritated, and displayed no interest whatever. "Listen, miss, what is it you want?"

The figure skater stopped, and made obvious eyes at Dr. Bydzovsky. Swaying her hips, she walked over to him and stood close. "What do I want? To get to know you better, you know? Or are you going with Mrs. Ejemova?"

"Aren't you a little forward?" Dr. Bydzovsky snapped and walked away to sit down on an antique settee. The lady followed and sat down right beside him.

"I am, a little. But only when somebody appeals to me, you know?"

She edged even closer to Bydzovsky. Bydzovsky moved away.

"Are you going with her, or aren't you?"

"What business is that of yours?"

Bydzovsky was losing his temper, but the girl said coolly, "Because I know quite a bit about her."

"Undoubtedly more than I do," said Dr. Bydzovsky. "All I do is supply her with tranquilizers."

"Ah," said the blonde, moving closer again. "I need someone to check me out, too. Wouldn't you be interested? In examining me? Or prescribing something for me?"

She placed her little hand temptingly on his leg, and the psychiatrist removed himself briskly, and cleared his throat. "Look, miss, don't bother. If that lieutenant sent you over here and thought you could get something out of me *this* way—"

The girl edged closer to him again. "You really know how to be wrong, lover," she said sweetly. Dr. Bydzovsky rose and walked over to the fireplace, and turned his back to her. There was a large framed photograph of the murdered man on the mantelpiece, with a fresh black mourning band across the corner. The blonde got up, stood beside Bydzovsky, and picked up the photograph. She looked at the psychiatrist and their eyes met. "I'm sorry," she said. "Forgive me. I didn't realize that he was your friend—and of course it's only been two days—"

She replaced the picture on the mantelpiece and added, "But I still think you're quite the icicle. Where did I put my super-coat? Oh, here it is." She belted it tightly around her waist and walked over to the door, the long coat rippling romantically behind her. She turned in the doorway and addressed the doctor for the last time: "But about Pelent and Ludvik—you know very well what that was all about, don't you doctor!"

"Good night," said Dr. Bydzovsky, and rudely shut the door in her face.

> Who killed Ludvik Arnold? And which of Father Knox's commandments has been broken? Remember to rely on reason— and not just on the process of elimination (perhaps an unfortunate term, in a tale of murder!)

Lieutenant Boruvka awoke with a dreadful hangover. Once again he had the unpleasant feeling that he'd talked too much the previous evening. He didn't so much fear that he'd divulged police secrets as that he might have hurt his position with his rediscovered friend.

At eight o'clock he was sitting at his desk, swallowing pills and washing them down with coffee, and considering writing a confidential letter to his sister in Kostelec; he would ask if Zuzana could come for a brief stay with her, say about eight months. As he listened with half an ear to Sergeant Malek's report, he decided against the idea, labeling it too romantic; at breakfast that morning Zuzana had remarked, "I wonder how I'm going to manage my final exams in track and field this spring, now that I'm knocked up!" Someone cynical enough to talk like that would probably turn up her nose at spending time in the backwater of her father's native town. And even if she didn't turn up her nose at it, even if she went, she'd only damage the good reputation he'd created for himself in that old-world community, when he'd stepped up to the correct (if inevitable) resolution of the unexpected consequences of his activity at the girls' high school. . . .

"The phone call appears to have been verified," the sergeant read from his notebook. "The Obdrzalek girl really did call somewhere at about ten in the morning, and her co-worker confirms that she spoke to someone she called 'Ludvik, love'—" the sergeant gave the lieutenant a meaningful glance, but found him staring out the window at the saint across the street. " 'Ludvik, love,' she called him, and she wanted to know if she'd left 'what he gave her' at his place. I'm quoting the witness verbatim." He looked back at his notebook. "Her name is Jana Kolemjdouci," he said, a little uneasily, and snapped his notebook shut adding, "That verifies what the Obdrzalek girl said. On the other hand, it could have been a trick. A prearranged alibi, you know what I mean, Josef? Setting it all up in case we traced the murder weapon back to her—"

"You know, Pavel," the lieutenant interrupted the sergeant's musings, "that seems much too sophisticated for Irena Obdrzalek. And besides, if there were that kind of premeditation, wouldn't she have used a different weapon?"

"Just what I was thinking," the sergeant chimed in. "And something else. Not a single one of those women has an alibi. For instance, the Pelent woman left work at two o'clock but she didn't go home, she just suddenly appeared at the scene of the crime at five. She can't explain what she was doing in the meantime. *Walking* around town, alone, by herself. That's an old one!"

"But she's a more likely candidate." The lieutenant's voice sounded tired. "She could have picked up the revolver during the party. She was a cravie, too—"

"She was a what?"

"That's a word that . . . our Zuzana uses. These young people are always inventing new words, mostly strange ones. I think the Pelent woman was after men. She was certainly jealous of Irena—"

"Absolutely, Josef! So we've got a motive the size of a barn!" exclaimed the sergeant, a proponent of the principle that it's better to commit ten miscarriages of justice than to let a single culprit get off scot-free. "We've got the motive, and we've got the lack of an alibi. We've got the opportunity, too. So now we can go nab her!"

The telephone rang, and saved the unsuspecting Milena Pelent from Sergeant Malek's fearsome nabbing.

"Yes?" said the lieutenant darkly, and Malek, who was tightening his belt in preparation for action, witnessed a rare occurrence: the lieutenant's face brightened.

"Hello, hello there, Miss Adam—all right, Eve, then," he said joyfully, and he listened to the distant voice, unforgettable in its timbre.

"Lieutenant, can you come down to Charles Square? Right away?"

"I'd love to. But I'm on duty—"

"But it's on duty that I need you. I'm here with Dr. Plechovec—"

"With who?"

"He's a taxi driver. At a cab stand in front of the clinic. And he knows something important—at least, I think it is—about that murder on Loreta Square. But we need you to come quick, because he's losing fares."

"I'm almost there!" exclaimed the lieutenant.

. . .

"No, I couldn't be mistaken." Dr. Plechovec shook his head. "I know it for sure. After all, I'm acquainted with Dr. Bydzovsky. As a matter of fact, I know him very well. He always walks home unless it's really pouring rain, and then he might take the streetcar. So it stuck in my mind when he took my cab home the day before yesterday."

"What time was that, do you remember?"

"We got there a few minutes after a quarter past four," said Dr. Plechovec. "I remember looking at the clock on the barracks, because I had a fare waiting at the Hotel Yalta."

"I see. Well . . . thank you," said Lieutenant Boruvka.

. . .

"Yes, it's clear he was lying," the detective said ten minutes later, at the Hlavovka Café. "But where's the motive, Eve? We don't have the slightest motive!"

The singer looked him in the eye.

"Mr. Boruvka," she said urgently, "take a look at me."

The lieutenant did.

"Don't you think," she said, "that if you were alone with me, say in a nicely furnished flat—and if you were single—and if I'd come there on my own, and I told you that you appealed to me—not that you'd fall in love with me or anything, I'm not that conceited. . . ." She was still trying to make herself look good, but as far as the lieutenant was concerned she needn't have bothered. "But what kind of man would you be if you didn't at least have a *twitching* to take advantage of the opportunity? Even if you held back for one reason or another?"

It seemed to the lieutenant that such a reason was beyond human imagining.

"And I'd be able to tell—with you, or with anybody," the girl went on. "But that Bydzovsky? He just sat there like a stuffed dressing gown—"

"Sat where?" The lieutenant felt an unpleasant suspicion coming over him.

"That doesn't matter." She shook her head impatiently. "The point is, the whole thing's perfectly obvious."

"Not to me," said the lieutenant apologetically.

"Of course not. I mean, you deal with normal people—"

"I don't consider murderers normal—"

"I mean normal in a different sense. Look, you saw that flat of Arnold's, didn't you? You'll find the same kind of things at Bydzovsky's, carpets and pictures, fancy furniture—the only difference is that he has flowers instead of nudes."

The lieutenant stared at her, with a pang of jealousy. When the devil had she been at the psychiatrist's? And why?

"And Pelent shared an office with Ludvik, day after day. But he only met him six months ago. Bydzovsky had known him much longer, but he couldn't spend entire days with him. It's like the divorces you get today—women spend the whole day at work with strange guys, they only see their own men in the evenings, all tired out—"

"Oh!" breathed the detective, trying to turn all his suspicions upside-down.

"And how about that picture! What men hold onto each other

like that? And both of them dressed to the teeth? Or those gifts! A naughty inkstand. A sexy book. Erotic slippers. Mr. Boruvka, the women haven't got anything to do with it. Not even that Irena of yours, though she was head over heels into that pretty boy. This kind of thing happens, you know? You said it yourself—"

"Who, me?"

"Yes, you, when you got me out of that foolishness of mine." The girl glanced urgently at the lieutenant's moonlike countenance, once again possessed by a feeling that something united the two of them. She thought of all those bars in all those perfumed cities, and of all those men—handsome, well-to-do, unreliable, strange. And of the moon over the tiled roofs which she had only just seen again, after almost two years' absence. And she realized the similarity. "Back then," she said softly, "almost two years ago, you said that under the influence of the erotic nothing is impossible in criminology."

"That's true," sighed the lieutenant.

The blonde shifted her gaze and looked around the cold, cheerless, almost empty café. The lieutenant gazed at her pretty face, which was gradually being affected by the first strokes of time's inconsiderate fingers. Still only very lightly, though—and besides, the lieutenant was blind in that direction.

"Even outside of criminology," she added gently, "nothing is impossible, you know."

The lieutenant's heart stopped.

"I—ahem—" he began gathering his courage, but then all of a sudden it was gone. "I wanted to tell you. . . ."

"Yes?" She looked at him hopefully with gray eyes, which almost everyone so far had found irresistible—if only for a while.

"That is . . ." His courage had definitely vanished, in the light of the majesty of his age—which moral people insisted on stressing so much. "My daughter—Zuzana—is in the family way," he wound up desperately.

The blonde also wilted, but she forced herself into a cheery, insincere enthusiasm: "Isn't that fabulous. Congratulations!" Then she noticed the lieutenant's face, and her extrasensory antennae grazed his aging soul. The girl caught on. "You're going to be a young granddaddy, then."

"That's a fact," he said mournfully. "Young I don't know, but granddaddy for sure."

"And so much better suited to being a daddy!" she teased merrily. "But run along now, before that poor bastard gets away from you."

. . .

They arrested Dr. Bydzovsky at the clinic. He didn't deny it any more. He had killed his lover out of jealousy, because the wrinkle-faced Pelent had come between them. Under the influence of the erotic, the lieutenant repeated to himself, anything is possible. He worked automatically, and every so often his head rang with that merry and—he wasn't entirely sure, but he was hopeful—perhaps naughty statement. Instead of paying attention to the interrogation, he left it to the very professional Malek, while he himself was tortured by a memory that for some unknown reason had emerged from the intoxicating green light of time gone by. He had spent an entire afternoon—a very long afternoon—sitting on an extremely isolated forest bench with a girl from the Fourth Form, a girl who in his opinion possessed not only the most beautiful red-ribboned braids in the whole world, but also the brightest mind. He had sat with her and talked to her without pause about Czech handball—he had played goalie with the S. K. Kostelec junior team—but the only sports that interested the pig-tailed pupil were dancing to swing and strolling in the woods, while he excelled at neither. He had talked and talked, it had grown dark, the spring sun had covered the two of them with the green and ruby shadows of the forest meadow, and he had kept on talking until the girl gave up and declared that she had to go home or her daddy would ground her. And so he had walked her home—talking about handball all the way. Now he realized bitterly that he had blown an opportunity of some sort back then. Perhaps a big one, perhaps a little one, but certainly a nice one. Irretrievably.

He was still thinking of that awkward long-ago afternoon the next time he and the singer got together, once again at the Lesser Quarter Café. She arrived in her mink coat, fresh from the hairdresser's. The lieutenant, stripped of what was left of his reason by the gorgeous mink, the fragrance (he had no idea that it was sandalwood, all the way from America), and the exquisite bangs, reported vaguely on his working day. It was a lengthy report, and finally the singer grew impatient and said, "The good Lord has quite a menagerie in this world, don't you think? It's a good thing the two of us are normal." Mercilessly, she stabbed the lieutenant with a gray dart.

The lieutenant cleared his throat and, with superhuman effort, screwed up his courage to take action.

"Or aren't you? But you are!" declared the girl, and fell silent.

"Ahem," he cleared his throat again, and dove in. "There's a— sort of an old movie playing—" he twisted his head back and forth as if his collar were too tight, "starring Gérard Philipe. You like him, don't you? Would you like to go . . . or don't you have— ahem—the time?"

"You asked me that once before, though." She gave him a disappointed look, but the lieutenant didn't notice the mischief victorious in the shiny gray eyes.

"You're right," he admitted, beginning to fall apart. "Forgive me—"

"But," said the blonde girl, "I *do* have the time."

Ab-solutions

1. An Intimate Business

The murderer—the director's spouse—is not mentioned until quite late in the story, and even then she is entirely outside the narrative—a sin against Commandment Number ONE. The reader knows that Weyr has a son, and must assume that there is a wife somewhere. It is never implied that he is a widower; in fact, his fear of having his womanizing revealed is mentioned several times. But the main clue is in Dr. Heyduk's testimony, in which the reader determines that he suffers from genetic sterility, and yet is supposed to be the father of a daughter. It is obvious from his testimony that the skirt-chaser Weyr knew Heyduk's wife very well; it is only a question of working out *how* well.

2. Mistake in Hitzungsee

This is of course a violation of Commandment Number THREE. The suspect is fairly obvious, although the clue to his motive lies back in the story "An Intimate Business." But while Monsignor Knox allows one secret passage in the kind of house where such a device might be expected—and as a former convent the Cloisters Hotel qualifies—*two* passages are, so to speak, going too far.

3. *The Man Eve Didn't Know from Adam*

When Eve walks past the cars, "a little spark" seems to smoulder inside her head, but she doesn't divulge it to the reader—a sin against Commandment Number EIGHT. It can, of course, be easily deduced from Eve's description that the murderer's car has the steering wheel on the right; in Italy they drive on the right, yet the girl ran up to the car and *around* the front to sit beside the driver. Furthermore, the tennis racket in Terra's Alfa-Romeo lies on the *right-hand* seat, beside the driver's seat on the left. The reader cannot determine the murderer—since Eve conceals the crucial clue that it is Sylvestri's Jaguar that has right-hand drive—but can deduce that Captain Potarot is mistaken when he accuses Terra.

4. *A Question of Alibis*

Although the motive is not easily deduced here, the identity and method of the murderer should not be too hard to work out. Careful attention to a number of clues (arrivals and departures, the inexperienced smoker and yellowed fingers, the mysterious Englishman who disappears without a trace, etc.) makes it easy to deduce that the commandment broken is Number TEN—the presence of an unheralded double.

5. *Why So Many Shamuses?*

A reader truly talented in the sphere of deductive reasoning should be able to determine the murderer in this morass of blood and passion, through pure logic. But Eve is guided above all by intuition—a violation of Commandment Number SIX.

6. *Miscarriage of Justice*

Many clues—his nervousness, his financial difficulties, his dexterity, the alarm clock, and the lavish insurance policy on his mother's life—indicate that Bob Cornhill intended to blow up his mother's plane. But the arson he is convicted of was in fact committed by Eve, the detective in this tale, when she removed the package with the bomb from old Mrs. Cornhill's suitcase and hid it under her bed, convinced that she had defused it. It's true that her crime was not deliberate, but I hope It will be forgiven for that, in the sphere of the purely formal logic of detective mysteries of the unrealistic school. The fire was labeled arson and arson is a crime; every crime must have a criminal; and so the commandment violated is Number SEVEN.

7. The Mathematicians of Grizzly Drive
Here, it's obviously the FOURTH commandment that is violated—though the reader who is mathematically inclined will find the solution no problem. I received some mathematical assistance from Professor Vaclav Chvatal, but he of course had no idea why I was so interested or what I needed it for—and bears no responsibility for any errors in the construction of the graphs, let alone for the not entirely proper solution of the equation.

8. An Atlantic Romance
Not only is there a Chinaman—actually a half-Chinese *woman*, Miss Abigail Wong—but she turns out to be the murderer—a flagrant violation of Commandment Number FIVE. (Incidentally, what the professor of phonetics overheard—translated into socially acceptable English—was "To hell with all this useless effort.")

9. Just Between Us Girls
In "A Question of Alibis" Zuzka played Watson to Eve's Sherlock; here she actually narrates the story, as Watson did. In the process, however, she overplays her role and displays far too much intelligence: a sin against the NINTH commandment.

10. The Third Tip of the Triangle
However enlightened we may (or may not) be today, in Father Knox's day homosexuality was seen as a breach of the divine order that started with Adam and Eve, a diabolical upset of the natural law—and so this case infringes on the SECOND commandment.